DEFIANCE

SKYE MALONE

Defiance
Book Eight of the Awakened Fate Series

Copyright © 2019 Skye Malone
Published by Wildflower Isle | PO Box 129, Savoy, IL 61874
www.wildflowerisle.com

Cover design by Karri Klawiter
www.artbykarri.com

Proofreading by Monica Bogza
www.trustedaccomplice.com

ISBN-10: 1-940617-61-8
ISBN-13: 978-1-940617-61-9

Library of Congress Control Number: 2019905984

**Join Skye Malone's mailing list to hear about new releases!
www.skyemalone.com/mailinglist**

PRONUNCIATION GUIDE

Dehaian (deh-HYE-an)
Driecara (dree-uh-KAR-uh)
Greliaran (greh-lee-AR-an)
Ivalaen (ih-val-AY-en)
Kreyus (KRAY-us)
Periantrea (per-ee-AHN-tree-uh)
Prijoran (prih-JOR-an)
Ruanir (ru-ahn-eer)
Strakirin (strah-KEE-rehn)
Teariad (tee-AR-ee-ad)
Venika (ven-EE-kuh)
Vetorian (vet-OR-ee-an)
Yvaria (ih-VAR-ee-uh)
Zekerian (zeh-KEHR-ee-en)

BAYLIE

There was once a girl with secrets.

Some she told her friends, some she told her family, and some she never told anyone at all. Many of these secrets protected people. Through secrets, she guarded her stepbrother, the thunderstorm in human form who'd once sacrificed his life to save others. Through secrets, she shielded her best friend, the mermaid who now lived with her boyfriend in his palace beneath the sea. Through other secrets still, she helped her stepfamily, most of whom weren't human but who'd spent their lives pretending to be. She was well-acquainted with secrets.

Some even protected her.

Secrets let her live a normal life: graduate high school, prepare for college, and have pleasant dinners with her stepfather and his family in their beachfront home. Secrets allowed her to dream of a career someday, and a house and family too.

They kept her safe.

They kept her secure.

They kept anyone from learning about the strange, dark

song that had called to her ceaselessly for the past year, the one that had pulled her from the dead-grass fields of Kansas to the sunny California shores. They denied the shadows that clustered around her bedroom at night, breaking things, moving things. The damage was only silly accidents, she'd say. Nothing that couldn't be replaced. She never let anyone know how the shadows tingled through her and tangled inside her, no matter how much it frightened her that their power grew stronger with every passing day.

There was once a girl with secrets.

But then, everyone has secrets.

I opened my eyes to a white ceiling and the feeling I'd been asleep for way too long. Machines beeped in rhythmic monotony somewhere nearby, and a utilitarian light panel glared in my eyes. Something constricted my chest, making breathing difficult, and my body ached like I'd run a marathon.

My gaze dropped toward the remainder of the room. Steel plates covered the windows to my right. The walls were made of scuffed plaster; parts of their pale blue paint were peeling. I was lying on a bed. Tubes and wires ran from beneath the white sheets to IV bags and machines and other things I didn't recognize. Against the metal doorframe, Jace leaned with his arms crossed and his attention on the ground. A brooding expression clouded his face.

Oh, this couldn't be good.

I tried to hold my breathing steady, but the machine at my side started beeping faster when my heart rate accelerated. I opened my mouth to ask Jace what had happened, but all that emerged was a dried croak like I hadn't spoken in a year.

Jace glanced up anyway. His pensive look cleared into surprise. "Hey."

He shrugged away from the doorframe quickly. From a tray near the wall, he took a cup of water with a straw. Walking closer, he held it so I could have a drink.

I eyed him warily. I didn't know much about him, besides the fact he was Ari's brother and spent most of the time looking angry enough to punch bricks, anyway. He'd barely spoken to anyone in the few days I'd known him.

He seemed anxious now.

I lifted my head, wincing as my muscles protested the motion, and then took a sip from the straw. I didn't like needing him to help me—he was little better than a stranger, for pity's sake—but my arms didn't want to move and my muscles felt utterly drained of strength. Even lifting my head was exhausting. I swallowed and then cleared my throat while he set the cup aside.

"What happened?" I asked, my voice hoarse.

Jace hesitated. "You were shot."

I stared at him. I'd been *what?*

"That… woman." His tone turned the word into something far harsher than the mild term he'd chosen. "Shannon. She broke out of the room Miguel had her in. Stole a gun."

It was hard to breathe, and not just because of the

constricting pressure on my chest that I was starting to suspect was a bandage. Memories shuddered back: a fire. A form jumping from the burning rooftop like Spider-Man. People shouting. Shannon turning toward me, something in her hand.

My mind retreated from the rest.

"Where's Noah?" I asked.

"You can't tell?" Jace sounded tense, like my question gave rise to some fear he had.

My heart pounded harder. In my head, I searched for that alien feeling of Noah's presence. It was so strange; I'd had so little experience with the connection between us, owing to the fact that he'd been God knew where for about a year. It only seemed to work if he was nearby.

There was nothing.

I wished I could unplug the heart monitor. The beeping kept getting faster.

"What *happened?*" I repeated, fighting to keep my voice steady.

"Shannon got to Ari," he said. "Did something to her. Ari, um… she took off. Noah went after her."

"Got to?" I repeated.

"Like that enforcer. Just touched her and…" Jace didn't finish. "The judges changed Shannon somehow. Best we can figure, they tried to do something similar to her like what they did to Ari—make her into one of those dehaian-enforcer hybrid 'strakirin' things—only she didn't hold out as well. Maybe she was too old. Post-adjustment or whatever. But her job was to 'trigger' Ari and finish what the judges started."

My stomach churned. "So when you say Noah went after her…"

"She headed for the ocean."

My gaze skittered across the chipped blue walls and steel-plated windows, not really seeing them. That explained the void where his presence in my mind had been. He could be halfway to China for all I knew.

I hoped he was okay.

Closing my eyes briefly, I made myself breathe. If anyone could take care of himself, it was Noah.

I forced my focus to the place around me. The equipment near the bed looked new, even if the room was a dump. Air conditioning rattled from the grate overhead, making the air drier than it was already. The chipped walls and steel plates gave the place an atmosphere like Miguel's hideout at the lighthouse in Calumet Bay—the place where those wizards I hadn't known *existed* a week ago hid from the judges that ruled their secretive society. But the air was different. Odd. Thinner, maybe. Almost—

I realized where my thoughts were heading and shied away immediately. I didn't want to go there.

"Where are we?" I asked Jace, holding my voice as steady as possible.

He hesitated. "Arizona."

I froze.

"You, um… you were hurt pretty bad and, um…" He exhaled. "It's been eight weeks since you were shot."

My mouth moved, but I couldn't make a sound.

"You lost a lot of blood. We weren't sure you'd make it for a while. And then…" His jaw worked around. "Then you just wouldn't wake up."

The damn heart monitor kept beeping faster and faster.

But I'd almost died. I'd really almost *died*. I'd practically been in a coma for eight *weeks* and—

No, it didn't matter. I hadn't died. I was fine.

Dad and Sandra had to be so worried, though. Peter, Diane, and Maddox too. I wondered if anyone had called them. If Noah—

"So Noah's been gone this whole time?" I asked. "He hasn't…"

I couldn't let myself finish. He'd been gone for a year. Eight weeks was nothing.

But I'd been *shot*. Did he know that?

Did he care?

I shoved the thought aside. Of course he did. And he was fine. He had to be. He'd just gone after Ari too.

A pained feeling twisted in my chest. I knew he cared about Ari. I would've had to be blind not to see that. And that was great. Relieving, really—and not just because of what had happened with Chloe. So much had changed for him in the past year, and it scared me. I wanted to believe he was the same; that maybe his body was different, but otherwise, he was just Noah. My stepbrother I'd known since I was little. My stepbrother who meant the world to me, who'd shared movie marathons and stupid jokes and funny memes with me, back before all our lives had gone to hell and I thought I'd lost him forever. But in all honesty, I hadn't known how much of him was left in there.

And how much only looked like him.

Finding he could still do something as *normal* as fall for someone was a relief. But for him not to come back even *once* to make sure I was okay after rushing off to—

"He's stopped in a lot. He's been really worried about you." Jace paused. "Good guy." He said it like he was admitting to something, and it sounded like respect. "We haven't seen him in about a week, though."

I drew a breath, attempting to be reassured by the words. That was different, then. A week was nothing. A week was no time at all. Noah had to be fine.

"You'd know, though, yeah?" Jace continued. "If something had gone wrong…"

I looked back up at him, discomfort moving through me at his tone. Till yester—*eight weeks ago,* the only people who'd known about my empathic link to my stepbrother were Chloe, Zeke, and Ellie. Maybe Olivia and a few other landwalker elders too. That'd been bizarre enough. I didn't have much choice in telling Jace either. But I wasn't sure I was okay with him knowing more about it.

His expression turned insistent, silently pressing the question. I fought off a frown. "Doesn't work like that. I can only tell things if he's close. It's not like with your sister."

Jace turned away. My discomfort increasing, I looked to the steel-plated window. Noah was *fine,* though. And if he was going after Ari, chances were she'd be fine too. I might not be able to tell where he was, but I'd know if he died. I'd know if he was in trouble. I was sure I would.

But I wondered where he was now.

❧ 2 ❧

NOAH

Two of the enforcers were dead, and the lone survivor hadn't made it far.

His hands on the metal pipe pinning him to the brick wall, the man snarled a curse at me. The abandoned factory around us was nearly empty, barring the bodies on the floor and the decrepit machinery no one had bothered to take with them. The sound of traffic carried from the streets of Vancouver outside, but none of the occasional police sirens seemed particularly interested in heading our way.

"Where is she?" I growled.

The enforcer shoved at the pipe. My grip on it didn't budge. I only barely looked human at this point, and most of it was for show, just to give the bastard something to talk to. Storm clouds made up the shape of my body. More extended through the cavernous building, churning along the ceiling and amid the open space of the factory floor. A twist of shadow held the pipe in place, shifting on it when the enforcer's hands did but pinning him nonetheless.

"Go to hell," the man spat.

I drove the metal pipe harder against his throat.

"Go on, kill me," he rasped. "You're already too late to stop what the masters have planned."

A scowl twisted the darkness of my face. The masters. Their plan. I was sick of hearing that—not that I'd heard it much. This guy and his friends were the first enforcers I'd seen in days, and they'd each said the same thing. Before that, the others I'd found hadn't been much help either. Each group proclaimed their allegiance to their masters and then killed themselves rather than talk to me. It'd been horrible.

I remembered a time when it'd been horrible.

A shudder ran through me. Eight weeks. Eight weeks of searching the coast and the ocean for any sign of Ari. Of tracing every reported "dehaian" attack only to find no sign of dehaians or strakirin at all. Of fearing the longer she spent with those bastards, the less chance I had of reclaiming the girl I'd known.

If I had any chance at all.

Desperation was a funny thing. The Beast side of me wasn't familiar with it. In all these centuries, there'd never been any-thing it cared about besides itself. Not until Ari, the girl who was like me but not like me, and who had come to matter so much more than I ever could have imagined. The Beast side of me wasn't sure how to handle the frantic, consuming fear of losing her that had gripped it whole.

And the greliaran part of me was beside itself at the thought of being here again. Of having psychos want to destroy some-one I cared about *again*. I'd lived this nightmare once already, and now, only a year later, here it was a second time like nothing had changed. Hell, it'd only gotten worse. My stepsister had been shot. She was still in a coma that no one could bring to an end, much less explain. And the girl I cared about had been taken.

Again.

Every passing day only made it worse. Every hour. Every minute in which I failed and failed and failed to find Ari. I hadn't even *seen* an enforcer for nearly a week after she disappeared, and when I finally spotted a couple of the bastards lurking in an alleyway in San Diego, something about them just *screaming* that they weren't fully human…

The Beast side of me knew all about hurting people. In that part of my past, I'd done more damage and killed more people than I could bring myself to remember. The way the Beast had been designed—*I'd* been designed—even meant that destruction felt good in a way. Like a drug, like a type of satisfaction that ran down to my core. As for my desire to control that, to hold myself back and stop from giving into that…

Desperation was a terrible thing.

"Let me explain something to you," I said to the enforcer. "Your masters? They needed me dead. They couldn't carry out their plan with me alive. So you think about what that means. How much of a threat your masters obviously consider me to be." I ground the end of the pipe into the brick wall. "And you fucking *tell me* where to find Ari Moreau!"

The man gritted his teeth, his hands straining at the metal pipe.

I kept myself from snarling. All threats aside, if this guy died, I was back to hunting down enforcers again.

And who knew how long it'd be till I found another one.

I sent a crackle of lightning through the pipe, not enough to kill, only enough to jolt him.

The enforcer spat curses at me.

I hit him with another bolt—stronger—and then let it die into a low-level current.

The man jerked. Started gasping. His eyes were rolling back into his head.

I let the lightning fade. I waited.

"Boathouse near Hortensia Beach. South of Tijuana."

Finally.

I released the pipe and started for the door.

"They *will* kill you, Beast!"

I ignored him. I could get to Tijuana in no time.

And Ari would be there. I'd find her. She'd be fine.

The enforcer yanked the pipe from the wall, sending it clattering to the floor. For a heartbeat, he stood there, his chest heaving, and then he charged at my human form as if to attack me from behind.

Cold contempt twisted through me. He thought I needed my eyes to see him coming?

Storm clouds snaked down like a tornado, snatching him up and then hurling him backward like a plastic toy. He sailed through the air and crashed into the bricks. At the impact, the decaying wall collapsed onto him like an avalanche, roaring in the stillness of the factory.

Blood seeped from beneath the debris.

I kept walking, the storm clouds pouring into me till only the regular shadows and darkness of the room remained. I stepped past the corpses, my shoes crunching over the gravel, while the rest of my body transformed back into a fully human appearance again.

I remembered a time when this had all been so horrible.

❧ 3 ❧

ARI

"Release."

Poison thrilled through me at the judge's command, the venom coursing through my veins in a rising crescendo of bliss. My nerves tingled in an ecstasy of rightness at fulfilling my purpose. My body was in heaven from the pleasure of it.

And I was in hell.

Inside my own mind, I fled from the flood of sensations surging through the monster that controlled my body, seeking the relative high ground of the farthest reaches of my consciousness. Like a tidal wave, it swept through her even as the poison rushed out into the captive in her hands.

Another one I couldn't save.

The man staggered, his body spasming against the restraints holding him. Blinding lights overhead revealed every line of agony on his face, every teardrop falling from his eyes. Sterile white floors and walls stood in stark contrast to the inky black poison spreading through his veins, staining his suntanned skin. Outside the large white room, beyond the wall of glass,

14

Judge Engle watched, while a host of lab-coated technicians waited behind him, studying monitors and taking notes as the man died.

Sandy brown hair, I told myself. Green eyes, or maybe blue-green. He'd looked fifty in human years before I… before I couldn't save him. I'd heard the technicians say he was a resistance member, which meant I could ask Miguel who he was, someday. I'd find his family, too. Tell them I was sorry. I'd make sure they knew what had happened to him, and that I'd made the judges pay.

Just like all the others.

The aftereffects of the poison swept up to lap at the edges of my safety zone, my tiny corner behind thick walls. Panic shot through me. The world blurred. My thoughts slowed and became fuzzy. Became cold. Became simple. And I wanted that. Needed to give in to their control. To let go and obey the masters as I'd been made to do. It would be so much better to surrender and—

"End it," Judge Engle ordered.

Spikes rushed from my forearms on command. My arm swung and blood splattered me. The dying man collapsed to the ground.

"Good."

The lull of the poison faded.

I wished I was still able to cry.

"Any indication of signal degradation with the hive?" Judge Engle asked one of the technicians.

"No, sir."

"Excellent."

Jace, I whispered to myself in the darkness. Maia. Dhanya. I remembered my family. Baylie, Miguel, his wife, Veronique, and the rest of the resistance. I still remembered them all.

And Noah.

Always Noah. The first one killed by the monster they'd turned me into, back on the beach, that night Shannon found me and finished the judges' plan to turn me into this. Noah, who had trusted me and tried to save me, only to have that horrible poison rip through him the moment he touched my skin, killing him right in front of my eyes.

I'd make the judges pay for his death. *Somehow*, I'd make them pay.

From behind the walls in my mind, I peered out again. I'd found this corner of safety in the moments after I left the beach and the lighthouse, while my body swam toward the judges' signal, obeying the command to return to them. The monster controlling my body came after me in the darkness, trying to destroy me before we'd even reached her masters. And she almost had. If not for this place, out here at the edges of my consciousness, she would have destroyed me entirely.

But from all I could tell, the monster controlling the rest of me couldn't find this place. This infinitesimal space of quiet behind walls that I held with every trace of strength I had left, like a barricaded corner in a dark attic, inside a house that was no longer my own. I suspected the place was a remnant of the link Noah and I had shared, somehow spared the corruption that the judges planned.

Because they'd done nothing but corrupt the rest of it.

Judge Engle turned away, waving a hand at one of the technicians. "Clean and prep Zero-Zero-One for transport."

Anguish tinged the tiny, safe corner of my mind. Not again. They'd moved me so many times since that first night in San Francisco when the thing that controlled my body swam past the Golden Gate Bridge and straight to where the judges waited in an old factory at the edge of the water. At their command, the monster moving my body climbed from the bay and let them drug me. When next I woke, I was in a tank.

And that's when I heard the drone.

The technicians came into the room, one of them carrying a bucket while the other held towels and sponges. They sopped lukewarm water over me with the sponges, washing the blood from my scale-covered chest and rinsing over the 0-0-1 tattooed in blocky numerals on my upper right arm. A moment later, they attacked my body with the towel, roughly drying me before retreating.

My body followed them from the white room.

The drone wasn't a sound. Not exactly, anyway. It was a pressure. A whisper-hum inside my mind, inside my blood and my bones. The force of an entire consciousness, separate from my body yet inextricably a part of it, occupying it like muscles beneath skin.

It was the strakirin.

The knowledge was instinctive. Something that went beyond my conscious mind and into the realm of pure awareness. Other strakirin were out there, waiting, killing, serving the judges. I had no idea how many—dozens? Maybe a hundred now?—but inside their heads and mine, we were tied together, like a mangled, horrific version of the empathic connection that had existed between me and Noah but *so* much deeper. Stronger, to the point where nothing was left of who we'd been.

There was only the hive.

It was a creature in its own right. A being made up of dozens of consciousnesses united and enslaved to a single purpose. It was amorphous, made physical only through the bodies at its command. Like an enforcer, it had no sense of a future, no memory of a past. The hive existed in the eternal now, where nothing mattered and submission to the judges was the only goal. The drone of its presence spread through every corner of my mind, save my safety zone, like black water, ebbing and flowing but never, ever gone. And like a deep and terrible ocean, if it swept over me, I knew I'd drown.

Whatever the judges had destroyed in me when their process was finished had become a part of the hive, and that was what controlled my body now. She was a piece of the overwhelming whole, moving me like a puppet, with no real individuality or distinction from the rest. The judges and the hive wouldn't grieve her death—*my* death—any more than I'd grieve the loss of a single hair amid the thousands on my head.

Even if I was the first strakirin the judges created, that didn't mean I had any significance to the hive.

But in the moments when she was distracted, when the hive that filled my mind was busy elsewhere, I crept out from behind my walls, seeking anything to give me a foothold to take back my body. In the ravaged, magic-blasted wasteland of my mind, I was insubstantial as a ghost, and yet, like a ghost, I still had some power. It was difficult, *so* difficult, but after days—weeks? Months? I pushed the thought aside; it couldn't have been months already—I'd finally managed to make my finger twitch.

It was small, but it was something. I'd owned this body once. I would again.

Beyond the brilliant white space where they made my body kill people, the monitoring room was a gray abyss of shadows with a large opening that led to the hallway beyond. Screens glowed, showing views of the white room from different angles, showing readouts from the small, plastic spheres attached to my temples. At a nod from Judge Engle, one of the technicians set to peeling the devices from my skin while another waited with denim shorts, pink flip-flops, and a floral-patterned tank top. The creature controlling my body pulled the clothes on and then started after Judge Engle out of the room.

"Wait," someone called from the hallway.

Judge Davenport, my uncle, the man I'd hoped to force to fix this once upon a time, strode through the opening that led to the hall. The embodiment of unremarkable, every feature on him seemed to define the word "bland." He wasn't tall but he wasn't short. He wasn't fat but he wasn't thin. His eyes were the color of dishwater, and his black suit washed out his skin to a shade of old newsprint. In the past, I'd marveled that he was Maia's father, given that her mahogany hair and brilliant blue eyes made her the vibrant opposite of him.

Now, I just seethed with rage at the sight of the man.

"Judge Davenport, I didn't realize you would be joining us." Judge Engle's voice was mild, as if only politely interested in the other man's presence. He waved a hand at me, never glancing my way, and at the motion, my body came to a halt.

"Change of plans," Judge Davenport replied. "Vancouver is gone."

Judge Engle stared at him for a moment, as if processing the cryptic information. "Any indication of betrayal?"

"Yes."

Judge Engle sighed, not appearing shocked, only disappointed. "How long do we have?"

"Long enough, but only if we move soon. Contingencies are in place, however. We're redirecting to the secondary location."

"Very well."

My uncle regarded me for the first time, his gaze flicking down to take in the tattoo on my upper arm and then back to my face. There wasn't a trace of emotion in his eyes. Nothing to show it bothered him that his own niece was in front of him.

Nothing to show he even recalled who I was.

"Zero-Zero-One." He directed the statement to Judge Engle. I couldn't read anything from his tone.

"Final checks."

"Ah." Judge Davenport glanced toward the white room. Technicians hauled the body away while others stood by with mop buckets, waiting to clean the blood from the white room's floor. "That was the man we captured in Bakersfield, correct?"

"Yes."

"Efficient."

"Indeed."

My uncle turned back, walking around me and eyeing me like I was a piece of meat on a butcher's rack. "No sign of divergence from the hive?"

"One hundred percent conformance, sir," a technician said.

"No deviation in signal at any time?"

In the darkness, I trembled. Had he seen something? Some hint I was still here?

The technician scanned the readouts on her screen. "No, sir."

A hint of a smile lifted the corner of Judge Engle's mouth, nothing warm in the expression. "It hasn't showed a single indication of nonconformity since arrival."

In my tiny corner of safety, anger prickled. After however many days—just days, surely, not months—of enduring their hell, I knew that *it* referred to me.

"A stroke of luck, then," my uncle replied. "You will recall I argued that it be put down. Not only is its continued existence an unnecessary risk, but our predicament persists because it remains alive."

Shock shot through me. He'd wanted me *killed*? And what predicament?

Judge Engle's mouth thinned. "And, as I argued, that would have been a waste of resources—not only due to the intelligence we've gathered about the resistance and the Delaney boy, but also given the continued emotional leverage value of the asset."

Guilt made me cringe in the darkness. They knew the truth about Noah now. They knew about his family. Baylie, his human stepsister. His greliaran dad and brother in California. His mom in Kansas. Anything I'd known, that monster did too. And she'd told them.

All of it.

But what did Judge Engle mean "emotional leverage value"? Was he talking about my family? Using me against them? As much as it hurt to admit, no one else was left alive to care about what happened to me, which didn't leave a great many options. But what *predicament* could involve them?

Anxiety gnawed at the edges of my guilt. Jace and the others had to be fine. Noah was dead, but they would be fine. I wouldn't lose anyone else while I was trapped here in this prison of my own skin.

"We have tested it extensively." Judge Engle gestured to the technicians. "There is no defect or cause for concern, no trace of the original subject remaining. Contingencies are in place to divert our adversaries, but if by some unfortunate circumstance, a situation *does* develop either at the target or en route, we have verified that Zero-Zero-One will behave precisely as ordered. I see no liability here."

My uncle was silent. I watched them both from over the edge of my mental walls, at a loss for what they were talking about.

"For all our sakes, I hope you are correct," Judge Davenport replied finally. "The project cannot be jeopardized."

"It isn't, and it will not be."

The judges regarded one another for a long moment, their faces unreadable, and then Judge Davenport turned his attention to me. "May I?" he asked the other judge coolly.

Judge Engle paused. "Of course."

My uncle extended his hand, palm up. "Give me your hand."

Caution filled my tiny corner of consciousness, but the thing controlling my body didn't hesitate. My fingers rested on his cool, slightly clammy palm.

"Good. Now, release."

What? That was the command to—

Poison swelled up and rushed from my skin, flooding into him. I gaped from behind my wall, aghast.

His body went rigid. Black lines shot through his veins, racing for his chest, his face. His eyes rolled back, the whites going gray and then black too while his mouth fell open in a silent gasp. But the look on his face wasn't pain.

It was ecstasy.

Another breath left him. The black lines faded away as he lowered his gaze to the room again. The smile on his face was stronger this time, almost a full-blown grin. "That never gets old."

"Indeed."

I stared from the darkness. The poison… they…

It didn't kill them.

Anguish threatened to overwhelm me, and despair followed close on its heels. I couldn't poison them. Even when I finally did manage to gain control of my body, it wouldn't matter.

I couldn't stop them with the evil, magical venom they'd put inside me, because the bastards had made themselves immune to it. More than immune, they *enjoyed* it. All this, and I couldn't—

I still had spikes. They weren't immune to those.

The thought was steadying. I clung to it.

"Will you be accompanying us to the secondary location?" Judge Engle inquired, starting toward the exit.

Judge Davenport turned, joining him. My body followed at the flick of his hand.

"Yes. I have a few hours before my flight."

"I presume the research continues to go well."

"The subjects are performing admirably, yes, though the pool is shrinking. We have achieved a conversion rate of ninety-eight percent, and incidents of malfunction have almost been eliminated. We've had to cease all vivisection, for fear of running out of subjects for further research."

"The unfortunate consequence of perfection."

"Agreed."

Strakirin, I realized. They were talking about strakirin. *Dissecting* defective strakirin…

I retreated further behind my walls, curling into as small of a space as I could. They wouldn't find out about me. I was safe. Judge Engle himself just said they hadn't seen any sign of Zero-Zero-One being defective.

They didn't know about me.

Enforcers waited beyond the monitoring room, and they fell in around the judges while both men walked down the long, gray hall. The floor, ceiling, and walls were all made of rough cement, with intermittent openings for other rooms to my right. From the corner of my eye, I caught glimpses of more monitors, more white spaces, all of them empty. The stinging scent of bleach carried on the cool air, hinting at more cleaning like what was happening in the white room I'd just left.

At the end of the hall, the silver doors of an elevator waited, whispering open at an enforcer's touch to the upward-arrow button on the wall nearby. The judges walked into the glistening interior, their black suits reflecting like dark blurs on the brushed metal walls. I followed and the enforcers did too, all of us turning once inside the elevator and leaving the judges at our backs.

My skin didn't crawl, but in my dark little corner, every bit of me was shivering with revulsion and the memory of adrenaline.

The elevator slowed. The doors whispered open again, revealing another hallway. With the judges still behind me, I trailed the enforcers down the slate-gray corridor and through another doorway, into the concrete space of a loading dock. A collection of delivery trucks waited there, logos on their sides for a meat and seafood distribution service.

Every time I thought the judges couldn't get any sicker than they already were…

On the far end of the loading dock, the oversized garage door began to inch open. Sunlight pierced the gray space, bright and brilliant and swallowing whatever lay beyond the opening in glare.

In the darkness, I whimpered at the sight. With all I had, I wanted to run toward the light, though the monster controlling my body merely continued on, climbing into the truck at an enforcer's direction, ignoring the path to relative freedom only a few yards away.

It wasn't just the fact she didn't run that hurt, because of course she didn't. But after who knew how long in this hell, I would have given almost anything to see the sun.

The metal bench in the back of the truck was cold beneath me, and when another enforcer pulled the door closed, the entire compartment plunged into darkness. An enforcer sat on either side of me. I could hear them breathing while, up front, the driver's side door opened and the truck rocked slightly when someone climbed in.

Doors slammed. The engine started. In the darkness of my own mind, I wanted to cry.

I'd get out of this, I reminded myself. I would. I'd sunbathe in the middle of the desert, a thousand miles from the nearest ocean. I'd never change form or lay eyes on a body of water bigger than a rain puddle again.

Peace filtered through my body like the cold calm of death. Tranquility lapped higher like a rising pool of acid rain.

The drone was getting louder.

Behind my walls, I threw everything I had into holding out the sensation, the whispers, and the pure *pressure* of that sound-that-wasn't-a-sound. It was growing louder with every moment, and that wasn't the only thing.

We were approaching the ocean.

Panic poured through me. I had no idea what ocean magic—straight-up, unadulterated ocean magic unlike the mangled monstrosity they'd taken from Noah and given me—would do to me or my defenses.

But if the way my walls were shuddering was any indication, it couldn't be good.

The truck bounced over the roads, rumbling on toward who-knew-where. An unintelligible murmur carried from the front—a judge or an enforcer speaking, from the sound of it. And with every minute that ticked past, the drone became louder, humming a monotone lullaby of peace through nonexistence while the sea traced razor blades over my skin.

I'd get out, I repeated to myself, holding onto my walls with all my might. I'd get out of this and never come near the water again.

The truck slowed, bounced over two obstacles that felt like speed bumps, rumbled on for a few more moments over a road that sounded hollow, and then came to a stop. Doors opened and then slammed. The enforcers on either side of me stood up.

"Follow," one of them commanded.

The rear door opened. Sunlight burned my eyes.

Salt in the air burned my skin.

I dropped down from the back of the truck, my flip-flops hitting rough concrete crusted with salt. Judge Engle and Judge Davenport stood nearby, both of them regarding the long stretch of industrial buildings and warehouses like the entire area had barely passed muster.

The ocean was only a few dozen yards away.

Inside my mind, I cringed. I'd missed the light, but I didn't want *this*. To be here, of all places, because I knew what was probably coming next.

I'd give anything to avoid what was coming next.

"Mister Marseilles," Judge Engle said.

In the darkness, I froze. *No.*

The monster controlling my body turned like a compass needle pulled toward the north.

Logan strolled toward us. His dark hair was wet and slicked back like he'd just come from a dip in the water, and skin-tight, green swim trunks were his only clothes.

Wait… not swim trunks. No more than the scales that covered me were a swimsuit.

They'd changed him. Made him a strakirin like me.

Killed the real him.

I didn't know what to feel. What to think. I never wanted him to come near me again, but this? Would I have wished *this*?

"How can I be of assistance, sir?" Logan asked Judge Engle, his voice devoid of any emotion.

But then, what if he was still in there?

From the darkness, I scrutinized him, searching for any sign that sick bastard was still behind that obedient, placid stare. The drone was a uniform nightmare, but somehow, I could feel Logan apart from it too. And he was… colder. Slimier. The magic coming from him didn't feel entirely like the drone, or entirely like the judges either, but like an oily mold congealed in between them, made up of them both.

"You are to go to the rendezvous point," Judge Engle said. "Osias will be waiting. Follow him along the border of Yvaria to the southwest. Our associates will give you further instructions once you reach the western territories."

Nothing else came from him, though. Not even a flick of an eye in my direction to show there was anything left of the bastard who'd tried to rape me, right before I blasted him away with enough magic to leave me drained for a week. Logan now appeared as dead as I did whenever I caught sight of my reflection.

"Of course, sir." Logan's expression was dutiful. He turned and dove into the water.

But then, looking dead was the point, wasn't it? It didn't mean anything. I looked like a walking corpse with spikes and poison.

I wasn't.

Judge Davenport glanced at me. "Follow."

Wait, what? No. I—

My body dove into the water. Electricity surged over my skin, through my muscles, and down into my bones, bending them, twisting them in a rush of magic that was so swift, it was over before it had the chance to be painful. My clothes disintegrated. My flip-flops dropped away. In only a few heartbeats, my body shifted from human-shaped to something else entirely.

Eel tail. Eyes like yellow-green stones, split by a line of pure black. Scales the color of emeralds. A gold fringe ran along the side of the tail, and I knew it continued around my pointed ears, shimmering with glittery bioluminescence that should have been impossible.

Just like the rest of it.

The thing controlling my body took off, flying through the water after the sound of the drone. It was out there, getting louder with every second, buffeting my defenses like a rising flood. And through it all, ocean magic wove like another, equally terrifying hum of power. One that threaded through my walls, threatening to fracture them, crumble them, reduce them to useless gravel.

A figure floated in the blue-gray murk ahead of me.

Alarm hit me. I couldn't see them, whoever they were. I couldn't see anything, and yet somehow, I knew they were there.

Echolocation. The dehaians had echolocation abilities, or some magical version of it.

And apparently I did too.

My body slowed. Logan came into view. His body had changed, same as mine, though the fringe around his tail and ears was darker, like burnished gold. His yellow-green snake eyes glowed faintly in the twilight.

There was nothing dead in his expression now.

"Well, well, Ariabella Moreau." He swam closer, his gaze raking over me. "Back from the meat grinder."

He grabbed my arm, yanking me to him. His chest pressed to mine, and his tail pushed at me as it undulated in the water, holding him afloat. His other hand lifted to my chin, pinning it in his grasp.

Panic and rage surged through my tiny corner of my mind.

"I bet if I told you to kiss me, you would. I bet you'd do anything I told you…" His attention flicked to the tattoo on my arm, and his lip curled into a sneer. "Zero-Zero-One."

Logan traced his fingers down my jawline, down my neck and lower, watching my face.

I was going to kill him. I was going to stab him, strangle him. I was going to electrocute every single inch of his skin and scales till nothing was left but charcoal.

The monstrous hive controlling my body didn't even turn my eyes from the empty water ahead.

"Do it," he ordered. "Kiss me."

No! I—

The hive mind obeyed.

I rushed up from behind the walls in the tiny corner of my mind, frantic to stop his grasping hands, to spit out the wretched taste of his revolting mouth. Killing him wasn't enough. Killing him a *thousand* times wasn't enough. I'd—

My hand twitched, a sharp jerk like a spasmodic attempt to shove him away.

Logan took his mouth from mine abruptly. "Ugh." He pushed me back.

I retreated behind my defenses again, watching Logan. Had he noticed that movement? *My* movement, a bigger movement of control over my body than anything I'd managed since this nightmare began?

Had the hive?

"They really did kill you, didn't they?" Logan's snake-like

eyes scanned my face again. He looked offended, and almost confused, like a kid who'd just discovered his toy was broken and he couldn't have his fun anymore. "God."

With a disgusted snort, he turned away. "Come on."

Kicking his tail hard, he swam deeper into the water. My body followed immediately, obedient to the command.

But it wouldn't do that forever.

I hovered in my tiny corner of safety, shuddering with relief. I would stop him. If he ever tried that again, I'd add spikes to that movement of my arm. And while, yes, I could still hear the drone, horrible and monotonous and getting louder, and up ahead I could feel the slimy, slithering magic that was Logan as well… I was still here too. The monster in my head hadn't come after me. My walls still held, even if only barely. And for a moment, just a moment, I'd had more control over my body than I had since this nightmare started. That was something.

More than something.

It was a start.

✺ 4 ✺

NOAH

The boathouse came into view, and immediately, it was obvious something was wrong.

For one thing, it was on fire.

I slowed, eyeing the wreckage. The smoke. The snapping flames and the burnt timbers where a building had been. Emergency vehicles surrounded the place; fire trucks with their lights flashing, ambulances with the same. Hoses sprayed arcs of water over the destruction, though they were fighting a losing battle. The building was a loss.

As were the victims of the blaze.

I drifted closer. EMTs were there. They were getting ready to load corpses into body bags. And the bodies were burned, some of them beyond recognition.

But one…

Waves of denial coursed through me, panic biting at their heels. That'd been a girl. Her face had been battered and bruised till it was unrecognizable. Her body was burned. But the remaining tufts of her dark golden hair were the exact shade of Ari's own.

It was all I could do to keep dark clouds and lightning from ripping through my invisible form. She couldn't be gone. Not now. Not after all this. Not after everything they—

The judges wouldn't have killed her. They needed her.

Or maybe they only *had* needed her. Something could have changed. Maybe they'd only wanted her temporarily. Or there could have been an accident. Her magic, that lightning she could summon, it might have—

No.

No, I wouldn't buy this. It was too much of a coincidence. Too neat and tidy. Only a short time after I finally found out where she was being held, she died?

The hell with *that*.

I scanned the scene below me. They must have known I was coming. They could detect me in this form, after all—at least when I wasn't deep in the ocean and masked by the magic there. So this was a diversion. They must have been trying to slow me down or get me away from her trail. They obviously didn't have the setup to capture me here. This must have been the next best step.

Make me think she was dead.

Not a single detail below me offered up clues about which way they might have gone. There were hardly any vehicles on the road, barring the emergency ones with their lights flashing around the wreckage of the boathouse. No tracks of any kind.

The judges could have taken her anywhere.

I spread out over the city, an amorphous and invisible

creature made only of magic, as I searched for a single sign amid the roads and crowds and people who had no idea of what really went on in their world.

Nothing.

Panic surged through me and then came rage. Weeks of searching, of hoping, and I'd missed her by minutes.

If she'd ever been here at all.

I swept south, then north, crisscrossing the coast like a desperate bloodhound without a hope of finding a trail. There *had* to be something. Some trace that would lead me to her. I'd tried everything I could think of for weeks, poking and prodding at the shattered remnants of our connection, calling for her in the depths of the ocean and in my mind. But nothing had worked. Nothing was—

Three mismatched vehicles were parked on a dock. Two black sedans and a white delivery truck with a meat and fish delivery service logo on its side. The collection looked like a joke, like a mob meeting, totally incongruous outside of a movie, except that half a dozen people surrounded the vehicles, scrambling to get into the cars. They were panicking, shouting, clearly eager to escape something.

And I recognized one of them.

Judge Engle, the man who'd started all this.

I dove down while the suit-clad judge slammed the door on a black sedan. The driver hit the gas the moment the judge was inside, and the vehicle lunged for the main road. Invisible, I sped after them, ignoring the other sedan and knocking away the empty delivery truck. The driver—an enforcer, most likely—yanked the wheel to the left, whipping the car toward a large warehouse and then racing inside.

It occurred to me that the building might be a trap.

It occurred to me that I'd destroyed the last one.

I tore into the warehouse. The steel walls crumpled like a crushed tin can. The roof shredded and the support beams shattered, raining debris on the concrete floor below. Old machinery and massive crates tumbled away from me like children's toys, rolling after the sedan still trying to escape. The car whipped through the building, fleeing the destruction cascading down behind it. Fleeing me.

Like hell.

They veered toward the exit, the sedan bouncing and screeching over the metal beams that dropped onto its path. In a swirl of black clouds, I snagged the vehicle, carrying it out from the warehouse and then slamming it into the brick wall of the building next door.

I let the car drop. It wasn't crushed. Crumpled badly, yes, and the airbags inside had all deployed. But I'd been careful not to kill the occupants. Dead people couldn't give me information.

The driver's door opened. An enforcer tumbled out, unable to keep his feet though he still tried to aim his gun. In the back seat, the judge pushed himself upright. Blood covered half his face, pouring from a gash on his forehead.

I drew down into human form. "Where is she?"

The enforcer fired his weapon. The bullets sped right through me, harmless.

I grabbed the man and hurled him aside. The rear door came off its hinges when I yanked it open.

Judge Engle glared up at me through bleary eyes.

"Where?" I demanded.

His lip tried to curl into a smirk, but he was losing consciousness and couldn't maintain the expression.

I'd hit them too hard.

"Never catch her," he whispered. "Made them to hide… even from you."

His eyes rolled back in his head. He slumped against the seat.

I hurled the car door aside with an infuriated snarl. I could wake him. He was still breathing, after all. I could rouse him again and again till the bastard told me what I wanted. And it still might take hours to get the information.

Even minutes would be too long.

I looked around. The other sedan was gone, and the warehouse behind me was a wreckage. In the distance, sirens wailed. It wasn't hard to assume they were coming closer.

Never catch her.

She'd been here.

I let my body vanish, rising higher into the air. Only a few people had been with the judge when I found him moments ago. A handful of enforcers and another guy, who looked like a judge too. But no strakirin. No Ari.

There was only one place she might've gone.

I dove toward the water, hoping I was right.

5

BAYLIE

The tile of the hallway floor squeaked beneath my shoes, and only Jace's arm on mine kept me steady. Eight weeks of being bedridden hadn't done my muscles any favors, and that was without the weird shakiness that held onto me and refused to let go. I wasn't comfortable with the help, though.

Jace was creeping me out.

It wasn't that he seemed like a bad person, necessarily. He had an edge to him, yeah. Like there was a chance he could be a jerk. But he also cared like crazy about his sister and was protective of his cousin and her fiancée besides, and I could respect that. He even qualified as attractive, with his light brown hair that flopped into his eyes like a little kid's if he didn't swipe it back. For that matter, his eyes were interesting too: an unusual shade of smoky gray I'd never seen on anyone besides him and his sister. At a good bit over six feet tall with a decent build, he might've been the kind of guy I'd try to get to talk to me, if life were remotely normal.

Which it wasn't. It hadn't been for a long time. And

38

interesting or not, he was one of these wizard people, a group I didn't want near me for a million reasons plus one. He was already paying *way* too much attention to me, what with his weird, single-minded intensity about staying by my side.

He almost seemed afraid I'd break.

"You really don't have to help me like this."

He didn't say anything as we continued down the hallway. Doors lined the walls on either side of us, most of them closed, though the one where I'd been staying at the end of the corridor behind us remained open. Beyond it, I could hear Veronique still talking in baffled tones with her assistants, comparing notes on what they'd found—or more specifically *not* found—in examining me. They'd checked me over for hours, taking readings, making sure I was stable—figuratively speaking, anyway. The fact I was capable of walking and mostly moving around on my own after weeks of being bedridden seemed to alarm them. Apparently, two months in a coma should have done my body more harm than I felt like it already had. If not for how I'd nearly had a panic attack at their tests, I'd probably still be in there, getting poked and prodded.

We reached a doorway that led to a stairwell. Jace turned, starting down the gunmetal gray steps.

"Jace," I said.

He grimaced. He also didn't let go of my arm.

"Look," I persisted, "you're a nice guy and all, but—"

"Huh?" He turned toward me in alarm.

Heat touched my cheeks. I just knew they were going red.

Jace stepped back so quickly, I had to grab the metal banister.

I stiffened my arms, bracing myself and praying I wouldn't collapse. Breaking my neck by falling down the stairs would easily be as embarrassing as proving I'd been wrong about doing this myself.

"I'm not—" He stared at me like I was an alien, and then he tugged his focus away, clearly attempting to regroup. "Listen, this isn't some… I just promised Noah I'd look out for you."

I blinked. This was Noah's idea? "Oh."

Jace went back to eyeing me warily, like the thought that I'd read something else into his actions was disconcerting as hell.

If awkwardness could've been sold, we would have made a fortune.

I shifted my focus to the concrete stairs. My fingers tightened on the banister, and I willed my legs to hold me while I started down the steps.

My knee buckled.

Jace moved fast, and then I was up against his chest.

I froze. Fortunes upon fortunes in awkwardness. Possibly enough to buy Switzerland.

He eased away, appearing torn between retreating and making certain I didn't fall. His hand didn't leave my arm, though, but from the look on his face, he seemed afraid I'd burn him or something.

My face blazed. At a plodding pace, we continued down the stairs.

"Sorry," I offered, my eyes locked squarely on the steps below.

He made a vague noise of acknowledgment. My insides

curdled with embarrassment.

The stairway turned and delivered us to a heavy steel fire door. Keeping hold of me, Jace shifted around to tug the thing open.

A cacophony followed, shoving through the opening doorway like a battering ram made of sound. People shouted to each other, barked orders at each other, held conversations and joked and called questions to each other. To a person, they rushed around like they were all in the middle of a thousand tasks, the purposes of which I couldn't hope to guess. The room around them was massive, like a gigantic waiting area in an office building. Steel plating formed the far wall, leading me to assume windows had been there. Solid, gray concrete scrawled with old graffiti made up the other three sides of the cavernous space, and the floor and ceiling besides. To my right, steel cabinets occupied the area behind what might have once been a front desk, while numerous landline phones dotted the desk itself. Computers were arranged on the left side of the room, and people sat in front of the machines, typing quickly. Other people conferred before various televisions in the corners. From what I could catch of their conversations, they seemed like they were dissecting the news reports playing there.

My eyes caught on the nearest television screen. News reports, sure, but suddenly Miguel's and Veronique's pictures were in them. I couldn't hear the reporter's commentary over the voices around me, but the words flashing across the screen were more than clear.

Fugitives. Most Wanted.

"No, not Atlanta. I said *Alabama*, you moron!" Declan strode through a doorway to my right. "Our intel isn't that specific yet!"

With a huff, he thumbed off the phone in his hand. He shoved the cell into the pocket of his white lab coat, only to stop as he spotted me.

"She lives," he commented dryly.

"Oh, shut it, Declan," Willa snapped, marching past him. "Hey, Baylie. Good to see you awake." Her red ponytail swinging, she tossed me a quick smile before turning her attention to the main room. The wounds she'd gotten when that bastard, Logan, invaded her home and killed her grandmother seemed long since gone, but her baby-blue eyes still held a razor sharpness that promised to take no prisoners. "Any news from Chicago?" she called. "Our people lost the prisoner transport after it caused that pileup on Lakeview."

"Nothing yet," a man by the computers responded.

Willa muttered a curse and kept moving.

"Baylie!"

Maia's voice came from the far side of the room, and suddenly, people around one of the televisions shifted as if to get out of somebody's way. "Excuse me. Sorry." She slipped by the others and then jogged toward us.

My eyes widened. Dressed in cargo pants and a dark olive green tank top with brown leather boots, she looked like a recruit from military boot camp. A hunting knife the size of a machete was strapped to the side of her leg, as if she was ready to hack her way through the Amazon.

Maia grinned, not seeming to notice my stare. "You're up! You didn't tell us she was actually *up*!"

She directed the last to Jace, who shrugged uncomfortably. "Veronique was checking—"

Dhanya walked in through another doorway. Like her fiancée, Maia, she was dressed in dark, almost camouflage-like colors and she had a long knife lashed to her leg. "Oh my God, Baylie?" She beamed at the sight of me, relief clear in the expression.

I tried to match her smile and couldn't even come close. "Yeah, hey. Um, what is all—"

"Dhanya?" a woman by the computers called. "We've got a report coming back from Vancouver."

The girl gave me an apologetic look. "Sorry." She glanced at Maia. "You—"

"I'm good, yeah. Go on."

Dhanya hurried toward the woman.

I looked to Maia, still wide-eyed and unable to hide it.

She saw my alarm this time, and she winced. "Dhanya's sort of their resource on enforcer info now. One of them, anyway. There were a few people here who trained for being an enforcer like she did when she was younger, but they..." She trailed off, looking uncomfortable. "Anyway, there aren't as many anymore. But she and the others have been helping Noah track down enforcers around the country, in case they have any information on Ari."

Oh.

I nodded, trying to absorb the information, even if I already felt like I was on total overload.

Maia gave me another smile, though this time, her attention flicked around the room too. "How about we head out to the courtyard, eh? Maybe get some fresh air?"

Without waiting for a response, she retreated toward a steel-reinforced door near the covered windows. Two men stood on either side of it with knives the size of swords. The effect was surreal, like I was suddenly trapped in some bizarre mashup of medieval times and a modern military nightmare, and for some reason, the realization suddenly made it hard to breathe. The men skimmed their gazes over me, coldly evaluating, and then they nodded at Maia and Jace like I'd passed some test. Maia tugged the door open and hurried outside.

The hot desert air hit me hard after the refrigerator-like air conditioning of the building. Blinking against the heat that seemed to want to zap my eyeballs into dust, I scanned the area. Industrial-looking walls of off-white concrete surrounded us on each side, like we were at the bottom of a four-story-deep box. Windows lined the height of the walls, though most of their glass was gone and only the steel reinforcements inside remained. Cement walkways cut winding paths through the dust and dirt of the courtyard, and dead sprigs of old landscaping still stuck up from several places. The only color came from the graffiti covering the walls, though from the faded paint, the art seemed fairly old.

Maia crossed to a low cement bench to one side of the walkway and sat down. Reluctantly holding onto Jace's arm, I trailed after her and sank down on the other end of the bench.

"Are you doing okay?" Maia asked, the moment I sat down. "I mean, Veronique said it could be weeks before you'd be up to moving much once you were awake."

I managed a nod. "I'm fine." I saw her gaze go to Jace, incredulous, and quickly, I cast a look around for something to distract them. I *was* fine. Who gave a crap if there wasn't a sane reason why?

"What is all this?" I asked.

Maia's wince returned. "Um, well… resistance headquarters."

At my expression, she shrugged. "We couldn't go back to the bunker at Fiona's. Even if enforcers haven't been seen there, Miguel says it's too dangerous to return now. But the judges don't seem aware of this place, since Harvey bought it through some shell companies about a decade ago, so we decided this'd be a safe location to set up shop."

"We?" I repeated.

She blinked at me, and I struggled to regroup. Right. The resistance she and the others were obviously a big part of now.

God, I wished Noah was here.

"What was all that in there?" I tried.

She looked from me to Jace as if seeking help. "Well, basically… war."

I struggled to keep my jaw from dropping.

"It started about two weeks after Ari left." Jace's voice was so quiet, it was chilling. "Three dehaian attacks—*supposed* dehaian attacks—on the ruanir. All in rapid succession, all in different parts of the country. The human authorities haven't seemed to connect the dots, and most humans online are just yelling about whether they need more guns or more gun control." He shook his head. "But meanwhile, the judges claim the dehaians have declared war on us. They say they had no warning, that this was an unprovoked strike. They say the dehaians are back, and they're hunting the ruanir down. But families died. Kids. And then more attacks followed, more spaced out, and in other parts of the country from the first ones—"

"It's been terrifying," Maia summed up. She caught sight of my expression. "Not because we believe them, but because of what it means. What's happened because of it."

I wasn't sure I wanted to know. "And that is?"

"Our people are panicking," Jace said. "The news you saw in there? That's twenty-four hours a day, played on stations ruanir receive through special modifications to their phones or televisions. It's the Judiciary's way of communicating important information to our people. And all it does anymore is talk about how the dehaians have come back, how they've reclaimed control of the Beast, how all the old legends are true, and how they're turning it on us again. The judges say the dehaians could be anyone. *Anywhere.* They even claim to have stopped a few attacks now, though of course we just have to take their word for that." He looked disgusted. "It's all one big propaganda machine."

Maia glanced at him. "That's not all, though."

Great. This was bad enough. A bunch of paranoid wizards in a world that didn't know they existed?

A bunch of paranoid wizards who were turning on dehaians? On Noah?

I wondered if anyone had warned Chloe and Zeke to keep their people away from the coast.

"The bastards are smart," Jace said. "Our people hide what we are. No one knows we exist. So for these supposed dehaians to figure out which families are ruanir and which aren't… it shouldn't have happened. Except now there are 'traitors' in the ruanir. Conspirators who heard the Beast was back and, rather than aid the Judiciary and our people, ran to the dehaians to cut a deal and save themselves instead."

"Miguel and Veronique," Maia supplied in a quiet voice. "Mostly, anyway. They're the ringleaders, according to the Judiciary. The rest show up on the news too, though. Declan, Willa, a bunch of others. Pretty much anyone the Judiciary believes is in the resistance—which means innocent people are getting caught up in this too. The judges have set them all up to take the fall for this."

I stared at them. "What about you guys? Noah?"

Maia bit her lip.

"Maia and I are there too," Jace confirmed. "We're the 'poor, misguided ones.' They're accusing Dhanya of being the one who 'misled' us."

"Dhanya?"

Maia shifted her shoulders with discomfort. "She's a threat to them. Given her history with the enforcers, she's got training and information the judges would prefer she didn't share. They're calling for her capture."

"What about Ari?" I asked.

Jace's jaw worked around. "She supposedly found out

about all this and 'did the right thing.' Ran to warn the judges. Volunteered to help them in any way she could."

His brow twitched coldly.

My skin crawled.

"They're not calling for our heads," Jace continued. "Not yet. We need to be 'saved' instead. We're the poster children for what could happen without the constant vigilance of others to keep their fellow ruanir on the 'right path'—like, if we, with our families' high positions in society could be turned against our people, what could Miguel and the rest do with those who've been *lazy* in their loyalty to the Judiciary?" He scoffed. "'Sign up to show your support of the Judiciary today.' And meanwhile, our families are paraded around, surrounded by judges and enforcers and pleading for us to understand how 'mistaken' we've been. Mom's just *loving* the attention." His tone was scathing.

Maia shifted on the bench. "Mine's not."

Jace's dark expression fractured into something apologetic before he turned away.

"She okay?" I asked warily.

Maia blinked fast, pain in her eyes. "I don't know. She doesn't *look* hurt."

"Surely your dad wouldn't—"

"Judges don't care," Jace interrupted, his attention on a nearby planter. An empty cube of off-white concrete, it still held dead sprigs that had probably once been plants. "If he thinks hurting her will get the Judiciary what they want…"

Nausea twisted my gut.

"She'll be okay," Maia said, like she was reassuring herself. I could see her hands tremble as she tangled them together on her lap.

"Yeah," Jace agreed.

Silence reigned.

"So…" I said into the quiet. "I'm guessing you guys didn't find him. Maia's dad, I mean."

"No," Jace said flatly.

"It was bait," Maia said, "like Miguel told us. Him being in Grayland, the fact I knew that information. The judges have plans within plans. That was just another one."

I didn't know what to say. Miguel's people had stopped us from going after the judge in Grayland, Washington. They claimed the Judiciary already knew we were coming. So hoping that he'd stay put after the judges had gotten their hands on Ari…

Long shot, to say the least.

"To hear them talk," Maia said, "they're just doing the best they can to counter the 'dehaian threat,' but within days of the first supposed dehaian attack, they were already spreading the word about their new initiative. Made it sound like real spur-of-the-moment-type stuff, like they'd just come up with the ideas in a frantic meeting or something. But it was all 'taking the fight to the dehaians' and 'defending our homes' and whatever."

"The strakirin," I filled in, not really asking.

Maia nodded. "And enforcers. The Judiciary's spokesperson announced the plan, broadcast a call for volunteers, and then, about a week after that… we saw her."

I glanced at Jace. The guy had three expressions: awkward, neutral, and seething rage. The latter—apparently never very far below the surface—was now back on his face in force. I could feel the tension coming off him like heat waves.

He looked like he wanted to kill something.

"They showed Ari on the news," Maia said. "She was in a lab. Miguel's people have been trying to dissect the video and the transmission data for weeks to determine where she might be. But she, um… she looked human at first but in that green swimsuit thing like when we found her on the coast. And then they had her dive into this tank of water, and she just…"

I shifted uncomfortably on the bench. I had no idea what a strakirin looked like. Noah only said he hadn't seen anything like one of them in his life.

Maia didn't seem to want to describe it. "The judges asked for others to join the cause, become like her."

I stared at her.

"We're not sure how many have volunteered. Hundreds, maybe, if even half the number the judges are claiming is true. But they're just kids. All of them, just kids. And anyone else who wants to 'help the cause' has become an enforcer. To hear the news, whole families have signed up to fight back against the 'dehaian threat' in one way or another, because who knows, right? It could be their family who's butchered by the dehaians next."

"What about Noah?" I asked. "What do they know about him?"

Maia went quiet, glancing to Jace.

"What?" I pressed, anxiety thrumming through me.

"Your family's okay," Maia said. "Ellie and Olivia too."

Oh, that wasn't a good answer. That was what you told people after a car accident. After a fire.

The looks on their faces weren't helping. Adrenaline pounded through my veins. "*Okay*, but…?"

I didn't know how to ask, or even what to ask. Had the judges hurt them? Had they tracked my family down? The judges had more money than God. Dad and the others could have gone halfway around the world and still not been safe.

"We're pretty sure Ari told them everything," Jace admitted, not looking at me. "Noah's family. Yours. Chloe and Ellie and the landwalkers." He paused. "You. Anything she knew. Miguel worried she might, so we reached out to Ellie not long after we got here."

"We found the number on your phone," Maia added apologetically. "Sorry."

I couldn't have cared less. "But you're certain she—"

"The Delaneys' house caught fire about a month and a half ago," Jace said. "Not bad, just a few rooms burnt. Bait for the Beast, we think. Or you. Someone broke into Olivia's house in Santa Lucina around the same time too; she saw them on security cameras."

My hands went cold. I could feel my heart in my ears, pounding.

A faint, tingling sensation shivered past the adrenaline in my veins.

I froze. No. No, no, no, that wasn't real. That wasn't—

It got stronger.

I pushed away from the bench, pacing out into the box-like courtyard with my legs as wobbly as paper and my heartbeat drumming in my ears. I wouldn't let this out. Couldn't. I'd hidden this for a year—the broken things in my apartment notwithstanding—and I'd hide it for the rest of my life if I had to. Squeezing my eyes shut, I made myself breathe and begged the feeling to go away.

The tingling sensation faded.

Maia was watching me, but there wasn't anything but pity in her gaze. "Miguel had already gotten the Delaneys to safety, though," she said. "Noah's family is somewhere in Michigan now, and your dad and stepmom are too."

Her expression was earnest. Jace wouldn't meet my eyes, even though he'd stood up like he planned to catch me if I fell.

But I didn't think they'd noticed anything. They thought I was just upset about my family.

And I was. Relieved too. I couldn't think what I would've done if they hadn't been okay.

But it raised another question…

"What'd you tell them?" I asked warily. I eased myself down onto an empty planter, not trusting my legs.

Maia shifted on the bench when Jace sat back down. The scratch of the gravel beneath her shoes sounded loud in the quiet. "Ellie told Noah's family that she had heard about some dehaian threats against them. She and Olivia finally convinced them to head back east just a few days before the fire. But Ellie also said that she didn't think your dad knew about any of this, so Miguel arranged for him to get a temporary-job offer out of state. Too good to resist."

"The judges can't track that?" I asked.

"Miguel used proxies and shell companies."

I nodded, distracted. That was good. Really. And maybe Dad wouldn't even need to know the truth.

Maybe Sandra, my stepmom, had told him about Noah and the others, though…

A pained feeling twisted in my gut. I tried to push it down. She wouldn't. Not after all these years. Things could still be ordinary after this.

Maybe.

I wrapped my arms around my middle. "Did they ask about me?"

Maia and Jace were quiet.

"Ellie told the Delaneys that you two were visiting some landwalker elders overseas," Maia said. "Last minute thing."

I stared at her. "And my dad?"

"Backpacking across Europe with friends."

She winced at my expression. "It was the best we could do. We couldn't risk them calling the police or raising any kind of fuss. The Judiciary might've picked up on it, and since we couldn't take you to a hospital and they almost certainly would have wanted us to…" She gave a helpless shrug. "Your family has been calling your phone, though. We haven't answered. We're just sending texts, trying to deflect concern for as long as we can."

"Two months," I said.

Her wince deepened. "It's been getting tense, yeah."

I turned away. As terrible a solution as it was, I couldn't blame them. What else should they have done? By now, the judges probably knew I'd been shot and were watching the hospitals as a result.

Though that still left the question of what to do now.

I looked back to Maia and Jace. "I have to call them."

Jace hesitated, while Maia's worried expression deepened.

"What?" I asked.

"It's just…" Maia started. "What're you going to tell them? The farther they stay away from this, the better off they'll be."

Like I didn't know that.

"She has to talk to them eventually," Jace said.

Maia frowned.

"Secure phone lines are inside," Jace continued before Maia could speak. "You can call from there."

"Thanks."

He gave a neutral nod. Rising from the bench, he eyed me for a second and then held out an arm, waiting.

I hesitated, but I didn't want to collapse on the way in there. My legs still felt made of Jell-O. Pushing up from the edge of the planter, I walked the few steps over to him and took his arm.

His gaze twitched toward me, but he didn't say a word. Keeping his hold on my arm, he started after Maia toward the exit, even as awkwardness hung around us like a fog.

The thick, metal door clunked shut behind us like a vault clos-ing. Their expressions like stone, the men on either side of it nodded to us as we came back inside.

"Maia!"

I spotted Dhanya rising from a chair and motioning urgently for Maia to join her.

"Uh—" Maia started.

"We're fine," Jace replied. "Go."

She nodded fast and hurried toward her fiancée.

"This way." Jace headed for the front desk. My legs waffling beneath me, I followed him.

A woman dressed in a leather jacket covered with military patches glanced up from behind the desk when we came closer. "She need something?" she asked tersely, returning her atten-tion to the shotgun she was cleaning. A man and a woman with knives clasped in their fists stood on either side of her, never taking their eyes from her or the gun.

"Just a phone," Jace replied.

The woman jerked her chin at a cream-colored, corded machine in a line of mismatched telephones. "Techs just checked that one."

Jace nodded, but the woman's focus had already moved on to another person who'd come up to the desk. The two people with knives remained behind her, their eyes on the gun like they expected it to sprout legs and run.

My gaze lingered on them. "What is all this?" I whispered.

"What's with the ones watching her?"

"Security," he answered quietly.

"Security for what? And what's with all the knives? She's—"

"Shannon wasn't the only one."

My stomach turned to lead. The woman who'd shot me, the one who'd been transformed into a monster by the judges.

I glanced at the rest of the room.

"There have been two others since you were hurt," Jace continued in a low voice. "People the resistance didn't know had been taken. And when they came back, they seemed fine—right up until they tried to kill everyone. We lost a lot of people… to them, to the friendly fire to stop them, to ricochets and missed shots and all of it. Most of these people are trained military, but when the enemy could be your buddy or that cute girl from the mess hall and, in all the shooting and confusion, you can't even be sure who the bad guys are… too many things can go wrong. Now, no one touches a gun unless they've got guards ready to kill them if they even *look* like they're going to turn traitor. Now everyone carries knives because you can't mow down fifty people with a blade. It's a trade-off. Maybe someone is compromised, and yeah, maybe they'll get their hands on a gun on top of everything else. But maybe they won't. And at least this way, the rest of us aren't armed fish shooting each other in a barrel." His mouth tightened. "The whole thing just sucks."

I turned back to him. That was about the most personal commentary I'd heard from him on this nightmare.

He seemed to realize he'd let that guard of his down. He pulled his attention back to the phones, his face going unreadable once again. "We'll get you a knife later. Whatever you're comfortable with."

I hesitated. Great.

Attempting to hide my uneasiness, I reached for the phone.

Running footsteps interrupted me. Miguel raced into the room, several other people in military fatigues coming behind him. "Location identified in Colorado," he called to the people by the computers.

Maia rose from a chair, Dhanya only a heartbeat behind. "Judges?" Maia asked urgently.

"Landwalkers." Miguel returned his attention to the others. "I need two teams. We've isolated a possible way in, but I need backup for the base location too. We don't know what'll follow us. Got it? Head out in ten. Now, move!"

The room erupted into chaos as everyone scrambled from their chairs and headed in a hundred directions at once. Jace moved fast, practically muscling me out of the way while the woman by the phones opened up a steel-plated door behind the front desk and the whole area turned into a free-for-all of people arming themselves with guns.

I retreated into a corner, Jace still holding onto my arm. "What's going on?" I asked.

Jace grunted as someone bumped him and pushed him against me.

"Sorry," he muttered, easing away from me.

I tried to find my voice again. It was difficult. We were still crammed close enough that I could smell him—and honestly, he smelled kind of good. A bit like the woods near my stepfamily's cabin, with a hint of spice.

I shoved down the observation and stabbed it to death for good measure. That sort of thinking was the absolute *last* thing I needed right now, for about a million reasons.

"Yeah, whatever," I managed. "What's, um—what did Miguel mean by 'landwalkers'?"

"Some landwalkers have gone missing."

"What? When?"

Jace hesitated. "A few days ago. It could be nothing, though. Coincidence."

I'd just woken up from a coma, and even *I* didn't believe that. "Is Ellie one of them?"

He shook his head. I started breathing again.

"She's helping find them."

"*Huh?*"

"She's helping."

"With what?"

"Finding the landwalkers. Those elders have connections, and she's got those weird abilities…"

He trailed off, seeming to see that this wasn't calming me down.

I tried to keep my feet under me, no matter how the room had started swaying. Ellie was helping the ruanir resistance, my stepbrother was God knew where, and my family was in hiding.

I started to wonder if I'd really woken up. Maybe this was an insane dream.

The way my heart was racing would seem to belie that.

"Okay." I swallowed hard. "But will Ellie be there, then? At this place they're all going?"

Jace hesitated. "Probably."

I struggled past him and headed toward Miguel, willing my legs to hold me steady.

"Baylie!" Jace hurried after me and caught my arm again. "What are you—"

"I'm going too."

He made an incredulous noise as he twisted to get out of people's way. "You just came out of a *coma*. You shouldn't even be *walking*, let alone—"

"I need to see my friend."

"They can bring Ellie here after this is done."

An angry noise left me. I couldn't wait. Not right now. Sure, it might be safer for me, but everyone around me had weapons, Ellie was some kind of resistance operative, and I'd just found myself in the middle of a war. Noah was gone. Chloe wasn't here. Jace and the others seemed nice and all, but I'd only *actually* known them for a few hours—my two months in a coma aside. I needed someone I trusted. I needed to know I hadn't lost my mind.

If I was even really awake.

"I'm not staying here," I told him.

"Baylie, you—"

"Jace, I won't—"

"Okay!"

I blinked at him, surprised at how he'd switched from arguing to agreeing without much of a stop in between.

"Okay," he said more calmly, not looking happy in the least. He glanced toward the opposite side of the room. Miguel and his people were heading for the door. Jace took my arm and started after the others. "Come on. You can call your family from Harvey's safe house."

ARI

My body sped through the water after Logan.

My mind was under siege.

In the darkness, I trembled, holding up my walls with all my might. I had no idea how long it had been. The twilight world of the ocean wasn't that different from the windowless hell of the judges' white room; there wasn't a hint of time in either of them. But with every mile of gray limbo that swept past, the drone grew louder. The ocean seemed to be feeding it, helping it, strengthening it. Magic from the horrible water all around me flicked through the cracks in my walls like a vicious snake's tongue, sending shocks through me while it eroded every defense between me and oblivion.

Endless, soothing oblivion where nothing would matter, not ever again…

Desperate rage filled me. I wouldn't end like this. I'd see my family again. I'd survive.

My God, I had to survive.

Vague figures floating in the distance registered on my

strange echolocation ability. We were closer to the ocean floor now, and hills with pockmarks like caves prickled at the edge of my senses too.

Logan slowed, but continued onward, and my body did the same. The figures came into view.

All of them.

I stared. Strakirin. Hundreds upon hundreds. Maybe even a thousand.

How many had the judges made?

The creatures hovered in the gray twilight water, their sinuous tails rippling slowly. Their bioluminescent fins glowed like a shifting fabric of glittering gold, and their yellow-green eyes shone, unblinking, unwavering, locked on Logan.

On me.

A jolt went through me again, followed by the lull of peace through surrender, as the ocean cracked my mental defenses and then the drone slipped through the gap. My world blurred with the desire to join, to obey the masters. To do as the masters commanded, *whatever* they commanded, because that was my purpose.

It would be so easy…

So easy…

I whimpered in the dark, trying to fight it. Slowly, painfully, I bolstered my walls again, but not before I heard a whisper weave through the drone, fading in and out like it was carried on a shifting breeze.

They'd been waiting for me.

A dehaian swam up from the caves below, heading straight

toward us, and two others followed. Shuddering in the dark corner of my mind, I watched them approach, their figures slowly resolving out of the gray twilight. A silver-haired dehaian man with gunmetal gray scales swam on the left, while a brown-haired dehaian guy with black and orange scales floated on the right.

Chills went through me when I recognized the guy in the middle.

The man arched a dark eyebrow at Logan. "*This* is what we were waiting for?"

He didn't look much different from when I'd first seen him, after I was kidnapped by the judges from in front of Baylie's apartment. He'd stood outside the tank that was holding me in the lab in Santa Lucina. He'd mocked me and Noah before the procedure to strip away my identity began, saying that the judges had had their eyes on me for a long while. Saying I was going to become something new and yet old, all at the same time.

I still wasn't sure what that meant.

But he'd been human-looking then. A dark-haired guy enjoying the power trip of having the Beast and me at the Judiciary's mercy. Now he had scales the color of sea foam and a tail crisscrossed by scars that looked like they'd never healed well. Another scar continued over his chest, long and ragged like someone had nearly cut him open once.

His eyes were the same, though. Black, scathing eyes over a mouth that hovered on the edge of a sneer.

To see them next to each other now, it suddenly struck

me how much he reminded me of Logan. He appeared cold. Contemptuous. Certain the world owed him, and ready to make it bleed if it didn't agree. If I didn't know Logan's father was an enforcer who'd died before Logan was even born, I would have thought I was looking at father and son.

"We've evaded four Yvarian patrols in the past hour alone," the man continued. "And your Judiciary had us wait for you to bring only *one?*"

"Ozzie, *chill.*" Logan scowled, putting a hand to his temple like he had a headache. "She's the last. The judges didn't want to leave any behind."

"These creatures are krill, child. *Plankton*, even. One more or less, what does it matter?"

"And if someone had found her?" Logan countered. "God, Ozzie—"

"*Osias.*"

A smirk flickered over Logan's face, though it was lost beneath another wince of a headache almost immediately.

"Why did they not send this one earlier?" the man with orange and black scales asked.

Logan shrugged. "I don't know. Maybe they wanted to run some final checks. Maybe they had some more of those resistance people to snuff out. What does it matter?" He started for the rest of the strakirin.

The dehaians didn't move.

Logan stopped. "Relax, guys. Zero-Zero-Whatever here is just the same as the rest of them. You think the judges would let her out if they weren't sure? She's ready. The strakirin will find the target, and then every single one of our enemies, here and on land, will die."

I froze in the darkness. What?

"The plan'll be fine," Logan continued. "You just tell me whether your part of it's working."

Osias regarded him darkly. "Yes. These *things* have been trying that out at my command for the past half hour. But can she do it too?"

Logan turned to me. "Block yourself from being detected."

My skin shivered. Behind my walls, I winced at the strange new feeling running through my body, like the faint buzz of a mild electrical current.

"Excellent." Osias grinned.

"Yeah?" Logan asked like he wasn't sure of whatever this was himself.

Osias' grin turned derisive. "Yes. She has that masking trait from the Beast, same as any of them. If I couldn't see her in front of me, I wouldn't know she was here at all."

Confusion moved through me, and then realization dawned. Noah was invisible sometimes. And maybe, when he was like that…

Oh, God. If the dehaians had that echolocation trait too, they *should* have been able to feel Noah, even if only from the disruption of the water. But maybe they couldn't. Maybe he blocked them from doing that somehow. Maybe he didn't even *know* he did… he'd never mentioned it.

I'd never asked.

But the judges must have taken something like that from

him, along with his magic. Given it to the strakirin. Made them almost invisible, in a way.

The implications rushed through me. No one would know the strakirin were there. If the dehaians' echolocation couldn't find them… in the deep, in the blackness that had to be down here, they'd have no warning. Not till the monsters were right on top of them. And with the speed at which those monsters could move…

No one would be able to stop them. Even if the dehaians figured it out, even if they brought entire *armies*, they wouldn't even know the strakirin were nearby till there was no escape. Add into that the ability to poison whomever touched them, their ability to electrocute anyone nearby with lightning, and the hive mind controlling them all…

I'd always been so scared of the dehaians, of how fast and dangerous they could be.

The strakirin would make them look like kittens.

"Cool," Logan said.

"And the rest?" Osias prompted.

"I told you. She's no different than them, Ozzie."

Osias gave him a heated look.

Logan smiled like he'd won something, though I didn't know what. "Osias," he allowed.

"For your sake, I hope you're right." Osias spun, swimming toward the strakirin, and called, "The others are waiting."

Logan watched him go, contempt twisting his lip. Shaking his head, he dismissed the expression.

His eyes twitched over to me. "Too bad you're already dead,

Ari. I would've loved to see your face when your family dies. Once we find what we're after down here…" He made a theatrically worried sound.

I trembled in the dark.

Chuckling, he glanced around to the other strakirin. Osias was already beyond them, swimming off into the murk. The strakirin didn't move, however. They didn't even look in his direction. Just as before, their focus was locked on Logan.

The drone got louder. He wasn't the only one they were watching.

But I needed to join them. To give in and drop my defenses. I needed…

"Come on." Logan motioned over his shoulder for me to follow and then took off after Osias. My body trailed after him, obeying the order.

The other strakirin moved as one to join me.

To *be* me.

Horror gripped me. Oh my God, I could feel them. Their strange ability to block echolocation or not, I could feel the strakirin in the water, but in a different way than the dehaian swimming ahead of me, or anything below or around us. I could feel their *bodies*. The way the water slid across their skin, just the same as it slid across mine. The way their tails moved. The way their lungs breathed in the depths. My mind was spread out into theirs and vice versa, and all the sensations poured into me as if they were my own. With Logan, it wasn't nearly as strong. Nowhere even close because I hadn't even noticed it at all, but for the rest…

I *was* them. They *were* me. My mind, my body…

Panic pounded through me. Too much more of this, and I'd go mad. I needed to keep it out. Buffer it. The overwhelming awareness was too much.

The ocean slammed against my walls.

I fumbled around in the tiny corner of my mind, straining to maintain my defenses while I hunted for something, anything to block the ocean and that sound-that-wasn't-a-sound. Memories only distracted; I wouldn't want to sacrifice them anyway. But then, if my walls fell, they'd go too. Everything was in danger of dying while the ocean pounded at my defenses, fueling the drone like it was mainlining kerosene to a wildfire.

Miles shot by beneath us, a blur of hills and canyons and garbage from the world above. Cracks spread through my walls. Ocean magic poured through the gaps, tearing them wider, bringing the drone with it.

I retreated, frantic. I didn't want to die. I needed to gain control of my body and get back to my family. They were in danger. My friends were too, along with every dehaian in the ocean. I couldn't die out here, alone in the dark, where no one would ever know what—

A faint sensation rushed across me, like a feather sweeping over my scales and skin, but the thing controlling my body didn't even seem to notice or care. Colors suddenly flickered in my mind, a rainbow blush like an aurora borealis in the darkness. Without even thinking, on pure instinct alone, I grasped after the impossible sensation. It was familiar. *Somehow* familiar.

But not enough to stop the wave of ocean magic pounding at the walls in my mind.

It tumbled over my tiny corner of safety, and I had nowhere else to run. The hive came with it, carried like venomous eels in a tsunami. The drone twisted and snapped at me, trying to tear through everything that was left of who I truly was, deep inside this crumbling corner of safety. The hive was everywhere inside my mind, surrounding me, choking me, and ocean magic powered it. Strengthened it. They'd been changed to survive it.

But so had I.

A chill wave rose up from inside all that was left of my true self, like ice water from the coldest depths of the sea. Colors swarmed inside me, spiraling about the tiny scrap of consciousness that was me, brushing me with feather-light kisses, leaving light wherever they touched. Ocean magic joined them, changing from a hell of consuming darkness to sparkling light when it absorbed into all that was left of my true mind. But the hive still had power too. It drew on the energy of the ocean as well, using it as fuel and attempting to consume its power before the magic could reach me. The drone tore at the lights surrounding me, trying to devour them, trying to choke my life away and leave nothing but cold emptiness as a memorial to where my true self had died.

My mind, my body, my entire existence had become a war zone.

Inside my head, I grasped after every trace of light, every scrap of ocean magic, struggling to bring them into myself even as I fought to keep the drone out. Everything around my body, the seafloor and the other strakirin, were nothing but snapshots amid the tumult.

The hive kept my body swimming like a puppet. The drone fought to destroy me once and for all.

Rocks flashed by. A valley too. Logan, his hand raised. The strakirin slowed. They didn't seem to be reacting to the war within me, but maybe they didn't see a point.

Maybe the hive simply believed it would win.

Words then. Osias, his mouth moving, the sounds warping in and out of intelligibility. "Pass… opportunity… see what they can do."

Alarm prickled through me, threatening to distract me from the war to stay alive. What did he mean?

Logan's words were garbled. "…supposed… stay unnoticed…"

Osias' response was lost, but I saw Logan grin.

My alarm grew, but I couldn't focus on the two of them. The hive was everywhere. All around, sapping my strength everywhere it touched, even as the ocean magic that reached me tried to build my defenses back up. A war of attrition, where every inch of ground ceded was me, where holding territory was all I could do.

And I couldn't sustain this forever.

Osias made a gesture, and the strakirin swam toward the ocean floor. My body followed them.

A weird sensation sped past the edge of my awareness, like static tingling over my skin. An image flashed through my mind, a snapshot of the world outside my body. The barren expanse of rocks changed. A village lay below us, seeming to have appeared out of nowhere. The immense boulders held stands of long, green-leafed plants across the caves on them, like curtains on the windows of houses. Lights in myriad colors glinted on strings between the rocks, like street lamps. Dehaians swam through paths between the boulders as if they were traveling down streets. Parents were there. Children. They looked up in horror when we came into view above them.

Oh my God, no.

Osias came up beside me, grinning, his words carrying past the rushing in my ears. "Kill them all."

Panic filled me as my body dove. Spikes slipped from the skin of my forearms, fanning out to stand up like a line of translucent knives. Lightning crackled over my hands and scales alike, just as it did on all the strakirin.

But that wasn't the worst of it.

A cold, slimy sensation poured out of my body, invisible in the water but with immediate effect. Shrieks of terror came from the dehaians. Paralysis overtook some of them, while others bolted wildly for nowhere, screaming as if they'd just seen their worst nightmare.

Fear. Another one of the Beast's powers.

Another weapon stolen for the strakirin.

I cried out with horror inside my mind. It was all I could do to hang on against the assault of the drone trying to destroy me. Ocean magic whirled in me, a blessing and a razor-blade curse all at the same time. The whisper-soft lights around my essence flared and spun, fighting to hold back the onslaught of the hive. But if I lost focus, if I let myself become distracted for even a moment, it would devour me. There'd be nothing left of who I was, nothing left to even *dream* of stopping this madness or escaping this hell.

And then the strakirin reached the dehaians, and in a swath of blood and terror, the dehaians began to die. Howls of pain rose. Scorching blasts of electricity came from everywhere. I shrieked inside my mind as my body cut down a man so fast, I only caught a glimpse of bone and flesh before he was behind me. Satisfaction thrummed through the link to the other strakirin, and thrills of pleasure too, all of it pounding at my mind in an endless cadence of surrender, surrender, surrender.

I wanted to sob. So many of the dehaians were dying, just like the resistance. Just like the countless men and women the judges had used to test me. And I couldn't help them.

I could never help anyone.

Poison flooded from the strakirin. The dehaians tried to escape, twisting fast as thought but still too slow in this game of tag from hell. Strakirin fingertips brushed skin, scales. More screams followed. More pleasure pounded through the drone.

More people collapsed and died.

Grief choked me as I tried to hold my ground against the hive snapping and snarling at every shred of magic surrounding me. There were so many strakirin, so much power behind the thousand-strong mind that cared for nothing, wanted nothing. A wasteland of emotionlessness, of hunger and sameness, whose only joy was found in delivering death at the masters' command. The hive couldn't be stopped. Couldn't be overpowered.

And against that, was only me. Alone in the dark, surrounded by a maelstrom that was devouring all light.

I had to survive this. I had to help my family. I had to break free.

My body spun in the water, and my eyes fastened on the next target. A tiny girl. Barely more than a toddler, with a stubby little fin and pigtail braids in her golden hair.

In the darkness, I choked. Oh my God, not a child.

My body took off after her. There was no way the girl could outdistance me. Her little blue tail thrashed, fighting frantically for speed while she bawled for her mommy.

And through my body, through my lips, the hive smiled.

I screamed.

The protective light swirling around me exploded outward. Ocean magic went with it, the strange kaleidoscopic power shredding the hive and the darkness like a supernova of blinding light. Every bit of myself, every trace of me, erupted in the blast, and I didn't care. Not anymore.

The hive had emotionlessness as its power.

I had rage.

The kaleidoscopic magic inside me crashed into the drone and didn't stop there. Countless days and weeks of anger and pain poured out of me, shrieking into every silence, every lull in that mindless, endless hum of submission, tearing it apart. Electricity, tension, and pure will to survive rushed through my bones, my muscles, and out to my limbs like magma from the core of the earth, chasing the hive from every inch of my body. They wouldn't have me. Not again.

Not ever again.

And then the hive was gone.

Breathless, I hovered in the water. I turned my head, lifting my hands in front of me even as I willed the spikes to retreat back into my skin. My tail moved when I wanted it. My fingers curled into fists at my command. I had my body back, and my defenses too. The walls no longer filled only a tiny corner of my mind but, instead, traced my skin like a shield ready to halt an invasion.

But I could still hear the hive in the distance, beyond my defenses. It was surprised. No, more than that.

It didn't know what to do.

A blue-scaled dehaian grabbed the little girl and bolted after the other survivors.

"No!" Osias shouted. "Kill the escapees!"

None of the strakirin obeyed.

"Something's wrong." Logan swam around, looking at the strakirin like they'd grown horns. "They're… something's…" His attention landed on me. His confusion flickered like he was suddenly seeing something about me, though God knew what. My shock, maybe. Or my fear. But stunned comprehension took the place of his bafflement. "She… oh my God, she's…"

On all sides of me, the other strakirin turned, their snake-yellow eyes finding me in the gray twilight. The drone bore down on my defenses like a physical weight, pressing on me to come back, to obey, to never leave. Staying was important. Staying *mattered*, more than I could understand.

A whimper escaped me. Fatigue pulled at me. It'd taken

almost everything I had just to drive them out. And now I… I had to… I couldn't… they needed me to…

Logan's voice cut through the drone. "Grab her!"

As one, the other strakirin charged at me. Panic hit me, washing my fatigue away in a flood of desperate adrenaline. At only a thought, at the barest flicker of an idea, lightning erupted from me on every side. The nearest strakirin died instantly, caught in the tangle of blue-white power.

And it hurt. Oh God, it hurt. Even with my walls, sensations still reached me. The agony of their skin burning to black, of their throats closing on screams. They'd been me once. I'd been them. Pieces of that shared experience were still there, waiting for me, reaching for me, screaming with their pain.

My lightning faltered. My arms wrapped around my middle while I shook from the residual agony. Blackened bodies floated on all sides of me, with Logan and Osias just beyond. The two of them stared, Osias horrified and Logan…

Fear quivered my chest. He was still connected to the strakirin. He must have felt the same agony I had. And now, hate curdled his expression, burning like acid through the nonchalant mask he always wore. I'd seen that expression once, when I blasted him away the first time he tried to hurt me. The expression of a sadistic child who believed it was his right to pull the legs from someone's body as readily as he'd take the wings from a fly, simply because he considered it fun.

Not only had I hurt him, I'd stopped the rush of pleasure from killing the dehaians.

I'd gotten in his way.

"Get her, dammit!" Logan snarled.

The order reverberated through the drone, and instantly, the strakirin surged forward. I struck out again, desperate, but the hive didn't stop. It wouldn't, not this time. Individual bodies were nothing to the hive. Vessels of a single mind, a single will. It could lose a hundred of them, and it would only send two hundred more.

Because it had been commanded to capture me. It *needed* to capture me. I had to stay.

I retreated, lashing out with lightning while looking around frantically for a way out. Live strakirin shoved past the dying. My magic couldn't hit them all, not when they used the dead as shields. Like a tumbling wave of poisonous eels, they rushed at me, closer, closer.

And if they got a hand on me…

Shannon flashed through my mind. The woman who the judges had sent after me, the one who'd only needed to touch me to trigger an onslaught of magic that had nearly driven me from my own body and mind.

I spotted Logan beyond the wave. He was in control of them. He was the one they obeyed.

He was the only target that would stop this.

I struck out with my magic, aiming at him. His eyes went wide, and instantly, other strakirin lunged to intercept the blast and give their lives for his.

But they weren't quite fast enough.

Logan screamed as a tiny flicker of magical lightning lanced past him, scorching a line across his chest. All around me, the strakirin faltered, suddenly torn between their orders and the only pain that seemed to actually matter to them.

But the pause wouldn't last. Even now, Logan was regrouping, the rage and hate on his face even stronger than before.

I spun in the water and took off, racing for anyplace away from here.

7

LOGAN

I was going to kill her.

Shaking hard with pain, I stopped myself from touching the burns on my chest. A line of my skin was blackened. Red too, like raw bacon. And, goddamn, it hurt like hell.

That *bitch*.

"What are you waiting for?" Osias shouted, gaping at me and then in the direction Ari had gone like his head was on a swivel. "Catch her!"

God, I was going to kill him too, the annoying bastard. I'd had about all of him I could take over these past few weeks. Constantly badgering me to leave, to get on with things even though all the strakirin hadn't been ready. He didn't care that it wasn't the plan, or that the judges didn't want a single strakirin left behind, just in case that idiotic resistance got their hands on one. No, Osias didn't care about any of that. All he cared about was Yvaria. His every waking moment seemed to be consumed with thoughts of revenge against the nation, its people, and especially its king.

Zek-something-or-other. The details hadn't exactly been worth my attention.

On a good day, his lack of objectivity was annoying. But when I'd just been hurt, it was inexcusable.

The surviving strakirin turned, locking their eyes on Osias. They felt my pain and my impulse to put the bastard out of my own misery as well. To his credit, the dehaian bastard seemed to notice their attention—not that he appeared to appreciate the perilousness of his situation.

"If she gets away, we're screwed," Osias growled.

Like I didn't know that. But I had bigger problems—like the fact my chest was burned and bleeding.

"Where the hell is that gel stuff?" I snapped back at him.

Osias glowered at me, but his attention still flicked toward my wound. He motioned shortly to one of his people. "Get the sieranchine."

About damn time.

While one of the dehaians slathered that glowing, glittering gel across the burn on my chest, I turned my attention to our surroundings. The bodies of the dead covered the ground, protected by the magical bubble curtain that surrounded the village from the desiccation effect that normally consumed bodies down here. I couldn't feel Ari racing away from us anymore; with the speed she had as a strakirin, she was probably miles from here by now.

But that didn't account for the failure of the hive.

Ari had felt like nothing before this, like just another mindless drone, and she'd been as responsive as a deflated blowup doll when I kissed her. So *nothing* should have been left of her in there. The procedure was damn near perfect. And I should know.

I could hear the entire hive in my mind.

I glared at them, silently cursing them for betraying me. They owed me everything. They were connected to me, after all. Not like they were to each other, of course. I wasn't one of them, even if I had their powers—but that was the point. I was the commander. The mind at the base of theirs, controlling them, powering them with my strategic skill, my brilliance.

The judges had designed it like this. The hive they'd created was like an enormous enforcer. A thousand mediocre minds, stripped of pesky individuality and memory, tied together through an amped-up version of that empathic link that had existed between Ari and the Beast. But the strakirin didn't only share feelings. They were the *same* being, synched together to the point where nothing of their individual selves existed anymore.

The hive wasn't sentient. Not exactly. Like a lobotomized dog, they existed to obey, to attack, to follow specific commands with almost no payoff but the magical rush of pleasure they received from the kill. There were a thousand of them, though. More, even. And with that many minds linked together, the judges had known that the hive would need a stabilizing force, someone with autonomy, to steer the monster in the direction they wanted. And that was me. The will at the heart of the hive. The mastermind.

Their core, and the only one still *myself* enough to be

considered alive.

Or so I'd thought.

I closed my eyes but my ability to see persisted, becoming a blurry image from a thousand angles through a thousand pairs of snake-like eyes. I could hear what they heard, see what they saw. The judges weren't fools—any pain the strakirin felt was barely a whisper when it reached me—but as for the rest…

"Any of you still in there?" I muttered.

Nothing changed. None of them even blinked. And more importantly, the drone continued just the same.

Huh.

She'd hurt it, though. Stunned the hive with her sudden reappearance as an actual person. Shockwaves had gone through the drone, bringing everything to a halt.

It shouldn't have been possible.

I hadn't picked up on her feelings, though. I hadn't had a single indication of what the hell was going on inside her that made her able to do that.

Clearly another failure of the hive.

"What did you say?" Osias snapped.

I opened my eyes. "Nothing." I glanced around at the dehaians. There weren't that many of them, although Osias hinted there were others elsewhere. Maybe a dozen here, all told. Maybe not even that.

"What are we waiting for, then?" Osias growled. "Your masters promised us Yvaria would burn, not that we'd give our enemies the very weapon we sacrificed to build."

My masters. Damn, this man was annoying. But he still had

a point. I had a mission down here, but I couldn't exactly let Ari escape. The dehaians getting their hands on her would be almost as bad as that resistance.

I turned back to the strakirin. With barely a thought from me, two dozen of them split off from the main group and swam toward us.

"Send some of your guys," I said. "These will go with them."

And, by proxy, so would I.

I ignored Osias' glare. Ignored him when he summoned his dehaian cohorts too. Several of them hovered nearby, waiting, while the rest set to hauling the bodies beyond the magical bubble curtain surrounding the village. The corpses would vanish once they hit the open water. No one would know what took out this place, not once we were done.

I liked the ocean for that at least. Bodies had a great way of disappearing down here.

And Ari would join them. She was out there, somewhere. Scared. Possibly hurt too—or at least she would be when I was done with her. If this miracle gel didn't fix the problem, I'd end up with a scar across my chest, thanks to her.

She'd blasted me away with her magic once, months ago. Now this.

My lip twitched. Forget killing her. When I was done, she'd *beg* me to let her die.

"The strakirin understand that capturing that girl is top priority, yes?" Osias said.

I turned to find him waiting, the other dehaians at his back. And I smiled.

"Of course," I told him, certainty at my words thrumming through my connection to the strakirin. "They know exactly what to do."

8

ARI

I fled through the ocean with no idea where I was going. Rocks shot past beneath me. Sand and valleys, mountains of garbage and endless stretches of nothing did too. It'd been all I could do earlier to hold out the drone. I hadn't been able to notice landmarks, or whatever the dehaians called them down here. The drone had devoured every ounce of my attention.

And now I couldn't hear the strakirin at all. The drone had dwindled to nothing as the miles fell behind me. After days, maybe even weeks, of that endless noise, the silence was eerie. And good. Undeniably good.

Except that I had no idea in which direction I'd been heading when I swam away from them.

And I had no idea where to go now.

Breathing hard, I scanned the water around me, only to be met with a gray-blue haze on every side. I hated the ocean. My *people* hated the ocean, and with good reason. It was dangerous. Deadly. Filled with sea creatures and dehaians and magic that would kill us all.

And it'd just saved my life.

The thought made me slow down. Ocean magic, the toxin we'd all been taught to fear, had saved me. It'd powered the hive, but it'd saved me too.

I felt numb at the thought. I didn't know what to do with it.

With how much it proved I was no longer even *remotely* ruanir.

But I was still me. In this messed-up body, yes, but at least I could control it now. And that was progress. That was something. So now all I needed was to get back to land and find the resistance. Surely there had to be some way to contact them.

Even if I didn't know what it would be.

I pushed the thought down before anxiety could bubble over my determination. I'd think of something. I'd find them, and they would confirm that my family was safe—because they would be. Jace and Maia and Dhanya would all be fine. The resistance would be able to help me. They'd capture a judge and get them to change me back somehow. I could warn Miguel and the others about the strakirin too. About how the judges were after something down here. All of it.

And they could do… what?

I stopped in the water, a chill creeping through my body. What *could* the resistance do about the judges' plans down here? Miguel and the others couldn't come underwater. They couldn't fight creatures with poison and spikes and impossible speed. Even the dehaians couldn't match that.

At least the dehaians stood a chance.

But how much of one? They were slower, not even close to

being as deadly, and—thanks to the stealth abilities the judges stole from Noah—the dehaians' weird, magical echolocation abilities wouldn't even pick up on the strakirin till the creatures were right on top of them.

But I could.

My arms wrapped around my middle, nausea swirling in me at the direction my thoughts were taking. I wanted to go home. Oh my God, I wanted to go home more than anything in the world. I needed to find my family, find the resistance, and track down those bastard judges and force them to reverse this.

But what if, in that time, the strakirin found this thing they were hunting for?

What if, once they did, no one would be able to stop them?

My whole body ached, and my tears joined the saltwater. Desperation crushed down on my chest, heavy with the sheer unfair weight of it all. Every muscle in my body cried out to swim like hell after the first sign of home. The ocean seemed to open like an abyss around me, a great chasm with my family on one side and the monsters who would destroy them on the other.

And me in the middle.

My nails dug into my sides. This wasn't fair. This wasn't right. I'd lost so much. My body. My memories, for a while. Noah. Damn near everything but my life.

But not my family. Not yet.

And right now, they needed me here.

I drew a ragged breath. Only the dehaians stood a chance against this. Not much of one, but more than the rest of the world. Only the dehaians had a hope of getting anywhere in time to stop the strakirin. And maybe I wouldn't even need to go further than warning them. They were dehaians, for pity's sake. They knew more about magic and the ocean than anyone. Maybe they already had a defense against that stealth power.

I could just warn them. Warn that king Noah had known. That would be enough.

Now all I had to do was find them.

I scanned the ocean. No fish, no plants, not even a whale or a shark—though God knew I didn't want to run into one of *those*. A tumble of hills and rough boulders clustered below me, tracing a path into the distance to my left and right like someone had crushed together two parts of the seafloor, creating a crumpled line. Garbage from the world above carpeted swaths of the hills, tinging the water with a nasty flavor but providing no clues on which way I could go to find dehaians.

Biting my lip, I considered either direction. I needed… east, maybe, whichever direction that was. West too, though that made my chest hurt with how it only took me farther from the California coast. But the other options—north and south— only meant that the next landmass I found would probably be made of ice.

There was also no way to know in which direction I was heading for sure.

I swam left. I'd find a hint of my direction before I went too far, I reassured myself. There had to be some kind of landmark or whatever around here. Surely even dehaians needed help with directions from time to time.

Shapes like strakirin appeared in the distance, and I came to a sharp halt. The forms were on the edge of my senses, getting clearer with every second. They didn't feel like the hive. The drone wasn't back either.

Not strakirin, then. Dehaian. They were on the horizon, heading this way.

I hovered, torn. Maybe they could help me. Give me directions.

Maybe they were with the strakirin, hunting me.

I bit back a whimper. I'd hide, then. Wait till they'd passed before following them. I could use that stealth ability and see if I could get up close enough to find out who they were really with before I let on that I was there.

Yeah. That could work.

Repeating reassurances to myself, I dove for the rocks. The boulders were far more massive up close than they'd felt in the water above, all of them easily the size of three-story houses, but between them, narrow gaps would allow me enough room to hide.

I hesitated at the opening to the tiny space, a new realization hitting me. It was dark down here, so very dark, but it wouldn't matter.

Not if I was *glowing*.

I looked down at my body. The fin around my tail, my hair, even my eyes were glowing with gold bioluminescence. Dehaians had eyesight like the strakirin. The judges had taken that trait from them, even if strakirin eyes looked totally different and far less human than a dehaian's.

The dehaians out there would spot me in a heartbeat.

I tensed, silently begging my cursed body to stop glowing.

The radiance around my tail vanished, and a strange sensation passed through my eyes, as if I'd squinted too hard at something and then released my muscles again.

Darkness swallowed me like someone had switched off all the lights in the world.

Fear froze me for a heartbeat. Reaching out, I fumbled at the gap between two gargantuan rocks and nervously slipped inside, praying I didn't cut myself on any of the garbage cluttering the seafloor down here. Could dehaians smell blood like sharks? No one had ever said. Trying to stay calm, I closed my eyes again and concentrated on the strange stealth ability the judges had stolen from Noah.

A shiver coursed over my skin. I barely breathed, hoping that meant the defense was working.

Seconds ticked by, turning to minutes. Desperately, I tried to keep from imagining what else might be down here with me in the dark.

Dozens of glowing eyes appeared in the murk above me. I stopped breathing completely.

They drifted to the left, vanishing beyond a black wall that had to be the rocks.

I stayed put. Time crept by.

A dehaian appeared directly in front of me.

I felt the water move like the dehaian was reaching toward me. My eyes changed back fast, bringing the world into sharp clarity.

It was already too late.

A ball of vines struck me, shot from a weapon that looked like a gun. The vines exploded over me, crawling across my skin and scales. With impossible speed, they wrapped my arms, my tail, and rendered me unable to escape. I twisted, fighting to snap them, while my body sank toward the seafloor like a stone.

The dehaian swung back with his spikes, getting ready to stab me.

"Stop!" someone barked.

The dehaian froze. He looked over his shoulder.

Another dehaian swam down to join him, his body language making him seem like he was in charge. Amber-eyed and dark-haired with harsh features like he'd been carved from granite, the man bore a savage scar down the length of his bronze tail, as if something had tried to cut him open once upon a time. A belt encircled his waist, a sheathed knife hanging from it. He wore an armband stitched with glistening thread, tracing out the shape of a mountain on the black fabric. The dehaian holding me and the dozens of others behind him all wore the same.

My breath caught. I recognized the shape. They belonged to that nation Noah had told me about, the one that the judges tried to pretend had attacked the ruanir. The one where that king lived. Yvaria.

Hope flickered in me, only to falter at the leader's cold expression. "Bag it."

One of the dehaians grabbed a handful of the vines and dragged me up from the sand, while another snagged something from a pouch attached to the belt at his waist. I opened my mouth to protest, and barely had time to see a black blob of what appeared to be fabric before the dehaian dragged it over my head.

Something clicked near my ear.

The ocean went dead. The water became sludge coating my skin and tail. I choked, and slime-like water slid into my nose and throat.

Panic hit me like a wall. I thrashed, shrieking and then gagging on the goop that the ocean had become. I couldn't breathe. Couldn't think. The poison in my skin flared like a fire, ready to burn anyone who touched me. Of their own accord, the spikes on my arms grew, slicing through the vines near them.

Someone jerked me. Shoved me back. Rock slammed hard against my back while something pressed on the vines, pinning me on the wall of stone. Sharp points touched the skin of my neck. Spikes.

They were enough.

The poison fled my grasp, racing down the spikes before I could stop it. Shivers exploded through me at its departure, terrible with how good they felt. My thoughts blurred, numbing my panic with familiar-horrible euphoria. I heard a muffled scream, and shouts followed. The grip on the vines holding me vanished. Unable to swim in the tangle, I sank to the rough sand.

Struggling past the buzz from the poison, I thrashed on the seafloor, banging into the rocks around me. The spikes on my arms slashed through the vines, freeing my hands and forearms if nothing else. I reached up, ripping the hood from my head. The ocean returned in a rush.

As did the sight of a guard swinging her spikes at me.

I twisted fast on the gritty seafloor. The blades struck the stone near where I'd been lying.

But I was between the boulders. Vines still covered my tail and tangled around my body, rendering me almost immobile. Dozens of guards were above me. In front of me. There wasn't anywhere to go.

"Shoot it!" one of the men yelled.

"No!" I cried.

The woman in front of me froze, a shocked look on her face like she hadn't expected me to be able to speak.

I gulped down a breath. Beyond her, I could see two dead men, blackened lines of poison marring their veins.

Their bodies were collapsing. Drying out and falling in on themselves, like the pressure of the ocean was crushing them into nothing. There wasn't any blood. They were just becoming husks, crumpling down into oblivion.

My gorge rose. Oh my God, did that happen to strakirin who died down here too? I'd taken off so quickly, I didn't notice, and if it did…

I shoved the thoughts away. I wouldn't die down here. I'd make it home. I'd be fine.

With effort, I tore my attention from the corpses, fastening it on the guard ahead of me. Those others… one of them had touched my skin with their spikes. The second must have tried to help his companion.

The remaining soldiers were staying far from them and me alike. They looked pale. Shaken.

"Please," I begged. "Don't touch me. I don't want to hurt anyone."

The woman regarded me warily. She turned her head, not taking her eyes from me. "Commander Damerion?"

The leader with the bronze tail swam closer. Spikes still protruded from his arms.

I pulled back against the boulder. "Please," I said to him. "Please stay away. I'm not sure I can control this if you touch me."

Damerion's glowing amber eyes ran over me. "What are you?"

"Strakirin. That's what the—" He wouldn't know what I meant by judges. "—the leaders of my people call me. Us."

"How many of you are there?"

I shook my head. "I don't know. Hundreds. Maybe more."

"What do you want?"

I didn't even know where to begin with that question. "Please, I'm on your side. I don't want to hurt anyone. I'm trying to warn you. Your king too."

Damerion's face darkened. "What do you want with the king?" All the soldiers appeared ready to strike me dead on the spot.

"Nothing!" I made myself take a breath. "I'm just trying to help. I… I know a friend of his. Of his girlfriend. I—"

"What friend?"

I hesitated, hoping they didn't hate him or something.

"Noah. The Beast."

Or I had known him, before the judges made me kill him.

Pain throbbed through me. I stuffed the thought down hard, never taking my eyes from the man.

Damerion's eyes narrowed, the anger in his expression strengthening.

"I'm not your enemy," I said. "I swear on my life, I'm not. But the other strakirin are going to kill people. Yours. Mine. Their leaders are after something down here, and there's a dehaian helping them—"

"Dehaian?"

"Yes. So please. I need your help. You have to stop them. You're all in danger. Everyone is."

He was silent. I didn't dare to breathe.

"Blindfold stays on," he said, like he was stating the terms of some agreement. "Vines do too. If you lose control of that poison inside of you, you die."

"But—"

"And we'll take you somewhere where you can give us more information."

I hesitated. That could mean anything.

That could mean torture.

"Please, I—"

"Or we kill you here." He drew the knife at his belt in a smooth, swift motion. A reflection of my glowing fins shone from the metal.

I froze, my eyes locking on the knife. "I-I'm not your enemy," I repeated, my voice breathless.

"Then you have nothing to fear."

I pressed my lips closed, his response sending fear quivering straight through me.

"Bring her," he ordered the woman beside him. "Don't touch her skin."

The woman hesitated. Damerion glanced at her.

"Sir, this thing killed—"

"Now."

The woman's mouth tightened. She swam toward me, and she paused for a heartbeat before reaching down to take the blindfold from the sand nearby. She looked like she expected it to be poisonous too now.

"You six stay with us," Damerion ordered several of the dehaians. "We're taking her back to Nyciena. The rest of you, follow the lieutenant to the village. Offer assistance, and see what you can find out about this attack."

A woman behind him motioned to the others around her. The soldiers swam quickly after her, as if eager to be farther from me.

Damerion ignored them, studying me, and I couldn't begin to guess what he was thinking. But at his nod, the first woman lifted the hood toward me.

"Please," I tried. "You don't have to do this. I'm not—"

Blackness swallowed my view of the world, and then a click followed. The water turned to sludge again, choking me. I lurched, panic bubbling through me once more while I struggled to breathe, to protest.

My words sounded like they were coming through mud.

Taking the vines near my neck, the woman hauled me up from the rocks. Dragging me with them, the dehaians set off into the ocean.

$$\mathcal{O}\,9\,\mathcal{O}$$

BAYLIE

When it came to resistance safe houses, I was starting to expect certain things. Barricaded windows. Rundown buildings with tiny black security cameras perched where they were hard to see. Remote locations seemed to be a theme too, at least with the ruanir resistance.

The place where Harvey and Ellie were hiding delivered in spades.

I eyed the surroundings while we drove up. Fences were the first impression. Stretching up at least ten feet and possibly higher, the chain-link barricade was surrounded by trees and undergrowth and topped by spirals of barbed wire. A rolling gate barred the rough and overgrown path that our convoy was trundling along. Beyond it, lay a compound like a small military installation, complete with sheds for vehicles and a block of a central building.

But the structures were weathered and falling in on themselves. Even the main building had half-collapsed in a pile of cinder blocks and rubble, with only the rightmost portion of the structure still standing. One or two faded scrawls of graffiti dotted the walls here and there, but even most vandals hadn't bothered to trek out this far. The buildings didn't look like anyone had been near them in years.

I knew enough by now not to believe that for a second.

The convoy of vehicles came to a stop. I braced myself on the side of the SUV while the others climbed out. My legs felt stronger, though the ride had taken its toll. We'd driven for hours, bouncing along a rough path through this forest somewhere in Colorado. Miguel had brought five vehicles: a mismatched trio of rugged SUVs, a Jeep, and a full-sized van. Declan had driven Jace and me in one of the SUVs, grumbling all the while about wasted resources, while people who looked like soldiers in civilian clothing rode with Maia, Dhanya, and Veronique in the other vehicles. I didn't know what Miguel expected when they went to find these landwalkers, but from the looks of it, he was ready for a fight.

We walked toward the central building, Miguel leading the way, but a door opened before we'd made it more than a few steps. Harvey peered out at us, his eyes sweeping the forest and the half-fallen building alike, and then he motioned for us to get inside. In the room behind him, I caught a glimpse of white walls, concrete floors, and an array of computers situated among a spaghetti-like tangle of cords. It was like the other resistance hideouts: decay on the outside, ready to withstand the apocalypse on the inside.

I suspected I'd never look at an abandoned building the same way again.

"Ellie's downstairs," Harvey said to Miguel. "She's found two possible locations, but there's a sixty-one percent probability that—" He cut off. I looked back to find him staring at me. "Y-you're awake."

"As of this morning," Miguel supplied. "Now, where are we headed?"

Harvey blinked, struggling to regroup. "Not far. Ski lodge, one hour west. Signs say it's closed for the season and under repair, but—"

Declan pushed past us on his way into the building. "Fine."

Jace appeared at my side, and his eyebrow twitched up in a silent, not-quite-question while he waited for me to take his arm.

"I'm okay," I told him in a low voice.

He didn't move. "And if you fall?" he replied, his voice equally low.

I fought back a scowl. Not looking at him, I took his arm and headed inside, trying to ignore the way that Harvey continued to stare. The room was bigger than it first appeared, with double doors at the far end that led to a hallway, if the view I could gain through the small windows on them was any indication. Crates for storage took up the rightmost wall, though space was left clear for a doorway there as well. Declan veered toward it and yanked the door open, revealing a dark stairwell. Ignoring us completely, he swiftly descended the steps. We trailed after him.

"Okay, but what about the northwest route?"

Ellie's voice carried from the basement, and a surge of relief hit me at the sound. I hadn't realized just how much I wanted someone I knew around me right now. Fast as I could, I headed down the steps.

We'd had a strange start to our friendship, Ellie and me. The granddaughter of a mad scientist who'd experimented on my best friend, I hadn't had much sympathy or interest in getting along with Ellie when we first met—as unfair to Ellie as that was. Sure, she could be shier than a rabbit, but she was also smart as hell and a genuinely good person too. But the insanity of finding out that greliarans existed and dehaians did too, all while trying to rescue Chloe and Zeke before Ellie's grandfather could kill them, had left my temper shorter than a firecracker fuse. It wasn't a good combination. But over the past year, she'd become one of my closest friends. With Noah and Chloe gone and the rest of my family just trying to leave the craziness behind, she'd been the only person I could talk to about everything.

Well, almost everything.

I pushed the thought down by reflex. That part didn't matter.

"It's too dangerous," Olivia replied. "If you would wait, we have made some progress on the weapons research—"

"There's no time. I know it looks bad, but I think if you read the report I sent—Baylie!" Ellie glanced away from her monitor and spotted me. On the screen, I could see Olivia, her black-framed glasses perched on her nose and a pencil stuck behind her ear. She'd let her short afro grow a bit longer since last I'd seen her, though otherwise, nothing had changed. An academic to the core, she looked like she belonged in a library rather than in the vaguely rustic-looking office I could see behind her.

"Baylie is there?" Olivia sounded alarmed.

Ellie blinked fast and cast a quick look back toward the screen. "Yeah, she—Olivia, can I call you back?"

Barely waiting for her mentor's agreement, Ellie switched off the computer program and then jumped up from her chair. "When did you—"

"This morning," Declan cut her off. "So where's the information on this ski lodge?"

Ellie blinked, glancing from him to me. "Directions are in the report." She motioned toward a folder laying on a chipped wooden table by a wall.

Declan strode toward it. Still watching him from the corner of her eye, Ellie hurried over. "Are you okay?" she asked me in a low voice.

"Yeah." I nodded. "Just a bit shaky."

She didn't look convinced. "You sure? Prolonged muscle inactivity like that, you probably shouldn't even be out of—"

"I'm fine," I cut in quickly.

Ellie faltered. "Um, okay. But what are you doing here? You're not, like, thinking of going with us, are you? It's not—"

"Us? You're going out there?"

"Well, yeah, I—"

"Ellie, why do you need to—"

"It's landwalkers," she said like that explained everything.

"Yeah, but you don't need to—"

"I'll be fine. It's a fairly standard assault plan, compared to the last couple times."

I choked. "What? Hold on. You've done this before? Like, raids or assaults or whatever the hell…" I ran out of words, staring at her.

Ellie appeared uncomfortable. "They didn't mention that?"

I shook my head slowly.

"Oh." She fidgeted with one of her fingernails. "Well, um, yeah. For about three weeks now, anyway. I didn't really *plan* on it. I was just visiting one of the hideouts, helping with the intel, and then there was an attack on our location, and the enforcers were coming and—" She seemed to see that the words weren't making anything better. "I have abilities, and they save lives. And these are *my* people this time. The landwalkers—*if* they're at this place—they don't know about the ruanir. They'll freak if wizards show up, claiming to rescue them." She shrugged. "I *have* to be there."

"But—"

"I don't go out on the front line or whatever; I work from a distance, and the others keep me protected." She tried for a placating expression. "Miguel and the others are really good at this. Did you know most of these people used to be military?"

I stared at her, speechless.

"I'm careful. I swear I am. But I need to do this. I need to help keep people safe."

"We going?" Declan called from the door to the stairwell.

Ellie winced. "Just a second," she replied, an edge to her voice I'd almost never heard. From her, it was as good as shouting at somebody.

She exhaled. "I've got to go. Can we catch up when I get back?"

I didn't know what to say. "Sure."

Ellie smiled, though the expression was more nervous than anything. "Take care, okay? Rest or…"

She seemed to run out of words. I managed a nod.

Her smile returning briefly, she hurried after Declan. He slammed the stairwell door behind them while she jogged upstairs.

And then it was just me and Jace.

I exhaled, working to regroup. I knew Ellie could look out for herself—mostly, anyway. After all, last year she'd taken on Noah's cousin, a muscle-bound and psychotic greliaran who would have killed us both. She'd taken him apart.

But that didn't mean I wanted this to happen again. My friends to rush off, putting themselves in danger again.

While I sat around and did nothing.

My face twisted. I was being ridiculous. Emotional. That coma had hit me worse than I thought.

Go figure. I'd only woken up from it to find myself in some sort of bizarre Land of Oz where my stepbrother, friend, and acquaintances were all soldiers in a *war*.

I turned away from the door, drawing a steadying breath and ordering myself to get a grip.

Jace was watching me. "You okay?" he asked, his voice totally neutral, like he was checking because he figured he was supposed to.

God, I wished people would stop asking me that. "Phone?"

I replied tightly.

"The one on the desk should be secure."

I nodded and retreated toward the old-school corded phone on the far side of the room. An electric-sounding dial tone greeted me when I picked up the receiver.

My eyes twitched back toward the door. Jace was still standing there.

"You, uh, want to give me some privacy or something?"

He hesitated. "Sure."

Another heartbeat passed before he pulled the door to the stairwell open.

"Just so you know," he added. "We didn't tell your family about Noah. About him being back and all. He didn't want us to."

Leaving me staring after him, Jace headed upstairs.

I let out a breath. Right. Okay. Secrets. Always secrets. What else was new?

Besides everything.

Shaking my head, I turned my attention to the phone and began to dial.

As phone calls in the History of Horrible went, that probably had ranked around the top one hundred. Maybe the top ten. I was fairly certain my stepmom, Sandra, would have my hide the next time I saw her. I was just glad my dad hadn't been around. He would've been even worse.

And as for Noah's dad and stepmom…

I gripped the handle to the stairwell door. I didn't tell them Noah was back. I'd kept that secret like so many others this year. And honestly, it wouldn't have done any good to tell them the truth, anyway. They'd want to help us or, at least, to look for him. Either would be bad, seeing as how the judges had already set fire to their house and probably wanted to do worse to them.

So I told them I'd been out of the country, like Ellie and the rest had said. Visiting elders from morning till night. And for Sandra, I'd spun a story about backpacking across France and Germany and Austria and any other country I could name. I told her I was safe, back in the States now but staying with Ellie, and that I'd come see her and Dad and my dog, Daisy, soon.

My heart was still racing from the slew of lies.

The empty stairwell greeted me when I tugged open the door. Taking a steadying breath, I gripped the staircase banister, willing my legs to hold me while I started up the steps.

At the top of the stairs, the other door opened. Jace gave me one of those unreadable looks for which I was starting to suspect he owned a patent, and then came down and took my arm without a word.

I eyed him askance, briefly weighing the satisfaction of arguing versus the discomfort that would follow.

It probably wasn't worth it. But I really needed to have a talk with Noah about this "having people watch out for me" thing.

We started up the stairs.

"Call go okay?" Jace asked quietly.

I took a second to respond. "Yeah."

He hesitated for a heartbeat, like maybe he wanted to say something else, but then he changed his mind. Silence hung between us, awkward as ever. The steps clunked heavily beneath my feet, and the vaguely dusty smell of the basement fell behind us when we reached the top of the staircase.

Maia and Dhanya were conferring in front of one of the monitors, something in their motions making me think they were staying busy more than anything. Veronique was flipping through screens on her tablet computer, a look of consternation on her face. But on a chair in a corner of the room, Harvey was frozen with one of his notebooks in his lap. His hand was poised mid-page turn, and his eyes were wide, staring at me.

"Hi," I offered for lack of anything better to say to him.

Harvey swallowed hard and attempted a smile. It looked like he was being tortured.

Attempting to ignore the expression, I walked toward the chairs on the opposite side of the room. Jace stayed by my side. "He heard Noah was your brother," Jace murmured while he helped me down.

The man's nervous expression clicked, even if it didn't make much sense. He had to know the Beast thing wasn't genetic. Plus, Noah wasn't even related to me by blood. And surely, by now, Harvey had figured out that Noah wasn't planning to hurt anybody here.

"I'm not dangerous, you know," I said to Harvey, though my insides quivered like they wanted to debate the statement.

"And Noah's not—"

"We heard you're connected to him," Harvey interrupted.

"So was Ari," Jace retorted, a hard note in his voice.

Harvey gulped. An array of fledgling responses rushed across his face, stifled before they could emerge. He returned his attention to his notebook.

I heard a quiet breath leave Jace, the sound vaguely exasperated. Tugging a chair around, he straddled it and sat down, staying a few feet from me. He regarded one of the screens next to him, studying its black-and-white images of the compound's surroundings.

I watched him from the corner of my eye. Three looks, and now he wore the unreadable, neutral one. I couldn't hope to guess what was going through his head.

Time crept by. The sound of pencil scritching came from the far side of the room, sporadic and anxious. Every so often, I caught Harvey staring at me, though he always hastily returned his attention to his notebook whenever he saw me glance his way.

I should've stayed in the basement.

The ring of the phone on the wall nearly sent me jumping from my skin. With a noise like his muscles had gone stiff, Jace pushed away from the chair and crossed the room to pick up the receiver.

"Yeah?" He paused. "How many?"

Anxiety bubbled through me.

"Okay, we'll be ready."

Jace hung up. "Six wounded," he said to the others. "One

dead. They'll be here any minute, and they need bandages ready."

Veronique nodded and headed for the storage boxes on the other side of the room.

"Ellie?" I asked, afraid to hear the answer.

"She's fine." Jace moved to join Veronique. "Enforcers took out an SUV, though. The passengers got away, but one of Miguel's people was killed covering their retreat."

I exhaled, torn between relief and guilt. Ellie was okay.

And someone else was dead.

Veronique hefted the lid from one of the storage crates and then tugged a large first aid kit from inside. She handed it back to Jace. "Over there, please." She nodded to the double doors leading to the hallway.

While he lugged it away, she pulled another kit from inside and then started after him. Pushing one of the doors open with her back, she disappeared down the corridor. Jace returned to the crate, retrieving several boxes of bandages from within. His attention on balancing the load in his arms, he nudged the lid shut with an elbow.

Still feeling shaken, I went to take some of the boxes from him. Harvey's gaze tracked me the whole way across the room.

Jace balked. "You really shouldn't—"

"I'm helping," I said, the words feeling like a bizarre echo of Ellie's from earlier. I couldn't bring myself to look at him.

From the corner of my eye, I saw his mouth tighten. I made an exasperated sound. He handed over a few more.

We walked toward the hallway. The boxes joined the first

aid kit by the double doors.

I turned to him. "What else will they need when they—"

A beeping sound came from a monitor on the far wall. Jace walked over to it quickly. He clicked a button, shutting off the alert.

"They're here," he said.

I shivered.

Veronique reappeared by the double doors. "If you want, you all could head to the—"

She cut off as the door opened. I blanched.

"There, put her there," Miguel called, pointing to a spot on the floor. Behind him, two of his people carried a third between them. Blood stained the woman's side, and her chest moved in rapid gasps. Another person followed, limping from a gash on his leg, while still another came through the door with one of his hands clutching his opposite arm. The limb dangled uselessly from a socket that didn't look the way it was supposed to, underneath his shirt.

Veronique jumped into action, snagging a box of bandages and hurrying toward the bleeding woman. I floundered and then grabbed one too. The cardboard ripped beneath my shaking attempt to open the flap.

"Over there," Miguel ordered. "Take that spot against the wall. Declan, can you stop that bleeding?"

I looked up and then backpedaled when several of the wounded started toward the space where I was standing. Declan strode after them, practically bowling me aside.

"Give me that." He snatched the roll of gauze from my

hands. Dropping into a crouch, he set to wrapping a deep gash on a man's shoulder.

I stared around the room, feeling patently useless. In the space of a few moments, the place had gone from empty to crowded with the injured. But like a well-oiled machine, Veronique and the others moved between their people, triaging the wounded, sending the less injured toward the hall, and bandaging up everything they could.

They looked like they'd done this *way* too many times.

I choked down a breath. There had to be something I could do too, though. Sure, my legs were wobbly. I could admit that—privately, anyway. But maybe there were more bandages in another crate or—

My eyes darted around. Wait, where the hell was Ellie?

"Baylie."

I flinched.

"Come on." Jace took my arm. "Let's clear out of their way."

I wanted to protest, but there wasn't much point. We *were* in the way. Veronique and her people needed the space.

Together, we wove past the injured to reach the main door.

The cool breeze of the forest stole the flush from my face. Gratefully, I gulped down a breath of the pine-laden air while my gaze skipped over my surroundings.

No one else was outside. Besides me and Jace standing here, there wasn't much to indicate anyone was at the entire property at all. Even the vehicles had already been hidden.

"Where's Ellie?" I asked Jace.

He glanced around. "Uh, she should be—"

Ellie hurried around the corner of the building. "Oh. Hey."

My eyes widened. A bandage was taped to her forehead, stark white against her dark skin, and another wrapped her forearm. I could see blood starting to stain it. Meanwhile, tiny cuts marred the rest of her face and arms alike. "Oh my God," I stammered. "Are you okay?"

"Huh?" Ellie followed my stare to her arms. "Um, yeah. Yeah, I'm fine."

She didn't sound fine. And she looked flustered.

"What happened?" I demanded.

Ellie shrugged and then winced, stopping the motion like it pained her. "Nothing. I mean, something, obviously, but—" She managed a strained smile. "It's fine. Mostly. The enforcers just came after our SUV really bad, and it, uh… it crashed."

Holy God, what?

She blinked fast and then turned her attention to the main building like she couldn't continue meeting my eyes. "Is Miguel in there?"

"Yeah," Jace replied before I could speak.

"Good. I need to talk to him. All of you, actually."

"Why?" I demanded. Goddammit, she shouldn't have gone. She shouldn't have risked herself for a bunch of strangers and been out there where monsters could get her and—

Tears burned in my eyes. I blinked them away, seething.

"What's going on, Ellie?" Jace offered in a tone much calmer than mine had been.

I hated him for it.

Ellie bit her lip. "Can we find Miguel first?"

Without looking at me, she skirted around us, heading for the main building.

"Baylie?" Jace asked.

"Don't."

He didn't say a word. I stalked away from him, distantly grateful for my legs finally consenting to carry me.

"—new intel," Ellie was saying to Miguel and the others when we came in the door. "A few of the landwalkers, they, um… They heard something while they were being held prisoner. It's about Maia's dad, that judge you've been trying to find?"

"What?" Maia asked.

Ellie's gaze darted around, anxious. "It's what we've been waiting for. They heard where he's going to be."

10

NOAH

Following the strakirin was impossible.

Following their trail of destruction, on the other hand, was not.

Invisible in the water, I hovered just inside the veil surrounding the ruined village. Dehaians zipped through it, darting past the rippling wall of bubbles that shielded the little town from notice by anyone.

That *should* have, anyway.

Wounded villagers sat on the seafloor, medics rushing around them with bandages and jars of glittering gel. Still more dehaians were coming from beyond the village, huddling together like they were trying to reassure themselves it was safe to return.

But as for what had attacked them…

I glanced to the side as another group of dehaians swam through the veil, passing several yards from my invisible form without giving a single sign of noticing I was there.

"—have a prisoner, sir," a cold-faced soldier was reporting

to another dehaian. "One of the eel creatures the survivors described."

I froze for a heartbeat and then drew closer.

"The thing was out on its own near the Rialan Wastes," the soldier said. "Claims to be on our side. Commander Damerion sent it for questioning in Nyciena."

Another soldier nodded. "Good. Any sign of others?"

The woman started to shake her head.

I didn't wait for the rest. The water swirled, and the magic barrier around the village warped as I raced through it, heading for Nyciena.

One of the strakirin on their own. One who claimed to be on the dehaians' side. That had to be Ari. It *would* be Ari.

I'd find her.

Miles of ocean sped by me, taking too long and filled with nothing useful. Wherever the strakirin had gone, they weren't on the direct line to Nyciena.

Which was good. And Ari wouldn't be with them. It was fine.

But I had no idea what I'd say when I saw her. Hi? How are you? That was just stupid. She'd had her brain mangled by a bunch of megalomaniacal wizards.

Wizards that would die when I got my hands on them.

Shudders rippled through me. I struggled to calm my rage. It wouldn't help anything right now.

Oh my God, what was I going to say to her?

The valley near Nyciena passed by me. I slowed down. I couldn't fly into the city at this speed. I'd sort of torn it apart a year ago. Making people think I was doing that again wasn't the best way to get answers.

I passed through the veil surrounding the city, noting a strangeness to the feel of the magic there. It wasn't the same as before. More… charged, somehow.

I pushed the thought aside. If it was a defense against me, it wasn't working, and if it was an alarm, then it was too late now. I'd already set it off.

The barren rocks and hillsides had instantly transformed when the veil fell behind me, sprouting lights and plants. Dehaians were everywhere, filling streets between boulders so huge they'd dwarf skyscrapers. I stayed in my invisible form, debating. I didn't like my chances for whether the dehaians would tell me what I wanted to know.

They'd probably just flee from me, screaming.

My attention skimmed over the city. The guards wouldn't have put Ari in the palace, though. Not if they didn't know what she was. They wouldn't risk the king. They wouldn't put her near the general populace either, given what they'd probably heard happened in that village. But as for where that left—

Soldiers rose up from a large stone formation near the palace. Their eyes swept the water as if they were searching for something.

Which they probably were.

My awareness drew down into my human form.

It took less than a heartbeat for them to notice me. They rushed in my direction.

"What's the meaning of this?" one of them demanded.

I weighed how to respond. Explaining myself to them wouldn't help. I doubted they had the authority to take me right to her. "I need to speak with your king."

The soldier hesitated. His head turned toward one of his companions, though he didn't take his eyes from me. "Find Captain Tiberion."

I tried not to scowl. Tiberion hated me. It didn't help that he had a decent reason—I was responsible for killing his previous king and leaving Tiberion himself with only one eye.

My odds of getting him to let me see Ari were slim to none.

"Listen, I don't have time for—"

"You will stay there!" The man's voice cracked with tension. Around him, the other soldiers shifted into more defensive positions.

I didn't move. They didn't stand a chance against me, and they knew it.

But I had no idea where to find her. No idea where to even begin. Through my empathic link to Chloe, I could tell that she wasn't around either, meaning that—beyond waiting here—my options were basically nonexistent.

My good options, anyway.

The Beast side of me churned with impatience. The desire to lash out, to force the issue, to *fix this* through whatever means necessary, was overwhelming. Ari was here. She *had* to be here, even if our shattered connection meant I couldn't feel her presence at all.

And they were between me and her.

I gritted my teeth. The last thing I needed was to convince

Zeke and the rest of Yvaria that I was their enemy by tearing this place apart again.

A minute crawled by. Tiberion swam from a building in the heart of the city.

"What do you want?" he barked the moment he came within a dozen yards of me. His single amber eye glared out at me while the other was lost behind a black eye patch that made me think of a pirate. The scars covering his pale chest and bronze tail helped with the impression—and almost all of them, I knew, were my fault.

"You captured a…" I wasn't sure what to say. They wouldn't know the word *strakirin*. "A creature. Green scales? Eel tail?"

Suspicion stole over the man's face. He knew who I was talking about, though. I could tell.

"Was it a girl?" I pressed.

"This doesn't concern you, Beast."

Anger boiled through me. "Yes it does, so answer the question."

Tiberion hesitated. "It looks like a female, yes."

Oh, God. "I need to see her."

"You don't—"

"*Now!*"

The water shook. The soldiers gripped their weapons tight while they struggled to keep from being pushed back by the sudden current.

I fought to rein the magic in. It was harder to control down here. The power from the ocean was so much stronger when I was inside it. "She's a friend," I managed more calmly.

Tiberion stared at me. I could see him weighing his options, and every second he took ate at me. Ari was here. She *would* be. The strakirin they'd found was her. And she'd be fine.

The Beast side of me growled bloody threats of retribution if she was anything even *slightly* to the contrary.

"I won't have you breaking it out," Tiberion warned. "That *thing* was part of an attack on a peaceful village just outside the Yvarian border. It is a prisoner of war."

"I won't."

He was silent for another moment. Shivers started to ripple through me. I wouldn't take her out of here as long as they hadn't laid a finger on her, or as long as it seemed like she wasn't in danger. She didn't need to be a fugitive from the dehaians as well.

But if they'd *hurt* her…

The Beast side of me snarled internally. I ordered myself to focus. "I swear, I'm only here to make sure she's safe. You can keep me under guard the entire time if you want." Not that it would matter. "I have to see her, Tiberion. She's not like those others. I have to know she's okay."

Tiberion's mouth tightened. "The king has ordered it to be kept in isolation till we figure out what it is."

My fists clenched at the way he kept referring to her as an *it*. I made myself continue, "I can help with that."

His jaw muscles jumped. "This way." Tiberion turned, swimming out across the city.

I followed. The other soldiers fell in around us, keeping their distance from me though spikes still protruded from their arms. Buildings passed below us, and then the edge of the city fell away.

Tiberion headed for a spire of stone surrounded by guards. Magic shimmered on the door at the base of the towering rock, and the water shivered around it.

I winced, uncomfortable.

He did something to the lock. The shimmering magic faded.

"In here," he said.

I trailed him inside. A black tunnel stretched out ahead of me, but almost immediately, its floor vanished into a canyon-like crevice. With his single eye glowing like backlit amber in the darkness, Tiberion glanced at me and then swam down.

More strange, quivering feelings covered spots on the walls, all of them roughly the size and shape of doors. From all I'd been able to tell, my senses were similar to a dehaian's under the ocean—some weird form of quasi-echolocation that let me pick up on rocks and fish and everything else in a certain proximity, even if I couldn't see it. Although I was fairly certain my eyes didn't glow, my eyesight was easily as good as theirs in the dark.

But down here, I was nearly blind. I suspected they were too.

At a spot like any other, Tiberion slowed. He reached toward the shivering feeling of magic in the water.

It faded, leaving a square space with bars on it like a cell door. Wavy lines of faintly shimmering, glowing gold moved in the darkness beyond the bars.

"Hello?" came a tentative voice.

Relief surged through me so strongly, I could barely hold on to human form. Ari. Oh my *God*, it was actually Ari.

A torch flared to life in Tiberion's hand. Blue-white flames reflected from the sheer walls and cast light into the barred cell ahead of me.

Hesitantly, Ari swam from the shadows in the corner of the cell. She winced, the golden glow in her eyes dimming at the light. She froze when she saw me. "*Noah?*"

I shivered at the sound of her voice. I'd missed it. Missed it more than I could describe. I'd been so scared I'd never hear it again.

I couldn't make myself say a word.

"You can speak to it from out here," Tiberion told me coldly.

The hell I would. I let my human shape vanish for the heart-beat it took to pass through the bars.

"You're…" Ari crushed her fist to her lips like she was trying not to cry. "You're *alive*."

Alive? I—

Understanding clicked. Her magic. The poison. The last time she saw me.

"Yeah," I managed. "Yeah, I'm fine. But are you—"

She retreated fast when I reached for her. "Don't."

I stopped, confused.

Pain and fear flickered over her face. "I don't want to hurt you."

I wasn't sure what to do, what to say. "Are you okay?"

She nodded fast, her faintly glowing hair waving through the water with the motion. "Yeah." She hesitated. "I mean…"

Anger boiled up when she trailed off. That pause could mean anything. "Have they hurt you?"

She shook her head. "No. I'm… I'm fine."

"What happened?"

Ari's attention flicked to Tiberion and the guards. "These, um… these are the dehaians you know, right?"

"Yeah."

"And you trust them? Their king?"

I hesitated. I wouldn't call it trust. More like an awkward arrangement built on a month or so of hell last year. "Something like that."

She was quiet for a heartbeat. "Please," she said to Tiberion, "I need to talk to your king. Your people are in danger."

Tiberion's face was like stone.

"Where's Zeke?" I asked.

"We are *not* requesting the king come down to—"

"Then bring her to him," I cut in. "Under guard. With me."

The man regarded me scathingly. "Our people have already briefed him on what this creature told us when we captured it. If anything else is needed, we will acquire the information from it here."

I heard the threat. It was difficult to keep from doing something about it.

"Ari," I growled at him. "Not *it*. Not 'the creature.' Her name is *Ari,* and if you touch her…"

Tiberion didn't respond.

I turned to Ari. "What did you tell them?"

"That the strakirin want to hurt them. That they're after

something to help them do it." She gave a tiny shrug. "There wasn't really time for more. The others could have been coming. And then they… they didn't really want to talk once we got here."

Shivers rippled through me, driven by fear and rage at what the words could mean. But she said they hadn't hurt her. She said…

I made myself turn back. Focus. Stick to the matter at hand.

Not kill anyone.

"Listen, Tiberion. If you want to protect Zeke, you have to let us see him."

He was silent, watching us both.

"She's not lying to you, and neither am I. The bastards who did this to her are targeting Yvaria. I know that; she knows that. But she might be your best chance to save your king and the rest of this country."

"Then we will interrogate… the girl… *here*," Tiberion replied. "We have no idea what she actually is, and until we do—"

He cut off as a man swam down from the levels above.

"May I speak with you, sir?" the guard asked.

Tiberion glared at me warningly and then retreated toward the opposite wall with the man.

I drifted closer to the door, listening.

"—Beast, sir. Right away."

Tiberion scowled. He returned to the door.

"Zeke wants to see me, doesn't he?" I asked dryly.

"It would appear the king has heard of your presence and

your insistence upon him seeing this… person. So, yes, he wishes to speak with you."

"Not without her."

"The king's orders—"

"Were to talk to me, yeah? And I'm staying with her. So either you bring both of us, or you explain to Zeke why you couldn't follow his command."

Tiberion's scowl deepened. I waited.

"Contact the king," Tiberion snapped to one of his soldiers. "Inform him of the Beast's demands."

The soldier swam off quickly.

Tiberion regarded me coldly, as if daring me to challenge him.

I gritted my teeth, waiting. If Zeke said no…

My gaze skimmed over the rocks, over the bars, and what I could see of the shadowy canyon beyond. I wasn't leaving her down here. I didn't care what Zeke decided. What bridges it burned. Ari wasn't staying here, locked in a cell, trapped in the dark with armed dehaians all around.

Of that, I was absolutely sure.

The soldier returned. I couldn't hear his whisper to Tiberion this time, but the result was more than clear. Tiberion looked like the last bastion of sanity in the universe had failed him, and now he had to go along for the ride.

"Very well," he grudged. "His Highness says she may come. But I will not allow her near the king without shackles, do you understand me, Beast? The entire time. And if she makes a move we don't like, she dies."

Ari's breath caught. Tiberion glanced from her to me and then turned to his companions, taking my silence for agreement, as opposed to what it actually was.

I really hoped I didn't end up destroying the city again.

The lock on the cell clunked. The door swung open, and a man swam in, manacles in his hands. The shackles were easily long enough to cover Ari's entire forearms, and their surface shimmered with magic similar to the door.

"It's okay," I told Ari. "I'll be right here."

She closed her eyes briefly, like she was bracing herself for something, and she bit her lip as she held out her arms. The guard clamped the bindings down.

"Let those spikes out," the man warned. "And these'll shock you. Let them out again, the shock gets worse. Try anything we don't like—" He showed her a small, round stone attached by a short chain to his belt. "Same thing. Understand?"

Ari nodded, trembling. Swimming with her arms held awkwardly extended, she trailed the guard from the cell.

I eyed Tiberion while I passed him. He met my gaze darkly and then motioned for me to follow his soldiers toward the exit. I did. We wouldn't be coming back here, though.

Not if I had anything to do with it.

❧ 11 ☙

ARI

Noah was okay. Noah was alive.

Oh my God, Noah was *alive.*

My heart pounded, every beat a throb of relief, exhilaration, and fear—for him, for me, for everything. I swam after the guards, my arms pinned in cold manacles that looked like something out of the Spanish Inquisition. Ahead of me, impossible flames burned from the torch in the guard's hand, blazing like we weren't swimming beneath an ocean. The fire cast bright, blue-white light on the canyon walls around us, revealing square doors to other cells. Some of the openings were shielded by magic, and some were not, and when we passed, murmurs came from within a few of them like the occupants were curious to know what was going on.

And meanwhile, Noah was alive.

I wanted to scream and cry and shout for joy at the sheer fact of his presence. I wanted to throw my arms around him, close my eyes, and lose myself in how he was here. *Not* dead. *Not* hurt. Somehow, by some miracle, he'd survived everything

125

the poison had tried to do to him. And now he was *here*.

Except that didn't mean he was safe.

I made myself keep breathing. The poison twisted beneath my skin, waiting for a slip in my concentration. It'd been difficult, back in that cell, to keep it under control when the guard put the shackles on me. The urge to let it out seemed to get worse when I was scared.

And, I admitted to myself, I'd spent pretty much every moment since I escaped the strakirin being scared.

I pulled my shackled arms closer against my body. I didn't have to touch Noah. I could just… just be so glad he was here.

The guards swam up past the edge of the crevice and started down a space like a hall, minus most of the floor. A door waited at the end, and when we reached it, the hostile looks that greeted me were enough to make the poison worse.

I bit my lip, trying to watch the guards and avoid their gaze at the same time.

The door swung open. The dehaians led the way out.

Into a city.

My eyes widened. When they'd brought me here, I was muffled by the blindfold. I hadn't seen a single thing except the cell. But this… it was like the village on steroids. Like Chicago, but made out of natural stone. My focus darted from each colossal tower of rock to the next, all of their sides dotted with wavy green plants and countless openings like windows and doors. Schools of fish drifted past like birds, while over it all, a blanket of magic hung like the shield I'd seen around the village, only a thousand times larger. Its surface glittered as if it held an entire galaxy of stars, and beneath it, dehaians swam everywhere—though, when we passed, many of them stopped to watch the guards.

And Noah. And me.

Mostly me.

My gaze fell from the onlookers to fasten itself on the ground. I didn't want to imagine what they were thinking. What they probably saw when they looked at me.

The guards continued on, guiding us through paths between the stone monoliths. The one with the chain on his belt stayed near my side, and I could feel the pressure of his focus. His body language radiated a watchful readiness to electrocute me if I made a single move he didn't like.

More than ever, I wanted to retreat toward land, wherever that was.

The soldiers slowed. "Prisoner to see King Zekerian at his request," announced the one Noah had called Tiberion.

Something shifted ahead of us. My eyes flicked up.

A mountain lay before us. Barren slopes met my gaze. Nothing moved on them at all.

Except the water.

Alarm crept through me. A line shimmered in the empty water, parting like a pair of curtains. The glistening magic pulled wide before us, revealing something completely different from the barren wasteland of a mountainside.

The place was hidden like the city. Dehaians swam everywhere, with every shade of scales imaginable. Deep green plants covered the spaces that looked like windows and doors, and lights sparkled in a multitude of colors among the leaves.

I looked back while we swam through the opening. Bubbles formed a shimmering fabric behind me, separating this area from the city.

My gaze went to Noah. His jaw muscles were jumping. His eyes darted over the mountain and everyone there like he was waiting for something to happen. Something to explode.

I shivered. It was so strange, not being connected to him like we had been. Not knowing what he was feeling. His tension was written all over his face, but still.

It was so… silent.

I started to drift closer, and then caught myself.

He glanced at me. His mouth tightened, an expression in his eyes like he wanted to reach out to me too.

But he didn't, and an ache settled in my chest at the realization that he probably would never be able to again.

I forced myself to keep breathing. This wasn't helping me. He was alive. It was enough. And I needed to concentrate, if only to be sure I didn't accidentally kill someone. "Where are we?" I whispered.

The guard beside me made an angry noise.

Noah gave the man a sharp look. "Palace."

He didn't say anything else. Nodding uncomfortably, I studied the mountain while we came to a stop at a stand of leaves large enough to be a massive door.

Or a gate.

The soldiers there eyed me warily. "Twenty-third level, southwest suite," one of them said to Tiberion.

Without a word, Tiberion motioned for the guards to swim upward along the mountainside.

I followed. I didn't have much of a choice.

At another opening, they pushed the leaves aside. I trailed the soldiers through, my eyes skipping over the room beyond the plants. The space was at least twice as tall as a normal room on land, with a ceiling that was easily thirty feet high. An opalescent bowl hung from it, with impossible blue-white flames flickering inside. But beyond that, there were no other features to note. The walls were empty; the floor was too. Opposite the windows we'd come through, another tall stand of plants grew from the ground, looking for all the world like a closed door. Guards hovered in front of it. The whole room seemed a few padded walls shy of being a cell, and besides the soldiers, only one other person waited there.

But at the sight of him, I froze.

The strangest sense of recognition flashed through me, though I was sure I'd never met him before. But I *did* know him. He'd been in that memory Noah had shared with me— the terrible one. He'd been holding onto that girl, keeping her back from the Beast.

He'd been there when Noah died.

I made myself continue into the room. This had to be him, then. Zeke. The King of Yvaria. Even without that memory, I suspected I would've been able to tell that much. It wasn't anything about the way he looked, exactly. Nothing to do with his dark hair or brilliant, sapphire blue eyes. He wasn't even wearing a crown or robes or fancy jewelry, just a silver wristband engraved with intricate shapes that looked like mountains, but without a single gemstone. There was just something in his bearing, something in the way the guards around him seemed to keep one eye to him all the time. He drew the focus of the room to him without even saying a word.

But he didn't look much older than Noah—at least, Noah's greliaran side. He couldn't have been more than a few years older than me.

"His Highness, King Zekerian," Tiberion growled at us.

Noah ignored him. "Thanks for seeing us," he said to the king.

Zeke's blue eyes flicked to him, as if noting how Noah included me in the statement. "I got the message Baylie sent through Diane a few weeks back," he replied neutrally. "And considering that you're here now, I'm assuming she has something to do with all that?" He twitched his head toward me.

The words didn't entirely sound like a question. Noah nodded anyway. "Yeah." He motioned to me. "This is Ari. She's a ruanir."

Gratitude welled up in me. He knew that wasn't true. I couldn't really claim to be a ruanir anymore, as much as I wished I could.

But it was kind of him to say that, nonetheless.

"The guards said she called herself something else."

"Strakirin," I supplied in a tight voice, nodding.

"That's what they did to her," Noah interjected. "The judges. The bastards in charge of her people. They experimented on her."

Zeke didn't respond. I couldn't figure out what he thought about this at all.

"Your Highness," I tried. I had no idea what to call him, and the fact he was practically my age made it all the more awkward.

It occurred to me that he could order his people to kill me on the spot.

That helped.

"Please," I continued, making my tone as unequivocally respectful as I could. "I'm not your enemy. I swear."

He regarded me silently for a moment. "You trust her?" His attention went to Noah.

"Completely," Noah replied.

I couldn't stop my eyes from twitching toward him. He shouldn't. There were a million reasons why he shouldn't, and the biggest was twisting under my skin like a plague, waiting to strike him dead.

If I lost control again…

Zeke caught the glance. "What?"

His tone was sharp. The guards around us tensed at the sound.

I hesitated. "Did your soldiers tell you about the, um… what happened out there?"

I couldn't meet Noah's eyes.

"I'm aware, yes," Zeke allowed.

My eyes lifted to his blue gaze, and suddenly it hit me. Zeke knew exactly what he was risking, being here. Talking to me. He could have refused to let me in the room with him, and from the expressions on the faces of the soldiers around him, that's precisely what they wished he'd done.

But he hadn't. I could kill everyone in this room with a touch, and he hadn't.

And given the question he'd just asked of Noah, I could only think of one reason why.

He was counting on Noah to stop me if anything went wrong.

I didn't know what to think. The fact this guy trusted his girlfriend's sort-of ex with pretty much the lives of everyone in this room… it made me wonder what had really happened between them all last year.

"I want to help you," I pressed on. "But you have to understand what you're facing. Your Highness… I was made like this to kill people. Dehaians, humans…" My chest quivered. "Him." My head twitched toward Noah. "The force you're up against is the same. They're different from me in only one way—they don't question. They have no pity. No mercy. If they're ordered to kill, they'll do it, even if their victim is a child."

The quivering in my chest grew worse. I could feel Noah's eyes on me, like he could see right through me, empathic connection or no empathic connection.

I hated it. I wished he wasn't here for this part, but there was nothing to be done.

"They're a hive mind," I made myself continue. "One will, one identity. They're not *people*, not anymore. They've been stripped of fear, of emotion, and they—" I shivered. "Their only desire is to obey their masters, no matter *what* they're ordered to do. I'm not entirely sure how I was able to break free of that, but I'm telling you, your subjects are in danger. The strakirin were designed to be stronger than you. Faster. You can go for days without food or sleep; they can go longer. They can mask themselves from your detection using some kind of skill they stole from the Beast, and a single touch from them can kill." I dragged in a breath. "They'll never stop, Highness. Not until every single one of them in that hive mind is dead."

Zeke's face was expressionless, but the guards' faces were far less so.

They looked like they wanted to shoot me right now.

"You have to get your soldiers ready," I said. "You have to go after them. The judges have dehaians on their side. Osias is their leader's name. He said he was taking the strakirin to meet others, so I'm guessing there are more. But they're after something. I don't know what, but it's out here somewhere, and they seem to think it'll let them kill all their enemies, here or on land. The judges don't want a war, Your Highness. They want a slaughter, and they'll do anything they can to get it."

I couldn't look at Noah. It was difficult enough to picture what he must be thinking of me without having to see his face.

"To what end?" Zeke asked.

"I don't know."

He was silent for a moment. "What can you tell me about Osias?"

I shook my head. "Not much. He was maybe middle aged. Dark haired. Dark eyes. Green, um…" My bound hands moved toward the scales covering me. "But lighter and not the same as… you know, me. Dehaian."

"Is this the guy from the lab?" Noah asked quietly.

I nodded, not meeting his eyes.

"He was there when they did this to her," Noah explained to Zeke.

"Do you know where they were headed?" Zeke asked me.

"Along the southwest border, heading for some western territories, I think. That's all I heard the judges say."

"You said they were a hive mind. Do you have any way to track them?"

Noah looked between us fast. "Zeke, you can't *seriously* be suggesting she—"

"Let her answer the question," the king interrupted, looking to Noah sharply.

Noah stared at him. His brow furrowed at whatever he saw in Zeke's eyes.

"Can you?" Zeke repeated.

I faltered. That… that wasn't what I'd intended to do. Warn the dehaians and then head home as fast as I could, definitely. But to use the hive, use the *drone*, to track them?

I blasted them out of my mind once. What if searching for them with their own horrible drone let them back in?

"D-do you not have a way to find them? With this stealth thing, I mean. Do you have a way of, you know, getting through…"

Zeke's expression shut down, and my fumbling words trailed off. They didn't. I'd bet money on it.

My heart sank.

"Enough." Tiberion looked ready to spit nails. "Answer the king. Can you track them or not?"

"Back off." Noah turned to Zeke. "You can't ask her to go after those things. If they got their hands on her again…"

Zeke looked away, something almost like furious desperation flashing across his face so fast, I almost missed it.

But it hit me like a bucket of ice water. Was this what Noah had seen a moment ago? This expression like there was a lot more going on here than met the eye?

It could mean anything. I didn't know this guy. I had no reason to trust him.

But then, Noah seemed to.

I swallowed hard. Zeke wasn't the only one counting on Noah in case something went wrong.

"I… I can hear them."

Zeke looked back to me.

"Not right now," I elaborated quickly. "Just, if I'm close and I don't…" Block them? Build walls to keep them out? I didn't know how to describe it. I forced myself to go on. "They make a noise in my head."

"Hive mind," Zeke said.

I gave a tight nod. "Yeah."

"Does it affect you? Does it interfere with the control you have over keeping yourself from becoming like them?"

I could feel Noah's gaze—and his anger too, our lack of an empathic link be damned. It was like a faint quiver in the water, radiating out from him.

"I don't know," I managed. "I'm blocking it out."

My worry was written on my face. I felt it.

Zeke seemed to see it too. He nodded, dropping his gaze away briefly, considering. "We will send soldiers after them. Try to locate them before they find whatever they're searching for, and then call for reinforcements to stop them." He looked to me. "Your assistance would be appreciated."

I could hear the question in the words. The request I could still refuse. It was more than I'd expected, to be given the option when his people were at stake.

And if I did say no…

I shifted uncomfortably in the restraints. They wouldn't hurt me. Probably not, anyway. Maybe they'd even let me go home.

And then they'd have the whole ocean to search, chasing an enemy they couldn't see till it was too late, who was after something that would kill them along with everyone I loved.

"I'll help," I said quietly.

The rage coming off of Noah was palpable. I shifted away from him, avoiding his eyes.

"Thank you," Zeke said to me. "Captain Tiberion."

"Sire."

"Remove her restraints. As of now, Ari is our guest, not our prisoner. We'll extend her the complete benefit of the doubt about not being our enemy until we have information proving otherwise, so I want her treated accordingly, understand?"

Tiberion was silent. Zeke waited, raising an eyebrow.

"Yes, sire."

"Then please escort her to a more suitable place to stay, and instruct Commander Damarion to prepare to leave."

Tiberion bowed his head.

"Zeke," Noah started. "What—"

"Stay for a minute," Zeke interrupted. "We need to talk."

Noah stared at him.

Zeke twitched his chin at his soldiers. Several swam toward me. One of them removed the shackles before motioning toward the window at my back.

I rubbed my wrists, risking a look to Noah. His incredulous gaze went from me to Zeke and back.

"Be there soon," Noah said, sounding a bit at a loss.

I nodded. Trying to believe this would be okay, I trailed Tiberion from the room.

12

NOAH

I watched Ari swim away, and more than anything, I wanted to go after her. Hold her.

And get her the hell out of here.

"Zeke, what the *hell* do you think you're doing?" I demanded, turning back to him.

For a moment, he studied me, that same guarded expression on his face that he'd had almost the entire time we'd been in here. "I'm trying to save lives."

I bit back a scoff. Save lives by risking hers. By possibly handing her back to the bastards who'd nearly destroyed her.

"Bullshit."

"I need your help, Noah, and Ari's too. This situation threatens a lot more than just her."

"So that makes putting her in danger okay, then?"

"I'm not saying that."

I waited, seething. She'd *agreed* to this. Why the hell would she agree to this?

A twinge of anxiety tugged at my anger, whispering that I

didn't know what she'd been through. What she'd seen.

That only made things worse.

"Look," Zeke sighed, "you don't know me that well, and to be honest, I don't really know you. Maybe that should keep me from trusting you, but… maybe that doesn't matter either. I trust Chloe. She believes you're a good person. That even after what you've become, you're still *you* in there—and that the creature who destroyed our city a year ago won't do so again."

He watched me as if evaluating my reaction. I wasn't sure what to say. People had died that day.

His brother had died.

I wouldn't do that again. Not without a damn good reason, and not like the Beast had.

"But," Zeke continued, even more carefully, "there's more to it than that. I'm trusting that, whatever your thoughts about Chloe after how everything went, you still wouldn't want her to get hurt. You'd protect her like you did a year ago, before…"

His eyes flicked over me, and I could read between the lines. Before I'd died and become this.

And he was right. I'd still do what I could to keep Chloe safe. The fact she'd ended up with him instead of me didn't mean I'd ever be okay with her getting hurt.

I wasn't that kind of monster.

"What's going on?" I asked in the calmest voice I could manage.

"Things have become more… complicated since last summer. Most of it's political. Allies becoming cagey about their support, mistrust even in places where there never used to be any. Chloe's heritage as the daughter of a Vetorian mercenary hasn't helped anything. Her biological father can be… frustrating—" Zeke sounded like he was using a lot more colorful of a term in his head. "—even if he hasn't let matters become bad enough to affect his chances of having a relationship with Chloe. But on other fronts… let's just say, I don't want to see the situation get much worse. You caused a problem a year ago, and I don't mean the storm aspect of yourself returning. This. You as you are now. The Beast, with *all* its power, in the form of Chloe's… friend."

"People think I'm under her control," I filled in. "And yours."

Zeke paused like he hadn't expected me to see the problem.

"The ruanir," I said. "Their leaders, all of them. They assume that too."

"Everybody seems to be waiting for Yvaria to turn the Beast on them. For us to attempt to take them over. And despite all the reassurances in the *world* to the contrary…" He scoffed, something like old frustration in his tone.

I wondered how many political arguments he must've had about this.

"And now you're here," he continued. "Back, and appearing in Nyciena at will. It's made matters worse. I wish I could just ask you to leave, but I know that won't solve anything. And I need every ally I can get."

I studied him, not sure what to say.

"We have an enemy out there, Noah. Chloe, me, all of Yvaria." Irritation flashed over his face. "And I can't find them.

My soldiers can't find them. Someone is spreading paranoia and mistrust, and it's only getting worse. Ambassadors have been recalled, trade agreements ended, threats made…" His mouth tightened. "The attack on those ruanir a few weeks ago, the one that was made to look like Yvaria was at fault… that was only the beginning. My mother's people in Lycera intercepted an assassin, one targeting their queen. He claimed to be Yvarian as well, right before he killed himself. The Olician ambassador's convoy was attacked on their way back home, and while they were able to drive the perpetrators away, those people appeared to be Yvarian soldiers too. And now a village on the edge of our border has come under attack. I don't know where this is coming from or who is behind it." He paused. "Or who I can trust."

My awareness stretched out, searching.

I still couldn't find her.

"And Chloe?"

Zeke twisted the silver armband on his wrist, an absent gesture that made me think he'd done it numerous times.

I suddenly wondered if she'd given that to him.

"She's gone to see her father."

"Does she know about all this?"

Zeke gave a soft scoff. "It's why she went. To reassure our allies, she said." He shook his head, humor fading. "She's good at this. And she's right. We need to secure every alliance we can. But it worries me. We're trying to stop this, Noah. Both of us. But if things go wrong…"

I watched him. I didn't know him well—he was right about

that—but I knew that look. I'd felt it on my own face enough times. Desperation and the fear for someone you love.

It was strange to see it from him, for her, someone I'd once felt that about too. Strange in a way I couldn't quite define.

"What can I do?" I asked.

Gratitude flickered over his face. "Find those dehaians—and these 'strakirin' as well. If what Ari is saying about this Osias guy is true, he's the best lead toward putting a face to our enemy that we've had. Finding him and the strakirin could stop this before it escalates." He was quiet for a second. "The Sylphaen were bad, Noah, with their spies and the fact their converts were everywhere. We've spent the better part of the past year repairing all that they destroyed. And now this…"

I didn't respond. I remembered, though. Those crazy cultists hunting Chloe had been a nightmare.

They were a big part of why I'd died.

"We need your help," Zeke continued. "Yours and Ari's. The situation here is deteriorating fast, and without knowing what this enemy wants—or who they even *are*—we don't stand much chance of getting ahead of this. I don't know how much longer it'll be till something goes truly wrong and one of our neighbors declares war."

A chill ran through me. I didn't want to agree to this. I *couldn't*. This was Ari's *life* we were talking about here.

But I also couldn't just walk away. Not with everyone I had ever cared about in danger.

Not with a war coming.

I felt sickened. Dehaians and wars… my Beast side

remembered the last one I'd been in, centuries ago. Remembered how bloody it'd been, how hellish. They'd tortured me into existence back then, all to create the weapon they wanted. If the dehaians started fighting, if things went badly, I could only too easily imagine some of them attempting to gain power over me again. The Sylphaen had already tried killing Chloe last year for that sole purpose.

And that didn't even bring into it the people who'd want to hurt Chloe, and anyone else near her, simply because they refused to believe I wasn't Yvaria's slave.

"Okay, I'll help. But not Ari. She stays out of it."

He was silent.

"You can't put her in danger like this, Zeke. If those things take her over again…"

I trailed off, fighting to rein in a surge of desperation and rage at the mere thought. The Beast side of me couldn't stand it. The greliaran side was the only thing keeping me from breaking something—possibly the mountain.

"You want Osias," I continued. "This is the deal. I'll find him. Bring him back to you. Ari doesn't need to be with me for that."

He seemed to weigh my response. "Is she safe here over a longer term? This hive mind—she says she can't hear them unless she's close. Do you know if it's the same for the others? Could they track her here?"

A scowl tried to twist my face. Hive mind. *God*, when she'd said that…

I pushed the memory aside. "I don't know. I'll find out."

Zeke nodded. "We'll protect her, either here or at one of the garrisons. She sounds like she's been through hell. I'll make sure she's safe and has whatever she needs."

Tension drained from me slowly, like it wasn't sure it should leave. "Thank you."

He nodded again. "Thank you too."

A second passed. Awkwardness sidled into the space between us, making it clear it was time to go. I hesitated, ready to head for the exit.

But the silence pressed hard on me, heavy with old ghosts.

"Zeke," I said. "About your brother."

He shook his head. "Kirzan killed Ren, Noah. Not the Beast."

His voice was quiet, like he'd spent a lot of time thinking about this. And, yeah, it was true that the leader of the Sylphaen had drawn the Beast here a year ago and baited it—*me*—into attacking Nyciena and Zeke's oldest brother.

But I'd still been the one who killed him.

Zeke seemed to read my pause. "You direct your anger at the person who wielded the weapon, not the weapon itself. Kirzan is dead. To me, that means it's over."

I managed a nod. That was that, then.

"The guards outside will lead you to Ari," Zeke finished.

I turned, not stopping on my way out of the room this time.

✺ 13 ✺

ARI

Hotel suites back on land had nothing on this place. Shelves of polished rock lined the walls, all of them covered with trinkets and baubles made of precious stones. Mirrors positioned behind them reflected the light from the opalescent bowl hanging from the ceiling overhead. Inside the fixture, blue-white flames flickered, casting a peaceful light on the whole room. Tall leaves had been pulled back like curtains in the archway to my side; past them I could see another room, one that held a wide, low-walled box filled with sand. Folded blankets of something that looked like seaweed lay over the foot of it, leading me to suspect that the whole thing might be a bed.

It was all so strange. So insane. More than the city, more than the cells, the bizarre not-quite-normalcy of this place brought home just how *far* from home I truly was.

I swallowed hard, my eyes going to the door. Guards were out there, and outside the windows too. They hadn't said a word when they delivered me to this room, but their intent was more than clear. I was supposed to stay put. As much as they were keeping any curious dehaians from bothering me, they were keeping me here too.

It was hard not to feel like a prisoner, albeit in a much nicer cell.

I turned away from the door, wondering when Noah would be coming back. It wasn't difficult to guess what Zeke wanted to talk to him about—at least, what I assumed he wanted to talk about. Me. This. The strakirin and the fact Osias was out there somewhere.

Going to track them all down.

My shoulders shifted uncomfortably, my skin crawling. I didn't want to go out there. I wanted to go home. Noah was alive, which was like a miracle, and my heart raced with the desire to flee back to land with him and stay there till the end of time.

But that wasn't possible. Not yet.

The thing that used to be my legs rippled in the water. The twitch sent me toward the ledge of the window, and for lack of anything else to do, I sat down. The tail curled beneath me, bending like knees and then bending more.

My stomach rolled at the feeling. I wanted my body back. My *real* body. I wanted to see my own eyes in the mirror again, not these snake things. I wanted my own skin, my legs, everything.

Every second in this twisted form of my own body… it just hurt.

I closed my eyes, drawing several deep and slow breaths in an effort to calm down. I'd go back soon.

Unless Zeke was lying.

Unless he was just as bad as the judges in that way.

My nausea grew worse, obliterating my attempt at reassuring myself, and my hands clenched around the sharp stone ledge. Noah trusted him—or "something like that" anyway. And I trusted Noah. He wouldn't let us stay here for a heartbeat if he thought Zeke was going to be like them.

People made mistakes, though. I had.

My tail twitched in the water, frustration boiling up in me. This wasn't the problem. It wasn't the *point*. Zeke wanted to find Osias. He'd as much as said that. He wanted to stop this.

At least, I thought he wanted to stop this. I could only assume he was in that room now, working to convince Noah that we should go out there and keep that weasel bastard Osias from siccing any more strakirin on little dehaian girls with pigtails. And that was good. I was one hundred percent behind that.

Except for the part where it meant I had to track the strakirin. Where it meant risking I might become one of them again.

I shoved away from the window entirely and swam into the middle of the room, only to spin back again. I wouldn't turn into one of them. I'd burned through that *thing* they'd made me become. I'd destroyed it.

I hoped.

Scowling, I spun again, swimming back and forth like I was pacing. No, the hive couldn't touch me. And if it tried to get back past my walls, I'd burn it again. I could feel the lightning inside myself as much as the poison, and on top of that, I had *more* than enough rage.

I'd be fine.

My heart was pounding, but the anger helped. I liked anger. It kept the fear at bay.

The leaves on the window behind me rustled.

I jumped a mile.

Noah stared at me, his hand frozen on the plants he'd pushed aside. Awkwardly, I sank back down through the water, my reflex having jolted me up to nearly the level of the light fixture.

"Are you okay?" he asked carefully.

"Yeah."

My voice wasn't convincing, I could tell. Neither were the spikes protruding from my arms. Noah just eyed me for a heartbeat and then nodded anyway before moving farther into the room.

I watched him warily. The silence was deafening, and not just because of the way neither of us spoke. I couldn't pick up anything from him. The empathic connection we'd shared was totally missing, and this weird emptiness had taken its place, dividing us like we were two lonely islands parted by a sea neither of us could cross.

I didn't like the feeling.

"So," Noah began. "I, um—"

"How long was I gone?"

He hesitated. My heart was pounding again, the question having burst out on its own.

"Eight weeks," he answered quietly. "Two days. About three

and a half hours."

A shaky breath left me. Oh.

"And my family? A-are they okay?"

"Yeah," he said. "Last time I saw them."

"When was that?"

He wasn't quite meeting my eyes. "About a week ago."

I made myself keep breathing. That wasn't bad. A few days, really. They were probably still fine.

Oh, God, let them still be fine.

"What about Baylie?" I continued.

The pause came again. Dread seeped through me.

"She's alive. She's in a coma. Doctors aren't sure why."

I didn't know what to say.

"Listen," he tried, "I just came by to… to make sure you were okay and to say that I'm going to need to be gone for a while, but—"

"Wait, what?"

"I'm going after Osias."

"What about me? Zeke asked—"

"I'll take care of it."

I stared at him. It wasn't that I doubted him. He'd found me here.

But the strakirin could hurt him. If they had magic like mine—and everything I remembered said they did—he could die.

"Noah, you can't just—"

"It'll be fine."

"Since *when*?"

"Since I don't want you near them."

I struggled for words. I didn't want *him* near them either.

"It won't take long." He sounded like he was attempting to make the words softer. "I'll head south and—"

"No."

He stopped.

"No, you can't. Not without help."

He opened his mouth to protest.

"I have to go with you. Those things are designed to keep you and the dehaians from knowing they're there, and—" I choked down a breath, and in my head, I inched closer to the strakirin abilities I could feel lurking inside me.

My skin shivered like a cool breeze had suddenly stirred around me. "Can you feel me in the water here? If you're not looking at me, can you tell I'm here at all?"

He hesitated, his jaw working around.

And he didn't respond.

"Yeah," I said, reading the silence. Another breath entered my lungs, fast and ragged, while I shoved the strakirin traits back down. "I'm the only one who can find them. You need my help."

"You're not going out there." The words were emphatic. Flat. Like there wasn't a chance in hell I'd convince him otherwise.

Fury boiled up in me. What, did he think he could *control* me or something? That he had the right to decide what I did and didn't do?

My heart began to pound, hard and fast and driven by adrenaline. "That is *not* your call."

Frustration broke past his stubborn expression. "Ari, you don't have to—"

"The judges are going to start a war, Noah, and when the dehaians come onto the land to strike back, they'll be hunting ruanir. My friends. My family. You think I'm going to just sit by and risk that they'll all die?"

"And if coming near them turns you into one of them again?"

"Is Zeke sending soldiers with you?"

His jaw muscles jumped. "Yes."

"Then I'll stay back. Just tell you and the soldiers where they are. I won't come close enough for the strakirin to get near me."

His face twisted like he was biting back curses in his head.

The sight only strengthened my resolve. I knew I was right. I wanted to go home more than anything in the world, but that wasn't an option. Not yet. At this moment, I was the only person in *possibly* the whole ocean who stood a chance of finding the strakirin. Or at least of surviving that discovery.

"I won't turn into one of them again," I insisted.

He looked up at me. I could see the questions in his eyes.

My temper flared higher. Maybe it was good we didn't have that connection anymore. It'd been more trouble than anything half the time, and it *definitely* would be infuriating right now. After all, he'd just know how terrified I was that I might be wrong. That I'd lose myself. That I couldn't hold out against them, all my efforts be damned.

He'd use that knowledge to try to stop me.

"I'm going," I snapped and swam for the window.

He reached for my arm when I passed him. I jerked away a heartbeat before he stopped himself too.

"You shouldn't do this," he ground out, not looking at me.

I clenched my teeth while my chest quivered. Fighting with him hurt. It wasn't what I wanted.

But I couldn't back down now.

"I'm the only one who can," I replied.

Without another word, I shoved past the plants and left the room.

✦ 14 ✦

BAYLIE

Maia's father, Judge Davenport, turned out to be staying only a few hours north of the resistance hideout in Arizona.

And everyone could see that was too convenient.

"—come at them from the north, where the terrain is best," Miguel said. "That should give us the opportunity to get close enough for decent surveillance."

"Then what?" Declan snapped. "They're practically on our *doorstep*, Miguel! We should move the Arizona hideout, get everyone to safety, and *then* focus our attention on—"

"My father could be gone by then!" Maia protested.

Declan tossed her a glare. "Or our people could be dead after they get done risking their lives for your little zombie cousin."

From the corner of my eye, I could see Jace shift position, like he was fighting the urge to punch the man.

"Declan," Veronique interjected, a warning note in her voice.

He turned the glare on her. "You know I'm only saying what everyone else is thinking. We're in this mess because of them."

"We're *in* this mess because the Judiciary wants to turn us all into mindless slaves," Miguel retorted. "If they hadn't used Ari, they would have used someone else, and the situation would be exactly the same." He pinned the man with a pointed look. "We will warn our people, but we *must* get our hands on a judge if we stand any chance of bringing this to an end."

Declan looked away, his teeth grinding.

"Now," Miguel continued. "I need three teams. One to handle scouting the perimeter and identifying any security they have. One to guard the—"

An alarm on the wall went off.

For a heartbeat, I froze.

But I was the only one.

The soldiers spun toward the monitors, their eyes darting over the black-and-white images in a frantic search for what could be triggering the alarms. Miguel grabbed for his walkie-talkie. "Report!"

A garbled shout and then static answered him. My heart hit my stomach.

Harvey came running up the stairs. "Enforcers!" he cried.

Veronique blanched.

"Weapons, now!" Miguel snatched his rifle from where it leaned by the wall. "Where are they?"

"Heat signatures to the west and south," one of the soldiers answered. "No visual yet. They—"

"There!" another soldier called, pointing to a screen.

I stared at the monitor, seeing nothing. Black-and-white forms of trees. Bushes. A fence and the forest beyond it.

Something moved.

A breath left me. It was so fast. A blink of an eye, and then it was gone.

"Stay or go, Miguel?" Declan called.

I glanced around fast. The place was like a fortress. Out there, the monsters were waiting.

But if they surrounded us…

Miguel scanned the monitor. More figures darted by, so fast my eyes only registered the motion after they were gone.

"Go," Miguel ordered. "You four," he gestured to several of his people, "come with me. We're the diversion. We leave via this exit, circle toward the secondary vehicle storage. The rest of you, protect the wounded, take the landwalkers we rescued with you, and then head to the primary storage behind this building. Lock it down if you have to, but try to get out. Veronique, Declan, go with them. Take Ellie and the others too."

The soldiers started moving for the double doors that led to the hallway. Staring at her husband, Veronique didn't budge. I could see the refusal on her face.

"It's the best plan," Declan said, his words directed at Veronique.

She didn't take her eyes from her husband, but anger joined her expression.

"Go," Miguel urged. "We'll join back up with you soon."

Gunfire came from outside.

"Come *on*," Declan called to Veronique.

"See you soon," Veronique said to Miguel, an order in her

tone, like he better do his damnedest to make sure that was the only outcome of this situation.

He nodded.

She looked to us. "This way."

We hurried after her. I heard the front door open behind us, and for a breathless moment, nothing followed. They were fine. We were fine.

And then the gunfire started.

"Run!" Declan ordered.

Without a word, Jace grabbed my arm, pulled it over his shoulders, and took off down the hall. The corridor was a blur of shadows. Industrial-looking lights glared in the larger space up ahead. When we reached the end of the hallway, I caught a glimpse of soldiers with wounded people supported between them. Others stood with guns at the ready. A double-wide door waited on the right side of the room, the thing bolted with steel bars like it was designed to withstand a battering ram, and a smaller door stood straight ahead. The left side of the room was a pile of rubble. Cinderblocks and ceiling beams had crashed down at some point, leaving a blockade that even an enforcer couldn't pass.

And then the soldiers pushed the larger door aside, took one look at the situation, and opened fire.

My breath caught.

"Go!" one of them yelled back to us.

We ran.

Declan shoved the small door open, sweeping the terrain with one swift glance before tearing outside. Concrete turned to gravel beneath our feet, and then to grass while we ran from the building. Undergrowth and bushes swiped at our legs, and my own breath sounded loud in my ears. I could hear gunfire somewhere to my left, but I didn't look for the source. Up ahead, one of the house-sized storage sheds waited, its walls brown with rust and age. And the soldiers were heading there. Only a few more moments and we'd—

A chopping noise tore my focus from the building. It sounded mechanical. Unnatural.

Loud.

I looked back.

A helicopter skimmed over the tops of the trees.

"What the hell?" I heard someone shout.

The helicopter banked hard and turned toward us.

"Get back!" a soldier shouted.

A rocket launched from the helicopter, straight at the storage shed. I saw a flash of light. Felt a pressure on my chest, like a giant had shoved me as hard as it could. Below me was nothing but air.

I slammed backward into the ground.

Pain burst through my hips and back, paralyzing me. Blinding me. My ears rang with a loud whine that drowned out everything.

Popping sounds penetrated the ringing first. Guns. Lots of guns.

Tingling spread through me in response, like ice water running through my veins.

No. No, no, no. This wasn't happening. Not here. Not now.

Frantically, I looked around, fighting to stay in control of this… this *whatever* it was. At my side, Jace was struggling up from the ground. The soldiers were already on their feet, aiming their weapons at something beyond us.

My eyes focused.

The vehicle shed was a loss. The roof had caved in. The building was in flames.

And the enforcers were jumping the fences.

My heart hit my throat. Panicked, I scrambled for my feet and grabbed Jace. "Get up!" I urged, pulling on him.

He staggered upright. Several yards to my left, I could see Ellie clambering up from where she'd landed in a bush. Closer to us, Maia tugged Dhanya upright.

Overhead, the helicopter circled for another pass.

"Take it down!" I heard someone shout. "Take it down!"

A weird feeling spread through the air, nauseating and clammy like the ground had opened up to reveal a bog. The cold tingling in my veins recoiled from the sensation. My eyes snapped to the right, searching for the source.

Declan was on his feet. His attention was locked on the helicopter. His hands were spread out, palms toward the ground.

The feeling grew worse. Stronger. All around us, the soldiers shot at the enforcers, desperate to keep them from making it beyond the fence.

Declan threw his hands into the air.

My guts felt like they were being ripped inside out.

The earth itself roared upward around him, engulfing the flying threat and sending it hurtling from its path. Careening wildly, the helicopter spiraled toward the trees and then disappeared into the forest with a deafening crash.

Declan sagged to his knees, gasping for air, and the clammy sensation faded. I swallowed hard, begging the nausea to disappear with it.

"This way!" a soldier yelled, gesturing toward another building in the compound.

Jace took my arm. "You okay?"

My legs shook. My whole body quivered like I was frozen from the inside. Struggling to conceal my queasiness, I nodded.

I couldn't tell if he believed me at all.

Another burst of gunfire came from behind us.

"Run!" Ellie shouted. She took off after the soldiers.

Clinging to Jace, I ran. From the corner of my eye, I could see the resistance soldiers firing at the forest. Black blurs sped by, so fast they could only be enforcers. I kept my eyes on the storage building. We were almost there. Just a bit farther. We were going to make it.

Enforcers raced from behind the main building, cutting us off. The soldiers fired, trying to slow them down, but for every one they took out, another was already in its place. Grabbing a soldier, an enforcer ripped the man's gun away and then hefted the man by the throat, holding him aloft as he thrashed, and black poison surged through his skin.

Ellie screamed. The enforcers had gotten past the soldiers. They were all racing right toward her.

Not us.

Her.

What the hell?

Panic gripped me. Ellie backpedaled, trying to escape, but the enforcers were fast, so fast.

"Hey!" I shouted, grabbing a rock from the ground and hurling it at them. It struck one of them in the head. He staggered but didn't fall. Blood pumping down his face from a gash in his forehead, he turned toward me.

Oh, hell.

"Ellie," I cried, "run!"

The enforcer charged at us. Jace tugged at my hand, yelling for me to run too. Soldiers aimed for the enforcers, trying to get a clear shot, but they weren't fast enough. Ignoring Jace, the enforcer snagged my arm. His yellow-black snake eyes met my own while his hand clenched down. I heard Jace shout. I saw the enforcer smile.

Electricity thudded through my veins like a lightning strike on the spot where I stood.

The air warped around me, driven by the percussive pulse of energy. The force of it ripped the enforcer away, hurtling him back and slamming him into the wall of the main building. Beneath my feet, the ground crunched downward like it had been punched. The tree branches overhead thrashed like a giant's hand had ripped up through them.

The electric feeling dissipated.

I gasped, looking toward Ellie.

The enforcers were gone.

I stared. The monsters were on the opposite ends of the compound, all of them thrown into trees or walls, and none of them were moving. Some of them were bloody, too bloody, and the sight made my stomach roll. The soldiers, the wounded, and the rest of our side were standing as they had been, like whatever happened hadn't touched them at all.

But they were all gaping at me.

"*Baylie?*" Ellie gasped. "What—"

My legs buckled. I caught myself with one hand on the flattened grass, but my whole body shook like adrenaline alone was keeping me alive. I knew this. I had no idea what I'd just done, but I remembered this feeling, this exhaustion when I'd wake up in the morning and everything in my bedroom would be on the carpet.

It'd never been this strong before.

"Get her up!" Declan snapped. "We've got to go."

He strode past me, tossing me a guarded look before he returned to scanning the compound. "Grab a couple of those bastards, and tie them up. We need whatever intel we can get from them."

"What the hell was that?" Miguel appeared around the side of the storage building ahead. "Declan, Veronique, did you—"

"Later!" Declan snapped.

I tensed, watching them both warily. I'd never heard Declan try to give him an order before, but Miguel simply paused like he was reading something in the single word. "Get inside," he called to the others, switching gears like nothing had happened. "Judges won't be far behind that chopper."

My adrenaline kicked up a notch. Pushing at the grass, I attempted to shove myself upright.

I stumbled like a newborn deer.

"Baylie." Jace appeared at my side. His hand reached for me, not touching me.

"It's okay," I tried. "I'm—" My legs faltered, nearly giving out. I gritted my teeth, fighting to stay standing. Damn this. Damn whatever the *hell* this—

He took my arm and slung it over his shoulders.

"Jace!" Maia protested.

He ignored her. "Come on," he said to me.

Gulping down a breath, I nodded. Together, we hurried toward the main building as fast as my legs would carry me. Around us, I could see the others watching me and the forest around us alike.

Miguel pulled the door to the building open. My eyes took a second to adjust to the shadows, and then alarm slowed me a moment longer.

A collection of military-style cargo trucks and rugged ATVs filled the space.

"Wounded in the back," Miguel ordered. "Kids and medics too. The rest of you, grab an ATV."

Jace and I hurried toward the back of the nearest truck. On unsteady legs, I clambered up to the seats affixed to the sides while he and the others did the same.

I could feel the others watching me. I glanced over, finding Ellie's startling green-brown eyes fastened on me.

"Why did they come after you?" I asked, breathless.

Ellie shook her head. "I don't know." She searched for words. "What was…?"

I hesitated and then shook my head too. I didn't know, not for sure. And I didn't want to.

All around me, the others stared. I locked my eyes on the door, the walls, anything but the people on all sides.

Several soldiers hurried past, hauling a bound and unconscious enforcer between them.

I trembled.

"Get ready!" Miguel called.

Anxiously, I looked toward the large garage door. Two soldiers took up positions by the control on the wall, one of them ready to press the button to open the door while the other took aim at the outside with his weapon.

Clunking heavily, the door rolled upward. The soldier swept his gun over the area, but there was nothing. No enforcers. No judges or helicopters.

The driver didn't wait for that to change. With a lurch, the truck surged forward and sped away from the compound.

❧ 15 ❧

NOAH

It'd practically been minutes since I found Ari again, and already we were having an argument.

Awesome.

Frustration boiling inside me, I moved through the water with Ari swimming several yards away. Two dozen dehaians surrounded us both, watching her, me, and the open ocean alike. Zeke had ordered them to protect her—a nod toward how little I wanted her to come, I was sure. I tried to be grateful for it, even if the way the soldiers eyed her like she might turn into a three-headed monster made me want to pummel them. But it wasn't the only problem.

The main problem was the fact she was here at all.

Gritting my teeth, I followed the lead dehaians while they veered down through the murk, staying close to the seafloor. Ari was being ridiculous. Osias and the strakirin could hurt her. *Had* hurt her. Hell, they'd damn near *killed* her, and it'd only been hours since she got away from them. What the hell was she thinking, coming out where they could try it all again?

The rational part of my mind muttered something about war and her family being in danger before slinking off to hide.

I scowled. It was still ridiculous. Sure, the dehaians were a hornet's nest. I knew that. Stir them up, and who knew how many people could get hurt? And fine, so the judges were a problem too, with whatever the hell they were after down here. She was trying to keep people safe. I would've done the same thing if it were my family. Hell, I *was*.

After all, Baylie had gotten hurt too.

Discomfort ate at the edges of my anger. No one knew why Baylie was comatose. It didn't make any sense. The resistance was trying to help her, though. They'd brought in doctors, even used some of their people to sneak her into a hospital for a CAT scan without the judges or human authorities noticing. They were doing everything they could.

But it didn't change the fact that she'd been hurt because of all this. That Ari had been hurt too, and she could be again.

That all I wanted in the whole damn world was to keep the people I cared about safe, and hopefully not die again in the process.

In the lead, the commander altered course toward the south, and the other soldiers followed. Commander Damerion, Zeke had called the guy. From what I'd gleaned in overhearing the other soldiers, he was Tiberion's brother, a fact which was equally obvious from how similar the two of them looked. Apparently Damerion had some kind of working relationship with the Vetorians, one that would make him valuable in dealing with them, considering we might cross into their territory.

Zeke hadn't gone into details, though.

I'd recognized him as well. The memory was blurry and filled with people screaming, but I knew where he'd gotten those scars on his tail.

He hadn't looked that happy to see me again either.

We continued on, hours crawling along, through the unchanging water. My eyes slid to Ari from time to time, no matter how I tried to stop them. She gave no sign of noticing the strakirin—at least, her nervousness appeared the same, as far as I could tell. It was bizarre, not having that link to her. We'd only been tied up empathically like that for a few days, but those were the only days I'd really had a chance to get to know her.

It felt like we were starting all over again.

And doing a fantastic job of it, too.

I buried another scowl and kept going.

It was probably long past midnight in the world above when Damerion finally motioned for the others to slow. At his direction, they dove toward a cluster of boulders on the ocean floor.

Several more dehaians rose from behind the rocks. I stopped, alarmed, but Damerion and the others didn't stop.

Warily, I drifted closer. Scars arrayed their skin and tails, the marks seeming ritualistic rather than random. One of them swam out ahead of the rest, heading for Damerion. Dark-haired with a mottled, cream and orange tail that made me think of a koi, he was leaner than the Yvarian soldiers, most of whom looked muscular enough to wrestle down anything that got in their way.

I remembered him. He was a Vetorian mercenary. He'd been with Chloe's father, Kreyus, last year.

Damerion seemed shocked to see him, but in an odd way. Not defensive. Angry. He snarled something I couldn't hear, to which the other man replied calmly. The mercenary's gaze flicked to me, though, an unreadable look in his eyes.

Still appearing furious, Damerion didn't say anything else. He motioned to his soldiers, who moved swiftly to set up a protective veil around us, before he swam for a smaller boulder nestled beside several larger stones. The Vetorian returned to the group of his people hovering a few yards away.

"What's going on?" Ari asked anxiously.

"Confirming where the enemy was seen last," one of the soldiers answered.

Ari hesitated. I wasn't sure that was what she meant. But then, I didn't know what to say. Chances were, she was probably still mad at me. Any reassurances would probably ring hollow as hell, and I really didn't want to end up in another argument—*especially* not in front of these people.

Damerion sank down by the small boulder. We drifted closer, and I kept an eye on the Vetorians, though they showed little sign of being interested in us. Their attention was on the soldiers setting up the defenses and the blue-white campfire the Yvarians were starting near the largest of the rocks.

Ignoring them, Damerion pressed his fingers to depressions on the side of a stone, and in response, the water shivered with magic in front of him. With a teal shimmer, the energy pooled into a dinner-plate-sized depression on the rock.

Ari's breath caught at the sight.

"Report," Damerion snapped.

Muffled voices answered him. I shifted closer still, till I could see the image of a man, faintly blurred but moving like a video signal transmitted through magic.

"—appear to have continued in that same direction, sir. They're just outside Yvarian territory along the southern border, heading west. We've tried to track them, but…" He shook his head. "The king is sending additional forces, but it's like fighting ghosts out here, sir. The only way we know where they've been is when our scouts or sentries disappear."

Damerion looked like he'd bitten something sour. "No sign of them inside the borders, though?"

"Not from what we can tell, sir."

That wasn't remotely reassuring.

Damerion seemed to think the same. His sour expression deepened. "Very well. Send a message to the outpost near the border crossing by the Cylian Pass. We'll be there in three hours."

The man nodded. Damerion took his hand from the boulder, and the image faded.

"Get food quick," he ordered the others. "We leave in twenty."

The soldiers nodded. Damerion ignored them, turning toward Ari.

"Anything?" he asked, his voice harsh.

She shook her head.

He nodded. "Eat if you're hungry." He jerked his chin

toward the containers of cubed, raw fish several of the dehaians were getting out, and then swam toward another group of his soldiers.

Ari didn't move. Hovering only a few inches above the sea-floor, she bit her lip, her attention darting from the others to the veil and then the open water beyond it.

I risked drifting a bit closer to her. "You don't want anything to eat?"

She glanced back at me, a flare of indignant anger some-how making itself apparent in her strangely snakelike eyes. But then it died. Blinking, she dropped her gaze to the sand. "I ate before I left land."

I hesitated, about a hundred questions crowding up. I wanted to know what'd happened there. What they'd done to her. When she'd broken free of them. I wanted to know everything, even if the answers were sure to make me want to kill something. But the awkwardness between us was over-whelming. And she didn't seem like she wanted to talk about it anyway.

"Oh," I said instead.

Her eyes twitched in my direction and then fled again. A silent moment crawled past, staring at us both.

"Excuse me, miss?" someone called to Ari.

Frustration boiled up at the interruption. I had no clue what to say to her, but that didn't mean I wanted our non-con-versation cut short.

The illogic of that didn't change my annoyance in the *slightest*.

"Yeah?" Ari answered.

A man swam closer. It was the Vetorian, the one I recognized from Kreyus's retinue last year.

"I know you," I said.

"And I, you," he answered smoothly. He turned to Ari, giving her a small bow of his head. "Ezio vel Oryan, liaison to Yvaria from the Ivalaen tribe."

Ari hesitated, her yellow-green gaze twitching to me.

"He's a mercenary," I translated.

His lip twitched. "I'm a diplomat."

Something in his tone made the title seem disingenuous, like he'd be one or the other if the price was right. Added to that was the look in his eyes. His expression was calm, even mildly amused.

But his eyes gave me the impression it was all for show. That beneath it, he was watching everything. Making note of everything. I couldn't begin to guess for what end.

"Why are you here?" I asked.

"Because this little adventure is heading west. The Prijoran Zone is out west. Praelex Kreyus spoke to King Zekerian and expressed the belief that if you ended up traveling there—which seems likely, given your enemies' current trajectory—it would be beneficial to have a guide, yes? Someone to make certain you don't accidentally end up in hostile territory?" He grinned. "Not all of the Zone's residents are as friendly as me."

"And Kreyus would *love* the other tribes to see the Beast working with Ivalaens, right?" I added.

His smile widened, but rather than respond, he simply

turned to Ari. "I've wanted to ask you, how were you able to break free of the rest of your kind?"

My frustration grew, in no small part because he was asking the very question I'd been unable to bring myself to raise.

Ari shifted uncomfortably. "Why?"

Ezio gave a quick look to Damerion when the man swam closer. "It could help us," Ezio explained. "If there's a way to disrupt that connection between the rest of them…"

He trailed off when Ari shook her head. "I don't think it'll work on them," she said.

"How come?" Damerion asked sharply.

I bristled at his tone, which couldn't have been more different from the mercenary's attitude. Polite patience was on Ezio's face, though it was belied by that strange intensity in his eyes. Meanwhile, Damerion seemed like patience was his last resort—if that. Behind him, the other soldiers had mostly stopped eating. Every one of them watched her now. I wanted to pull her away, if only to keep people from staring.

Though I really wanted to know the answer to this too.

"They're not like me." Ari's words were the only sound for a mile around. "I, um…" Her gaze darted toward me again. "The treatments were interrupted for me. They didn't get to finish the whole process the first time around. I think maybe that let me keep more of my own mind than the others did."

Ezio gave her a skeptical look, and then his eyes flicked to me like he'd caught her brief glance in my direction. "Then what about those stealth abilities I heard that you described to King Zekerian? How do those keep us from picking up on them? Is there any way past that?"

She hesitated longer this time. "I don't know. It's... it's like him. How you can't feel him in the water when he's not, you know, like this."

"Can you?" Ezio asked.

"Not—I mean, no."

Again, I was certain Ezio caught her faltering. He barely paused, though, before turning his attention my way. "So you *can* hide from them? In your other form, that is?"

"And?" I replied. "I can't find them any more than you can."

"No, but you're not exactly... this." He gestured to me demonstratively. "Could you surround us? Or go ahead of us? Level the playing field so they can't detect us either?"

I was silent. I wasn't sure what to make of how he'd asked that. Practical. Cold but detached, like it was simply another box he was ticking off on a checklist.

I looked away, my jaw working around, and my attention landed on Ari.

A small measure of my resistance died. Whatever his motivations, he might have a point, at least for how I could protect her.

"Stay put," I ordered him.

Ezio's brow twitched up.

I shifted form fast, disappearing from view. My awareness changed too, sight and sound instantly coming from everywhere at once. I moved between the others and Ari.

She tensed.

"Is it working?" Ezio asked her.

"Sort of."

"What do you mean?" Damerion demanded.

"I can't feel him there at all, and you're… blurry. Like, I can feel the rocks and the seafloor just the same, but you're just…" She appeared to search for another word and then settled for the same one. "Blurry. If you were farther away, it'd probably be hard to know you were there."

I drew back into human form. Ari didn't meet my eyes. Looking uncomfortable, she dropped her gaze to the ground.

"Well," Ezio commented to Damerion. "There's that at least."

The other man nodded.

"Why is that?" Ari asked me. "Why do you have that ability?"

I hesitated. I had no idea.

"Weapon," Ezio said like it was obvious.

Ari gave him a confused look.

"The Beast was made to be a weapon for the dehaians," he elaborated. "Maybe they meant it to guard them against their fellow dehaians too, in case they wanted to attack other nations or tribes after they got done with their war."

I fought the urge to shift my shoulders with discomfort, in no small part because I suspected he was right.

"But what about this hive mind?" Ezio continued to Ari. "Does the Beast's other form block them from picking up on you?"

Ari hesitated. "Maybe."

Ezio waited, but she didn't say anything more. "How much

area can you guard?" he asked me. "How far can we spread out through the water before we need to be concerned you'll be unable to block us from detection?"

I saw Damerion's jaw muscles jump. I could just guess he was thinking of the attack on Nyciena last year. "Miles," I answered. "If I want to."

Ezio glanced to Damerion, and then paused at the man's expression. "Huh," he commented. "Well, that'll help."

"We should get moving," Damerion snapped.

Ezio eyed him briefly before nodding, his face carefully neutral. "As you say."

Behind them, the other soldiers rose from the seafloor.

"I want you ahead of us," Damerion said to me. "You tell us where they are and block them from detecting us, but you stay clear of my people. Got it?"

Anger boiled in me. I wasn't one of his soldiers. I wasn't some *thing* he could just order around. "And if you all are in danger?"

Damerion swam closer. "Then we will handle it." He glared at me. "I lost too many people in your attack last year, Beast. Good people who *cannot* be replaced, and I will not lose any others. Not to you." His voice was thick, tense. "You're here for one reason: King Zekerian ordered it. But I will not have you endangering my soldiers—"

Ari gasped and spun, locking her eyes on the water to the south.

"Strakirin?" Damerion demanded.

Ari seemed to struggle for words. Her skin was bloodless,

and I could see her trembling as she nodded.

"How many?"

She shook her head. "I-I'm not sure."

"Take cover," Damerion ordered the others. "No one moves till we lay eyes on the bastards, and then we take them out, understood? Leave any dehaians alive for questioning. You." He glanced to Ari. "Stay out of sight."

Ari's attention was on me. "Their poison—"

"I'll be careful," I told her. "Go."

She gave another tight nod and then darted toward the boulders where the others had gone to hide.

"Beast?" Damerion snapped.

I tossed him a glare and then took off.

If there was a trace of life in the ocean around us, it had gone into hiding, as if everything for miles around had picked up on the presence of the strakirin.

Even if I couldn't.

Scanning the area warily, I let myself spread out through the water—a sensation that would have been relaxing if not for what could be waiting out here. But nothing moved. A hush seemed to fill the water, ominous and strangely cold.

Seconds slid past. I expanded my awareness farther, scanning for any sign of life.

A dozen shapes materialized from the near-black murk ahead of me. My focus locked on two forms toward the rear of the group. Dehaians, unlike the others, who were all strakirin. But neither of them were Osias. The closest had silver hair, while the second had scales in a mottled pattern of black and orange. The silver-haired one eyed the strakirin ahead of him like he was disgusted with their existence, though the ocean around him got a fair amount of the glare as well.

The strakirin came to a stop. To a person, they looked similar to Ari. Emerald scales, snake eyes, tails like an eel. They were young too. Probably not a one of them was over twenty. But there was something eerily unified about them, beyond their appearance, beyond their ages.

Hive mind, Ari had said. I could see it, somehow. It was in how they moved.

Their snakelike gazes swept the water, and tension joined the swearing in my mind. They shouldn't have been able to pick up on me. Ari had said they—

"She was there," one of the strakirin whispered, pointing toward the camp far in the distance.

"*Was?*" the silver-scaled dehaian demanded.

"Her presence has disappeared," another strakirin replied. The way they spoke was dreamlike, as if they were only another interchangeable mouthpiece for the same mind. "Something seems to be hiding it."

My tension eased a bit. Well, okay, then. That worked.

The orange-and-black-scaled dehaian gave the strakirin a brief glare, and then returned his attention to the distant camp. His lip curled, nothing good in the expression. "Close enough. Maybe they're trying a new defense technique. Doesn't matter.

You know what to do." He jerked his chin at the strakirin, motioning them toward the boulders anyway.

Anxiety surged back again. I drew away, staying ahead of the strakirin while my mind raced. Damerion was being an idiot. If the strakirin reached the camp, it'd be chaos. Soldiers would die. Ari might be hurt, or overwhelmed by that hive-mind hell. I couldn't let them have her, not again.

I could kill them.

I hesitated. I could. The Beast side of me argued I should. They looked like kids, yes, but they would hurt Ari. Maybe kill her. And I could do it fast, long before their poison had a chance to sink in. They didn't even know I was here. It'd be easy. It'd *been* easy for weeks.

That didn't make it right.

Discomfort boiled inside me while my attention flicked back toward the camp. Killing wasn't supposed to be easy. It was supposed to be horrible. And it had been—once. And what I'd done, what I'd *had* to do, just to find Ari…

It was horrible too.

Would Ari feel it if I killed them? Would it hurt her?

I retreated farther, uncertainty gnawing at me while my Beast side raged that I should attack them now. I had the power to stop this. End this threat. Ari could be killed if I didn't. I had to protect her.

But then, what *about* Ari? She hadn't wanted to be this. She hadn't chosen it, not like enforcers or the judges or even these two dehaians. And, yeah, I'd talked with the resistance, heard their reports of recruitment and all that the judges had done… but it wasn't like the judges hadn't lied before. Ari said the strakirin were a hive mind, that they weren't individuals anymore, but… these strakirin had been kids, for God's sake. What if they hadn't exactly chosen this either? What if they were innocent?

They'd slaughtered those villagers.

But the dehaians had ordered them to do that. They didn't have a will of their own, not after what the judges had done. You blamed the one wielding the weapon, not the weapon itself, right?

Unless that weapon was about to kill people you cared about. Unless by leaving that weapon alone, other people could die. A weapon was still a weapon, and I could stop them right here, right now.

It'd be simple.

And possibly murder.

Dammit.

I reached out, invisible in the water, and snagged the dehaians. Damerion was right about one thing. We needed information. We had to know what they were planning. But I didn't have to kill.

Not yet.

The dehaians shouted in alarm, and the strakirin faltered, seeming at a loss while the water itself swirled to grab their leaders. Hanging onto the dehaians, I whirled and took off, racing back to the campsite while I fought to keep from taking any magic from the men in my grasp. I could do the same for Ari and the rest. Grab them, be careful not to drain them, and then swim like hell. After all, I could move faster than any dehaian. Maybe than a strakirin too.

But I also didn't have much time.

The strakirin sped through the water behind me, and a wave of impossible cold raced ahead of them. In my grasp, the silver-haired one twisted, fumbling something from a pouch strapped to his side. A box, and before I could knock it away, he'd already flipped it open.

A white stone lay inside, cushioned by green fabric and held down by a strip of green seaweed. Suddenly, the weirdest feeling rippled through me. It wasn't like the poison. It was like…

Screaming. Blood. Pain and raging tides and searing flames, rising like the memory of a nightmare, swallowing everything in a blur of death, and I didn't want to be here, didn't want to be here, didn't want to—

My awareness of my surroundings returned.

The silver-haired dehaian was gone. I'd lost him.

And the strakirin were flying at me, even closer than before.

I tightened my grasp on the other dehaian, coming perilously close to crushing the man, and raced for the camp. I drew down into human form so fast, the water around the campsite roiled. My fist gripped the dehaian's arm. The man struggled, unable to break my grip, and he swung with his free arm, stabbing at my body with his spikes.

I barely noticed.

Damerion rose from behind a boulder. "Beast, what—"

"They're coming." Without another word, I let my body vanish. I swept around the soldiers, the mercenaries, the dehaian man, and Ari alike, carrying them away from the campsite.

And they were fine. Safe. I wouldn't take any magic from anyone. Not if I concentrated.

The strakirin raced toward me. The silver-haired dehaian was still nowhere to be seen.

"Beast!" Damerion shouted.

I ignored him. I flew through the water, struggling to balance speed with the safety of Ari and all the people in my grasp.

But, God, the strakirin were fast. They surged closer, trying to slash at the soldiers I held. Wave upon wave of ice buffeted me, seemingly pointless because what did cold matter to me?

And then the soldiers began to scream. Began to thrash and howl like their worst nightmares gripped them. I struggled to hang onto them, costing me precious speed.

The strakirin slashed at me, at the soldiers. Poison raged from every one that touched me, burning like hell.

"Damn you!" Damerion shouted. "At least kill them!"

No.

I swam faster. The strakirin started to fall back. Farther, and then farther still. I fought for every ounce of distance I could gain. A few moments later, the strakirin were at the edges of my senses, and then they faded entirely. Miles and minutes and empty stretches of nothing passed before I finally began to slow.

I released everyone except the mottled-scaled dehaian and then drew down into human form. "Are you okay?" I asked Ari.

She nodded, looking pale. I started closer. She flinched back, a frightened look on her face.

I stopped.

The mottled-scaled man twisted in my grasp, trying to break free. I ignored him, looking to the soldiers.

They looked shaken too, but only a few heartbeats passed before they regrouped. They weren't injured, at least physically, anyway. The strakirin hadn't been able to reach them. And the poison was fading from me already, thanks to the immunity Ari had given me a million years and a few weeks ago.

"Gods of the ocean *damn* you, Beast!" Damerion snarled. "*Now* you're a coward?"

I turned to him, fury mounting inside me. "*What?*"

The commander hesitated.

Satisfaction twisted through me. Good call.

I shoved the mottled-scaled man at the other soldiers. They grabbed him, keeping one eye on me and their commander.

"You murdered countless dehaians a year ago," Damerion seethed at me, "and now, in the face of our enemies, you force us to retreat without stopping a single one. Those things killed innocent dehaians too. Are you simply happy for *any* of our people to die?"

I didn't move. The Beast side of me raged, and the greliaran too. My awareness flickered, broader, less human and less in control. The poison was still draining, and concentration was difficult. I was certain my eyes had gone black, and possibly some of my skin too. I could see his soldiers all around me, staring at us both. Ari hovered nearby, doing the same.

She looked terrified.

My rage cooled, turning to something dark, something

cold. I moved through the water, closing in on the commander. "I died to save the girl your king loves. The girl I loved. I died too."

Damerion stared at me.

"My name is Noah, Damerion, not Beast. And I won't kill unless I have to. I'm not the monster you knew."

I turned away. My awareness still flickered, not entirely contained. I wasn't ready to trust my back to him, even if he couldn't hope to hurt me.

Old, sort-of-human habits die hard.

Damerion didn't move. I could still see him, after a fashion, despite how my back was turned, but I couldn't read what was on his face. After a moment, his jaw worked around. "Are there more of them nearby?" he asked Ari. "Are they coming?"

"I-I don't…" She bit her lip briefly. "I don't think so."

Damerion scowled.

"What about dehaians?" Ezio asked me, swimming closer. "Were there any besides this scum?" He jerked his head toward the mottled-scaled man.

"One. He got away."

Damerion stared at me.

"He had something," I gritted out. "A white stone in a box. It felt…"

Like death. Like the nightmares I didn't even *have* anymore, because I wasn't greliaran or human or anything that slept. It'd overwhelmed me, distracted me, and given that dehaian bastard a chance to get away. I didn't know how to explain that.

Or even if I wanted to.

"A stone?" Damerion eyed me like he couldn't believe what I'd just said. "You let him go because of a *stone*?"

The Beast side of me snarled in the back of my mind, but I didn't respond to the implied insult. What was I going to say? I had no idea what had happened.

I also never wanted it to happen again.

Damerion shook his head in disgust. "Fine. We head for the next stand of boulders we find and set up a perimeter—"

"Wait." Ari looked alarmed. "You want to—"

"Our mission is to destroy our enemies, in addition to bringing their dehaian allies back to Nyciena." Damerion glared at the ocean around him. "We don't retreat."

"You can't destroy them *here*," I argued. "*I* barely outran them. You think your people can stay out of their reach? Damerion, if the strakirin lay one hand on you, then you die. You can't—"

"Don't you tell me about what they can do. That one already killed two of my men."

He jerked his head toward Ari, not taking his eyes from me.

Oh, to hell with this. How the fuck *dare* he—

"Commander Damerion," Ezio interjected, swimming in between us like he had no sense of what I could do to him. "We have one prisoner. Perhaps it would be best not to risk losing him, but instead, to take him somewhere more defensible for questioning first."

"And what *exactly* do you suggest?" Damerion retorted, still glaring at me.

Ezio was quiet for a moment. There was something in the

way he looked at Damerion that I couldn't quite read. Loaded and angry, but strange.

If Zeke thought Damerion had a good diplomatic relationship with the Vetorians, I would've hated to see what the other Yvarians were like.

"The garrison at the Cylian Pass," Ezio replied. "We can question this one," he nodded toward the mottled-scaled dehaian, "and protect ourselves at the same time."

Damerion gave him an irritated look.

Ezio met it flatly, but I could see the warning in his eyes.

Damerion didn't speak for a moment, and then he scowled. "Very well." He glanced sharply to the soldiers. "Patch up the wounded with sieranchine and then head out!"

The soldiers scrambled. From the supplies, one of them drew out a jar of something clear and glistening. I vaguely recognized it from a year ago. Dehaian medicine. Magical stuff. Healed wounds almost instantly—short of fatal injuries, anyway.

Damerion swam off, and Ezio followed him. I turned away to find Ari hovering motionless in the water, her eyes locked on the jar, and her face somehow even more bloodless than before.

"Ari?"

She drew a sharp breath like she hadn't for minutes on end. "What?" Blinking, she looked at me as if she'd just woken up to find herself here. "Are… are you okay?"

"Yeah."

She didn't quite seem like she believed me.

"I promise. But, Ari, are you sure you're—"

"I'm fine."

For a heartbeat, I hesitated, not trusting her response any more than she'd appeared to trust mine.

"Those strakirin—"

"I said I'm fine." She spun and took off after the others.

Irritation snarled through me. Right. Sure she was. That's exactly how someone looked when they were fine. More likely, she just didn't want to talk, which was just…

I shook my head.

Awesome.

∽ 16 ⌒

LOGAN

The ruins of the village lay all around us, and this time, no one had survived.

I smiled. The residual sizzle of poison and pleasure tingled through me in a lingering high better than any drug I'd ever tried. The strakirin had slaughtered everyone. They'd cut down dehaians so fast, I'd barely been able to watch the death before the rush of it hit me.

It was amazing. No, forget amazing.

This was *fun*.

I stretched my arms out at my sides, faintly surprised not to see myself glowing. More than what seemed normal, anyway. This was Christmas. My birthday and every other holiday in the world too. No cops. No human or ruanir legal systems to worry about, either. Just whatever I wanted to do, to whomever I wanted to do it, at the hands of a thousand monsters that obeyed my every command.

This was *heaven*.

The strakirin hovered in the camp, the drone peaceful and

sated like they were sharing in my pleasure. But then, of course they were. They were happy because I was happy. Around them, Osias' dehaians moved like they were afraid to get too close. That was good too. I wouldn't kill them, not unless they deserved it. But so far, they were proving more useful alive, so they could stay that way.

God, I wanted to do this again.

I looked around, wondering where the next village was. We were supposed to be causing confusion, after all. Destabilizing the region and all that. Osias' dehaians were taking care of the last touches of that part now, placing armbands and weapons from some dehaian territory or another into the debris. In the great mystery of who had destroyed the village, the little tokens would scream "I'm a clue!" and then the dehaians would turn on each other.

But surely, a few more destroyed villages would help.

"—creepy bastards."

My attention flicked to one of the carved-rock hovels these dehaians called home. Closing my eyes briefly, I caught a blurry image of two of Osias' men. A copper-scaled guy and a green-scaled one.

Copper-scales was glaring balefully at my strakirin.

The green-scaled guy made a shushing noise, casting furtive glances to my strakirin too. "What if they can hear you?"

Copper-scales scoffed. "They won't do anything."

"What if *he* can?"

Clever dehaian.

Maybe I should kill him.

The copper-scaled guy only scoffed again. "You sound like a child afraid of the waves. That one…" He laughed. "God of tides, have you seen him? He thinks he's in charge of this. That he's making it out alive. You can see it on his face."

What?

Green-scales made another frantic shushing noise. Shit. Some of the strakirin had moved closer because I wanted to hear more.

I made the strakirin look away.

"What are you talking about?" Green-scales hissed.

Yeah, what?

"Osias knows the real plan," Copper-scales continued.

Oh, he did, did he?

"Those wizard bastards let him in on the whole thing."

I doubted that. But it also didn't matter. That slimy dehaian bastard thought he was going to get one up on me?

That was almost funny.

The strakirin turned back. I didn't care if they suspected I could hear them now. I wanted to know what the *hell* they thought—

Something was wrong.

I looked back to the west. A prickling feeling crept over my skin. The strakirin. Something was wrong with the—

A commotion came from that end of the ruined village, drawing my attention. A silver-haired dehaian, swimming like he'd been racing for his life to get here. My strakirin, the ones I'd sent after Ari, trailed him at a slower pace.

Memories flickered in my mind. Water coming to life,

grabbing the dehaians, ripping them away and carrying them into the distance while my strakirin chased.

What the hell?

Osias and the others sped toward the dehaian. Through the strakirin nearby, I could hear Osias demanding to know what had happened to the other man he'd sent along.

"The Beast, sir. It was the Beast. It—" Gasping, the silver-haired dehaian struggled to keep speaking. "It grabbed us."

"You saw it?" Osias replied.

The silver-haired man shook his head. "No, sir. But I… The water. It attacked us."

Osias spat something in a dehaian language, furious. I ignored him.

The Beast was *here*, in the ocean. I knew the judges had been tracking it. The damn thing had been spotted everywhere from New York to San Diego in that human form the judges said it possessed—a teenage boy or whatever, as bizarre a choice as *that* was—and where it went, enforcers died.

And now, on top of that, it was invisible too.

Bastard.

I turned to the strakirin. What had they—

No sooner did the thought cross my mind than I saw a flash of memory again. My strakirin hunting Ari, picking up on her from far off. There'd been others too, just for a moment. A sense of vaguely dehaian shapes in the distance. And then it was gone. Instead, there'd been a few moments of nothing. Utter silence.

Then the water attacked. My strakirin gave chase, racing

after the dehaians while the water carried them away. Poison surged from my strakirin's skin, and the water quivered. Spasmed, even, almost like a...

My lips curled. Almost like a *flinch*.

I could hurt it. The strakirin had been made with poison inside them, poison designed—among other things—to kill the Beast. Ari had failed to do that, it was true, but then, she'd only been one little strakirin.

A thousand-strong *swarm* of them, however…

"Ozzie," I called.

His face darkened. He cut off mid-order to his men, his gaze sliding to me with a wealth of threat for the nickname.

Whatever.

"Where would they go?"

His brow arched, his contempt obvious. I'd make him pay for that, once I was sure I didn't need him anymore. "They?"

"She's with dehaians. The Beast too. Where would they try to hide out around here?"

"How do you—" He cut off, his eyes flicking over the strakirin.

Whoops. So much for that secret.

But the hint of caution creeping into his expression was worth it.

"What dehaians?" he asked. "What did they look like?"

"Your guys didn't go close enough for me to see." I nodded at my strakirin.

The caution in his expression grew.

Perfect.

He was clever enough to attempt to bury it quickly, though. He turned to the silver-haired guy. "Which direction did the Beast go?"

"East, sir. Toward the Cylian Pass."

Osias' mouth tightened.

"What?" I prompted.

"An Yvarian garrison is there. If she's with soldiers, they'd go there."

Soldiers. Now that could be fun.

"We go," Osias said, turning to his people. "Make for the—"

"What?" I cut in. "You want to run?"

He stared at me.

"Swim," I amended. "Whatever. The *Beast* is out here. You want to leave that thing—"

"We're leaving nothing."

I stared at him.

"The signal. Is it calling you? Calling *them?*" He jerked his head toward the nearest of my strakirin.

Signal?

"Once we're close enough, it will call her, same as you, and if she's with that creature, it will follow. We do not need to chase her or some ancient mistake of a being. We *have* a *mission.*" He snarled the words through a clenched jaw.

I ground my teeth. Sure. Mission. Fine.

But I could *hurt* that thing, dammit. Hurt it and feel the rush of a thousand strakirin's pleasure at the kill.

There was no way I was going to pass that up.

"Don't you want to create confusion?" I bargained. "Chaos?

Don't you want to watch Yvaria burn from the inside out?"

Osias was silent. I held back a grin. Human or dehaian, everyone was the same. Find the levers, watch them twitch.

"Take down a garrison, Osias. With my strakirin, we could obliterate them in minutes, and you could pick your nation to blame. Or leave no evidence at all. Think what that would do to those bastards."

The gears turned behind his eyes. I could see it.

"The mission is paramount," he said.

"And we'll get to it," I agreed. "But this is important too… right?"

I had him. He hadn't said anything yet, but I knew I had him.

"Move out!" he yelled at his men.

I buried a smile. That was more like it.

Time to show the Beast what I could do.

17

BAYLIE

For almost an hour, we continued racing along backroads and nearly indistinguishable dirt tracks before Miguel called for the vehicles to stop. Forest still surrounded us, and mountainsides too. In a cave concealed behind overgrown bushes, Miguel's people made quick work of hiding the ATVs, and then we were on our way again with the soldiers crammed into the trucks with us.

We didn't see another enforcer for the entire time.

Another hour found us back to civilization, rolling down the road like a military convoy, till we reached an industrial-looking area on the outskirts of a town. Behind a warehouse with a sign for a medical supply distributor hanging on the side, we pulled to a stop.

The door to the warehouse opened immediately, and Willa appeared. Her red hair was lashed back in a ponytail, and like every other time I'd seen her, she was dressed in clothes that looked like she'd just stepped out of military boot camp. Her blue eyes swept over us, sharp and assessing, before she said,

"Inside. We have a space set up on the main warehouse floor. Landwalkers can stay in the back. We're contacting the elders to arrange safe passage for them elsewhere."

Carrying the wounded, the soldiers hurried past her. Behind those soldiers came several others, a trio of chained-up enforcers cautiously supported on gurneys between them.

I watched them warily. No one wanted to touch the enforcers, and with good reason. They weren't awake yet. At least, I didn't think so. But once they were…

"This way," Miguel said to us, walking past.

"Where are we?" Dhanya asked, her attention never quite leaving the enforcers.

Miguel's gaze flicked toward me briefly, and I could see the considering look in his eyes. It made me want to run away. They'd told him. What they could, anyway. Even I didn't know what this was. But I'd seen that look in his eyes before. He'd turned it on Noah from the moment he'd learned my stepbrother was the Beast.

And now he was turning it on me.

"Property of a friend of the resistance," he replied and walked away.

Biting my lip, I trailed the others toward the building. I could still feel them watching me, and I was fairly certain it wasn't my imagination that no one came too close. No one besides Jace, anyway. Alone of all the others, he lingered nearer to my side, appearing ready to catch me if I fell.

Suddenly, it reminded me of how Noah had watched Ari weeks before.

The thought was uncomfortable. I tried to ignore it.

I continued past the door. My legs weren't as shaky as they'd been before, though I couldn't say I felt anything close to normal. My muscles still quivered, but with a feeling of residual adrenaline tingling through them. It took concentration to keep the world from swaying like a boat on the ocean.

But I was better than I had been, and who cared why. The fact I felt stronger was all that mattered. That and staying safe if these people decided to turn on me.

Adrenaline tingled stronger through my veins.

The inside of the warehouse was smaller than it had appeared, owing mostly to the crates and pallets occupying much of the floor. Past the rows of supplies, I could see what might have been an office on the far side of the room, along with a few other doors leading to God knew where. In between them all, a metal stairway climbed till it reached a door with an exit sign perched above it.

"Take them that way, away from the others," Miguel called to the ones holding the enforcers. He nodded at a door near the stairway.

The soldiers returned the nod, and carried the enforcers toward the door. Maia and Dhanya watched them, not taking their eyes from the enforcers till the door closed behind them.

Maia put her hand on Dhanya's back in a comforting gesture and murmured something in a low voice. I couldn't make out the words.

Dhanya nodded.

"You two don't need to be here for this," Miguel said,

motioning for the two of them to head for the stairway. "Offices upstairs have monitors for the outside security. You can help us watch the property till we're ready to move."

Curiosity hit me. Why would they need to leave?

Maia only nodded, though. She and Dhanya walked toward the stairs. I glanced around, not sure what to do. I didn't want to stay here. I didn't want to be surrounded by soldiers.

Upstairs was the only option. Soldiers blocked every exit. There wasn't anywhere else to go.

I started after the two girls.

"Hold up." Declan stepped forward. "What are you going to do with that one?" He jerked his chin at me.

Miguel didn't respond.

"You saw what happened out there," Declan persisted. "She's related to the goddamn Beast, Miguel. She's *connected* to it. We need to question her. We need to understand how that works or if it—"

"We will."

Miguel's words were flat. The way he was watching me made me shiver. I couldn't read anything in his eyes. "Are you doing okay?" he asked me levelly.

My gaze darted around. Everyone was staring at me. Even Maia and Dhanya had stopped on their way to the stairs. I shivered with the urge to run. Hide.

Something.

"Baylie?" Miguel pressed.

I nodded. "Yeah. I-I'm okay."

"What happened out there?"

I shook my head, one shoulder rising and falling in a lop-sided shrug. "I don't—"

"Bullshit," Declan interrupted. "She's lying."

"Quiet." Miguel didn't take his eyes from me. "They said an enforcer grabbed you right before… whatever it was that you did. Is this connected to them?"

My breath left me. I shook my head fast. "No."

"Has it happened before?"

I didn't want to answer that.

Declan seemed to read something in my silence anyway. "Then why *exactly* did you hide this?" His tone was scathing.

"I didn't—"

"Don't lie to us!"

"Declan." Miguel gave him a sharp look.

"*What?* Our people are dying, Miguel! Half the time from traitors the judges planted in our goddamn midst! We're being driven from hideout to hideout, losing ground all the time, and now suddenly, this supposed *human* just *happens* to have magical powers too? That's not suspicious to you?"

Soldiers adjusted their grips on their weapons. I could read their expressions. Cold. Ready to fire.

They agreed with him.

"Yes," Miguel acknowledged, watching me. "It is."

Ice shivered through my veins, tingling with electricity like crystalline sparks, and I wanted to whimper with fear at the sensation. This couldn't be happening. I wanted to wake up. This was worse than when they found out about Noah.

Bullets wouldn't kill him.

Declan made a self-righteous harrumph. "Damn straight it is." He stalked toward me. I backpedaled, but there was no way out. Soldiers were blocking all the doors.

"Stop."

Miguel's voice brought everyone up short. Breathing hard, my heart racing, I froze too.

Declan stared at him. "We have to lock this one up till we can—"

"No." Miguel's voice was calmer than a windless lake. "We don't. We hear her out. After all, we all started out human once too."

Declan sputtered. "*Loosely*! And what the hell does that have to do with—"

"Perhaps something changed for her."

I trembled. He was closer to the truth than anyone so far, but there wasn't any way in hell this truth would set me free. They could lock me up. Test me. I didn't know these people beyond a few days of madness, and no one in this place was safe.

Except maybe Ellie.

I glanced to her, desperate, but my brief moment of hope died at the scared, hurt questions in her eyes. Why hadn't I told her? Why had I hidden this? And for the first time in my year of hiding, I knew the answer.

Because maybe it would've made me into something she would have studied too.

Something inside me broke at the realization. At the admission. At the truth. I didn't have friends. Not even family, not really. I only had people from whom I was hiding things.

Secrets upon secrets. I didn't know where the secrets ended anymore.

My gaze skirted away. There wasn't any getting out of here, but I wanted to. These people, staring at me like I probably had stared at Chloe, at Noah, at everything else that had gone insane in my life.

And now I was part of that too.

The stairs beckoned like a path to escape.

Declan scoffed. "Changed for her?" he repeated. "*When?* Come on, Miguel, you can't seriously want to let this girl stay—"

I bolted for the stairs.

"Oh, no you don't," Declan warned, blocking my path.

"Let her go," Miguel said.

The man stared at him like Miguel was insane.

I was shaking. I felt raw. Emptied and it hurt.

The dark, sparkling ice inside me quivered, whispering terrifying promises of how I could *make* him move.

"She's been here the whole time, Declan," Miguel said, "and she hasn't done a thing to harm us. Quite the opposite, given how many casualties we could have taken today without her help. Your concern is noted, and you'll get your answers. But we're not going to do the Judiciary's work for them by tearing into our allies without a distinct reason, understood?"

Declan's jaw muscles jumped. His dark eyes flicked toward me, weighing and cold and angry all at the same time. But then the look faded.

He stepped to the side.

I raced past him, trying to ignore the way Maia and Dhanya backpedaled from my path. I took the stairs two at a time, running for who knew what. A place away from them. From anything.

The door opened onto a narrow hallway with offices lining either side. Past a door to my right, I saw Miguel's people seated in front of monitors, though the soldiers went still at the sight of me. It was easy to read their expressions. They must have heard about me. Everyone must have by now.

My eyes began to burn with tears. I moved faster, striding past them into a room at the end of the hall. The door thudded shut behind me. Not turning around, I pressed my hands to the cold, metal surface, my chest heaving with ragged breaths.

I wondered how much longer I would've had, back in Santa Lucina, before this came out. Before Diane, Maddox, or Peter learned what had happened to me.

How much longer I would've had until I accidentally hurt somebody.

I bit my lip, my eyes squeezing shut. No, I'd been doing okay. I'd been keeping it… well, not exactly under control, but…

Oh, hell, I'd been falling apart.

I swiped a hand over my wet face, trying to stop the tears. I could've killed someone today. Someone besides those enforcers, anyhow.

My God, I'd *killed* people today.

Nausea churned, choking my throat. I swallowed hard and

pushed away from the door. The room was tiny. Some kind of old office with linoleum tile that had once been speckled beige and walls the color of an avocado. Both were chipped, with entire chunks missing from the drywall to reveal wires underneath. Gritty dust filled the gaps in the linoleum. The panel light overhead had been broken open at some point, showing the bulbs inside, but thankfully it still had power. With the only window in the room covered by sheet metal, the office would have been a blackened cave if not for the light overhead.

I walked farther into the room. There was an old desk ahead of me. Vandals had taken a knife to the wood surface at some point, carving out initials and symbols and other things I couldn't read. A chair sat behind the desk, teetered to the side due to the wheels missing on its legs. Its leather back was slashed; stuffing had spilled out on the seat.

I sank down onto the edge of the desk, gripping the wood like it was a lifeline to reality. My whole body was still shaking. Ever since I woke up in Arizona, the shaking felt like it hadn't stopped.

A knock came on the door. "Baylie?" Jace called.

I didn't respond. I couldn't. Of all the people…

"Baylie, I'm coming in, okay?"

I wrapped my arms around my middle. Imprints of the desk's edge throbbed on my palms.

The door crept open. Cautiously, Jace leaned his head in. I turned away, smearing the rest of the tears from my eyes quickly.

Jace eased into the room, guiding the door shut behind

him. "Declan's an asshole," he said quietly.

I scoffed. That was an understatement.

"You're not…" Jace made a frustrated noise. "He didn't have the right to talk to you that way. I'm sorry."

Some of the hurt drained. Declan's actions weren't Jace's to apologize for, but the words still helped.

He took a step closer. "Are you okay?"

No.

I shifted my grip on my arms. At least that had been his first question. Not, what the hell are you?

Or worse.

From the corner of my eye, I saw him check around, but there wasn't anywhere to sit except beside me. After a moment's consideration, he sank down into a crouch, propping his elbows on his knees.

I didn't move.

"What *was* that, Baylie?" he asked softly.

I was silent. I didn't want to talk about this. Not with him. Not with anybody, not anymore. I'd tried with Noah, but he was gone, and Ellie would just pester me with questions till I felt like a cross between a monster and a lab experiment.

I didn't want to talk. I just wanted this to go away.

Even though it never did.

Tears stung. I closed my eyes.

"You're not a freak, okay?"

I tensed.

"And no one is going to hurt you or… whatever. I promise."

I glanced in his direction, not quite looking at him. The

words were gentle. Like the way someone would talk down a wild horse or something.

But they sort of helped.

"Please," he urged. "Just… what was that?"

I hesitated. "I don't know."

Silence followed for a moment. "Does Noah know about it? Is it, like, because of him?"

A breath left me, edging toward a laugh though nothing was funny. Just ironic. So terribly ironic.

"Baylie?"

"No, he doesn't know. I tried to talk to him, but…" My shoulder rose and fell.

"But you're connected to him. So is it—"

I pushed away from the desk, retreating toward the steel-covered window, wishing it could give me an escape.

"I'm sorry," Jace said.

I glanced back to him.

"I don't mean to push."

Everyone else did.

I watched him, wary. He seemed to mean it. He just looked… sad. Like this whole thing was a mess and he hated that.

"Why not?" I asked softly.

He gave me a quizzical look.

"Why not push?"

"Because I'm doubting this is your fault."

My temper flared. "It's not Noah's."

He held up his hands, not saying anything.

"It's not," I insisted. "My stepbrother didn't do this."

But the creature he'd become did.

I looked away, wrapping my arms around myself again. Jace's shoes scratched on the gritty linoleum. From the corner of my eye, I watched him get up and walk over to the desk. Easing down onto the edge, he regarded me.

"You're okay, though?" he asked.

"Why do you care?"

He paused. "Because I told your stepbrother I'd watch out for you." His tone was so neutral.

"I'm fine." Even I didn't buy that lie.

"You collapsed out there, after what you did."

"I said I'm *fine*."

He was silent.

My chest ached. I didn't know him. I'd practically just met him.

But some part of me wanted to tell. Some part of me was desperate to let it out and let someone know and stop bottling this terror and darkness and crazy nightmare inside, if only so it could stop eating me whole. I hadn't been able to bring myself to tell Ellie, and I wouldn't dream of telling my family. And as for Chloe...

I shied away from the idea, my heart aching. She'd try to make this normal, but not the normal I wanted. The normal I loved. The normal I'd had a year ago, before I ever made the dumb decision to visit my stepfamily in California for a vacation, only to watch everything I'd known go up in smoke. She'd make it into a new normal, *her* normal, where being different was a good thing and didn't really matter at all.

Except it did. It so, *so* did. It was horrible, and terrifying, and meant I could never let my guard down, not for one second, because if anyone who was *truly* normal found out... if they saw this thing I could do...

I trembled. I loved my best friend, but I couldn't tell her this.

But I felt like I was dying of secrets.

"It happened a year ago," I admitted softly. "And yeah, it's because of the Beast. Not Noah. Just the Beast."

I risked a glance toward the desk. Jace was silent, but he inched an eyebrow upward, curious, waiting.

"The Beast came after us. After Chloe, really, but the rest of us were there. Me, Noah, Ellie... and Joseph. He was this..." I searched for a way to describe the turtle-like wizard we'd met on the coast.

"A ruanir," Jace said. "Old one, from the last dehaian war." At my confused look, he continued. "My dad mentioned him a few times. Sort of the crazy old uncle of our kind."

Oh.

"So the Beast came after you?" Jace prompted.

I took a steadying breath. "Yeah. We'd gone to Joseph to find a way to stop the Beast from finding Chloe, but Chloe's magic messed up Joseph's defenses. She didn't mean to do that. It just happened. But because of that, the Beast found us. These greliarans did too. Noah's cousins. They killed Joseph, but he had a bunch of magic stored up at his house, kind of like the resistance had back at that bunker at Fiona's but older. Joseph said it was like what had existed a long time ago. And when we were escaping, the Beast struck that magic and…" I shrugged. "Boom. Our car was hit by the blast wave. Noah and Chloe… it just ripped through them. Made him go greliaran and her shift like a dehaian in a heartbeat. And me…"

"What?"

"Nothing. I'm human, right? What's going to happen to me?"

I trembled, the sarcasm burning. I'd felt weird after that. Shaky and strange. I'd thought it was shock. A result of attempting to stop a bunch of psychopaths from killing the people I loved.

Maybe I'd just hoped that's what was.

"It wasn't till later that we realized that Chloe, Noah, and I had this weird empathic connection with the Beast. That something about that explosion had tied us to it, and then later, tied us to Noah once he became what he is now. And I tried to deal with that—go back home, get through my last year of high school. I figured I was just sad because my stepbrother was basically *gone* and my whole life had changed in one little, stupid summer. But the entire time, there was this odd feeling, like it was more than that. Like something was just…"

"Changing."

I looked back at him. "Yeah."

He paused. "So then what happened?"

I turned away again, exhaling. "Nothing. I wanted normalcy, you know? I mean, I'd learned that my best friend was a mermaid, my stepfamily were greliarans, and watched my stepbrother turn into this storm thing, all in the space of one summer. I couldn't handle any more weird. And Chloe was so distracted by dealing with her family and her long-distance relationship with the new King of Yvaria that she wasn't exactly hard to fool. My dad and stepmom were the same, given how her son had just vanished. But I was in pretty bad shape by the end of the school year. Shaky. Tired." I grimaced. "Hearing things."

"Hearing things," Jace repeated.

"I don't… I'm not sure how else to describe it. It was like a song playing somewhere in the distance, but only in my head. And if I tried to focus on it, it'd be gone. But if I didn't… it was like part of my mind was elsewhere all the time. Like the majority of *me* was off doing something else inside my own head."

He was silent.

"I thought I was going nuts. I had no idea what was happening to me. Chloe didn't describe anything like this; Ellie didn't either. And Joseph… he'd babbled like crazy when we met him, but never about that." I ran a hand through my hair, and my fingers caught on tangles and bits of grass. I dropped it down and wrapped my arms around my middle again, trapping my fingers. "I just tried to ignore it, but it wouldn't stop. None of it. I felt like I couldn't even stay inside my own house anymore. Like the noise in my head or the shakiness in my body was just *pulling* me toward the coast and Santa Lucina and everything that'd happened there. By the end of the school year, going back there was all I could think about, even if I didn't have a clue why."

"But you did go back," Jace said.

I nodded. "And it got better. Not *quieter*, just… less distracting. As if I wasn't hearing the noise from some far-off place anymore, but like it was around me, so I didn't have to strain to pick up on it—and that was good." I hesitated. "But other stuff got worse."

"What stuff?"

I shifted my shoulders, uncomfortable. "Things started moving in the night. Breaking. I'd wake up to find half my bedroom on the floor. And every time it'd happen, I'd be so freaked out, but I'd have this odd feeling too, like I was exhausted again. Like something had been sapped out of me."

"Magic," he translated quietly.

I swallowed hard, not saying anything.

Jace scooted over, making room and nodding to the space beside him on the desk. I hesitated for a heartbeat and then walked back. Sinking onto the edge of the desk, I watched him warily.

"I don't know what happened," he said, "but if I had to guess… Baylie, I think that blast made you into a ruanir. Or something similar to it, anyway. But more like the old-world ruanir than anything we've seen in centuries."

I stared at him.

"What happened that day at Joseph's—" Jace shook his head. "That much magic should've killed you. It *would've* killed any of us, and probably your dehaian friend and Noah too. But a human, up against all that?" His hands made a small motion, like the outcome should have been obvious. "Except that wasn't just any magic. That was the magic of an old ruanir. The Beast's energy was in that blast too, and from what Ari's told me, the Beast changes things. So you ended up connected to it instead. Ended up with its magic and old ruanir magic inside you too. It had to be an accident, but… still."

I couldn't breathe. My insides wouldn't stop shaking.

"I'm guessing it acted like a jump start. When we're young, it takes us damn near our first decade to build up enough magic to start using it—and forget about doing something like you did back there. But that blast changed you. Made you into what you are now and brought you up to a strength that equals the strongest of us. Maybe even surpasses us, from what I saw out there. We've never been able to do anything quite like that. But then, everything you're describing…" He shrugged. "Baylie, it's *like* us. *You're* like us. The stuff moving. The strange feelings. Even thinking you're hearing things. When we're kids, once we've been exposed to it enough, we start to just *feel* magic. We pick up on it like some sixth sense. Like you, feeling as if you're hearing music in your head."

"Ocean magic," I whispered.

"Maybe, yeah. If that's what he collected, then…"

I managed a small nod. "The way magic used to be, he said."

Jace let out a breath. "That had to be so strange, having that come out of nowhere."

I scoffed. Strange wasn't the half of it. I'd thought I was having a breakdown.

"And you've still never told anyone?"

I shook my head.

"Why?"

I didn't respond.

"Your best friend's a dehaian," he pressed. "Your stepbrother's the Beast, and Ellie's a landwalker elder. I'm sure they would under—"

"It's not that."

He waited.

I closed my eyes. It was too hard to explain. I'd hidden this for a year; hidden what I might *be* for a year. I'd been too scared of it. I'd just wanted it to go away, or at least I'd wanted to keep going on like nothing else had changed.

Because too many things had changed.

"Baylie?"

"Because magic ruined everything," I snapped.

He was quiet.

I scowled, tears trying to rise. "Life was fine, you know? Like, sure, high school sucked and Chloe's parents were nuts and whatever, but… but it was good. And now, one year later, my best friend's a mermaid who lives someplace I can't ever go and my stepbrother is a storm monster who seemed like he might never come home. And as for what we all went through last year? Yeah, I can't tell that to *anybody*." I shook my head, struggling to hold in the trembling rage at it all. "My own father doesn't even know about this stuff, Jace. He just thinks Noah's traveling and that Chloe and I decided to attend college on the coast."

"Why didn't you tell him?" Jace asked.

I shrugged, pain joining my anger. The Delaneys and my stepmom—Noah's mother—had all decided it was better to keep things quiet. They'd wanted to protect Noah and the rest of the family as well. And as for why I'd gone along with it, why I hadn't said anything to Dad… the decision felt too hard to explain.

Like everything.

"Your dad was the only one who could still carry on like things were normal?"

I turned toward him. Jace's brow twitched up, questioning.

Maybe it wasn't so hard after all.

"Yeah," I agreed softly.

He nodded, returning his attention to the ground.

I didn't take my eyes from him. He wasn't like he had appeared on the surface, all brusque anger and coldness. At least, not entirely. Beneath all that, he was starting to seem like something else. Thoughtful. Compassionate, even.

It was strange.

He glanced back up, his gray eyes meeting mine. "Well, for what it's worth, it seems like you got a good handle on it. The magic, I mean."

I dropped my gaze away, not sure that was the right description. I'd never used it intentionally before today. I was only lucky no one else had gotten hurt.

"You doing okay here, though?" he asked quietly.

I twitched my shoulder in another shrug.

"Shaky," he filled in.

"Yeah," I whispered.

"I'm not surprised."

I tensed, suddenly wary.

"Our people—*your* people. The people you're sort of like. We get drained after an output of magic like that. It leaves us shaky. Tired. And I'm thinking that's why you've been so worn out this past year, especially after things would move or break. You were struggling to replenish what's inside you."

He shifted around on the desk, turning toward me further. "But then, when that happens to us, we also help each other. We share magic so nobody ends up too drained."

I didn't like the sound of that. I didn't like the sound of even admitting I was dealing with magic, let alone what he described. And besides that, it seemed… personal. Close. Like what Noah and Ari had done that had ended them up sharing memories or whatever.

And intimate too. Disturbingly so.

"I don't think I—"

"You don't have to if you don't want to. I'm not trying to push. But we're hundreds of miles from the ocean. We may not be going back soon. This could help you." He paused. "Me too."

"Jace, we don't even know if that's what this is. And besides, you guys use *land* magic, not ocean. You can't—"

"I can try."

I choked on a scoff. "But that stuff is *poison* to you. If you—"

"I know."

I stopped, staring at him.

"Look, I understand the risks, okay? But what I'm

suggesting…" Jace grimaced. "It's not entirely charitable. I want to help you. I do. I promised Noah I would, even if he wasn't aware of this part. And I've gathered that you don't like the idea of me looking out for you, and that's fine, but… Baylie, my magic isn't going to hurt you. It's not toxic like the ocean, and maybe it'll help you hold out till we can get back there. But you can do something that none of us have been able to do in centuries. Declan and Veronique and the rest, they've figured out *something* with that ocean magic project of theirs, but from the look on your face at that bunker—from the looks on Noah's and Ari's faces too—I'm guessing it's not the same as what you can handle for yourself. But I want you to teach me how."

I shook my head, not taking my eyes off him. "I-I *can't*. I mean, I don't know how this even—"

"This is how ruanir kids learn magic, by our parents sharing it with us. By our friends sharing it too. We're *good* at learning magic like this."

"But if something goes wrong, you could—"

"My sister's in trouble," he interrupted, his voice becoming harder. "She might be dead. And if she isn't, she still won't let me *near* her, because she's terrified I might absorb some of that ocean magic inside her." His face tightened like he was fighting something back. "I *get* the danger, okay? But you're not the same as Ari. You're closer to something like us, meaning this is the best chance I've got to figure this out. So please. Help me. And let me help you."

His gray eyes burned into mine, and I didn't know what to

say. He could die. He could end up like those judges. I didn't have a *clue* what I was doing to make this work, and he wanted me to pull off what a centuries-old storm monster had done by accident?

Was he *insane*?

A breath left me, and I couldn't hold his gaze any longer. He wasn't crazy. He wasn't at all, because I recognized that look. That desperate, pushed-to-your-limit-but-you-kept-going look.

I'd seen it a year ago, every time I looked in the mirror.

I reached out, taking his hand. His palm was harder and rougher than I'd expected, but not in a bad way. Just as if he'd spent time outdoors growing up.

I shoved the observation aside. "What do we do?"

He seemed to start breathing again. "Just don't let go."

"You're sure this won't poison me, right?"

A heartbeat passed, and then Jace shook his head. "My ancestors used ocean magic and then learned how to tap into what's in the land. They were never poisoned. It's only the other way around that's dangerous."

He sounded like he was reassuring himself as much as me, and it left my stomach in knots. I made myself take a breath. "Okay."

The corner of his mouth lifted in a grateful smile. His other hand took mine as well. Something inside me quivered at the skin-to-skin contact.

"Ready?" he asked.

I nodded. My stomach was doing flip-flops.

And then my breath caught. The feeling of his hands shifted in mine, like the warmth of his skin was suddenly sinking through my own. And something in me changed in response. Something in the not-quite-sound inside my head. The music slowed, like the band or the orchestra were falling asleep.

But I didn't like the feeling. I wanted it to stop. To go back to the way it had been, as terrifying as that was. Sure, I wasn't as drained, but what filled me now was vaguely nauseating. Like lukewarm soup. Like room-temperature gruel.

I dragged my gaze upward.

Jace was in agony. His face was twisted, his eyes shut. His breathing came in harsh jolts, like he was fighting to make his lungs work.

I gasped, my fingers starting to release his.

"No!" His hands clenched on mine.

"Jace…"

He shook his head, his brow furrowed tightly. My stomach churned. My skin crawled like ants were swarming all over me, while the magic came at me stronger and stronger. Bile climbed my throat.

Jace broke away from me. Collapsing sideways, he crashed down against the top of the desk.

My stomach lurched. I couldn't help him. Frantic, I ran toward the bathroom I'd spotted several doors down in the hall.

I made it there just in time.

Ragged breaths escaped me as the heaving stopped. Swallowing hard, I swiped my mouth with the back of my hand and then walked unsteadily back to the office at the end of the hallway.

Jace was still breathing. I could hear him, his rough gasps slowing down as the seconds passed. He lay on the desk, supporting himself by one elbow braced on the dusty top.

On shaking legs, I walked back toward him. "Jace?"

He didn't answer. I sank onto the other side of the desk, watching him warily. He was staring at the scarred wood, blinking as if to clear his eyes.

"Jace?"

"I'm okay."

I studied him, not quite sure I believed the words. I didn't know what poisoning looked like, or how much ocean magic it took before someone ended up like the judges. It had to be more than one dose, though, and hopefully whatever the hell was in me was different anyway.

That didn't do much to make me feel better.

"I'm sorry."

I blinked. "What?"

"I said I'm sorry." Jace swallowed hard. "I shouldn't have pushed it. I just…" He closed his eyes.

"Did it help?"

A breathless scoff left him. "I feel like crap, but maybe that's a good sign."

I looked away.

"Seriously," he insisted, "if nothing else, I deserve it. I didn't mean for that to hurt you. I didn't think it would. I'm sorry."

I glanced back down at him. His eyes were still closed, and frustration showed on the lines of his face.

"It's alright," I said.

His eyes opened. He looked over at me, questions on his face like he doubted my words.

I shrugged. "Have to do what you can to help the people you care about, right? Even when it feels like you can't do much at all. I know what that's like."

He watched me for a moment, his gray eyes unreadable. "You okay?" he asked finally.

I hesitated. "I think so."

Jace didn't look reassured, but he nodded anyway.

"So what now?" I asked.

He shook his head. "I don't know."

"Should we see if Miguel will head back toward the coast?"

He looked confused.

"Find out if this changed anything," I explained.

His mouth tightened. "Or at least help you."

"I'm fine."

"You just threw up."

I grimaced.

"I'll ask Miguel," Jace said. "But I don't think he will. Not unless they get something out of those enforcers to change their plans."

I looked away. Right. The judge, the one their intelligence said was in Arizona.

"And I'm guessing Maia and Dhanya will want to follow up on that too, so—"

I glanced back, confused.

He paused. "I think Dhanya recognized one of them."

"Did she say—"

"No, but there was something about the way Dhanya was watching them. Her cousins and uncle are all enforcers, so… they could be one of them. I might've misread her expression. I'm not as close to her and Maia as Ari, but…" He shrugged.

I was silent for a moment, taking in the little nugget of personal information. "Want to go check?"

He paused. "You want to go back down there?"

My mouth tightened. Of course I didn't. The way Declan had looked at me, the way *everyone* had… I never wanted to see that again.

But I also wanted to get out of here. Back toward the coast, yes, but also outside. The music was starting up in my head again, pulling on me to go toward the ocean. Even the outdoors would be better than this warehouse.

Besides, I couldn't stay up here for the rest of my life.

"Have to, eventually, right?" I slid from the desk and then looked over, waiting for him.

He pushed himself up from the wood top. "Yeah." Taking a deep breath, he straightened and regarded the door. "Here we go."

❧ 18 ❧

ARI

We traveled for hours, and the entire time, I didn't feel like I could breathe. The strakirin could be anywhere. I couldn't hear them, feel them, or see them at all, but it didn't matter. They'd almost found me. Us. They'd chased us at impossible speeds while Noah carried us through the water, and they'd come so close. So horribly close.

I didn't think I'd ever stop looking over my shoulder. Not till the hive mind and the judges and all the dehaians helping them were gone.

Maybe not even then.

A cavernous opening appeared in the seafloor ahead of us. The dehaians dove toward it and didn't slow even when another form materialized from the depths.

"Commander Damerion." The person came into view. A soldier of Yvaria, with weapons strapped to his back.

"Activate all garrison defenses," Damerion snapped. "Now."

The man nodded fast and then darted back into the canyon. Damerion and the others followed him. Wariness bubbled through me as we passed over the ledge. Below us lay a cliff wall, pocked by caves and not much else. There were no stands of plants like I'd seen in the village or the capital. A few dehaians slipped from the cave entrances only to dart back into others. It appeared that the "garrison" was nothing more than a bunch of people hiding in caves on the edge of an abyss.

And then we drew closer, and my confusion turned to alarm.

Magic glistened on the stone wall, like the teal shimmer on that boulder Damerion had somehow used for a video conference, only about a thousand times larger. It was faint, and you couldn't see it till you were right on top of the place, but the entire canyon wall was coated with magic like a defense.

My eyes tracked over symbols carved into the rock. Formed of chiseled dashes and swirls intermixed with jagged lines, they didn't look like anything I'd seen the ruanir use. The purpose behind them was anyone's guess, though it wasn't a stretch to imagine it was unpleasant.

Several dehaians swam from one of the cave entrances, hurrying toward us. Everything about them screamed soldier, and the way they regarded Damerion only reinforced the impression. While the ones at the center of the group waited for Damerion's orders, the rest scanned their surroundings for enemies and barely looked toward us.

"Take this one to a cell," Damerion ordered, motioning to the dehaian prisoner. "I want everything he knows about this, understand?"

The soldiers nodded. Two of them grabbed the man, while a third led the way back toward the caves.

"Escort the girl to a secure room," Damerion continued to several other guards. "Post soldiers outside every entrance."

"Dammit, Damerion," Noah protested, "your king told you she wasn't a prisoner—"

"I know exactly what King Zekerian told me. And that includes keeping this girl protected from her own kind. If those strakirin come here, what would you prefer? For her to be in a secured location or in a tent on the canyon top?"

Noah glowered.

Damerion turned back to his soldiers. "I want the wall defense activated as well. These things can avoid detection like the Beast. This is the best chance to test the new security measures that we'll get."

One of the soldiers darted back toward the caves.

"What security measures?" I asked, my stomach twisting while I watched the soldier go.

Damerion eyed me like he was weighing whether to respond. "The king issued a command that the Beast was not to be viewed as an enemy. At least, not until we had evidence this—" He glanced up and down Noah. "—*version* of the Beast was a threat. But that doesn't mean we didn't make preparations for that eventuality."

"Is it similar to what's around Nyciena now?" Noah sounded on edge. "Because I felt that, and it didn't slow me down at all."

"That was only an alarm to let us know you were there—which worked perfectly. This is something else entirely." Damerion's brow rose pointedly. "You both should get inside before we turn it on."

I hurried after the soldiers while they swam for the wall. Noah followed me. We passed through an entrance, and I caught sight of torches lighting the way farther into the long hallway with flickering, blue-white light. Other soldiers eyed us coldly when we trailed Damerion's people in, though none of them said a word about Noah's presence or mine.

A strangely electric feeling buzzed to life in the water behind me. I turned sharply, looking back at the tunnel entrance. The feeling intensified, pulsing from my skin like I had a faint sunburn.

Nothing appeared different, though. My skin crawled.

"I take it the security measures work," Ezio commented, swimming past me.

I shuddered. His lip twitched, though the expression held some sympathy. "You willing to stop by the central security station?" he asked Noah. "Give them a description of that other dehaian?"

I kept myself from glancing to Noah when he hesitated. "Sure," he replied neutrally.

Ezio nodded. "Make sure you set her up with a room far from this, eh?" he told the guards.

Without waiting for their agreement, he swam down a hallway nearby.

"Come on," one of the soldiers snapped.

I swallowed hard, feeling Noah's eyes on me. Locking my attention on the soldiers, I followed them away from the entrance.

They didn't stop till they reached a rough doorway so deep

within the tunnels, I felt like we'd swum half the distance back to the capital.

"You may stay here," one said, motioning to the plants blocking the door.

I managed a nod. Pushing past the leaves, I swam into the room.

Nothing but silence was waiting for me.

Letting out a slow breath, I scanned the room. Smaller than the one I'd briefly stayed in at the palace, the space had a lower ceiling and was only about twenty feet wide and long. Despite the mat and cushions of woven seaweed on the floor, it seemed like it'd previously been a storage area. Shelves were carved into most of the walls, with large stone jars and boxes lining them. Industrial-looking sconces dotted the spaces between the shelving, and blue-white flames flickered behind metal-wrapped glass. A sign hung on the wall, something about its layout making it seem like a caution of some kind, though it was written in a script I'd never seen.

I crossed to the mat and sank down. My tail idly curled around me in a circle, contorting in an unnatural, stomach-twisting way. I grimaced, working to ignore the sight. I knew it was uncomfortable to sit any other way or to attempt to make it stop. I'd already tried.

Minutes ticked by. Nothing in the room changed.

My gaze crept to the door. The drone of the strakirin was almost silent here—due to their distance or the security measures on the walls, I wasn't sure. But meanwhile, Damerion and his people would make the dehaian talk. They'd get the information they needed, either to find Osias or learn what the judges were after. Or both.

We wouldn't be here for long. And the other dehaian Noah had seen… he wouldn't find me.

None of them would.

I shifted with discomfort. I recognized the man Noah had captured, vaguely anyway. He'd been there, briefly, in the testing facility where they'd kept me. He'd watched me kill a resistance member—a woman, that time, with long brown hair and eyes so dark they seemed black—and he'd grinned while she died.

It made me wonder how many others I'd seen were actually dehaians in human form.

I was glad Damerion and Ezio hadn't insisted on my presence while their people interrogated him, though. I'd seen the way the guy looked at me while the soldiers were bringing him here. Like I was a malfunctioning puppet, kidding itself into thinking it was a real girl. Like I could be compelled to return to the hive at any time.

I had to believe he was wrong.

The leaves on the door rustled. Noah swam into the room.

I tensed, feeling caught off guard for no reason I could define. His presence, maybe. The fact I couldn't pick up on it the way I once had.

Something.

He hesitated. "Sorry. I… I was just coming to check if you're okay."

I wasn't sure how to respond. Okay wasn't a term I'd apply

to myself right now.

Not that I wanted him to know that.

"I'm fine."

A heartbeat passed. A ghost of a grimace crossed his face. "And I wanted to apologize for earlier. Arguing with you back at the palace."

I toyed with the edge of my fin, and then stopped sharply when I realized what I was doing. "Okay."

Silence followed the word, and I didn't know what to do to fill the quiet. He hadn't wanted me to come. I wasn't sorry I had—though, yeah, I'd hated fighting about it.

But admitting that suddenly felt like backing down. Like giving an inch and maybe suggesting he could convince me to do anything but what I was doing now.

A tiny part of my mind suggested Noah would never try to control me. He was protective, yes, but there was a big difference between that and the hell I'd just gone through. And it was probably right.

I shoved it down anyway.

"Was that it?" I asked.

He hesitated. "Yeah. But look, I didn't..." He grimaced. "Back in Nyciena, I wanted to say that I'm here for you, okay? I'll listen. Whatever happened, if you need to—"

"It's okay. I don't... I'm fine."

Words weren't cooperating, and for so many reasons, I couldn't make myself look at him.

"Yeah," he tried. "But if it'd help to—"

"I said I was fine." My eyes darted to him hotly.

He went still. I tugged my attention back to the mat beneath me, fighting to rein in the flare of temper. I couldn't talk about it. I couldn't even think about it.

Because if I didn't, then it couldn't touch me. It'd be like it never happened. I could stay here, in the present, and everything that the judges had done… just wouldn't matter. I'd get home. I'd be fine. I could go on with my life and—

The sensation of my spikes sinking into a victim's body flashed through me so fast, it was as if time travel was another strakirin ability. I was there. Every molecule of my body was instantly in that place, the bright, white lights bearing down on me, the blood hot on my skin, and the smell—

My fingers curled into the seaweed mat as if the green strands were ropes, holding me in the present.

"Listen." My voice shook. I steadied it with effort. "I'm pretty exhausted—" It was a flat-out lie. I wasn't remotely tired, but that was its own issue. "—so I'm not really in the mood for… I'd like to get some rest."

I motioned with a jerk of my hand to the door, not looking at him.

He didn't move. I bit back the urge to snap at him again.

"Are you still hearing them here?"

Rage snarled through me. Goddamn him, I didn't—

"Ari, look." He swam closer, his voice urgent like he'd seen something in my expression. "I'm not trying to push you. It's just… the things you described to Zeke, they sounded—"

I shoved away from the mat. "Dammit, Noah, I said I'm fine. I don't need you fretting over me like a mother hen."

He straightened, his body rigid with anger. And the sight was suddenly painful, like my lungs had gone raw in my chest. This was messed up. This was all *so* messed up. I didn't want this. I didn't know *what* I wanted, except to erase the past eight weeks of my life, or maybe even go back to the moment when I'd met him and begin from there again.

"Please." I struggled to make my tone gentler. "I just—"

"Yeah. No, I get it."

He started from the room.

I felt like my heart was being ripped out. "Noah, please."

He stopped. He didn't turn around.

"I'm sorry," I managed.

He looked back toward me. I dropped my gaze away fast.

A moment crawled by.

"You can talk to me," he said quietly.

I didn't know how. Where to begin. Or if I even wanted to.

"What did they make you do, Ari?"

My breath caught. I looked up at him. How did he—

His eyebrow twitched up, as if he'd read my alarm. "Not that hard to guess."

I retreated, my hands clasping my arms protectively.

"They're the monsters, Ari. Whatever happened, it wasn't your fault."

My head shook. How could he know this? We weren't empathically linked anymore. At least I didn't think we—

In my mind, I reached for all that was left of the space that had been him. Us. The effortless, almost organic connection of weeks ago.

Nothing. It was black. Cold. Dead.

He was just guessing.

The realization made me hug my arms to my middle even tighter. He didn't know. He couldn't. And what he was saying…

The list of the dead scrolled through my mind. Faces. No names. Countless looks of horror as the life leached from their eyes, bleeding out through wounds the judges had made me inflict over and over and over—

Noah reached for me. I pulled away.

"It wasn't your fault," he repeated.

"How many resistance members are missing?" I asked softly.

He was silent.

I looked back up at him. "How many?"

His expression started to close down, and my heart drained away with it. Cold settled in my chest, numbing me.

If I let it, this would hurt later. If he left, if he blamed me… later, this moment would hurt like hell.

But not with the cold. Not now.

"They made me kill them." My voice was hard and dead like stone. "Over and over. Men. Women. The judges made me stab them or poison them while they begged for their lives. And then a rush would come. A feeling that made the whole world go blurry and soft, and I couldn't hide from that, not all the time. But it felt good. It felt good to make them die."

Expressions chased themselves over his face, too fast to read.

"They used to experiment on me too. The judges, when there weren't resistance members to kill. Sometimes it'd be magic, and sometimes it'd just be knives, and when they were done with the knives, they'd have jars of that gel. Apparently, they got it from the dehaians. And they'd put it on my wounds, wait for me to heal, and then they'd start all over again."

"Ari…"

"And I'd hide from that." My voice started to shake, rising higher. "I would. I'd hide in this deep dark corner of my mind, but I couldn't do a damn thing to stop them. And I'd make lists, every time someone died. I'd do everything I could to remember their face, their eyes, anything about them so that maybe someday, if I made it back home, I could tell Miguel, and then he'd be able to tell their families that I didn't do a *damn* thing, but at least I knew what had happened to their—"

Noah crossed the distance between us and wrapped me in his arms.

I'd started crying. I hadn't even noticed.

"It's not your fault." His hand rubbed small circles on my back. "I swear, Ari, it wasn't your fault."

A sob ripped from me. My fingers clutched him. My whole body was shaking.

"You got out," he said. "It's okay. You got out."

"I couldn't stop them."

His cheek rested against the top of my head. His arms tightened on me. "But you got out."

The taste of my own tears filled the water. An eternity seemed to pass before I could stop myself from sobbing.

He didn't let me go the whole time, and it wasn't till far too late that I realized that was a mistake.

My breath caught. "The poison." I tried to pull away.

"It's okay."

"But—"

"You won't hurt me."

I stared at him.

"I'm here because of you," he said softly. "Because of how damn determined you were to show me how to feel alive again. Sharing magic with you gave me a defense against that poison. That's why it didn't kill me, that day on the coast, and why the other strakirin couldn't kill me either."

A tiny breath left me.

He drew me closer. I caved into his arms again, desperate beyond words to feel him holding me. Desperate to be home on land so he could be holding *me*, and not this strakirin thing they'd created.

"You saved me, Ari. You always have."

I shut my eyes, my fingers curling against his back to hold him closer.

"I'm so sorry," he said, his voice rough. "For what those bastards did, I…" He shuddered. "But you're *not* a monster, Ari. You're just—"

"What they made," I finished.

His hold tightened on me. "A girl who has some extra stuff to deal with."

A rough breath left me, not quite a scoff, not quite a sob. I wanted it to be that simple, even if it felt like it never could be.

"How did you find me? Did Zeke or the dehaians tell you where I was, or…"

He was silent.

"Noah?"

"I was hunting them," he admitted. "The judges. I've been hunting anyone who might know about you for weeks. Mostly enforcers. But I heard you might be at that dock, so I—"

"Vancouver."

He didn't respond.

"T-the judges. They said Vancouver was gone and something was north of us."

Again he was quiet, and something heavy and dark filled in the silence. "A few enforcers were there. One of them gave me your location."

I bit my lip, caught by the tone and his words alike. The Judiciary hadn't wanted him to find me. That'd been clear from the look on Judge Engle's face when he heard the word Vancouver. So the enforcers would never have betrayed their masters by telling the Beast where to locate me. They would have tried to keep their silence no matter what.

I pulled back to see his face. He avoided my eyes.

And I could read it. What he'd had to do to get them to talk.

"I needed you back," he said, his voice tight. "I promised Jace I'd find you, and I just…" His jaw muscles clenched.

I reached up, touching his cheek. He still wouldn't meet my eyes. "You're not a monster either."

He didn't believe me. I could see it on his face.

I didn't know what to say. He *wasn't* a monster. But the silence lingered, full of darkness for which I had no answers.

"You… but you're okay?" I tried. "Now?"

He paused. "Yeah." His voice was as soft as mine.

"Thank you for still coming for me, even after I—"

He looked back at me sharply. "That wasn't you."

I hesitated.

His green eyes were intense. "I mean it, Ari. That wasn't you." He reached up, taking my cheek. He seemed lost for words. "And there wasn't a chance in hell I'd ever leave you."

My chest ached. I searched for a response, for any kind of way to answer the deep, oh-so-true look in his eyes.

I had nothing. I traced my fingers over his cheek, down his neck and his powerful arm, my breath gone at the pure joy of simply touching him again. But it was so quiet now. I'd never been this close to him with such silence between us inside. Only my own emotions, only my own reactions.

Two lonely islands drifting closer but never joined the way they had once been, forever held apart by a cold and silent sea.

My gaze met his again, questioning. His thumb slipped over my cheek. Cautious and careful, he leaned in closer, waiting for me to pull away.

I didn't.

Noah's lips brushed mine, the touch so soft, so gentle, like the first time he'd kissed me. His hand slid down to my side as his lips moved on, ghosting across my cheek, my neck. With his other hand, he lifted my own, and he lay kisses down my green skin and my watercolor scales, across the space on my forearm where the deadly spikes could emerge.

His eyes closed briefly and then lifted to find mine again. "I missed you," he whispered.

The ache in my chest grew worse, but now, suddenly,

hesitancy joined it too. He'd kissed my arm, kissed the place where those horrible spikes could emerge… but what was he thinking about? Those? Was it intentional?

Or was he thinking of me before?

I wasn't the same as I had been, in so many more ways than just what I'd done. Snake eyes. Green skin. Pointed ears and a too-sinuous tail that bore no resemblance to the beautiful mermaid legends that the dehaians had inspired. Was he thinking about that when he kissed me, when he touched my skin? Of me, before? Of the way I'd looked before?

Was that why he closed his eyes?

I nodded, and my words came out choked. "You too."

He reached up, his fingers tracing over the gold fringe around my pointed ear. My breath caught. The frill was so sensitive; I hadn't realized it. Hot shivers ran through me at the sensation of his fingers there, pooling in my middle, and, God, I wanted more.

Noah paused as if he'd seen my reaction, and a smile tugged at the edge of his lips. He leaned in closer, moving to kiss me again.

I pulled back. "Noah."

"What?"

I searched for a way to explain. "I… I just…"

"I didn't mean to push you."

"You didn't. I just…" God, words were failing me. Or maybe it was just the look on his face. The concern mixed with alarm and disappointment. It was killing me. "It's not you, okay? It's…" I waved a hand at myself, wordless.

"Huh?"

"I look like… I'm not *me*. Does that bother you? I mean, I'm… I'm one of those *things* that… And when you look at me, and you're seeing that, does it—"

"Ari, you're beautiful."

I turned away. He took my cheek, gentle and insistent. I dragged my gaze toward him.

"But…" I tried. "My eyes, what they did to my body, it's not—"

"That doesn't change anything. The differences in your eyes…" He shrugged like it was irrelevant. "They're you. You're in them." He grinned. "Temper and all."

A small and vaguely desperate laugh left me.

Noah chuckled too. "You're still you. Still the determined, intelligent, funny, incredible girl I met on the beach a lifetime and a couple months ago. And—" He hesitated, his expression an elaborate dance of things he was struggling to say. "And as for your body…"

There was something in his tone. My chest quivered—from hope or fear, I couldn't tell. "What?"

"This strakirin thing, it's just… it's not…" He trailed off like he couldn't quite figure out how to continue. His hand rose. A question flickered across his face as if he was waiting for me to protest, and then he moved carefully onward to brush the golden fringe around my pointed ear again, his gaze tracking the motion.

My eyes closed of their own accord, my face instinctively turning toward the motion.

Gently, his fingers continued onward, tracing lightly along my neck, my collarbone and shoulder, and down my arms till they slipped over to rest on the scales of my hip.

I trembled, my insides burning at how good that simple contact had felt.

"You're beautiful, Ari," he whispered. "Like this, in human form, all of it. And I'm attracted as hell to you."

The trembling grew stronger. I drifted closer to him while he took my cheek again.

His lips touched my own, gentle at first, and my heart began to pound. But he didn't stop. The kiss deepened as his hands slid around me, pulling me to him.

Peace and longing tangled through my veins. It felt like an eternity had passed since my body was last against his like this. It felt as if I'd finally found home, even if we were countless miles from anything I knew. Like, even though I couldn't feel his emotions or his reactions from the inside like I had before… it didn't matter.

That wasn't what I'd been missing. Not entirely. Not even close.

As if by instinct or some deep knowledge of how good it would feel, my tail twined around his legs, pulling me even tighter against him. He tensed briefly, and then a groan left him, the sound heavy with desire. His fingers dug into my back, into my hair, his magic keeping us afloat while his mouth moved over mine, hungrily, desperately.

My pulse raced. My tail squeezed around him, harder. He gasped.

His body vanished. Water surged around me, engulfing me like I was suddenly caught in a current, but then changing. Becoming focused. It swirled over my body, tight and intense, holding me up in the water and setting my skin and scales on fire wherever it touched.

"Yeah," I breathed. "Oh my God…"

Noah was behind me now, shifting effortlessly into human form. His lips traced a hot line down my neck to my shoulder while his hands slid over my body. I leaned my head to the side, giving him more room, giving myself over to the sensation.

"How…" he managed between kisses, "can you feel so…"

I gasped something inarticulate as an answer, more of a desperate plea for him to continue than any kind of words. My hand reached up behind me, tangling into his hair to keep him close.

I'd missed him. More than words could describe, I'd missed him.

Another groan escaped Noah's throat. He vanished, and water swirled all around me once more, coursing across my body, lingering and racing and then lingering on me again. I gasped, my back arching at the incredible way my scales and skin seemed to respond to his touch. At the feeling of him all *over* me, teasing along the sensitive edges of my fins, rushing across every inch of my body. He continued on, to the point where I could barely keep from crying out, and then he was in front of me, kissing me again.

Maybe this form wasn't so bad after all.

I moaned while one of his hands slid down to my backside

and his other raked up through my hair. Everything was going so fast, but I didn't care. It was like the desperation of eight weeks—*weeks*, for God's sake—of being away from him was all coming out at once.

"Don't stop," I begged breathlessly. "Don't—"

"Hey, make sure you check the relay by the outer perimeter."

I gasped, breaking away from Noah as the reality of where we were suddenly crashed back in.

"Yes, sir," came a response from beyond the cave opening.

Noah retreated from me, composure stuttering back onto his face in fits and starts that seemed like pure willpower. I shuddered, trying to do the same.

Ezio pushed past the covering over the cave entrance. He paused at the sight of us.

"What is it?" Noah asked, his voice carefully neutral.

The briefest hesitation followed before Ezio spoke. "The dehaian talked. I think you'll both want to hear what he has to say."

My heart climbed in my throat. That sounded ominous.

"Sure." I wondered if Noah's tight tone was my imagination. "We'll be there in a moment."

Ezio glanced between us again. I ducked my gaze away.

"The guards will show you where to find us," Ezio allowed. He turned and swam from the room.

A breath left me. I looked over to find Noah watching me.

My pulse second-guessed its attempt to come back down from racing. He was incredible. Like this, on land, all of it.

God, I wished Ezio hadn't come in when he did.

"You okay?" Noah asked quietly.

I wasn't sure how to describe what I was. Overwhelmed? Disappointed?

Strangely relieved that it hadn't just been the empathic connection between us that caused our attraction?

I gave a small shrug. "Interrupted again, huh?"

A look of wry amusement crossed his face, though it wasn't quite able to hide his disappointment. "Yeah."

He drifted closer. He reached up, his hand sliding gently around me and then drawing me to him. His forehead rested against mine, and his other hand rose, cupping the back of my neck, holding me to him as his eyes shut.

"God, I missed you so much," he whispered, his voice choked.

Warmth bubbled through me. I slipped my hands around him, my body moving in the water to keep me close to him. "I missed you too."

"I'm here for you, okay? Whatever you need, if things—" He took his forehead from mine, and his gaze roamed over my face briefly, as if to encompass whatever might go on in my mind. "If it starts to get bad for you. I'm here."

I hesitated, trying not to feel broken at the words. But then, that wasn't how he was looking at me. Even after everything I'd said, there was nothing but understanding and compassion in his eyes, and somehow, it made me feel better.

"Thank you," I said.

He gave me a small smile, and his hand moved to trace along my ear again. A short gasp caught me as wonderful shivers raced through my body.

"So… to be continued?" A hint of uncertainty lurked beneath the desire in his voice, like he wasn't sure what I'd think.

My insides quivered. "Please."

Noah's smile broadened. He leaned in closer, kissing me, his lips lingering on mine and making warmth spread through me that had nothing to do with magic.

At least not that kind.

He drew back. "Somewhere we won't be interrupted, yeah?"

A smile tugged at my lip. My thoughts exactly.

❧ 19 ❧

BAYLIE

From the moment we appeared at the top of the steps, I could see most of the room staring at me.

It didn't get any better all the way down to the warehouse floor.

I gripped the railing at the end of the staircase, scanning the room. Declan was gone. Miguel and Veronique too. The soldiers still blocked the doors, though, and they all seemed more interested in me than anything else.

I tried not to stare at their guns.

Ellie hurried toward me. "Are you okay?" she asked.

I nodded.

"You two okay?" Jace called to Maia and Dhanya.

The girl glanced to her fiancée and then hurried toward us. "Yeah, we're good. Just—" She twitched her head back toward the room where the enforcers were being held.

"Creepy?" I tried.

The hesitance in their eyes hurt, like the enforcers weren't the only thing creeping them out.

"Yeah," Maia agreed awkwardly. "But it's not really that. It's Dhanya. She, um…"

"One of them is my uncle."

My breath faltered at the confirmation of what Jace had suspected.

"It's not like it does us any good," Dhanya continued, frustration in her tone. "Enforcers have their memories taken so they won't have any qualms about the judges' orders. Impartiality and all that. It means he won't recognize me, let alone give us any advantage. But…"

"Still weird," Maia filled in.

Dhanya's mouth tightened, but she didn't say a word.

"What happened, Baylie?" Ellie pressed, keeping her voice low. She gave a wary look to the soldiers.

I was glad I wasn't the only one not wanting to be overheard.

Though I wondered for the first time if she'd tell them about me anyway. She was some big resistance operative now, right?

I wondered how that stacked up against being my friend.

Jace looked to me, questioning. "You, uh…?"

"Magic," I said softly.

"Is this from the Beast last year?" Ellie asked.

"What? How did you…"

She shrugged awkwardly. "That's when you all ended up connected to the Beast, because of all that magic. It changed Noah and Chloe, and you were there, so…" She trailed off at my staring. "I'd wondered if that did anything to you, but you never said anything, so I didn't ask."

I was speechless.

"Is she always this perceptive?" Jace asked, seeming taken aback.

I nodded distantly. "She's basically a genius."

Ellie appeared embarrassed. "I don't… I'm not really…"

"Are you going to tell them about me?" I asked her. "About why this happened?"

She blinked. "Do you want me to?"

"No."

I could see the others' discomfort. It wasn't like there were many options now.

"Just…" I tried to find the words.

"Wait on you?" Ellie offered.

I nodded, relieved.

She echoed the motion. "Definitely."

"Miguel won't push if he doesn't think you're a threat," Jace said. "I'm pretty sure of that."

"But Declan…" I started.

"Yeah, he's a jerk," Ellie said.

I stared at her. I'd never heard her insult anyone.

"We'll stay away from him," Jace said.

One of the doors to our left opened. The soldiers stepped aside, making space for Miguel when he stepped out. His focus skimmed over the room, and then he walked toward us.

"We're ready for you," he said to Ellie.

I blinked. Huh?

Nervousness flitted across Ellie's face, but she nodded and started toward the room he'd just left.

"Wait, what?" I stammered.

Ellie glanced back, not answering.

"Enforcers don't talk," Miguel said. "Not easily. Sometimes ever. But with her gifts…"

"They discussed it while you were upstairs," Maia explained quietly.

I stared at them. Just how involved in this resistance *was* Ellie?

"It'll be okay," Ellie tried.

Seriously?

I didn't even know what to say, but at something in her eyes, the fight drained out of me. Maybe because I wasn't even sure what I was fighting anymore. This was her life. She could risk it. Everyone else I knew had.

And I'd stood by the sidelines. I'd done nothing, because there'd been nothing I could do. I'd wanted to help Chloe, help Noah, help anybody last year, and all I'd been able to do was stand there and watch them almost die.

"Fine," I said. "But I'm coming too."

Ellie blinked, alarmed.

"Baylie," Jace started.

"Can your people stop them?" I asked Miguel. "If those enforcers attack or—"

"They can shoot them, yes."

I heard the careful phrasing. Shoot them, sure. And if that failed, then what? I'd seen those things today. They moved as fast as cheetahs, and bullets didn't take them down easily.

But I had.

"Do you think you can help with that?" Miguel asked

carefully.

Yes.

No.

Oh my God, what was I thinking? I wasn't a wizard. I didn't know what I was. But my friend was walking into a room full of monsters, and my choices were to stand out here like the epitome of uselessness, praying they didn't kill her, or walk in there hoping I could stop them if they tried.

The black ice crackled and sparkled inside me again. Not as much as before, no. But some.

My heart pounded. "I can try."

Miguel gave me a single nod and then motioned toward the door. "This way." His focus flicked to Jace, including him in the direction, before he turned his attention to the others. "Dhanya, if you want to—"

"Yeah. I'll come too."

He nodded again and then headed for the door.

Dhanya reached out without looking, finding Maia's hand. They walked after Miguel.

Leaving Jace with me.

I didn't look at him. There wasn't any point. I could guess he wasn't happy with this.

Taking a quick breath, I followed the others into the room.

The enforcers were arrayed against the wall, in chairs that looked like they'd started life at a dentist's. But metal reinforced them now. Each joint, each bend of the chair was braced by thick bands of steel. Additional bands, nearly a foot wide, trapped the enforcers' arms while others wrapped over the enforcers' legs and chests.

Even with their bodies pinned by metal, the men in front of us were terrifying. To a person, they watched us with eyes that looked like they belonged on snakes. One of them was darker-skinned like Dhanya, while the other two were pale—a redhead and a blond, both with buzz cuts. Their faces were like mirrors of each other. Cold, empty, not remotely afraid. And then the darker-skinned man smiled, nothing in the expression. Nothing human, anyway.

It was like watching a mannequin turn deadly. That empty. That soulless.

I glanced to Dhanya. Her expression was stoic. Her eyes never left the enforcer on the right, but her hand was clenched on Maia's own.

"You ready?" Miguel asked Ellie.

She nodded and started toward the men. I found myself following her, even while everything in me protested like crazy. Something about those men made me want to run screaming. Some ancient instinct, maybe. Something that kept my ancestors alive.

And yet here I was, walking toward it purely because my friend was too.

I took a breath and stopped when Ellie did. Black ice tingled inside me. Anxiety always made it worse.

This was enough to make it hard to keep the energy inside.

Jace appeared beside me. He glanced to me briefly, something in his expression challenging me to tell him to go away.

I said nothing.

Ellie took a deep breath and drew herself up. Her eyes locked on the closest of the three.

"I wouldn't bother, little girl," the darker-skinned enforcer said.

Ellie flinched. She was more worried than she was letting on, I realized. I didn't know whether that made me feel better for her sanity, or more worried that this was going to hurt her.

She'd taken apart the greliaran who tried to kill us last year. He was still in psychiatric care, last I'd heard. Heavily medicated too, and he couldn't sleep with the lights off.

But then, Wyatt didn't have *poison* inside him.

"Hello, Dhanya," the enforcer continued.

A tiny gasp came from behind me, a barely audible intake of breath. I looked over my shoulder to Maia's fiancée.

I couldn't tell if she was breathing anymore. The enforcers weren't supposed to have memories. That's what everyone had said. They remembered nothing of their lives before the judges made them into… this.

"I have been told about you," the enforcer continued. "The failure. So close to being among the chosen before you ran back to the herd. But fear not, you will have the opportunity to return soon and join us with gratitude and eagerness." The enforcer's snake-like eyes skimmed over the rest of us. "All will serve as they should."

Shivers ran through me.

"Hello, Uncle Indrajit," Dhanya replied, cold and controlled. She might be so tense she wasn't breathing, but she sounded utterly emotionless.

I wondered if it was the training to undergo the conversion to an enforcer coming out, maybe as self-preservation.

"You know that title is untrue, initiate."

"I am no initiate." Heat touched Dhanya's voice.

"You are, and you will rejoice in that fact soon. Know this. The masters are aware of your betrayal. Of the way you help their enemies. They are coming for you. Your masters will claim you again, initiate, and your gratitude will know no bounds when they—"

"Enough," Miguel snapped. "Ready?" He looked to Ellie.

She nodded. Her eyes narrowed, focused on Indrajit. The enforcer smiled and smiled, till suddenly he drew a sharp breath. His smile flickered, twitching toward a grimace.

"What are the judges' plans for the strakirin?" Ellie whispered. I doubted the man could hear her.

But he answered anyway.

And she did too.

"I don't know," Ellie and Indrajit said at the same time, their words so in sync that it was like one person speaking with two voices. "The masters did not need to inform me of such things."

Nausea churned in me, not just from the way he called the judges "masters," but from hearing the title come out of Ellie's mouth.

Ellie took a shallow breath. "What do they know of the resistance?"

"They know much." Again, voices in sync.

I struggled not to shift my feet, if only to get away from this thing and the way it spoke with the voice of my friend.

"*What* do they know?" Ellie pressed.

"I only go where I am commanded. I am only told what is needed. I serve."

From the corner of my eye, I saw Miguel shake his head, frustration clear in his expression.

"Do they have any leads on our locations?" Ellie whispered.

"Assuredly."

"What are they?" Ellie pressed.

"That is for the masters to know."

"What hideouts have been compromised?"

"I do not know," they replied together.

Ellie's mouth tightened with irritation. Indrajit's did too.

"Where is Maia Davenport's father, Judge Davenport?" she asked.

A heartbeat passed. Then another. Indrajit's face twitched, and I cast a short glance to Ellie. Tension showed around her eyes. Her breaths were short, quick.

"Oakland." They ground the word out together. "California. Blue house. White… shutters." I could hear Ellie breathing harder. "Fourteen… two… zero five Elm…Str…Str… *Street*."

Ellie gasped for air. "Why are they after the landwalkers?" she whispered fast. A bead of sweat trickled down her temple. In the chair, Indrajit flinched. His jaw muscles jumped when his teeth clenched.

"Ellie?" I tried.

She made a hissing sound, shaking her head fast. "*Why?*"

"They," the two of them responded together, "aren't."

Confusion flickered past the tension on Ellie's face. "But

why—"

"They're… after…" Ellie stopped speaking with a gasp, leaving only the enforcer.

"You." Indrajit stared at her with inhuman eyes.

Ellie stumbled backward. I grabbed her, and Miguel did too. Shaking hard, she didn't look at us. "It's so dark in there," she whispered, almost as if to herself.

"Are you okay?" I asked.

She exhaled. Her gaze crept back up toward the enforcer. She straightened, not answering.

Indrajit smiled. "They've been searching for you." If not for the sweat on his forehead, he would have looked like nothing had happened at all. "They will claim you; it's only a matter of time. The puppet master. Many of your brethren do not have your power. The masters know that now. They know they need *you*. We almost had you at the camp when you came to rescue your kind, and again before… *that* intervened." His attention slid to me. "The unexpected one. They will have both of you. The masters will take your powers, and you will increase their greatness and glory. Try any tricks you want, child. The time will come when you serve the masters too."

I trembled. I wanted his snake-like eyes off of me. I wanted to run, hide, get away, and never be near this *thing* again.

"Outside," Miguel ordered. "Now."

It was all I could do not to bolt out of the room.

Miguel shut the door once we were all out. "We need to get you both into hiding."

Ellie shook her head. "What? No. I can still—"

"You heard him, yes? Even when you were…" Miguel searched for a term. "Doing what you do?"

Ellie was silent.

"They're after you, Ellie. You specifically. And now that Baylie…" He frowned. "We can question them our way. It's not as fast, but it works. But we *can't* risk waiting and hoping the judges won't hear about Baylie too." He shook his head. "The Judiciary will come after you both. They've already tried, which means we have to get you out of here." Ellie opened her mouth to argue, and he cut in before she could speak, sympathy softening his stern expression. "You've helped us, Ellie. More than you know. But you need to let us help you too."

"But… what about the landwalkers? Or the ones the judges might've changed? You need me to help check—"

"We'll figure it out."

She gaped at Miguel. "No! I can't leave and just *hope* you all won't die if—"

"They're after you now. Your gifts won't help us if the judges get their hands on you. And that isn't bringing into it what they'll do to you."

"The judges take elements of things, Ellie," Jace interjected quietly. "Aspects, traits. It's how they made the enforcers and the greliarans."

"I know that," Ellie retorted. "That's not the poi—"

"Story is, the process is like torture," Jace finished. "The ones they use almost never survive."

Ellie shifted her shoulders like she was trying to shake off the words.

"We have to get you both safe," Miguel said.

"Where?" I asked.

Miguel paused. "We could send you back to your families."

A protest stalled in my throat. I didn't want to do that, and not only because the fact the Judiciary might track us there and then hurt my family left my stomach in knots. To go back and see Dad, given what I sort of, maybe *was* now... What if he saw that? What if I had to do something to protect us and he...

I didn't want to imagine the look on his face. The confusion. The horror. Dad was the only one left in my world who didn't know anything about magic or wizards or dehaians.

For him to find out I was weirder than them *all*...

Ellie sighed in resignation. "Olivia's been wanting me to come stay with her for weeks. We could go there."

"Is she in a secure location?" Miguel asked.

"Yeah. Very." Ellie nudged the toe of her shoe on the concrete. "Lots of the landwalkers are, now that the judges started hunting us too."

Miguel didn't say anything for a moment. "Declan!"

The man turned away from a conversation with one of the guards. Miguel jerked his head for the man to come closer.

"What?" Declan asked when he reached us.

"New job. Don't argue. I need you to go with Ellie and Baylie, keep an eye on them while they stay with that landwalker elder, Olivia."

Declan looked incredulous. "Excuse me? You want me to babysi—"

"You're the strongest we've got," Miguel interrupted. "And if the judges get their hands on these two and yank out of them what they can do…"

Declan was silent for a moment. "Fine." The usual rancor was missing from his voice. "When do we leave?"

"Soon as possible."

The other man nodded. "Let's go, then." He gave us a brief glance and then headed for the main warehouse door.

"Get your things," Miguel said to both of us. "And call Olivia from a secure line and let her know to be expecting you. Odds are the judges aren't aware of this place, but if I'm wrong, I don't want to risk you sticking around a second longer than you have to."

Ellie nodded and then headed for the stairs.

"Do we need to go back in there?" Maia asked with a worried look to the room holding the enforcer.

Miguel hesitated.

"It's okay," Dhanya said. I couldn't tell if she was directing the words to Maia or Miguel. "I might still be able to help."

A heartbeat passed before Miguel nodded. I didn't think he wanted to agree.

Even if it seemed like Dhanya's words might be true.

"Can I talk to you both for a second?" Jace asked Maia.

Maia gave him a confused look, but she followed him when he paced a few steps away.

Leaving me with Miguel.

"So," Miguel said. He left the air empty, like an invitation for me to say something.

The silence pressed on me.

"Do you know what it is?" he asked. "This ability?"

My gaze slid to Jace. He was talking in a low voice to the others. Maia shook her head, protesting, but Dhanya put a hand to her arm, saying something I couldn't hear.

"Baylie?"

I blinked, turning back to Miguel. "I don't…"

My mouth moved, wordless. I'd never been good at lying, not really, even with all the practice I'd gotten this year, pretending that this was nothing, that all the broken things in my apartment were simply the result of being "clumsy"…

"I'm not sure," I admitted. "Jace thinks that, uh, maybe I'm—"

"Hey." Jace walked back up to us. "Ready?"

I paused. "What?"

"I'm going with you."

I glanced over to see Maia and Dhanya still standing where he left them. "Are they coming too?"

He followed my gaze. "No, they're, um… they're needed here, right?" He directed the question to Miguel.

The older man regarded him for a moment. "They would be helpful, yes."

"Right. So… ready?"

I faltered. "I don't need you to protect—"

"I know." He gave me an intent look.

It took a second for the reason to click. This was about the magic. My magic. His. And that sharing thing.

He still wanted me to teach him whatever the hell it was I could do.

Protests rose in me. I wasn't a wizard. I wasn't like them. And sharing… sharing *magic* like that had hurt him last time.

It had made me puke.

Of course, now I felt better. A lot better, actually. The shakiness was going away faster than it ever had before.

I shifted my weight uncomfortably. I didn't really want to think about that. But meanwhile, Jace and Miguel were watching me.

"Okay," I agreed. "Yeah. We should, um—"

Ellie came down the stairs, a backpack hanging from each shoulder. She offered one to me. "Clothes," she explained, and then she glanced to the others. "Olivia's going to be waiting for our call once we get up past Missoula. She'll guide us on where to go from there."

I swallowed back my nausea and made myself nod. "Great."

Ellie wasn't quite buying my tone, I could tell. But she headed for the exit anyway.

Missoula? Wasn't that in Montana? My God, we might as well be heading for the moon.

But really, that wasn't what made me feel sick. I wasn't upset about the distance, or about the time it'd take to get there. All that really bothered me was how far we'd be from the ocean.

And after everything that had happened in the past two summers, nothing could have made me feel less human.

20

NOAH

With Ari at my side, I followed the soldiers through the laby-rinthine halls of the garrison. We hadn't spoken since we left that storage room they'd given her as a place to stay. We were staying close, though, with her hand still in mine.

I caught her glancing at me, and despite the fact it made it hard to concentrate, I looked over, giving her a smile as I met her golden eyes. She smiled in return, something bashful but happy in the expression.

Warmth filled me at the sight. I loved her smile.

I pulled my attention back to the guards while we contin-ued around a corner of the hallway. I'd meant every word I said to her in that storage room. All the ones I'd said and all the ones I couldn't get out. She was beautiful, and while, sure, it'd taken a second to get used to the change in her appearance, it wasn't like I didn't have experience with people looking differ-ent than humans. I'd grown up in a family of greliarans. Chloe was dehaian. And Ari…

I didn't know what those judge bastards had intended, but

on her, this strakirin thing just looked hot.

My gaze flicked to her a second time, sliding quickly along the curves of her breasts and sides before I could yank it back again. I needed to focus, in no small part on this dehaian we were going to see. It'd been a feat of will simply to keep my attention on Ezio when he interrupted us. After the eternity of these past weeks, to have Ari in my arms like that had been unreal. Beyond a relief. Like a miracle I'd needed to survive, more than the magic around me.

And as for what we'd been doing…

The Beast side of me growled deep inside, and I knew that, for once, the reaction had nothing to do with anger. Far from it, because that part of me had enjoyed this just as much as the rest. More than that. What we'd been doing was as much the Beast's idea as any greliaran side of me because, my God, talk about instinct. I hadn't been thinking when I let my human form go. Just feeling and acting on it and…

I wondered what else we could do like that. I wondered what it would be like if we ever had our empathic link again.

Desire surged through me, driven by memories and my Beast side and my imagination alike, before my mind registered the thought fully and brought everything up short.

Did I really want that connection back again?

Yes.

Maybe. I mean, that closeness, that understanding, that pure intensity… I missed it. I hadn't expected to, back when it first happened, but now some part of me *longed* for it. The Beast side of me had been created to have that empathic connection ability, albeit as some dehaian measure of control. Yet what happened when I was linked to Ari had gone beyond mere empathy and become something else entirely. Something wonderful. Something more than my Beast side could ever have imagined.

And I wanted that back desperately.

But for the greliaran side of me, the desire—hell, the *need*—was tangled up in a knot with fear, because we'd been losing ourselves. We'd been sharing memories, sharing parts of our histories without even realizing it was happening. We couldn't even be apart without pain.

But if *I* recreated it… not the judges, not their magic, but *me*…

From the corner of my eye, I saw Ari look toward me. I realized I had slowed down.

"Sorry," I managed.

I made myself keep moving. I didn't even know if that was a possibility. Chloe and Baylie had been an accident, and their connection to me wasn't like what I'd had with Ari anyway. And there was what Ari *was* to consider. The massive unknown that was what the judges had done to her.

I could kill her.

Chills crept through me. It wasn't only that—though that was more than horrible enough. I didn't know what the judges had done, but I remembered what she said. Hive mind.

I had a sneaking suspicion of how that came to be.

We rounded the corner of the hall. Near the opposite end of the corridor, Ezio and Damerion were waiting. Gripping Ari's hand harder, I struggled to push the thoughts away. We weren't exactly among friends here. I needed to focus.

And besides, I didn't want to think about this anymore. I didn't want to imagine all the things that could go wrong and that could take her from me so soon after I'd found her again.

Ezio showed no reaction at the sight of Ari's hand in mine, but Damerion blinked, his perpetually angry countenance faltering into disbelief before he buried the expression. I hesitated, but didn't move to release her. It was dangerous, making clear what she meant to me. If they wanted leverage…

But they also knew what I was. What I could do. Now that Ari was speaking to me and letting me near her, if those two and all their soldiers finally saw *exactly* what she was to me, they might be reluctant to try anything that could hurt her.

"Where is he?" I asked.

Ezio nodded toward the hall behind him. Damerion turned, swimming down the corridor without a word.

The dehaian was tied in a corner of a small room, and nothing else occupied the space with him. A chain wrapped around his tail, essentially stopping him from moving more than a few inches beyond the stone wall, while shackles around his forearms accomplished much the same thing. He had a bruise beneath his left eye and another one on his ribs, and his face looked haggard.

None of which stopped his disgusted expression at the sight of us.

"He says they're looking for a weapon," Damerion said to us, not taking his eyes from the orange-and-black-scaled dehaian.

"We *have* a weapon, you bottom-feeder," the man spat.

Damerion thumbed a small stone at his belt briefly. The dehaian lurched. Ari's hand clenched on mine so hard that, had I been human, it would have been painful. My face tightened at the sight as much as at the slight aftertaste of electricity to the water, though the latter was so faint that the others didn't seem to pick up on it.

"You told the interrogator it was missing pieces," Ezio said. "Something to do with the strakirin. So what is it? Tell us more about that."

The dehaian attempted a glare, but the bruise beneath his eye turned the expression partially into a wince. "We'll find what we need. Once we locate the source, your repulsive country will fall."

I glanced to Damerion and Ezio, but they didn't press for more. "What source?"

The man snickered. "You're the Beast, aren't you? A 'human' boy, miles and miles under the water; you'd have to be. Didn't even bother to hide it with dehaian form. Bit obvious, don't you think?"

He turned to Damerion again. "Your pet can't stop us. You think the strakirin are the only tool at our disposal?" He made a contemptuous noise. "You Yvarians have no sense of history. Never have."

"What is that supposed to mean, scum?" Damerion retorted.

I glanced to Damerion again. Something about his tone seemed to hint he hadn't heard this part before.

The prisoner's hateful amusement deepened.

Damerion pressed his thumb to the stone on his belt. The dehaian began to lurch and didn't stop. Garbled sounds escaped him. His body thrashed against the wall.

Ari made a choked noise and looked away. I pulled her closer, holding her and resisting the urge to turn away myself. But it was horrible to watch. It made me feel sick.

I'd done worse than this only days before.

Damerion stopped. The dehaian stilled.

"Bastard," the man hissed.

Damerion ignored the insult. "What history?"

Contempt twisted the man's face, along with a sickened sort of satisfaction. "Driecara."

Every muscle in Damerion's body seemed to go still. Ezio looked at him, alarm fracturing his stoic expression.

I glanced between them, wary. The word sounded familiar. I couldn't remember why.

"Driecara was destroyed," Damerion said.

The man smiled. "But the will of its king lives on."

Rage suffused Damerion's face. "You lie."

The prisoner shrugged a shoulder like Damerion's belief made no difference. He turned his attention to me. "Tell me, Beast, what will happen to you when your bitch mistress dies?"

I froze, my Beast side becoming so silent, it was like everything in me was processing those words.

"What's that supposed to mean?" Ari demanded.

The man ignored her, grinning at me. "Will you suffer when we cut her throat in her sleep and fill the water with her blood? Will you feel pain too?"

I didn't move. Didn't speak. The darkness of the Beast's true form stirred deep inside me, ready to rise up, ready to lose this shape and do more damage than the little device at Damerion's belt could ever hope to achieve.

This bastard wanted to kill Chloe?

Like hell.

I started toward him, but Damerion got there first. Unhooking the device from his belt, he held it up in front of the dehaian's face. "Explain yourself, scum."

The man's gaze returned to the commander. "We know what Yvaria will do." His tone was almost conversational. "Your king has his father's blood in him. When his Vetorian whore dies, he'll lash out too. He'll tear into his allies, refusing to trust any-one because, even if he knows we were behind her death, we still could be anywhere. That's our power, commander. The power your blunt-force nation of murderers will never understand. We are the unknown. The darkness. The question behind every shadow, leaving you wondering if—just *if*—we are there." His grin was a twist of contempt. "You thought those obsessed cult-ists, the Sylphaen, were bad? That their infiltration of Yvaria was terrifying? They were nothing. Pitiable children, playing at adults' games, scrambling to control an ancient magic that we have already replaced." His smile broadened, cold and cruel. "Hear me, commander. Hear me and know. King Torvias sought to destroy us and failed. Starvation could not stop us. Persecution did not tear us down. And now we are coming for you. At our hands, your beloved Yvaria will destroy itself from the inside, devoured by fear and collapsing on its own contemptible core. This is what we understand, what the ruanir Judiciary understands." He chuckled. "Everyone can become a weapon if triggered in the right way."

I stared at him. This was too horrible. Too obscene. This was what it had all been for, the spies, the assassination attempts. Everything Zeke had been talking about, that day in the palace.

War.

And they wanted to start it by killing Chloe.

"Oh my God," Ari breathed. Pale as a ghost, she shook her head as if she desperately wanted to erase all of this.

Ezio swam toward the dehaian. His gaze was locked on the man, and the look in his eyes was chilling. His laidback demeanor had disappeared. So had any pretense of calm.

The cold, lethal mercenary was all that remained. "Where is this threat to the valya Praelex? Where are your people coming for her?"

A smirk began to emerge on the dehaian's face.

My eyes went black. He damn well would—

Ezio struck so quickly, his spikes were gone before blood began to rise in the water.

The dehaian choked. He wasn't dead. Wasn't even injured that badly. Thin red stripes crossed his neck, deep enough to break the skin but no more.

"You think Yvaria is dangerous?" Ezio told the man quietly. "That the Beast is the biggest threat to your plans?" He smiled, the expression cruel. "Then you are the one without any sense of history, my friend. We know a thousand ways to hurt. A thousand ways to make you *wish* we would let you die. And so you've made a terrible mistake, haven't you?" The smile vanished. "You forgot what it means to threaten a Vetorian."

The dehaian stared at him, the defiance in his eyes failing to fully mask a new tinge of anxiety.

Spikes crept back out on Ezio's arms. "Leave us," he said, the words clearly directed at us despite how he didn't take his eyes from the prisoner.

Damerion barely hesitated before starting for the door. "Come on." He motioned for us to follow.

I didn't move. Damerion's voice was strangely firm, like the Yvarian commander didn't have a single qualm about leaving this Vetorian mercenary in here alone. Like it didn't matter that this was his king's girlfriend; he was ready to let Ezio be the one to gather the information.

But I wasn't. This was Chloe, and war, and more potential bloodshed than my Beast side had seen in centuries—or my greliaran side had ever seen at all. I had to stop this. I needed information to do that.

And I knew I could get it.

"Now, Beast."

I looked back. Damerion's expression was like iron. Whatever Ezio was about to do, Damerion was only waiting for us to leave so it could happen.

And Ari was beyond him, watching me.

I hesitated, my discomfort returning hard and fast. I could get the information, sure. I could, and then Ari would see that side of me. That part of me that didn't resemble human in ways that had nothing to do with black eyes or storm clouds. That part I didn't know how to feel about, because in the past eight weeks, my life had suddenly become a teetering scale of ends and whether or not they justified the means.

But these people were going to murder Chloe to start another war.

"Noah?" Ari prompted, a thread of worry in her voice.

I was scaring her. I hadn't even done anything yet.

My gaze slid back to the dehaian. I'd also seen the look in the man's eyes. He was afraid of Ezio, of Vetorians.

The Beast side of me growled he wasn't afraid enough. We needed information. They were going to start a *war*.

But it would hurt Ari too, seeing this.

I made myself swim toward the door, despite how my Beast side was still snarling. Ari didn't need to see that from me. Ezio would get the information we needed. I didn't need to be that. Not in front of her. Not now, not ever.

Hopefully.

Pressing his hand to a lighter patch of stone on the wall, Damerion sealed the leaves of the door behind us, turning them to a hardness like wood.

"You're just going to leave Ezio in there?" I asked, unable to silence my doubt completely.

Damerion gave me a dry look. "I trust him, yes."

That wasn't an answer.

"What's Driecara?" Ari asked.

Damerion's expression turned cold. "A dehaian nation. A dead one."

"That guy didn't seem to think so," I said. "What—"

"He's lying," Damerion interrupted. "Driecara is gone."

"But what *happened?*" Ari cut in before I could speak. "He said something about what the king's father did. What's that?"

The commander looked away. A muffled cry of pain came from the other room, cutting off quickly.

Ari winced, glancing toward the sound. "Damerion?"

His jaw muscles jumped. "King Torvias destroyed Driecara as retribution for the murder of his youngest child."

Ari stared.

"The Driecaran king was in a dispute with King Torvias, so his spies took Torvias' daughter to force his hand. And to add *motivation*, they hid Princess Miri somewhere beyond the ocean because, in those days, we would not survive outside the water for long—and children survived the shortest time of all. Our king only had a few days to capitulate to Driecara's demands, and when he didn't… the Driecaran king let her die and ordered his spies to leave her body for our rescue parties to find."

Ari recoiled, as if to retreat from the history he described. Damerion didn't seem to notice, something old and dark in his eyes.

"In retaliation, King Torvias summoned his army and went to war. And when it was done, they were gone. The king, the notorious spies for which that nation was known… and the nation itself. Almost none of its people survived."

I watched him, at a loss for what to say. But the name clicked now. Driecara. Zeke had mentioned that last year. And later, Chloe's biological father, Kreyus, had said something about

Zeke's dad being a genocidal tyrant and murdering a nation too. But Kreyus was manipulative. A ruthless mercenary who would've let Chloe die if not for the discovery that she was his daughter. So I'd honestly thought the statement was hyperbole. Something to dig at Zeke while we were negotiating Kreyus's supposed "help."

Not *this*.

"Did you…" Ari's voice was strained. "Were you there?"

For a moment, I didn't think Damerion was going to respond. "I was one of those who found the princess's body."

"And for the rest?" I asked.

Damerion turned to me, anger igniting in his eyes. "You would judge me, *Beast*?"

I met his gaze silently. He looked away.

"Were you?" Ari asked softly.

Damerion closed his eyes. "Yes. For parts of it, at least."

A small sound left Ari.

"We were monsters." His focus slid to the door behind him and whatever was happening back there. "Monsters in every sense of the word. Driven by rage and the refusal to deny our heartbroken king, we won a war. We did as we were ordered. But the cost…" He shook his head. "Something in us died in those massacres. Something that should have stopped us, but it didn't, and it died as the price. But our king now, King Zekerian, son of Torvias and brother to the murdered princess? He sees that. He *knows* it. He keeps in service only those of us who know that too. The others, the ones who would ever relish such horrors again, he has let go. He has started resettlement programs, returned territory we took, and given restitution to any Driecarans who survived. Yvaria is rebuilding its soul, miss, in the hands of our young king. It's reclaiming what it could and should have been." He looked back to Ari. "There is no forgiveness for what we've done, those of us who were there. No action or atonement enough to *ever* absolve us of our crimes. But we will live the rest of our lives, trying. We will fail, but we will keep trying."

The leaves of the door behind him stirred, loosening from their wood-like tension. "That hell must never come again," Damerion said. "Not in my lifetime nor any other. And I will be *damned* if I let that scum and his allies change that fact."

Without another word, Damerion swam through the leaves and back into the other room.

I watched him go. Ari came up beside me.

My hand found hers. I didn't know what to say about the look I'd seen in Damerion's eyes. What to make of the old ghosts and the fierce, determined loyalty mixed there.

I only knew I agreed with him.

I'd be damned if I let these bastards use Chloe to start a war.

21

ARI

I trailed Noah back toward the room holding the dehaian prisoner, my skin crawling from the nightmare Damerion had described. An entire nation wiped out. A whole people.

And a child. These Driecarans had murdered a *child* for their own political gain.

But then, the Yvarians had murdered a tremendous number more than that.

I shuddered. My entire life, the dehaian world had been amorphous to me—part dark fairytale, part ancient history. I'd never really thought about it, the fact they probably had their own wars too. That horrible things happened down here beneath the sea.

The leaves parted around us, and my eyes found the man on the other side of the room.

He looked like he'd been put through a marathon at the point of a gun.

I stared. His body hung in the chains, as if without them he'd collapse to the ground. Only a few new wounds covered him—a gash here, a slice there—but his face… his eyes…

They weren't seeing us. They were locked on the ground like he'd accidentally stumbled on a gateway to hell and he couldn't unsee its horrors.

My stomach twisted with nausea for what had been done to him, what I'd left the room and let happen, and for all that he had been planning to do. Was *going* to do. My gaze shied from him, only to land on Ezio. He hovered a few feet from the prisoner. Tinges of the cold, frightening expression that had taken him over when the man threatened Chloe still touched his face.

So many horrible things beneath the sea…

"We have a problem," Ezio said, directing the words to Damerion. We might as well have not been in the room at all.

"What did you learn?" Damerion asked.

"Teariad, tonight. The valya Praelex has stopped there on her way to see her father. The Driecarans have infiltrated the royal retinue."

Damerion muttered something heated in a language I'd never heard. "Who? How many?"

"He doesn't know. They work in cells to avoid compromising the mission; no one but Osias has all the information. But they're close to her. That much, this one *did* know." He twitched his head to the prisoner.

Damerion nodded once and then sped from the room.

Noah moved to follow him.

"Wait," Ezio called.

I looked back while Noah stopped.

"He said he recognized you," Ezio told me. "That he'd seen

you before."

I hesitated. "He was at the facility where the judges had me."

"Were there others like him at this facility? Other dehaian spies?"

My shoulders rose and fell awkwardly. "I don't know. Maybe. Everyone looked human."

"Would you recognize them?"

My gaze skirted back to the dehaian prisoner when I realized where Ezio could be going with this. If I knew who the spies were, if I could spot them on sight, then that could help Chloe.

And everybody.

"Ari?"

"Yeah. Maybe."

Ezio nodded, glancing to the dehaian. "He also spoke of something called the Judiciary and their plans."

My blood went cold. "What?"

"Tell her."

The man flinched like the sound of Ezio's voice hurt. "The relics," he rasped.

"What relics?" Noah asked.

"Stones. White stones. They're from the old world. From the time before the wizard war. The judges had them. The Judiciary isn't as distant from the dehaian world as they would have their people imagine. They knew about us. About Driecara. They approached us last year after the Beast's return."

The man shuddered. "The relics had been dormant for a

thousand years, but they started to reawaken when the Beast returned. They began to give off energy that led the judges to create tracking devices, new technology, ways to trap the Beast." His attention twitched in my direction, not making it to me fully before fleeing. "And to create the strakirin."

Shivers crept through me. "The stone in the box. The one that dehaian had."

Noah nodded.

"Keep going," Ezio said to the prisoner.

The man nodded jerkily, eager to comply. "The Beast's power was a catalyst for the creatures, but it was only part of the equation. The relics will guide us. They'll show us the way. The energy they give off is only getting stronger the closer we get to the source."

"Source of what?" I asked nervously.

"Everything. What made the relics, what helped the judges create the strakirin. The judges needed a way to reach it, harness it, and once we find it…" Old anticipation spasmed across his face, the expression fractured by his current fear of Ezio. He looked like a terrified former junkie remembering his favorite drug. "The power it will bring us and the judges will rival that of the ocean gods."

"And what is this power?" Ezio demanded. "What will it do?"

The man shook his head. "Only Osias knows. He's the one the judges told. They'll feel it, though. The strakirin. They're made from it. When we start to get close enough, they'll feel it too. The source will draw them to itself."

My skin crawled at the look in his eyes. Hungry. Fanatical.

"That was only the beginning, though," the prisoner continued. "The judges need to destabilize the ruanir world and ours too. Regime change takes chaos, takes fear. Otherwise you look like the threat, not the savior. So they need war. They need both the ruanir and the dehaians to demand each other's destruction. They've already started on land. But when the Vetorian's daughter dies…"

Indecision tugged at me like I was a rope between two horrible outcomes vying for control. I had to go. I had to chase Logan and the strakirin down and let Zeke's army stop them from finding this… this *whatever* it was. If the judges got their hands on what they were looking for, my family and the entire ruanir world could be destroyed. I had to stop them.

And in the meantime, Chloe could die.

I hugged my arms tighter to myself. I didn't know her. I didn't know any of these dehaians.

Nameless faces crowded in on me as if my thoughts had summoned ghosts. Dozens. More. Pain and pride and unbelievable sorrow filled their eyes while the life drained from them and their blood pulsed out onto my skin through wounds torn by my spikes.

I squeezed my eyes shut, trying to crush the memories away.

I couldn't have stopped their deaths. It'd taken the ocean magic pouring through me before I'd had enough strength to break free of the hive and take back control of my body. But this… but now…

I turned to Noah and Ezio. "How fast can we get to this

Teariad place?"

Noah looked to me. I could see his worry.

"How fast?" I pressed.

"We could be there in a few hours, top speed." Ezio glanced to Noah. "But I'm guessing we'll get there faster with you."

Noah hesitated. "Yeah."

"Good," Ezio agreed. "Then let's—"

A shrieking sound ripped through the water. Veins of blue-white light snaked through the ceiling, the walls, tangling through the stone surface like the caves had suddenly become chambers inside a giant's heart.

"What the hell?" Noah shouted.

"Security system." Ezio darted for the door. "We're under attack."

I looked to Noah. Attack? But the strakirin weren't here. I couldn't even hear—

And then I did. Like a whisper. Like the brush of a feather at the furthest reaches of my mind. But that meant they were far away. Too far to—

A scream punctuated the murmur of the drone, sending me thrashing back in the water like I'd just been stabbed.

"Ari?" Noah swam toward me.

The noise faded as fast as it had arrived. I looked to Noah. "What—"

Pain lanced through me. Burning. Bleeding. Blackening flesh in the cold depths of the sea.

Death.

Gone.

Noah grabbed my arm. I turned to the dehaian. "What is this? What are they—"

I cut off, gasping as the surge of sensation ripped through me again, only to vanish.

The man lifted his eyes from the ground, unsteady and trembling. A trace of his old contempt showed through, his lip curling, scorn in his eyes. "You're all going to die."

I stared at him.

"Like hell," Noah snarled. He grabbed me, pulling me with him as he sped through the water toward the door.

The hallway outside was in chaos. I couldn't see Ezio anywhere. Soldiers darted through the halls so fast that the water they displaced pushed me when they sped by. Noah yanked me back while another dehaian raced at us. The man jerked to a fast halt, coming within inches of slamming into me.

"What's going on?" Noah shouted over the shrieking alarms.

"Attack!" the man cried. "Those things—"

Another surge of pain hit me, and then a second followed on its heels. I doubled over.

"Where's Damerion?" Noah demanded of the man while he pulled me to his side to keep me from sinking.

"Main security."

Noah didn't wait for more. Holding me close, he took off through the hallways, heading in the same direction Ezio had directed him hours before.

I was grateful. Every few seconds, another shock of pain would flash through me, only to vanish as quickly as it had come.

But they were getting more frequent. And the strakirin drone was getting louder.

We rounded another turn in the maze of the garrison. Several dehaians rushed from an opening halfway down the hall. I heard Damerion's voice coming from inside, nearly lost amid the shouts of soldiers.

"—Nyciena! Tell them we're under attack!"

Pain lanced through me again. My vision blurred, and there it was. The feeling of burning, of death, and beyond it…

Cold. Water on skin, on scales. The droning sound of dozens of minds, unified as one.

They knew I was here.

I choked, the words lodged somewhere in my throat beyond a scream. Noah and I were in the main security room now. Past the blur of my vision, Damerion hovered. Soldiers flashed by, lost to the darkness, to speed, to pain. Blurred shapes that might've been images of dehaians moved on the walls, held inside magic like I'd seen in that communication device Damerion used at the campsite.

"—throwing themselves at the gods-damned barrier!" Damerion yelling at Noah like he was answering a question.

A strakirin rushed closer, filling up the murky image hovering on the wall. Pain surged through me again. I heard Noah and the others shouting, fragments of nonsense, filled with near panic.

"—get out of—"

"—trying to break through—"

"They know," I gasped. "They know I'm—"

Here.

The pain vanished. The drone didn't. Strakirin flooded past the garrison defenses through a gap torn open by the repeated kamikaze attacks of the swarm.

And the hive mind came with them.

"They've broken through!" a soldier cried.

I knew it.

The strakirin flooded into the halls, twisting through the tunnels like poison in a vein, and dehaians died in their wake. Pleasure rippled through the strakirin, the coursing satisfaction of obeying what they had been made to do. They surged toward me, invisible and distant in the maze of tunnels for now, but coming.

Oh my God, they were coming.

Noah grabbed me. I didn't even have to speak. The look on my face must have been enough.

"Get out of here!" Damerion shouted at Noah. "Take Ezio and the girl and get to Teariad!"

"What?" Ezio demanded, incredulous.

Damerion looked at Ezio, his expression loaded with pain. "Save your valya Praelex." He turned to Noah. "Go!"

Noah hesitated, aghast, but then he was moving. Disappearing. I felt him surge around me, saw him grab Ezio the same way, and then the room was behind us, the soldiers parting as if driven aside.

"No!" Ezio yelled, thrashing but getting nowhere in Noah's grip. "He'll die back there! They'll all die!"

Stone walls and alarms and other hallways flashed past, fast as thought, faster than I could have hoped to swim. I couldn't hear the strakirin anymore; Noah's magic kept them muffled in a way that felt like I could finally breathe. Noah was only a force around me, invisible as the water itself and holding me in his grip while we shot through hallway after hallway, racing for an exit.

"Stop, damn you!" Ezio shouted. "Go back! Don't do this!"

Noah didn't pause. More hallways passed. Soldiers too, with swords and knives and spikes bared.

And then the strakirin were straight ahead.

I gasped, flinching back and bracing myself as Noah charged at them. The strakirin pulled up short, their green-yellow eyes locking on me. The drone returned, slithering past Noah's magic and my defenses, honing in on me with a terrible, terrifying weight. They needed me. Wanted me. I didn't understand. I had to come back.

And then Noah hit them. A snarl tore the water as lightning sliced around me. He had to be in agony. Had to be suffering as the poison flooded from them. I could see Ezio, blades out on his forearms, slicing at any strakirin that came close, but even as the strakirin fell away like leaves, the drone didn't change. The individual strakirin didn't matter. They were only vessels for the hive mind. And it... I...

I had to go back.

I had to go...

I...

Noah burst from the tunnels. A sizzle of pain whipped across me, burning like fire, and then gone when we passed by the vestiges of the defense system. The canyon opened up around us, rough walls pitted by countless cave entrances, their extent lost down in the depths of the endless valley. Surging upward, Noah fled through the strakirin swarm, rising toward the cliff's edge.

"Dammit, stop!" Ezio cried.

The strakirin whirled behind us. The garrison was only part of their interest. I was the rest, and I was leaving. It didn't matter if Noah was around me, muffling me from their senses.

Not now that they could see me.

"They're coming!" I gasped.

Noah accelerated. He burst out into the open water above the canyon, a cloud of dirt and sand erupting from the cliff's edge in his wake. Rocks and sand and debris flew past, blurring with our speed. We needed to get beyond their echolocation if there was any chance of losing them now.

Clearly, Noah knew it. He veered upward, leaving behind the ocean floor and the damage he was doing there. The water churned in our wake, and a rumble filled my world. I could feel the water pushing at us, and I couldn't imagine what the pressure would be like without Noah there.

The strakirin faded from my awareness. The darkness paled, becoming a shade of deep blue-gray. We weren't far from the surface.

Noah slowed. His grip vanished from me, and the water swirled as he drew down into human form. "Are they still—"

The deep thud of a concussion rolled through the water, jolting us, like an explosion miles below. I froze, staring.

Noah did the same. "What the hell?"

"Contingency."

I looked to Ezio. His voice was flat. Toneless, like all the life had drained from it. His gaze was locked on the water below us, and his expression…

Suddenly I knew more than I could put into words, and it was terrible. What must have happened. What Damerion had done.

And more than that.

"They have contingencies for everything." Ezio paused. "Had."

He murmured something in another language, his eyes closing. But I saw nothing but determination on his face when he turned to Noah. "We should keep moving. The valya Praelex is still in danger." Without another word, he started swimming farther into the blue-gray murk.

"Any strakirin?" Noah asked me tightly.

I shook my head. "I can't feel them. And the… I can't hear them either."

Maybe they were all dead.

Hope filled me at the thought, but a strange discomfort followed. I wanted them stopped. Killing them would probably be the only way to do that, and if that explosion meant they were gone…

The pull of the hive haunted my memory. The way they'd needed me, wanted me, begged me to return even if I couldn't understand why it mattered that I stay.

"Can you change to human form?" Noah asked, drawing

me from my thoughts.

"I think so."

I hoped so.

He paused like he'd caught my uncertainty, but he didn't say anything about it. "If any of them are left and they start to get close, shift like that. I can fly. They can't. I'll get us out of here."

I nodded.

Ezio was a dozen yards ahead of us. Pity and pain twisted inside me at the sight of him continuing determinedly onward. He'd cared about the Yvarian commander. It had been clear on his face. And to lose someone like that so quickly, so suddenly… I couldn't imagine what it felt like.

Noah came up close, waiting till I started moving before setting off after Ezio. My stomach twisted.

I never wanted to find out.

❧ 22 ❧

LOGAN

I hurt.

More than hurt. Only my heartbeat in my throat, throbbing like I was going to choke, was enough to let me know I was alive.

Sort of.

I opened my eyes to a fog of dirt and grime hanging so heavy, I felt like I'd been buried. My mind ached. Every thought, every twitch of neurons, felt like electrical sparks biting at my gray matter. My body was a swath of pain-filled flesh, several hundred near-corpses wide. I could feel every piece of sand on a tail, every cut on green-stained skin.

A few hundred strakirin, floating limply or lying on the sand and grit.

And hundreds more below.

Gone.

A groan escaped me when I pushed up from the ground. I lay on the edge of the canyon, across from what had once been a garrison. Up until a little bit ago, anyway. Now it was nothing.

A pancake stack of dirt and rock. Inside were my strakirin.

They were nothing more than paste.

With a weak kick of my tail, I propelled myself higher in the sand-filled water. I could feel them, the survivors, their hive mind raw and jarred by the flood of pain. The drone had become a stutter, like an old and broken film still struggling to play.

I needed Ari. I had to find her. She had to come back.

The thought drew me up short. What? Why the hell would I need *her*?

As quickly as it had come, the impulse faded.

I shook my head in some faint hope of clearing it. The drone was getting stronger again. My strakirin felt my presence. They were getting stronger because I was strong, and my survival was all that mattered.

A form stirred in the murk, eerily close yet I hadn't picked up on it till now. Damn this dirt and sand. But the form was dehaian, and a moment later, it emerged from the muck.

"You're alive," Osias said.

"No thanks to you. What the hell was that? Why didn't you warn me they—"

He gave me an arch look. "You didn't think they'd have security measures?"

"They killed themselves!"

"Not all of them."

I scoffed. Right. Ari was—

I cut the thought off. What the hell? Who cared about Ari, or whatever was left of her? The *Beast* was still out there. Some of my strakirin had seen her and a dehaian guy flying through the water without twitching a muscle, and at speeds that even my strakirin couldn't match. Only one explanation.

That damned invisible ocean monster had carried them away.

"Enough of this," Osias said. "We need to finish the mission."

"Excuse me?"

"You lost us half our forces on this fool's errand. If we—"

I advanced on him. "*I* lost. *Me?*" Poison curled under my skin. This was what outliving your usefulness looked like. And I wanted that surge, that fix, that rush I felt after killing. It'd take the edge off of the residual pain.

What the hell did I need this guy alive for, anyway?

"As matters currently stand, the Beast is unkillable." Osias held his ground, the idiot. "It's too fast, too strong. Until we can—"

I grabbed his arm. "*I* lost…"

A flicker of actual fear flashed through Osias' eyes.

Excitement thrilled in my chest like a hummingbird flutter. I could feel echoes of it from my strakirin all around. I loved the sight of that fear. They did too.

We wanted to feel him die.

"You need me," Osias said hurriedly. "You think *this* is power?"

I hesitated.

"I heard the judges' plan," he continued.

My hand tightened on his bicep. "I heard people too. Your

people, talking about how I'm not going to make it out of this alive."

His expression didn't even flinch. His eyes didn't show a hint of reaction. Oh, he was good. Not as good as me, but good. You'd think he knew they'd talked all along.

Had he?

Curiosity made the poison inside me pause, hovering just beyond his skin. It could have been a setup, the fact I'd overheard his people. The man was devious as hell, for someone who wasn't me. But to what end?

"That isn't true." Osias shook his head. "The judges have something more in store for you. Something great. I don't have all the details—"

Bullshit. My hand clenched down harder on his arm.

"But I have to perform the ritual," Osias persisted. "It has to be me. None of the others know it. And if you kill me…" His gaze darted to the side as if to encompass the other strakirin. "This is all you'll ever have."

Like *this* was so bad.

I snickered. The drone of the strakirin filled me, obedient and waiting for my every whim and command. Poison flowed through me, shivering toward where my skin met his, promising a thrill beyond any drug I could name. And then a second thought caught me.

Was I really going to pass up more power?

The poison paused again.

"You will get your chance at the Beast," Osias said. "But we *must* finish the mission. If we do that, then the next time you see that creature, I promise you, it will die." He studied my face. "Power and the Beast dead. Isn't that what you want?"

I gave him a long look. Levers. That's what this was. Pull the levers, watch people twitch.

And he was trying to play me.

"You cost me hundreds of strakirin," I growled.

"They're only vessels. You're clearly the one who matters." Osias glanced to the west. "With my help, you could be more powerful than you've ever imagined."

Now he was bargaining.

True, but I could let him think it was working. For now, anyway. There was no chance in hell he'd pull anything over on me, not when "me" was hundreds of pairs of eyes and ears strong. I could always kill him later.

It'd still be good to make a point.

"You know what I could do if you double cross me," I told him. "Right?"

A shriek came out of the fog of sand. My strakirin swam closer, emerging from the murk with a dehaian in their grasp.

I reached out my other hand, and they brought him. It only took a brush of my fingertips, and then his screams began.

I never took my eyes from Osias while the man died.

"Of course," Osias allowed.

"Good." Shivers raced through my body and coursed over my skin. "Then you have a deal. Now let's go find me that power."

23

ARI

The empty ocean stretched around us like we were floating in deep space. No one spoke while we swam, following Ezio's course. The silence was oppressive, heavy with the weight of what we'd just left behind.

I watched Ezio from the corner of my eye. His expression had turned to granite, cold and impervious to anything, and his eyes looked dead.

I hoped I was wrong about him and the commander, for his sake.

But I doubted it.

"So… Damerion," I started quietly.

I saw Ezio flinch at the name, the motion so slight that if I hadn't been watching, I might have missed it entirely.

"He, um…" I didn't know how to say it. What dehaians thought about couples like I suspected they probably were. "He wasn't just a, um, friend… was he?"

Ezio looked over, his focus moving from me to land on Noah for a long moment before briefly returning. "No."

He resumed staring at the water ahead.

"I'm so sorry."

Ezio gave no reaction, except to blink a few times.

Silence returned, broken only by distant cries of whales too far away to matter to our course. I grimaced at myself. I shouldn't have asked. He was in pain, I could tell, but he wasn't like me. I'd thought maybe to talk about it would help, but—

"We met in Kansas."

I glanced over, but Ezio didn't meet my eyes. He was watching the water like he could see history in its shadows. See the person he'd lost.

"Last year, when the Praelex went to visit his daughter for one of the human holidays. Christmas, I think they call it. I was there as part of the Praelex's security detail. He was part of the king's." Ezio was silent for a moment. "It's not forbidden, an Yvarian and a Vetorian. Not *common*, no, but with the king and the valya Praelex as they are…" He made a shrugging gesture with one hand. "As long as we never give anyone cause to question our loyalties, King Zekerian and Praelex Kreyus allow us to—"

His expression crumpled with pain, and my heart ached for him.

He'd been talking as if Damerion were still alive.

I swam closer, reaching out to take his hand before I could stop myself.

Nothing happened. No poison, no magic.

Ezio looked over at me. "I'd heard people on land weren't as understanding about relationships like Damerion and I…

had."

I wasn't sure what to say. "Some of us are."

He gave a small nod. "Thank you."

"I'm sorry for your loss," Noah offered quietly.

Ezio watched him for a moment. "Me too."

Silence fell. The whales drifted closer, prickling at the edges of my senses, swimming in a pair with a young one nearby.

"The valya Praelex. You…" Ezio seemed to reevaluate his words. "There was a time before you were the Beast."

It wasn't quite a question.

"Yes," Noah said.

"And now that you are, has anything changed?"

Noah's gaze slipped to me. "Some things."

Ezio followed his glance.

"He's still a good person," I assured Ezio quietly, certain of my words even if I'd never asked Noah. But I knew I was right all the same. "He wouldn't want her to get hurt, whether or not they… you know…" I wasn't sure how to finish that sentence.

Ezio looked between us. "I see." He adjusted the belt around his chest. "Teariad is several hours from here. Even at dehaian speed—"

"I'll get us there," Noah said.

Ezio nodded. "Good."

Noah disappeared.

"Can you hear me, Noah?" Ezio called.

Noah drew back into human form, several yards from where he'd been. "Yeah, I can hear you."

Ezio paused. "Then you heard me before."

His meaning clicked. The tunnels. The garrison.

When he'd shouted for Noah to stop.

I bit my lip, uncertain what to say. Noah couldn't have stopped. The strakirin would have killed Ezio. Poisoned Noah. Taken me. If he'd stopped, in our own ways, we all would have died.

And leaving was what Damerion had wanted him to do.

"Yes," Noah replied quietly.

Seconds crept by.

"Head north," Ezio said. "The valya Praelex will most likely be at the palace. Center of the city."

Noah vanished again. Water moved around me, taking hold and carrying me forward without the need for me to move a muscle.

I looked over at Ezio. He was back to studying nothing. The ground maybe, beyond our senses though it was. Or what it now buried.

Time slipped by, the hours slowly piling up and full of nothing much in the ocean around us. The emptiness was a relief, in a way. The strakirin were nowhere to be found, and maybe, just maybe, that meant most of them were gone.

Including Logan. Possibly Osias too. Without those two leading them, maybe the strakirin wouldn't be able to find this source *thing*. Maybe the threat of that would be over.

It seemed too much to hope for, but that didn't stop me from clinging to the thought all the same.

Noah dove, and the shift in direction brought my attention back to our surroundings. Nearby, Ezio seemed to become more alert as well. We had to be getting close to Teariad, even if I couldn't feel anything around us to indicate that fact. The rocky ocean floor lay just at the edge of what I could sense, but that was it.

A tingling feeling swept past me. Suddenly, the empty ocean turned into an aerial view of a city teeming with life. With nausea-inducing speed, Noah slowed only enough to keep from destroying anything nearby with the effects of his passage. We swept over the city, neither Ezio nor I swimming or even moving, a dehaian and a creature no one here had probably ever seen before, both held in the grip of an invisible force that was moving faster than a dehaian.

The dehaians beneath us stared up in shock when we flashed by.

At the edge of the city, the palace came into view. Craggy rock walls ended abruptly in a sheer plateau that towered above the metropolitan area, smaller than the mountain palace in Nyciena, but still impressive in its size. Leaves like those I'd seen in Nyciena covered openings on the sides, dozens of them, like curtains on windows.

Noah flew past it all, veering around the plateau and heading for the far side like he knew exactly where he was going. For a moment, I couldn't figure out why, and then I remembered. I hadn't been the only one with a connection to Noah.

Two people still did, and Chloe was one of them.

Something in my chest twisted, weird and uncomfortable, like my heart was trying to go through my lungs. I struggled to push the thought away.

We circled to the far side of the plateau. There were more leaves here, but fewer openings, as if the windows they obscured were larger. Or maybe the rooms were too.

Noah's grip vanished.

I flailed and spun at the sudden absence of the force that had been carrying me. At my side, Ezio did the same, confusion flashing over his face for only a heartbeat before anger took its place.

"Dammit!" He kicked hard in the water, taking off in the same direction we had been traveling.

I sped after him, my confusion unchanged. Why had Noah let us go? What did he—

Lightning erupted from behind one of the curtains of leaves ahead of us, shredding through the greenery and lashing out into the water.

Shock made me falter. Strakirin?

"Venika!" I heard a girl shout.

A gray-haired dehaian woman shot from the window like she was swimming for her life. Ezio grabbed me, pulling me back when more lightning surged from the opening after the fleeing dehaian.

"What the—" I started.

"The valya Praelex possesses powers like the Beast," Ezio explained shortly, watching the window.

Oh.

Plant debris swirled by the window, as if caught in a new current in the water. Noah appeared amid the shredded leaves, staring inside the room.

Ezio took off. I swam after him, catching up in a moment. We neared the window, staying clear of it in case more lightning appeared.

"I'm okay," a girl said from inside the room.

Noah nodded once and then raced after the fleeing dehaian.

"Guards!" the same girl shouted. "I need help! Venika's hurt!"

"Valya Praelex?" Ezio eased around the edge of the window.

I trailed him warily. The apartment was a disaster. Burn marks scored the walls near the window. Gemstone decorations and carved trinkets were scattered across the floor. To my left, a man was crumpled, scorch marks all around him. A burnt aftertaste filled the water, acrid and sour. To my right, a dark-haired woman lay propped against the wall near the entrance of a bedroom. Scars covered her, ritualistic like Ezio's and matching some of his too. Beside her, a red-headed girl crouched, her cream-colored tail bent beneath her.

My insides lurched unexpectedly, twisting weirdly like my whole body had suddenly become an uncomfortable place to be. This wasn't like when I saw Zeke, or when I saw other people Noah knew.

This was Chloe, the girl he'd loved. The girl he'd died to save.

And she was beautiful.

I retreated in spite of myself, backing toward the window like maybe I could rewind time and just… get out of here or something. I wasn't even sure why. I'd known she was beautiful. I'd seen her in his memories. But for some reason, those memories hadn't affected me like this.

Chloe's hands clutched a wound on the scarred woman's side. Blood filtered into the water around her palms, dark amid the pale blue light of the single lamp nearby. She looked up, and relief filled her face at the sight of Ezio, only to vanish into shock when she saw me.

I wanted to disappear through the floor.

The injured woman lurched, choking, and Chloe's attention snapped back to her. "Goddammit!" she shouted, her voice breaking. "Someone get in here and—"

Dehaians raced in. From the moment they passed the doorway, half of the group had their eyes locked on the wounded woman. They sped over to Chloe's side, ignoring us completely.

The other dehaians took one look at me and raced forward, spikes emerging on their arms instantly. I swam backward swiftly only to bump into the wall.

"Whoa!" Ezio darted between me and the dehaians, his hands raised. "She's on our side!"

I stopped. The soldiers did too. The doctors ignored us, one of them taking Chloe's place in holding the woman's wounds closed while the others hurried to draw out supplies from the bags they carried. Jars of that sparkling, faintly glowing gel emerged, and bandages and stitching thread too.

Chloe relinquished her hold on Venika, moving away cautiously and watching the doctors and me in equal measure. "Who, um… Who is—"

Noah swam through the window opening, another dehaian trailing after him.

I blinked. The woman didn't look conscious, but she floated behind him all the same. She had scars like Ezio. Like the woman on the floor and some of the dehaians currently glaring death threats at me as well. Vetorians, then. All of them.

"Take her," Ezio ordered the other Vetorians, gesturing to the woman floating behind Noah. The Vetorians hesitated and then moved to do as he said. The others, Yvarian soldiers from their armbands, seemed torn about obeying Ezio.

Specifically his commands about me.

Ezio ignored them. "Are you okay, valya Praelex? Were there any others?"

"No, I—I mean, yes, I'm fine. Venika took the, uh… they hit her before they…" Chloe seemed to give up. "How did you know?"

She directed the question at Noah more than anyone.

It was strange, seeing the way she looked at him. Even if I hadn't known them at all, I would have been able to tell they had a history. The connection between them—a connection that had nothing to do with quasi-empathic powers or magic— was so clear.

My hands clasped themselves together in front of me, barely restraining my urge to wrap my arms protectively around my middle. I wasn't sure what I was feeling all of a sudden. Jealousy? Of what? Okay, so she was gorgeous, but she was dating the dehaian king. Noah and I had been… well, *close*, to put it mildly, only a short while ago.

And people couldn't pine for their exes? Use others to get over them?

Noah wasn't like that.

I couldn't tell what Noah was like anymore. Not from the inside, not like I had.

She could.

The thought hurt. I wanted that connection back, and she still had it, even if I knew from what Noah had told me that their link was only a faint shadow of what we'd shared. I wanted it too, though. Wanted what we'd had, even if it was only a shadow. Something in me ached for that feeling again. So this wasn't jealousy. Not just jealousy, anyway. There had to be another word for what I was feeling.

It came to me.

Loneliness.

And in some ways, that was almost worse.

"A spy, valya Praelex," Ezio supplied. "Interrogated at the garrison at the Cylian Pass. He told us of the assassination plot against you."

Chloe blinked. "You were at a garrison?" she asked Noah.

"Long story," he said.

She seemed to process the words. "But none of the soldiers…" She glanced around as if to encompass the fact none of them were here.

I didn't know what to say, and Noah didn't seem to either.

"There was an attack." Ezio's voice was quiet. "We were the only ones who made it out alive."

For a heartbeat, Chloe seemed taken aback, and then I watched a change come over her, like the shock was being shoved back to let necessity take its place. This was a girl who'd witnessed Noah killed by an ancient monster, who'd survived God-knew-what before that, and suddenly, that history was written all over her too. I didn't know what they called her down here—princess, lady, or valya Praelex, whatever that meant—but in a moment, I could see the truth. Like the king, she drew the focus of the room to her and carried a presence no one else here could match.

So *that's* who Noah had loved… and who he was still connected to.

An ache took up residence in my chest, cold and alone.

"Have you checked on Ina and Egan?" Chloe directed the question to the Yvarians, a laser-like intensity in her green eyes. "Are they okay?"

One of the soldiers nodded. "We dispatched guards to protect them the moment… *he* arrived." The woman seemed to stop herself from motioning toward Noah.

Chloe nodded. "And has the king been notified about this attack on the garrison?"

"There wasn't time," Ezio said. "But if your soldiers would—"

"Do that," Chloe ordered the soldiers immediately. "Please."

At this, at least, the Yvarians didn't seem to hesitate. One of them darted from the room.

Chloe watched them go, and then her gaze slipped toward Venika. The doctors had slowed the bleeding. They seemed less agitated too, as if their efforts were going well. Their attention wasn't as locked on their patient anymore. Several of them were checking around as if assessing the situation and whether they could move her. But like the Vetorians and the soldiers, I could see their wariness whenever their attention came anywhere near me.

I wanted to retreat, although there wasn't anywhere to go. I felt like the snake-eyed, eel-tailed elephant in the room. Like a monster barely in control, and the fact nearly *everyone* short of Noah, Chloe, and Ezio was looking at me like I might be one didn't—

Contempt flashed through the eyes of one of the Vetorians, so strong it brought my thoughts up short. It wasn't like the others. He seemed like he knew me. Like he *hated* me. And I recognized that look. I could swear I'd seen it somewhere.

"So was this another tribe in the Prijoran Zone?" Chloe asked Ezio. "Were Triya and Ilya working for them? They've been my bodyguards for almost a year now, but—"

The man lunged at Chloe.

I was moving before I registered the impulse. His spikes came out, aimed for her back, but I was faster. In a heartbeat, I was across the room, weaving past Chloe and the doctors and the soldiers alike. I felt the water stir when Noah surged toward us too.

My hands got there first, pushing the man back into the wall. Poison thrilled through me, wonderful like Noah's hands on my body and terrible like cold, black ooze. I craved it. I hated it. I had been made to do this, and I'd never asked for it. I wanted to cry while the venom poured into the dehaian like cold black ecstasy that would make him start to die.

Except he didn't.

His lips curled. With a swift motion, he twisted his arms

beneath mine, gripping me close. Though moments before I'd pinned him to the wall, now he held me fast, seeming to grow stronger with every second. The dark lines of my poison raced through him, climbing his neck, his face.

The black venom stained the whites of his eyes. He met my gaze, his satisfaction clear.

"Thanks, darling," he hissed.

Horrified, I tried to pull away, but his grip didn't budge. He drove me back from the wall while his mad gaze went beyond me to Chloe.

He started to shove me away like I was nothing.

Noah swept around me from all sides, propelling the man into the wall again and breaking his grasp on me. I watched, breathless, while the man struggled.

But he still didn't die.

I stared. Oh my God, this was like Judge Davenport. This dehaian was like the judges now. Any of the dehaians who'd sided with them probably were the same. My poison didn't kill them.

It supercharged them.

What the hell had the Judiciary done?

The water swirled, drawing down into Noah's human form. In his grip, the man continued to fight.

"Bitch of Yvaria!" the Vetorian shrieked at Chloe.

"Someone get those shackle things!" Noah snapped to the room at large.

Several dehaians shot off down the hallway.

The man thrashed, still trying to break Noah's hold on him.

"Praelex Kreyus ordered this! His support for your king is a lie. You shame the Ivalaen people with your foul—"

Noah slammed the man back into the wall so hard, I felt the water shake. The dehaian sagged in his grasp, not dead, but seriously hurt. His chest lurched while he struggled to breathe.

Whoa.

Pinning him down, Noah looked back. I followed his gaze to Chloe.

She stared at us.

Soldiers rushed into the room, metal shackles in their hands. Two of them started for me, and I retreated fast with nowhere to go.

"Not her, you idiots!" Ezio snapped. "Him!"

The Yvarians hesitated.

"Now, goddammit!"

They moved toward the Vetorian attacker uncertainly. Even when barely conscious, the man looked like a nightmare of poison, with black lines crisscrossing his skin where veins would be.

"Careful," Noah said. "Don't touch his skin."

The soldiers eyed him, clearly debating whether to follow his orders too. Common sense won out, though. They clasped the manacles around the Vetorian man's forearms, even if they seemed uncertain that they shouldn't chain me up too, just in case. Another soldier unholstered a weapon that looked like a gun, firing it at the man's tail. Vines erupted over him, tangling around him till he couldn't move. Staying clear of touching the man, the soldiers dragged him by a chain linking the manacles and pulled him from the room.

Keeping an eye to the barely conscious Vetorian, Noah moved to my side. "You okay?"

No.

"Yeah," I said, painfully aware of how he wouldn't feel the lie. "Yeah, I'm fine."

He didn't look like he believed me anyway.

"What—" Chloe started.

"My lady," one of the soldiers interrupted. The remaining Yvarians moved to surround Chloe, all while watching me. "This… *creature*… aided that man. We must get you—"

"*What?*" Noah protested.

My heart climbed in my throat.

The soldier frowned. "The power she gave him strengthened his attack."

I shook my head. "No. No, I was trying to—"

"To what? What was that?" The soldier turned to Chloe. "My lady, I must insist we take this creature into custody." He gestured for the guards. "Her and the Vetorians. We—"

Noah moved in front of me. "You won't *touch* her, do you—"

"Stop," Chloe ordered.

The soldiers froze. Noah looked over to her.

"Who are you?" Chloe asked me.

I floundered, my heart pounding. "Ari. Ari Moreau. I'm—" I didn't know how to *begin* to explain. "I'm not your enemy. I swear. I was trying to stop him. I-I didn't know he'd… I didn't know."

Chloe was quiet for a moment, and then she glanced to

Noah. And I saw it again. That look, the same one that had been in Zeke's eyes.

Trust.

"Your father did not order any attack, valya Praelex," Ezio said into the silence. "I swear to you on my life, that man was lying. And Ari isn't our enemy, as she said. What happened there…" He seemed to run out of a way to explain.

He wasn't the only one.

"But this *was* the Vetorians," Chloe said, a question tangled up in the statement.

"No," Ezio replied. "This was…" He grimaced, eying the Yvarian soldiers and the Vetorians alike.

"Is there somewhere we can talk alone?" Noah prompted.

Chloe glanced at him. At me.

"No," the soldier protested. "My lady, you cannot—"

"Yeah. Sure." Chloe turned back to the doctors still surrounding Venika. "Is she…"

"She is stable," one of the doctors said. "We need to get her to the infirmary, however."

Chloe nodded. The doctors moved to carry the woman from the room.

"Clear out," Chloe said to the soldiers while the doctors left. "Please. You all too." The last was directed to the Vetorians.

"My lady," the soldier protested.

"I mean it." Her eyes twitched to Noah. "I'll be okay."

"King Zekerian would not wish us to leave you—"

"The king isn't here." Her voice hardened. "I am. And he told you to follow my orders."

The soldier hesitated.

"Go."

With a sharp nod, the soldier turned and motioned to the Yvarians to leave. Ezio gave a jerk of his head to the Vetorians, and still watching me, the mercenaries swam after the Yvarians. Ezio trailed them, only to pause by the door and press his hand to a slightly lighter patch of stone on the wall.

The leaves on the door stilled, becoming like wood.

A short breath left Chloe. "Okay. What's going on?"

"Driecaran spies," Ezio said, swimming back toward us.

I could tell instantly she knew exactly what that was. "But they're…"

"Apparently not. At least, not all of them."

"Is that who you are?" she asked me. "Did they—"

"No." I shook my head fast. "No, I'm not. I… It's hard to explain."

"Ari's one of the wizards I told you about," Noah said. "The one I met in Maine."

Chloe's brow twitched up like she heard something else in the words, and she looked between me and Noah like she was seeing us for the first time.

I shifted uncomfortably. He'd told her about us? Me? Why? And why was she looking at us like—

"You didn't say the wizards could…" Chloe seemed to struggle for words. "I mean…"

"The others can't. The leaders of her people did this to her as part of an experiment. They didn't tell her what it would do, only that she'd be helping protect her family and friends."

Noah paused. "They lied."

She studied him for a moment. It hadn't gotten past her, I realized. The fact he'd left out a lot in that swift explanation.

But then that look of quiet trust came back, even if I could tell she wanted to know more.

I wondered again what had happened between them all last year.

"And that man?" Chloe asked.

"That hasn't happened before," Noah said. "Ari…"

"We have poison," I told her. "Inside us. I saw him lunging for you and…"

And I hadn't even thought, hadn't planned. Simply reacted, like a strakirin would. Like the creature that had owned my body until just a short time ago.

My stomach twisted.

"You saved my life."

I looked back up at Chloe. I gave a small shrug, uncertain what to say.

"Ari has been helping us," Ezio said. "The leaders of her people and the Driecarans are working together to start a war. That's what this was. What the man we interrogated at the garrison was doing too. An attempt to destabilize Yvaria and the rest of the oceanic nations as well."

"By killing me and making it look like Kreyus was responsible." She turned away, going quiet.

Noah shifted uncomfortably. "They wanted to drive Zeke to—"

"I know."

Silence fell. Discomfort nagged at me, suddenly making me want to swim for the window. For the open water beyond the city. And maybe just keep going.

I fidgeted. That wouldn't help anything.

Chloe looked over her shoulder to me. "You said we. '*We* have poison.'"

My mouth moved for a second before I found the words. "The judges—the leaders of my people—made more. After me."

"Those ones aren't on our side," Noah added quietly.

"They might be dead, though."

At least, some part of me hoped they were.

Chloe let out a slow breath, clearly processing the words. "And if they're not?"

"Then they're going to be chasing a weapon," Noah said. "Some source of power the judges think will let them… well, basically rule the world."

Chloe stared at him.

"We were chasing them," I told her. "They—um, *we*—have these stealth abilities like he does." I twitched my head toward Noah. "No one else can see past them, but I… I can. Commander Damerion and the other Yvarians were going to stop them, or at least call reinforcements once we found them."

Chloe stared at me too. Escaping out the window became even more tempting.

She turned to Noah. "Do you know why I'm here?"

"You're on your way to see Kreyus, to try to strengthen the alliance between the Ivalaen and Yvaria. Zeke told me."

"Did he tell you about the attacks? The ones made to look like Yvarians did it? Besides the one on Ari's people, I mean?"

He nodded.

She echoed the motion. "And now they're pretending to be Vetorians. This is everywhere, isn't it?" She directed the question toward Ezio as much as us.

"We don't know how far their reach extends," Ezio admitted.

The words seemed to confirm something for her. "Then we need to get to Kreyus. Now. If these others like Ari are still alive, you're going to need backup, and I…" She chuckled, nothing humorous in the sound. "I'm not going to let these people use me to hurt Zeke. *Ever.*"

"Yes, valya Praelex." Ezio headed for the door.

Chloe swam after him, only to pause before passing me. "Does it kill anyone to touch you?"

I blinked. "N-no." Honesty won out. "Not if I'm careful."

She paused. "Okay." Chloe extended a hand. "It's nice to meet you, Ari. Really. I'm—" Her eyes twitched to Noah for a second. I wasn't sure why. "I'm just really glad to meet you."

Uncertain what was going on, I took her hand and shook it. She smiled. The expression didn't look unfriendly. Just… glad, like she said.

I didn't know what to make of it.

She released my hand and swam for the door.

I turned to Noah, confused.

He was watching her like he wasn't sure what that'd been about either.

"Are you okay?" I asked quietly. "When you grabbed that

man, did he…"

Noah glanced at me. "No. No, I'm good."

I nodded at the words, though I wasn't sure he noticed it. Still appearing distracted, he headed for the exit, checking only to make sure I was with him.

I bit my lip and followed, still wishing I could swim away from this.

✺ 24 ✺

NOAH

In the end, I shifted form and brought the others with me across the long distance to Kreyus's location. It was faster, after all, and safer too. The strakirin couldn't detect Ari that way, plus we needed to save what time we could over the miles and miles of seafloor.

And I didn't want to get caught up in conversation, regardless.

Chloe had been acting odd right before we left. Looking at me and Ari in this way that made it seem like she was saying something without saying something, even if I had no clue what that could be. I supposed I might have been misreading it. She might have simply been friendly to Ari—which was good, really. Of course it was good. So maybe they'd been fine.

Ari had looked nervous.

Well, but that made sense, though. Her appearance worried her, which was understandable even if unnecessary. She *was* the only strakirin most of these dehaians had ever seen. And then there was the whole "tried to stop a guy only to have him go

Terminator" thing to consider. I would have been nervous too. So maybe I was overreacting. Reading too much into… something. I didn't know what. Probably nothing.

Chloe had still seemed odd.

A magical veil brushed the edge of my senses, indicating a settlement nearby, and the sensation was almost a relief. My thoughts had been spinning in useless circles for so long that, if I were still greliaran, I would've had a headache. Meanwhile, my Beast side seemed so uncomfortable with the flood of emotions and confusion that, if it could have reconsidered this whole "the two of us working together to be alive" thing, it might have.

It didn't know what to make of these feelings. I'd loved Chloe. I had. But that didn't help make sense of what was going on inside me now.

The Beast side of me would really rather focus on the straki-rin. The enemy. Something I knew what to do with—even if, most likely, that just meant kill. We were in potentially hostile territory, though, hunting monsters that could kill people with a single touch. Right now, that felt better than dealing with what was in my head or whatever remained of my heart.

Slowing to a speed that wouldn't hurt the others, I let them go and then drew back down into human form. "So Kreyus will be where?" I asked immediately.

"Center of the city," Ezio said. "This way."

I followed him, moving too quick and outdistancing Ari and Chloe within a heartbeat.

Aggravation gnawed at me, and I slowed back down, cursing

myself silently. The Driecarans had infiltrated the Vetorians, the Yvarians, and probably everywhere else in the damn ocean at this rate. And that didn't even bring into it what the murderers-for-hire ahead of us would think of Ari the moment they laid eyes on her. This wasn't the time to be excitable, or distracted.

A jumble of garbage long ago discarded from the world above came into view, but at its heart rested a sunken aircraft carrier, hulking in its size and in remarkably good shape considering its location at the bottom of the sea. Several hundred yards off lay part of a plane wreck too, the body of the plane cracked open like a nut. Only one wing remained attached, sticking up in the water like a grave marker. Both the ship and the plane rested against a collection of boulders so enormous, they had to be at least a hundred stories high.

The tingling sensation of a veil passed around us, and the barren seafloor around the debris came to life, revealing a city that Ezio and Chloe called Periantrea. Home of the Ivalaen clan, or at least, one of their homes in the vast expanse of the Prijoran Zone. There were stalls inside the plane wreck, with what looked like everything from weapons to food for sale. Tall, thin leaves blocked countless caves in the sides of the massive boulders, while other plants blocked openings in the sunken ship. In jarring contrast to the permanence of the boulders or even the wreckages, tents filled the area around the structures. Fire pits with blue-white flames dotted the spaces between the tents, leaving an impression as if the majority of the city was prepared to relocate at a moment's notice. Dehaians swam everywhere, calling back and forth in the plane wreck market, chatting in the pathways between the tents. Like Ezio, scars covered all of them, and weapons too.

Vetorians. Not that there'd been any doubt. Though how many of them were Driecaran spies in hiding…

Drifting back, I stayed closer to Ari and Chloe, avoiding both of their gazes. Around us, I could see people stopping to stare at me, at Ari, even at Chloe while the three of us trailed Ezio toward the sunken aircraft carrier.

Uncomfortable didn't *begin* to describe this.

We swam toward a gaping hole in the side of the ship, the opening blocked by leaves. Two guards hovered on either side—seeming redundant when everyone around us was armed—but they were probably only there to make it clear that someone important was inside. Mostly for show and all that.

Very lethal, and mostly for show.

"We are here to see Praelex Kreyus," Ezio said to them. "Please tell him his daughter has arrived."

The two men glanced at each other, then to me and Ari.

"You brought the *Beast*?" one of them asked Ezio archly.

"Apologies." Ezio beamed, his sudden smile like the glint of sunlight on a knife. "I didn't realize I worked for you." He gave the statement a moment to sink in. "Now, as I said. Please inform the Praelex that his daughter has arrived."

The men glared, but after a moment, the one who'd asked the question turned and slipped past the leaves into the ship.

Ezio ignored them, surveying the camp.

A minute crawled past. The man returned.

"He awaits you inside."

"Wonderful." Ezio swam through the opening and inside the ship.

I could feel the two guards scowling at us while we followed him.

From light fixtures on the walls, tiny blue-white flames flickered inside the remains of lightbulbs long since shattered. The hall was narrow—and an easy spot for an ambush, the Beast side of me observed. On either side of us, doors hung from their hinges or were missing entirely while pipes stretched overhead, their use unknown. Holes peppered the ceiling, and more dotted the floor. Whatever had killed the ship only explained part of the damage. Age and the seafloor were slowly taking care of the rest.

A single guard waited outside the door at the end of the hall, two swords crossed over his chest and his focus somewhere in the space beyond us all. Without a word, he sheathed one of the blades and then took the door handle, twisting it open for us to go inside.

The room beyond him was as lavish as anything I'd seen in Nyciena.

I blinked, my attention darting over the space while we swam inside. Blue-white flames lit the enormous room, burning inside jewel-encrusted stands bolted to the floor. Chandeliers hung in rows along the ceiling, glistening with gemstones of a thousand colors. More gems had been sewn into richly colored tapestries on the walls, each stone catching every scrap of light and casting it back in a riotous rainbow.

I suddenly knew what it would be like to be inside a kaleidoscope.

Thick rugs covered the floor beneath us, all of them woven of deep shades of green, purple, and bronze. Cushions clustered at various points in the room, providing seating for attendees and guests—in other words, probably us—while Kreyus himself sat upon a metal throne formed of intricate twists of steel accented by gold and silver. Two more guards hovered nearby, and like the ones outside—really, like the gemstones and the braziers and the throne itself too—their purpose seemed to be only for show.

When I'd met Chloe's father last year, he'd been hiding out with his Vetorians inside barren caves in Yvarian territory, most likely sleeping on a camping mat. Besides weapons and enough Ivalaen mercenaries to take on an army, he'd had nothing at all.

And he'd looked equally deadly. The decadent display was artifice. A game to project to visiting dignitaries how powerful and rich his people truly were. Even the ship itself played into the vision—steel and defensive on the outside, albeit damaged, but a war machine all the same. But none of the show really mattered. None of it was necessary. There was nothing soft about Praelex Kreyus. Nothing weak either. Sitting on a steel throne or on a rock in a barren wasteland, he still radiated the message that he was a force to be reckoned with and entirely in control.

"You have an interesting interpretation of the order to keep my daughter safe, Ezio vel Oryan." Kreyus's gaze ghosted over us indicatively, pausing only slightly longer on Ari than on the rest of us.

"It wasn't his fault," Chloe interjected before Ezio could speak. "The garrison at the Cylian Pass was attacked. Ezio had learned my life was in danger. He, Noah, and Ari helped save me."

"Indeed."

I couldn't read anything from Kreyus's tone.

"And the ones who threatened your life?"

"In Yvarian custody in Teariad, Praelex," Ezio said. "There were… complications. But several are dead and the survivor is secured."

"Triya and Ilya," Chloe explained. "They tried to kill me. Venika stopped Ilya, and I, uh, did too. But there were others. Ari and Noah stopped those."

"I see." Kreyus was silent for a moment. "And where is Venika? I notice she has not accompanied you."

"She's alive," Chloe replied. "Hurt, but alive. The doctors in Teariad are helping her."

He nodded once, but like everything else, I couldn't read what he thought of the statement. Did he care that Venika had been hurt? Was that why he asked? He and Venika had been involved with each other; I remembered that from last year. And if he trusted her enough to have her be his daughter's bodyguard, I assumed they still had some sort of relationship.

But the man was a closed book—one wrapped in chains and padlocked for good measure.

Kreyus's attention turned to me. "What a pleasure to see you again." He smiled, the expression measured. "Noah."

His tone was the same. Just this side of neutral, just that side of friendly, but not quite either.

I gave a small nod of acknowledgment. We were all friends here.

Right.

The Beast side of me growled, taking stock of the room, the exits, the chance of grabbing everyone before Kreyus could order his people to hurt anybody.

Kreyus's smile grew. "And would this be Ari, then?" he asked Chloe, twitching his hand toward Ari.

Chloe nodded.

"Interesting."

I didn't like his tone.

"And now you are all here. May I assume this is because you wish my help as well?"

"Yes, Praelex," Ezio said. "We require forces to continue pursuing those we know are responsible for the attacks against civilian and political targets in Yvaria and beyond. We believe they may cross through Ivalaen territory, searching for a weapon. With the Beast's help, we intend to stop them."

"Ah."

I waited, but nothing else came. "Well?" I prompted.

Kreyus regarded me.

"You agreed to help Zeke," Chloe said, her voice meticulously calm. "To provide support in figuring out who is behind these attacks."

His gaze slid to her. Chloe watched him. A tremendous amount seemed to be unspoken in that single look, and I couldn't interpret a bit of it.

What a difference a year made.

Kreyus smiled, his attention returning to us. "True. Of course, we did not discuss the Beast himself appearing in my city with a creature I doubt anyone has ever survived seeing."

Alarm prickled through me. How would he know that?

Ari shifted uncomfortably.

Kreyus regarded us as if curious and yet mildly amused. "Is my statement untrue?" he asked innocently. "I have, after all, heard reports of strange creatures passing near Yvarian territory. Rumors, only, and those who send distress signals do not survive to elaborate upon their stories." He paused. "The latest story came in mere hours ago."

A small breath left Ari. I kept myself from reacting, as best I could. But they were alive. Some of the strakirin had survived.

If Kreyus was telling the truth, anyway.

Kreyus appeared to know exactly how his words affected her—and the rest of us. "Given that I have never laid eyes on someone quite like her, for Ari to be anything other than one of these creatures seems… well, entirely unlikely, wouldn't you agree?"

The Beast side of me growled internally.

"Will you help?" Chloe asked, a hard note in her voice.

Kreyus's focus returned to her. She didn't blink.

He smiled. I'd swear there was a hint of pride in the expression. "I will keep my promise. Of course," he added, "it will take some time to gather enough forces."

I bit back a scoff. Seriously? He had a camp full of—

He seemed to read my expression. "My people here are needed for the defense of this encampment, and for the defense of the locations to which they are traveling. But worry not, Noah," he said my name like a concession to politeness, like he'd just as soon call me Beast, "it will only take a few hours, perhaps a day at most. And I'm certain you'll help us if we need to defend ourselves in the meantime."

"Thank you," Chloe said before anyone else could speak.

Kreyus smiled again. "Your tent remains as always, my dear. And for your… allies… I will have other tents prepared."

A pause followed. I knew what he wanted, and it annoyed me, but I said it anyway. "Thank you."

His smile broadened. "Indeed. Ezio…" He gave a sharp look to the mercenary. "…stay. I wish to hear more about these betrayers who threatened my daughter's life."

Chloe turned while Ezio nodded. She motioned for us to leave ahead of her.

"A pleasure meeting you, Ari," Kreyus called, "and seeing you again… Noah."

I left. Outside, one of the mercenaries was waiting as if they'd been there the whole time.

"If you will come this way?" the woman said to Ari, gesturing down a row of tents. "We have prepared you a place to rest."

Ari nodded. "Thanks."

I wasn't sure what to do, so I followed.

"Noah," Chloe called from behind me.

I hesitated before glancing back.

"Can we talk?"

I didn't know what to say.

Ari bit her lip, clearly uncomfortable. "I'll be down there."

Before I could protest, she swam after the woman toward a smaller tent at the end of the row. The woman held the flap for her, saying something I couldn't hope to pick up without my long-gone greliaran hearing. Ari nodded and then disappeared inside without a backward glance.

Leaving me nowhere to go.

I crossed the distance to Chloe. She nodded toward the decorated tent behind her and then pushed past the flap to go inside. I followed. The interior was like a cloth-walled version of the rooms in a palace, complete with decorations on tables and cushions for sitting.

Chloe was hovering in the middle of the space, her fingers clasping and unclasping near her waist.

"What did you want to talk about?" I asked.

Chloe cast a quick look to the door. "That's her? The, uh… the wizard girl you helped get back to her hotel a few weeks ago?"

She wanted to talk about Ari? I made a hedging noise, suddenly fighting the urge to drift backward toward the tent flap. This wasn't what I—

"It is, isn't it?" Chloe prompted, watching me.

I wondered what she could feel through our connection. I wasn't coming close to it, and hadn't, beyond using it to discover where to find her in the palace back at Teariad. It'd been different a few weeks ago. Maybe even different a few days ago.

But now, when Ari was right in front of me and yet I couldn't feel anything from her, when every moment with her was proof that the link I'd shared with her really was gone… something inside me shied away from my connection to anyone anymore.

Chloe was waiting for an answer.

"Yeah."

She hesitated. "You really care about her."

Forget the connection. I wasn't really comfortable with this non-conversation anymore. "Look, I need to—"

"I'm happy for you."

I hesitated.

"And it's good to see…" she continued. "I mean, that you… you're…" She seemed to give up whatever she'd been trying to say. "I'm really happy for you."

I didn't know how to respond. "Okay."

A second dragged past, full of the pressure to say something, but I didn't know what.

I turned for the tent flap. "I'm going to—"

"Noah."

The hurt in her voice pulled me up short. I glanced over my shoulder at her.

"We never had a chance to…" She crushed her clasped fingers to her lips. "After what happened last year, or even when I saw you a few weeks ago at the palace, I didn't…" Her eyes closed briefly. "I just wanted to say I'm sorry. And thank you."

I blinked, incredulous. "For what?"

"For everything. All of it, Noah. Every—" She cut off, her voice breaking. "Every single thing you did. We're alive because of you. All of us. You know that, right?"

I wasn't sure what to say.

"But it cost you so much. I used to be able to feel you out there in the water sometimes, in the distance, and it hurt. I worried that… that maybe you were just becoming a remnant of the person I knew. A ghost—"

I tensed, anger flaring up to hear my old fears now coming from her.

"But you're not," she hurried to add. "You're just you, aren't you?"

There wasn't much question in the question. More like simply an opportunity to agree.

"Mostly."

She hesitated. "I hated to think I'd killed you."

Confusion hit me. The Beast killed me. I killed me. It was still a mess in my head, how half of me killed the other half and yet didn't. But never in any of it had I thought she'd been to blame.

I'd made my choices. Then the Beast made one too.

"You didn't," I said.

Her hurting expression lingered.

"Chloe, you didn't."

A moment passed before she nodded. "And Ari, she… you're happy?"

My mouth moved, no words coming out. I didn't know how to answer that, or whether I even should. I'd loved Chloe. Died to save her. I'd dreamed of the two of us together, back before everything went sideways and life as I'd known it was gone forever. To tell her I'd let that go, that somewhere along the line, I'd found myself moving on… I didn't know how.

But I didn't feel the same about her anymore. I cared about her, yes, but it was different now. And I knew she didn't feel the same about me either—

At least I thought she didn't. I looked back up at her, suddenly wary of where this might be going. "Are you happy with Zeke?"

She appeared startled. "That's not what I—Noah, I wasn't—" She stopped. "I love him."

It didn't hurt.

I blinked, the realization slowly suffusing me. It didn't hurt. It really didn't. Those words, the truth of them that I could hear in her voice. It wasn't painful.

It was just… good.

I nodded. "I'm glad."

She watched me and then nodded as well, a tiny motion. "I *am* happy. I mean, the royalty thing is weird as hell, but—"

I chuckled in spite of myself.

Chloe grinned.

The moment hung between us, weirdly calm. Weirdly comfortable.

"I am," I said to her. "Happy, I mean. It's just…"

Lonely.

My mouth closed on the statement. I couldn't say it. Didn't want to explain. There was an ache inside where the link had been between me and Ari, one that felt like part of myself was gone now. One that, no matter how close I was to her, never seemed to go away.

But that felt like too much to share.

"Hard," I finished. "With these judge bastards after her and the strakirin…"

Chloe nodded. "If there's anything I can do…"

"Thank you."

She smiled.

Outside, voices carried as one of the Vetorians called to another. I shifted slightly in the water, glancing toward the sound. "I should probably get back—"

"Yeah."

I hesitated, feeling awkward, and then started for the tent flap.

"Noah."

I stopped and looked back.

She smiled again, that cock of her lips that used to make my heart stutter.

Now it was only friendly to see.

"I really am happy for you," she said.

I could hear that she meant it. I smiled back. "You too."

The Vetorians eyed me when I left Chloe's tent, but none of them seemed inclined to do more than watch while I drifted along the barren strip of seafloor that led down to the tent where I'd seen Ari go. I wondered if they would stare less if I tried to make myself look like a dehaian, or maybe walked like a human, though both felt awkward in different ways.

They'd probably stare regardless.

I reached the tent and hesitated, unsure what to do. I couldn't exactly knock, but it wasn't like she'd be changing clothes or something.

The thought was distracting. "Ari?"

"Yeah?" She sounded distracted too.

"Can I come in?"

She hesitated. "Sure."

I pushed the flap aside, peering into the tent. It was sparser than the one Chloe occupied—logical, considering she was the daughter of the Vetorian king or whatever—but it still had cushions on the floor and short tables and a roll of woven seaweed in the corner that dehaians used like camp beds.

Ari was seated on the ground, her eel-like tail wrapped around her with more of a sinuous bend than any dehaian could hope to achieve. "Everything okay?" she asked.

"Uh, yeah. I was just checking if you were alright."

"I'm fine."

I wasn't sure what to do. I floated in, letting the tent flap drift shut behind me. "Look, if you want me to see if they could find you somewhere farther out or, you know, closer to the center of camp…"

I was floundering. I didn't know what she wanted. Which I would prefer, if I were in her shoes.

Or whatever.

Ari shook her head. "This is fine."

She bit her lip. I waited.

"Your talk with Chloe go okay?" she asked.

I didn't quite glance to the tent flap. "Yeah."

It had. It really had.

But for some reason, Ari looked nervous.

The lack of empathic connection between us felt like an impassible gulf inside me, full of emptiness and confusion and problems for which I had no solutions.

I tried to ignore the feeling. "Look, if you were resting or—" I cut off as tension flashed over her face. "What?"

"Nothing. I wasn't…" She made a "whatever" kind of noise. "Dehaians don't need sleep, right? Or strakirin too, apparently. At all. Ever."

I blinked.

"I rest," she said. "But not like…" Her head twitched to the bed.

I recognized the words. I'd said them, after all, not long after the judges first connected us. After Ari and I first met.

"Like me, then?" I asked.

Ari nodded, seeming uncomfortable. "But yeah, if you need to get back to…"

"Huh?"

"Well, if she had things she needed you to—"

"Who? Chloe?"

Ari shrugged, a sort of pained look flitting through her eyes.

"She just—" What the hell was this? "Why would she—"

Ari rose from the ground with a small undulation of her tail, only to turn away from me. "Sorry. Right. No. Yeah. Just—" She didn't quite look at me, her pained expression strengthening.

"I'm fine here. Thanks."

I was lost. Missing something. Now that the connection between us was gone, I felt as flatfooted as the guy I'd been a lifetime and one not-quite-death ago, trying to understand a girl who wouldn't tell me what was upsetting her.

Or what I could hope to do about any of it.

"What's wrong, Ari?"

"Nothing."

Bullshit.

Water moved around me. I crossed the distance toward her.

She turned away further, and I stopped.

"What is it?" I pressed.

Her shoulders sagged. "Everything."

Indecision held me for a second, and then I reached out, pulling her gently around toward me.

She wouldn't meet my eyes. "I miss you." Her voice was so soft I could barely hear it. "That's all."

My chest ached. I lifted a hand to her chin, urging her face up toward me.

Her green-yellow eyes were full of pain.

I kissed her. I didn't know what I was doing. Didn't have a plan or a hope that this would help anything at all.

But maybe it could do something.

She tensed for a moment, only to melt against me. Her lips parted, inviting me in, and I immediately took her up on the offer. My hand slipped up through her hair, the glowing golden strands twining around my fingers, and it was amazing. A faint tingle of magic coursed through them. I didn't even know if she was aware of it.

And then she pulled away.

I blinked at her, confused. She turned, avoiding my eyes again, her hands coming up to smooth at her hair as if the water wouldn't make the strands float in a thousand directions no matter what she did.

"What?" I managed.

"I'm sorry, I just—" She gave up on her hair. "I know you just got done talking to your, you know… I mean…"

I couldn't keep the confusion from my voice. "Chloe?"

That pained expression came back.

A possibility slowly spread over me. I felt like the world's biggest idiot—miles-wide magical form notwithstanding.

"Are you thinking Chloe and I…" I didn't want to guess it. "What?"

"Nothing. I wasn't—"

A sound of disbelief escaped me. She kept saying that, and I knew it wasn't true. I swam closer to her.

"Ari, she's in love with Zeke." I took her hand. "And I'm…"

The words stalled. I didn't even know why. Because they were huge. Because they were important. Because the first and last time I'd ever said them to a girl, I thought I was saying goodbye to her and to a life I'd never get to have, right after I'd sort of died.

Because they felt different this time around.

The realization brought with it a strangely peaceful feeling. It wasn't that I hadn't meant it, last time when I told Chloe I loved her. I had. And if things had worked out between us, if our paths had stayed together, those feelings would have probably remained.

But our paths hadn't. We hadn't. I'd changed, my life had changed, and in her own way, she had too. And when we didn't pass through all those changes together, ultimately, we'd changed into two people who still cared about each other and probably always would, but who didn't fit that way anymore.

Then I'd met Ari, and it all fit again. This new person I'd become, not only because of the Beast, but because of life and growth and all those things… fit with her. Had a home with her inside whatever remained of my heart. It wasn't the same as it'd been with Chloe, but that was okay because *I* wasn't the same.

And the feeling was amazing. Breathtaking. And every bit as real and true and good.

"I'm not in love with her," I said. Ari looked up at me. "I'm in love with you."

Her lips parted, her mouth falling a tiny bit open, while she stared at me with those green-yellow, utterly still-her eyes. "But," she floundered. "I thought maybe—"

I bent and kissed her again. "Thought what?" I asked when I drew back.

She blinked, seeming to search for an answer. "I don't know." Her gaze skipped over the tent and the cushions and everything around us. "You have that link to her and not to me, and I didn't know if—"

"That doesn't change anything."

For once, empathic abilities didn't mean a damn—but only

to the point where I could tell she wasn't sure of my answer. I could see it all over her face.

"Ari, that's not why I have these feelings for you."

She turned away, drifting farther in the water.

Anxiety wormed into me. "Do you not—" My mouth moved, a needle of pain stabbing me. "I'm not saying you have to feel the same way, I'm only—"

She whirled toward me, alarm in her eyes. "It's not that."

I waited, unsure whether I wanted to hear the truth.

Her fingers twisted around one another, wringing each other into a chokehold. "Do you miss it?" she asked softly.

"Miss…?"

She looked at me like she couldn't believe I didn't understand the question. Like it hurt that I didn't. "The connection."

I wasn't sure what to say. Yes? Desperately and more than words could describe? But it terrified me too. It could hurt her. Those judges *had* hurt her. And the strakirin…

"Do you?" I asked back.

She nodded.

It was so hard to see the pain in her eyes.

"We could," she started, "you know, try to see if—"

I was already shaking my head no. "It's too dangerous."

"But what if it isn't? What if…" Her hands gestured in frustration only to drop to her sides. "I was trapped, Noah. The monster they made me into was in *all* of my head. It was everywhere… except one place. One tiny place, and I think I know what it was. You. The last trace of that space in my mind where you and I were linked. It saved me. So what if, you know…"

I wanted to believe her. I *did* believe her. It just didn't change the rest of it. "But the strakirin. What the judges did. Ari, that's what the hive mind is, isn't it? Our connection. Same thing."

She looked away.

"I'm right, aren't I?"

She ground her teeth, glaring at nothing. "I hate this."

Confused, I waited for her to go on.

"I hate the… the *quiet*. The feeling like—" Her jaw worked around. "Like there's this space inside of me that's dead now. Cold. *Wrong*. Like an old, dried-up tree trunk or something, and it used to be so alive."

I knew exactly what she meant.

"I want it back, Noah. Chloe has it. Baylie has it. And maybe it's stupid or childish or just damn jealous, but I want it too. I miss that feeling. I want that part of myself back again."

"But the hive—"

"Isn't this!"

My mouth slammed shut.

She glared at me. "The space in my mind that saved me wasn't connected to them. It wasn't *them*. It was us. You. Me and you and what we had. And it's empty now. And I feel it, like somebody cut off a limb. I feel it every time I look at you, and I just—"

I moved through the water and wrapped my arms around her. She curled her fingers into a fist against my chest in frustration. Holding her close, I ran my hand over her hair, smoothing the faintly glowing strands down even as others floated back up again.

"What if this is part of us, Noah?" she whispered. "What if everything changed a year ago? This empathic connection ability you have, the one the dehaians built into the Beast when they first created it—what if it changed when you became like you are now? And then, when the judges forced me to take in your magic and changed me like they did, I became a little bit like you too? And then when they linked us up like that… what if they weren't twisting something around? What if the strength of that connection wasn't only something they created? What if this is… natural to us?"

I didn't know what to say. Natural? Something like me was anything but natural, and that didn't even bring into it what the judges had done to her. To think we had some innate part of ourselves meant to connect like that with someone, with *each other*…

It was impossible.

But God, I wanted it to be true.

The Beast side of me stirred, ready to reach out for her. Ready to find a way to reconnect us, even if every time before had been an accident or the judges' design. There had to be a way, it whispered. She was like me, but not like me. The Beast side of myself had known that for so long.

But I had no idea how to do it, or even if I should.

Ari shook her head. "Maybe I'm crazy. I just—"

"Miss it."

She looked up at my whisper. "Do you?"

I turned my face away, my jaw clenching against the desire to say yes. More than yes. That it felt like something inside me had died when the connection between us broke apart.

"Noah?"

"I almost lost you," I said softly. "I saw that… that *thing* they tried to turn you into take over your eyes, your face. The face I—" I faltered, the memory gripping my words in a choke-hold. "I love. And it was terrible. I went for weeks, afraid you might be dead. That they'd decide they didn't need you alive. That I wouldn't be able to bring you back again. And now that I've found you…"

I shook my head. "I want it back, Ari. I do. But we were losing ourselves to that, even before Shannon triggered the rest of what the judges planned. And I will *not* risk losing you again. I can't see that thing take you over again, or be the reason you disappear for good if something goes wrong. I can't." Everything in me ached. "Please."

She was quiet for a long moment. So quiet I wasn't sure she'd respond.

"Promise me something, then."

"What?"

She looked up at me. "If anything happens, if the strakirin find me and I… I start to lose myself to them… Try. Please. For me, because maybe it might stop them, and maybe it might save me, and maybe…" Her gaze flicked away for a moment like she was searching for answers. "I don't want to die, Noah. I don't. But if I do, I'd rather die as Ari and I'd rather die with you. Because they're death too."

I stared at her.

"*Promise* me, Noah. Please."

I didn't know what to say. That wouldn't happen. It couldn't. The strakirin taking her back. Ari dying. It was too horrible.

Her expression grew beseeching. Desperate.

And there wasn't anything else I could say.

"I promise."

∽ 25 ∾

BAYLIE

"Slow down, goddammit," Declan swore. "You're going to run us off this pathetic excuse for a road."

The resistance soldier driving our SUV slowed, though only by a little. Nervous energy radiated from the man like heat waves—a sort of creepily accurate description, given the fact that I could see sweat dripping from his temple. In the rearview mirror, he kept casting quick looks at us, and had ever since we left the resistance hideout.

Though, really, who was I kidding? He'd been almost entirely watching me. Word traveled fast, apparently, and his first question to Declan had been about whether or not I was "safe."

Me. *Safe*.

My stomach twisted, and quickly I turned my attention back to the window and the dark night outside. Pine trees raced past, black blurs way too close for comfort. Branches swiped the sides of the white SUV, almost certainly scratching the paint job, not that the soldier seemed to care. We'd been speeding down the gravel track leading to Olivia's hideout in northwestern Montana for the better part of an hour, without any sign of civilization or our destination alike.

An itch crept over my skin, and absently, I scratched at it. I knew it was nothing—nothing physical, anyway. It was the same feeling I'd struggled with all year, the same feeling that had dragged me from Kansas all the way to California.

I needed the ocean.

"You okay?" Jace whispered.

I nodded. What else was I supposed to say? That I felt like crawling out of my own body? That I wanted to cry because the air felt too heavy, too sluggish, too lacking in something I couldn't even identify?

A hand brushed mine, and my breath caught. I glanced over. Jace's fingers were only an inch from my own. A solemn expression on his face, he was watching me. Beyond him, Ellie was doing the same.

I could see the question in his eyes. I shook my head, a tiny jerk, and pulled my hand away.

"We're here," Ellie said softly.

I turned back to the front. The wall of trees on either side of us finally broke, revealing a broad expanse of yard beneath a sliver of moon and distant stars. Small, round bushes like green balls lined the pale gravel drive, leading up to an oversized, two-story log cabin of a house. A wraparound balcony circled the second level, while the sloping roof turned several of the upper floor windows into triangles. A porch light glowed near the front door, and golden light spilled from windows through-out the house.

The soldier pulled the SUV to a stop and climbed out faster than anyone else. Declan muttered something under his breath, too low for me to make out the words, and then followed.

"Lot of help he's going to be," Jace said, watching them both go.

I wasn't sure which one he meant. Maybe both.

Probably both.

We got out. The night was quiet around us, with only the faint noises of summer bugs and bats fluttering in the darkness. Our feet on the gravel drive sounded so loud while we walked toward the house, and I couldn't help the way my eyes went to the shadows of the forest around Olivia's new place.

Nothing moved there. Nothing I could see. There wasn't any reason to think the judges would have followed us, either.

The reality of that didn't stop my stomach from twisting.

At Declan's order, the soldier approached the door first and knocked.

Olivia answered a moment later. "Hello!" She gave us all a surprised look. "You certainly made great time. I wasn't expecting you for another hour."

Declan cast a dry look to the soldier.

"Come in, come in." Olivia motioned us through the doorway. "We're just having some late night tea."

Declan stopped. "We?"

"Ah, yes. Several of the other elders are here." She continued inside.

Declan stared after her and then followed.

I didn't move. The elders were here. *Here*. Maybe that was

about the judges, or safety, or a total coincidence. Or maybe…

"Did you tell her about me?" I turned to Ellie.

She hesitated.

Holy hell. "Ellie, you said you wouldn't—"

"She guessed."

My temper faltered. "What?"

"When I called and said you were coming too, she…" Ellie made a helpless gesture. "Guessed something was different."

"W-why?" A better question hit me. "*How?*"

"I don't know. But I didn't say anything," she added hurriedly. "I just… didn't answer her questions."

And Olivia read between the lines, I finished silently. Though *what* she read was anyone's guess.

I glanced to the door. "Are you sure it's safe here?"

Ellie hesitated. "Yeah. I mean, it's Olivia. We can trust her."

The weirdest feeling of déjà vu struck me, like we'd been here before. Like we'd had this conversation before. But it wasn't me… before.

It was Chloe. It was last year.

Ellie winced like she could see what I was thinking. "I know. But Olivia wouldn't betray us. And we can probably trust the others too."

When my doubting expression didn't change, she shifted her weight uncomfortably. "I'm actually not the only one who can do what I can do. It's rare, but… there are a few. Ever since the elders heard what the judges did to Shannon, that woman who hurt Ari, the ones who have similar abilities to me have been testing the others. Using their abilities to be sure no one has been… changed." She looked toward the house. "Angelica's been here for days, so, you know, it should be okay."

I stared at her, incredulous. The elders didn't see the *thousand* things that could go wrong in that scenario, starting with this Angelica person or anyone else like Ellie being the very people the judges changed in the first place?

"But…" I tried to find the words. The judges weren't even the only thing we had to worry about. The elders didn't exactly have the greatest track record either, even if they'd never come close to the nightmare that was the Judiciary. But one of their members—Ellie's *grandfather*, no less—had experimented on Chloe and tortured Zeke last year. Some of the elders had sided with him on it all too. "If she told them about me…"

"We stick together." Jace came up beside me, his eyes on the house. "Until we're sure they don't have plans of their own."

I watched him, wary of how the words reassured me. I didn't know him that well. I barely knew him at all, a few days of chaos and a few creepy minutes of sharing magic notwithstanding.

But still, the words reassured me.

"Yeah," I agreed quietly.

He glanced at me, meeting my gaze flatly. They were like steel in the moonlight, those eyes, their stormy gray color turned to near-black metal.

Shivers ran over my skin, strangely warm.

"You all okay?" Olivia appeared in the doorway.

I flinched, the moment shattering. Taking a sharp breath, I looked toward the house.

"Yep," Ellie replied, only a heartbeat of hesitation in her

voice.

Together, we walked inside. The walls, ceiling, and floor of the entryway were all wood, much like the outside of the house, but polished and smoothed till they shone. The hanging light fixture overhead was shaped like an old-school lantern, with light bulbs instead of candles, while the deep green runner carpet extending the length of the hallway looked like a dream of grass. A staircase climbed up to the second story, affording me a view of little beyond a wall up there, while through an open door near the end of the first-floor hallway, I could hear the clink of dishes and the low murmur of conversation.

Guess that's where the elders were, then.

"So, introductions, yes?" Olivia extended a hand to Declan. "I'm Olivia, one of the elders of the landwalkers. And you are?"

Declan eyed her hand, and then his attention twitched to Ellie, weighing.

"You've heard something about us, yes?" Olivia's smile broadened. "We're safe to touch, I promise."

He took her hand, shaking it briefly with an annoyed look, as if he didn't like the fact she'd seen through his hesitation.

Jace and the soldier introduced themselves too, though the soldier kept his hands firmly at his side and only greeted her with a terse jerk of his head. Olivia's smile didn't fade at all.

"Good to see you again, Baylie," she said, turning to me.

"You too."

"How are you feeling?"

I hesitated. "Fine."

"Good, good. Just let me know if you need anything, okay?"

I wasn't sure how to respond.

Olivia motioned along the hall. "Well, this way." She smiled and then started down the corridor. We trailed her till we reached a doorway.

Half a dozen people were inside. Books and files were scattered across the long dinner table, till I could barely make out the polished wood surface. Laptops sat on the papers, askew on the uneven surface. On the few screens facing me, I could see maps, spreadsheets, and something that looked like visual displays of chemical formulas.

My skin crawled, and my eyes flicked to the people inside the room again. I recognized one of them from last summer, a white woman with long brown hair who looked like she belonged in an old photograph of the original Woodstock. Robin, I thought her name was. She'd helped us when we'd been on the run from Ellie's mad-scientist grandfather. But the others here were strangers. An Asian woman with soft eyes and a hint of what might become a welcoming smile on her face. Beaded jewelry wrapped her wrists, and multiple pendants hung from her neck, all of them ranging from assorted crystals to something that looked like a large abalone shell. A black man and woman were to her left, the man slightly in front of the woman like he was protecting her. Both held their gazes locked on me. They looked like they'd just stepped out of some upscale suburb, and like they might be a couple or related, if how close they were standing to each other was any indication. On the other side of the table was a white guy in paint-spattered pants and an equally paint-spattered t-shirt bearing the logo of a siding company I didn't recognize. The white woman next to him was dark-haired and thin like a sliver of metal, with eyes that were fixed on me like black lasers. Her dark pantsuit added to the severity of her appearance, turning her skin to a dead shade of white porcelain.

I shivered, tugging my gaze away.

"So," Olivia began. "I'm sure you all are tired, and we have rooms ready for you upstairs whenever you're ready to go to sleep. But if you could give us a moment, we have a few questions."

Of course they did.

I tried to keep the thought from touching my expression, but it was difficult. The elders always had questions. Questions upon questions, and not all of them asked nicely.

Some things never changed.

"This is inappropriate," the white woman in the pantsuit said sharply. "Have they been scanned?"

Olivia glanced at her. "We will get to that, Angelica. But Ellie has been with them, and I'm certain she—"

"The entire time?"

I couldn't quite suppress a glare. My God, that was my point exactly. They just never quit.

"Enough, I am sure." Olivia looked to Ellie for confirmation.

At Ellie's hesitation, Angelica scoffed, the sound somehow managing to be ladylike and derisive all at once. She strode past Olivia, heading for us.

I backpedaled at the same time that Jace stepped in front of me. My attention flashed between them while adrenaline made the darkness inside me flow toward the surface.

No, bad plan. Very bad—

The woman paused only long enough to pin her laser gaze on Jace, and then I heard him gasp.

"Angelica!" Olivia snapped.

Jace shivered, tension radiating through his body. He looked like his every muscle had gone rigid. Like he couldn't even breathe.

"Hey!" I tried to step around him, to get between him and the woman. "What are you—"

My arm brushed his.

A mudslide shoved past my skin. Magic as thick as a swamp poured into me, frantic and searching, reaching for me through that small contact, through that brush of skin on skin.

Instantly, cold swept out of me, rushing beneath the muddy sensation. Cold like the ocean, like the sea beneath the earth, surged out to steady the loose and frantic land magic, turning it into an island floating above the depths. And I knew it. I knew *this*, the person who held this inside themselves as if it wasn't sludge or mud at all. Just stability. Just earth, as solid and calm as the ground beneath my feet. And it wasn't like last time. It wasn't like trying to share magic or whatever Jace had done, as if we were the same thing. This was an orchestration of magic, a balance between two forces in a way that hadn't been there before. Different from each other like the earth and the sea, but able to exist together in equilibrium because they knew each other now.

And something foreign, something *else* was trying to push

through that earth.

Push through something that mattered to me.

Darkness lashed through me before I even registered the impulse, jumping from my skin to Jace's and racing through him like electricity through a wire, chasing the invader.

And finding it.

Light flashed like a circuit popping. Angelica shrieked. Stumbling back, she crashed into the table, catching herself on its side.

Jace gasped, sucking in air like he'd been on the edge of suffocating. He stumbled slightly, his arm pressing further against mine. The land magic coming from him spread across the power inside me for all of a heartbeat, warm and strong and gradually becoming more stable.

Shivers rolled through me that had nothing to do with cold. This felt… *good*.

The land magic began to retreat. Jace turned to me, eyes wide.

Heat rushed up my cheeks, turning them bright red I was sure. He seemed flustered as well, and I didn't know what to say. The light was gone, but the air burned with ozone. The darkness inside me drew back too like the ocean receding from the shore.

"Whoa," he whispered.

Angelica made a choked noise. I glanced over. She braced herself on the table, great gulping breaths rocking her chest.

Meanwhile, all the other elders stared at the ruanir.

"You okay, Angelica?" the black man asked, his voice wary.

One hand clutched to her chest, the woman looked up at me. I could see the fear in her eyes.

"She…" Angelica stammered. "The girl. She's not…" The woman pushed herself up from the table only enough to backpedal around it, away from me. "What the hell is—"

"Wizard," Declan replied.

Shock pulled my attention to him and away from the landwalkers gaping at me. A few hours ago, he'd been calling for my interrogation, and now he was saying I was one of them?

His gaze twitched to me and then back to the elders. And it clicked. If the landwalkers thought I was one of the ruanir, they'd leave everyone else alone.

A cold feeling moved through me. He was efficient, Declan was. Maybe too much so.

Because what if Angelica was right?

Shivers crept through me. I tried to push the worry away. If the soldier or Declan had wanted to betray us, they could have easily done it on the road here.

Unless they'd wanted to reach the elders too.

I shoved the worry down harder. I hated this. I hated that my life had become this. Paranoia. The possibility of betrayal.

Over and over again, the possibility of betrayal.

"Yeah, wizard," Jace seconded, shifting his weight so that he remained between me and the landwalkers. He was so close that, even if he wasn't touching me, I could feel the heat of him.

Despite everything, the warmth felt strangely good on my skin.

"Wait, Baylie is one of them too?" Robin's gaze ran over me, alarm in her eyes. "She didn't show any sign of that last—"

"Indeed," Olivia interrupted. I couldn't tell from her tone whether she believed Declan one way or the other. "Well, things can change."

I swallowed hard. Robin eyed me like she wanted to dissect me, through questions if nothing else.

"She's *not*, Olivia," Angelica insisted, almost frantic. "That wasn't like the boy. That—"

"You saying we're lying?" Jace snapped.

"I know what I felt! That *girl* is not—"

"We brought these people here for safety and shelter," Olivia cut in. "Not interrogation."

Angelica gaped at her like she was insane.

"My apologies," Olivia continued to Jace. "That was uncalled for. Are you okay?"

Jace eyed the others for a moment before he nodded, still appearing wary of all the other elders in the room.

Which was fair.

"Good." Olivia took a breath, smoothing her blouse down like she was trying to restore order to the world through the motion alone. "Well, again, I am sorry for that. We have had some trouble with your judges and their attempts to sway our people to their cause through, shall we say, forcible means. But if we turn on one another, we might as well do their work for them."

"Agreed," Declan replied coolly.

Olivia treated him to a pointed look. She didn't miss much. I remembered that too. And I doubted she trusted his agreement as far as she could throw it.

But she carried on, regardless. "Excellent. Then, if you would, we have a few questions, which I promise we will ask respectfully."

"What questions?" I asked.

"The kind that relate to this." Olivia motioned to the array of papers and books and laptops spread across the table. "We are working on a project that we believe will benefit us both, and we would like your assistance. Specifically—" She glanced back at Declan. "We would like to sample your magic."

"What?" Jace protested.

I couldn't blame him. Not after what Angelica had just done.

Olivia appeared unperturbed. "We believe we have made progress in a strategy that will allow the landwalkers—and by extension, our allies among the ruanir—to defend themselves against your Judiciary."

"A weapon," Jace said.

Olivia tilted her head in tacit acknowledgment.

"How?" Declan demanded.

"Well, that is what we need a sample of your magic for." Olivia smiled. "Our research can only get us so far. Without real-world application—"

"You want to test this weapon on one of us." The refusal in Declan's voice was blatant.

Olivia's expression didn't falter. "Not exactly. What we want is something slightly more complicated, but safer for all concerned. We believe we can extract some of your magic into a testing apparatus that we have developed with the dehaians. As you may know, we have been working with them to combine landwalker and dehaian abilities in the hope that our people could change form as the dehaians do." She turned the smile on Ellie briefly. "For that, we needed a way to test combinations of power that wouldn't harm a living being. Hence, our testing apparatus."

I swallowed hard against the knot of anxiety in my throat. She made it sound so normal, so obvious and simple, yet…

My skin crawled.

"What are you going to do?" Jace asked.

"We are going to ask you to direct some of your power into the collection devices we've developed. The dehaians are relative geniuses at creating devices that hold and focus magic—their lights, the defenses around their cities, their weapons all contain concentrated magic in one way or another. They've built a civilization upon it. From what I hear, you all are skilled at directing magic into storage objects as well. Jewelry and the like, yes? So this should be a relatively simple proposition. And then we will see how this magic reacts to what we have discovered."

"Do the dehaians know about this weapon too?" Declan asked.

My temper flared at the accusation in his voice. "They're not against us."

He treated me to a flat look.

"The Yvarians didn't—" I started.

"No," Olivia interrupted. "They don't. This is a recent development. We haven't informed them yet."

"Will you?" Declan shot back.

Olivia hesitated. "Only if required by circumstance."

"What the hell is that supposed to mean?"

"That if you turn on us," the Asian woman interjected, "we'll need all the allies we can get."

Declan glared at her.

"We are not enemies." Olivia held out her hands in a calming gesture. "Nor do we need to become so. It is true that our people fought a war, once upon a time, and it is through that history that we have found this potential defense. But we have no desire to start that war again."

Declan didn't seem convinced.

Olivia's mouth tightened briefly. "Prior to the deployment of the Beast, there were battles between the old world dehaians and the ruanir. Defenses and weapons were created. For your people, the greliarans were an example of that. For ours, well… That is what we think we have discovered. A way our dehaian ancestors might have defended against the ruanir at the time. However, while our records are… reasonably extensive, they are not without gaps. A thousand years is a long time to keep any history, especially records from the middle of a war. We are uncertain this will work. We could use your assistance to develop a weapon tailored to your judges, and no one else."

"What *kind* of weapon?" Jace asked.

"One that disables their magic. One that would weaken them to the extent that they could not harm anyone else."

"And the enforcers?" Ellie added.

"We are seeking a way to target them too."

"What about the strakirin?" Jace's tone was sharp.

Olivia hesitated. "We would appreciate your assistance with exploring options regarding that."

Jace didn't respond. *Options.* It sounded so cold.

And frightening.

"We do understand, however, that your judges' magic is not like that of a regular ruanir," Olivia continued. "It is perhaps older. More linked to your past, or some bastardization thereof. This presents us with the possibility of isolating that kind of power and affecting it without causing damage to anyone else."

Her dark eyes skimmed over me briefly, and my stomach twisted. My God, how much did she know?

"So that's why you allowed us here," Declan stated, only the barest hint of a question in his tone. "Why they're all here. Because you want to test our magic."

"What we *want*," the white guy with the contractor t-shirt cut in, "is a weapon that will stop your judges from flaying open any more of our people like frogs in a high school biology class."

Distaste flickered over Olivia's face.

"Have there been more attacks?" Ellie asked anxiously.

"Two," Olivia replied. "We were unable to save them before… well." She let out a breath. "Given we've learned that the judges seek to acquire the elders' particular type of gifts, we can hope the Judiciary will spare the others among our people, at least for a while. But in all other respects, it is obvious that time is *clearly* of the essence. We cannot be certain the Judiciary will not find one of the elders and take what we can do, no matter how well we try to hide."

I fought the urge to look to the curtain-covered windows, as if I could somehow make sure a judge or an enforcer wasn't lurking outside.

"What do you need us to do?" Jace asked quietly.

I looked over to him. He was watching Olivia, his expression somber.

"Direct some of your magic into the collection devices we have, and then provide us with any information you may possess on the differences between the judges' powers and your own. If you are willing, then we can start tomorrow, first thing after you've all had a chance to rest."

Jace nodded.

Declan scowled. "You don't have the right to agree to this, boy. Not for all of us. You give them that magic and—"

"And more people don't die. My sister might be saved. Those bastards who've been tearing the resistance apart for the better part of two *months* don't get to keep on killing. Or were you bullshitting Miguel when you complained about how the judges have been ripping into your people for weeks, driving them from hideout to hideout all the damn time?"

Declan stared. I could see Jace's chest rising and falling, his breaths coming short and fast.

"If they have a shot at making a weapon," Jace finished, "we need it too."

Declan was silent for a heartbeat. "I supervise," he said shortly, turning to Olivia. "Every step, every stage. Understood?"

Olivia nodded.

Declan echoed the motion with a single jerk of his head. "Show me what you have so far."

Olivia glanced at Robin, who shrugged and then motioned to the papers. "Research," Robin said. "Lots of it. Are you familiar with magical quantum displacement theory?"

Leaving them to their discussion, Olivia walked toward us. "I'll show you where your rooms are. Unless you'd like to stay?"

Jace turned and headed for the door. Olivia smiled, amused, and then started after him.

"Olivia," I blurted before the woman could walk fully past me.

She paused.

"You, uh… you asked Ellie about me. About…" I floundered, not really sure what had been said. "About whether this was about me, before we came. Why?"

Olivia cast a brief look back to the dining room, where Declan was listening to a description of the papers in front of him. He looked like a teacher whose student was trying to explain why a dirty napkin was their homework.

Displeasure flickered over Olivia's face, but she said nothing, motioning instead for me to follow her into the hall. "We have been tracking surges of energy," she said when we stopped again, several feet from the door. Ellie hovered nearby while Jace paused on his way to the stairs and then returned. "We don't have the technology that Ellie told me the Judiciary has, the panes of magic-charged glass that allow them to locate Noah when he is not in human form. But we have been able to hack into several weather stations and other such monitoring equipment. Some of our people are quite efficient at such things, and that enabled us to keep an eye out for odd disturbances."

"Humans see this?" Jace asked. "Saw her?"

"Magic is still energy," Olivia replied. "Take, for example, how Noah can appear as a thunderstorm. An approximation of one, anyway, albeit powered by magic rather than weather systems. But last year, during the Beast's hunt for Chloe, humans *did* detect that, after a fashion. Earthquakes beneath the water, so-called 'freak' storms that appeared and disappeared for causes unknown. They just didn't quite know what to make of it."

My stomach churned. "But… the judges. Can they—"

"The disturbance we noticed today was tiny," Olivia said. "Barely more than a few pixels-worth of color, flickering for a moment on our screens. I doubt the judges would have seen much more—but even if they did, that was hundreds of miles from here, and it ended as quickly as it began. There's no reason to think they could track you to this place."

I tried to believe the words, but it was difficult. The judges could have seen me. Seen this. Seen whatever the hell I had done. And sure, that didn't mean they could track me. After all, they couldn't track Noah when he wasn't, you know… like he could become. But what if something had changed?

What if they'd seen what just happened between Jace and me?

"And as for why I asked about you," Olivia continued. "The satellite images of the location where we spotted that flicker of magic showed devastation. Buildings destroyed, the wreckage of what may have been some kind of aircraft. And when Ellie called me shortly thereafter to report there had been an attack and she needed a place to hide not only for herself, but also for you specifically… well." Olivia gave me a kind smile. "Let's just say it was a hint something had changed with you. You were hit with quite a significant degree of magic last year, after all. You, Chloe, and your stepbrother. The effect on the two of them was clearer, but you…" She shrugged slightly. "I have been wondering, this past year, what effect that might have had on you."

"So are you saying I'm like him?" I asked weakly. "Noah, I mean?"

"No. I'm saying you might have become something else entirely. Something new to this world."

I stared. "What do you—"

"Olivia," Robin called from inside the dining room, her voice heated. "Could you please explain to this man the concept of *sharing*? He seems to have missed that lesson in preschool."

I heard Declan retort something low and heated, his angry words not carrying beyond the doorway.

A scoff escaped Olivia. "My apologies. Your rooms are upstairs, first and third doors on the right. I hope you don't mind sharing, girls. There wasn't enough space for everyone to have their own room."

"It's fine," Ellie assured her.

Olivia smiled briefly and then headed back into the dining room.

"Sleep, then?" Ellie suggested.

I nodded distractedly, barely hearing her words. Declan had called me a wizard, even though I was pretty certain he thought

I wasn't. Jace thought I might be old ruanir. And meanwhile, Olivia said I was something new. It all left me basically nowhere. As anything.

Undefinable.

"Hey." Jace leaned around, catching the corner of my eye and snapping me out of the daze. "It's okay. We'll figure it out."

I watched him, at a loss for what we could do. Share magic again? Yeah, that hadn't worked. What happened a few minutes ago, on the other hand…

My face started burning, and I covered it up with a quick nod and a hasty retreat toward the stairs. I didn't have any answers. I didn't even know what I was.

I just hoped the judges couldn't track me too.

26

ARI

I wasn't sure how long it'd been. Hours, maybe, while we lay curled up together on the seaweed mats that the dehaians seemed to use like camping beds. Time was hard to tell down here, without any sun or moon to make the hours clear. There was only twilight, eternal twilight, though I knew that without my weirdly enhanced vision, it'd be as pitch black as being trapped underground.

I nestled my cheek closer to Noah's chest, keeping my eyes closed. At any moment, the mercenaries Kreyus agreed to provide could be ready, and then we'd be on the move again. And that was good. I loved this peace, this calm, but I knew we needed to go. Based on what Kreyus had said about the rumors and reports he'd received, it was clear some strakirin had survived. Anxiety about what they were hunting for down here still nagged at me, urging me to swim for the open water, swim farther out into this vast expanse the Vetorians called the Prijoran Zone. We had to get to whatever the judges wanted first.

But it wouldn't do any good to race off without help.

Or so I told myself.

Noah pulled me a little closer, as if—even without the connection between us—he could still feel my tension.

I sighed, attempting to relax. We hadn't said much for a while, only listened to the sounds of the camp around us. The dehaians continued on, bringing in food, repairing tents, calling out questions or bantering with each other, regardless of the time. Some part of me wondered if their lack of need for sleep had evolved because they didn't have the same morning or night as humans.

But even they weren't anything like us.

The thought was painful. I was glad Noah had promised that if the hive tried to take me, he'd do what he could to restore the link between us. It wasn't what I wanted—on so many levels—but it was something, at least.

It might just save my life.

I shifted against Noah, hating the turn my mind kept taking. I was fine. Here and fine and I wanted to soak in every second of this quiet, peaceful time with him that I could. So what if the strakirin were out there? Maybe they were hurt. Maybe they'd lost those relics and had no clue where to go. Racing pell-mell into the deep wouldn't help any—

Someone shouted outside, and my eyes flew open. Pushing away from the mat, Noah sat up, his gaze locked on the tent flap.

Another shout followed, then more. They didn't sound anxious or agitated, exactly. Eager, maybe—though, with mercenaries, that could mean anything.

"Strakirin?" Noah asked me.

I shook my head. "I don't think so…"

I moved aside while he rose up and crossed toward the tent flap. Anxiety sidled back again, nibbling at the edges of my mind, irrationally urging me to ignore this and go because we were running out of time. I shoved it down and swam after him.

A group of Vetorians shot past when Noah pushed the tent flap aside. He looked toward the direction they had gone and then eased from the tent, holding one hand out to keep me behind him.

The camp was in an uproar, though I couldn't see why for a moment. And then I spotted them.

Dehaians. But in the lead, a strakirin.

I flinched at the sight, before my eyes registered the remainder of the details.

Ropes. Lots of them. The strakirin—a boy, maybe—had his arms pinned by a web of vines like the ones that had held me, back when the Yvarians had found me outside the destroyed village. The web wrapped around his chest and condensed into a stretch of ropes at his back that ran to a dehaian several yards behind him, like a leash. Vines covered the strakirin boy's eyes as well, blinding him to his surroundings, even if I wasn't sure that would stop his echolocation from working. Only the strakirin's tail was left free to keep him swimming, though his scales were bloodied by a long, deep gash.

"What the…" Noah murmured, incredulous.

I trailed Noah warily. The strakirin's head moved like he was searching, scanning, listening for something.

And then the boy's head turned toward me. His scanning motion stilled, and the blindfold seemed to mean nothing while he looked straight down to where I floated by Noah's side.

Noah muttered a curse. He moved like he wanted to pull me away but wasn't sure it'd do any good.

"You okay?" he said to me.

Shivers coursed through me, but they were only nervousness. At least, I hoped so. I couldn't hear any other strakirin nearby, and this one didn't seem to be enough on his own to break past the way I was trying to block the hive mind out.

"Yeah. I think so."

Noah drifted closer. I pulled my gaze away from the strakirin, looking instead to the dehaians while they swam closer. Bandages patched some of their sides, their tails, even their faces. A few of the dehaians lagged behind, their arms across the shoulders of their companions as if the support was the only thing keeping them afloat.

Near the center of camp, I spotted Chloe waiting at the edge of a crowd of Vetorians. Ezio hovered at her side, and though Chloe looked wary, he seemed strung tight like a thread about to snap.

"What is this?" Noah asked them both when we came closer.

Chloe glanced at us, worry in her eyes. "Not sure yet. The perimeter guards let them in. Said they're Yvar—"

Ezio gasped and then shot upward like he'd been fired from

a gun, racing for the group of dehaians. I stared, alarmed.

And then I spotted Damerion.

At the center of the group, he was giving orders to the dehaians around him, though he cut off at the sight of Ezio. Even at a distance, I could see the relief on his face.

The soldiers parted farther, letting Ezio through. The Vetorian swam up to Damerion, coming to a stop only a short distance from him. Ezio's entire body seemed to vibrate with tension. Damerion said something, and I saw Ezio nod, the motion short, sharp, tense. Ezio reached out, clasping Damerion's arm, and the commander froze, his eyes darting down toward us. Ezio spoke, drawing the commander's attention back, and after a brief hesitation, Damerion gripped his hand where it held him.

Realization hit me. Damerion hadn't wanted us to know about the two of them. For a moment I was confused, and then it clicked.

Damerion was military, Ezio was a mercenary, and both of them were only too familiar with people using loved ones as leverage. Neither of them had fully trusted us—and Damerion had distrusted Noah most of all. He'd tried to protect the person he loved by pretending there was nothing between them.

The look in his eyes now said something else entirely.

Ezio spoke again, and Damerion nodded. The two men swam down toward us together.

"Thank you," Damerion said to Noah immediately. "For saving him. You didn't have to listen to me. You did."

Noah hesitated. He gave a brief nod. "What is this?" He

gestured toward the strakirin above us.

"A necessity. Without Ari, there was no way to track the strakirin with any certainty. Thus far, we believed the boy seemed more interested in following the signal that Driecaran scum spoke of than in attacking us. Though, to find you all directly on our path…"

I could hear the implication. And meanwhile, the strakirin hadn't stopped staring at me.

"We're just glad you're alive, commander," Chloe said.

He turned a small, grateful smile on her. "Thank you, my lady. Some of us managed to reach the rear escape hatch from the garrison before the defense protocols brought the caves down. Others were not so fortunate." His expression tightened briefly, a hint of the emotions hiding beneath his military training. "Thankfully, most of the strakirin were killed in the collapse. This was the only one we found, pinned beneath a boulder at the edge of the destruction."

My eyes skirted back up toward the strakirin. The boy was still staring at me. He looked like a bloodhound, chained and leading its owners on.

Or like a puppet, and somehow he made me feel like one too.

"What forces do we have here?" Damerion asked Ezio.

"The Praelex has agreed to send several contingents with us, Ivalaens that he has known since before the Driecaran massacre. People we can trust."

Damerion nodded. "How soon can they—"

A jolt shot through me like an electrical shock in the water.

I choked on a cry, my eyes snapping toward the city limits and the endless ocean behind me.

Overhead, the strakirin prisoner started to shriek. I looked up to see him thrashing in his bonds and tugging frantically against the hold of the dehaians. He wanted to go that way too.

"What's going on?" Chloe asked.

I opened my mouth to answer, but the words never made it out, not before a second jolt hit me. The howling of the strakirin hive came with it, crashing against my mind like a sudden, inexplicable tsunami from nowhere. Across my body, my skin and scales burned. My breath scorched my throat and my vision blurred while the drone fought to break past the wall in my mind.

That way. Oh my God, we had to go that way *now*. We had to—

Hands grabbed me. I'd taken off toward the edge of the city. I struggled to pull away—it wasn't safe; *I* wasn't safe—before I caught a glimpse of the fact that Noah was the one holding me. Shock filled his eyes. His grip trembled on my arms like he felt something of this too. But it was impossible. We weren't empathically connected anymore. He shouldn't—

"What the hell, Ari?" he asked.

I twitched my head in a frantic shake, all the motion I could manage. Relief flickered in me for his presence, though, and for the fact he was keeping me from swimming like hell for the open ocean right this second. But we still had to go. We had to, and I didn't even know why. But it was *important*. Vital. My God, I'd die if we didn't—

The impulse drained.

I choked on a breath, my vision clearing further while the compulsion to leave suddenly melted away, returning to whatever normal was for me these days. The shrieks of the strakirin behind me faded as well. I looked over to find it hanging among the tatters of its leash like it had exhausted itself. Five dehaians held the rope, all of them clearly having been fighting to keep the strakirin from swimming away.

"Ari," Noah said.

"You felt that too?" I rasped.

He was silent for a heartbeat while he helped me back toward the others. "Something. I don't know. What happened?"

"I'm not sure. I…" A terrible, sneaking suspicion settled into me, sending goosebumps over my skin and turning my stomach to lead. The signal. The Driecaran had talked about a signal. And all I'd wanted to do since Teariad was swim deeper into the ocean, though I'd believed it was simply anxiety every time.

And now this. "I think they found it."

"Did that tell you what 'it' is?" Chloe asked.

I shook my head.

"We have to go," Damerion said. "Now."

I wanted to tell him he sounded like a strakirin. I doubted he'd find it funny.

I closed my eyes, fighting back the hysteria bubbling through me while I tried to shore up the wall in my mind to keep the drone out. But holes had been blown through my defenses, great gaping ones as if from cannonballs. I felt like I was patching them with tissue paper.

Tears welled in my eyes. I struggled to make them stop.

"How soon can Kreyus have those Vetorians ready?" Noah asked.

"Now."

I opened my eyes to see Chloe's father swimming toward us. His cold gaze twitched between me and the strakirin above—weighing, evaluating—and I could read his displeasure in the way his mouth thinned.

"Commander Damerion. I see you felt fit to bring this creature here without my permission."

"Our mission required it, and King Zekerian *did* have your blessing to assist with that mission."

"As you, my daughter, and her friends continue to remind me. Clearly, I will have to be more stringent in my stipulations regarding my agreement next time."

Chloe looked away with a wince.

Damerion ignored the tone. "Which way?" He directed the words to me.

I pointed.

"Then with your blessing," Damerion continued to Praelex Kreyus. "We will take those additional forces you promised and go."

"Quickly."

Damerion nodded once.

"Then they are waiting beyond the western camp perimeter."

"Thank you." Damerion motioned for his soldiers to swim onward. The strakirin lingered, hanging in the vines, but a tug on the leash roused the boy after a moment.

His blindfolded face turned toward me again. "Key…"

I froze. His voice was a rasp. A rough whisper. I could barely hear him over the water. And what he was saying made no sense.

"*Key*…" he said again, louder, more desperately.

Noah's hand tightened on me. I looked over to find him staring at the strakirin, alarm in his eyes.

"What?" I asked. "Does that mean something to you?"

"Shannon."

Fear sent a twinge through my chest at the name of the woman who'd done this to me, who'd finished what the judges wanted. "What?"

"She said that. About you. After you left."

My mouth moved, wordless.

"Do you know what it means?" Chloe asked him.

Noah shook his head. "She, uh…" He appeared uncomfortable. "She died before she could explain."

Chloe bit her lip, glancing between us, and I could only guess at what she was thinking.

"Perhaps you should stay behind," Damerion suggested.

I looked over to find him appraising me and the strakirin carefully.

"Yeah," Noah agreed.

"You wish to insist this girl stay in my city, presumably without the one… *being*… who seems immune to her powers?" Praelex Kreyus raised an eyebrow. "With my daughter and my people unprotected, should anything go wrong?"

I struggled not to shift with discomfort. I wasn't a monster.

But I had no idea what had just happened. What would happen when the other strakirin finished whatever the judges wanted with this… whatever they were after.

"I'm not staying," I said before the others could respond.

Noah started to protest.

"I'm not." I didn't want to add that I wasn't sure I *could*.

"If we lose that boy—" Ezio twitched his chin toward the leashed strakirin. "—we've lost our only guide. Without Ari, that is. And I'm guessing that one isn't exactly chatty."

He waited for Damerion to confirm or deny it. The commander looked away.

Ezio nodded like that was answer enough. "Right. So the boy can't tell us what's going on with the others, or even where they are. We'll be heading after the Driecarans at a disadvantage." He splayed his hands in a helpless gesture. "This is why Ari came along, and why King Zekerian insisted on her presence in the first place—to find these bastards and figure out what they're up to. Ari has to come. She's our only option."

Noah scowled.

"I'm going," I insisted.

"And if this is a ploy?" Damerion asked. "If they specifically need you there for some reason? That one called you a *key*, for gods' sakes."

I hadn't thought of that. And it didn't make any sense. The judges never let on that I was any different than the rest. In fact, they'd repeatedly tested me to prove the opposite.

But when had any of this made sense?

"Then Noah will stop me," I said. "Them. Whatever."

"Ari—" Noah began.

"I don't know what just happened," I snapped. "But if I *can't* stay here and the Vetorians try to stop me from leaving…" I hated this. "Praelex Kreyus is right. If I lose control, people could get hurt."

"And if you go, you could too," Noah countered quietly.

I looked away.

"We need to leave," Ezio urged.

"I have to do this, Noah." I started toward the edge of the city, not wanting to continue arguing. Not wanting to see Noah's face, because I knew he didn't agree.

For that matter, I didn't either. Not exactly. I didn't *want* to do this, to go out there. I could still feel that strange impulse pulling me toward whatever had just happened, and it made me want to swim as hard and fast in the other direction as I could.

But the strakirin had found something, which meant that— by tandem—the judges had too.

My family needed to be safe.

There was no turning back now.

❧ 27 ❧

BAYLIE

My eyes popped open to blue twilight and the green glow of an alarm clock. I lay motionless, searching by sound more than sight for what had woken me up. The room was quiet except for the soft sound of Ellie breathing deep on the other side of the queen-sized bed. A sliver of early morning sky showed in the gap between the thick curtains on the far side of the room, indigo blue with the hints of coming dawn.

But something had woken me. Something had… changed.

Shivers crept over me. I pushed away from the mattress, glancing over my shoulder to see if I was disturbing Ellie. She shifted a bit, but gave no sign of waking up while I eased away from the bed and then changed quickly into the first outfit I could grab from my backpack of clothes. Cerulean blue t-shirt and some equally blue jean shorts. Whatever.

My skin wouldn't stop crawling.

I inched the door open and then slipped out into the hall. A half-dozen doors lined the stretch to the staircase, and all of them except the one to the bathroom were closed. At the end of the hallway, another window showed the first hints of day creeping over the horizon, lightening the sky into shades of lavender.

But nothing else happened. No change, no noise, no hint of what had woken me up. I looked around, at a loss. Something was weird, but nothing around me showed evidence of that. I didn't even know *what* was weird. Just… something.

I crept along the hall, uncertain whether I should try to find Olivia. Maybe Jace too, though the thought of sneaking into the room where he was sleeping did strange things to my stomach. But odds were, if anyone was awake, they'd be downstairs still working, so that's where I should probably go.

Yeah.

I continued past Jace's door, determinedly *not* looking at it, and then onward down the stairs. The light felt like it was getting brighter with every second, the sun rushing up to get on with the day. I turned at the base of the stairs only to pause when I spotted the first-floor hall.

The walls were covered in sheets of paper.

Eyeing the pages tacked by pushpin to the wood surface, I walked toward the dining room. More chemical formulas. Graphs too. One whole swath seemed devoted to photocopies from old manuscripts. Notes and annotations in red and blue and green ink filled the margins, while twine crisscrossed between the tacks holding the pages as if to link them all.

It looked like a conspiracy theorist had done the decorating, though if there was a pattern here, I couldn't quite see it.

The crawling of my skin began to fade. The feeling of

something's changed drained away, almost like static on the radio being turned down low enough that it could no longer be heard. But nothing around me seemed to be the reason why. The hallway was silent. The house was too. Sunlight slipped through windows in the rooms at the end of the hall, lighting the papers with pale gold and casting the space in a calm, early morning glow.

The feeling was just… gone.

I continued down the hall, ducking the strings between the papers while the wood floor chilled my bare feet. I peered around the open doorway to the dining room.

Declan was there. Alone.

I paused. He sat at the table, papers still scattered in front of him. The books had disappeared, and the laptops were stacked two high on a folding table in the corner, each computer plugged in with its charging light pulsing. On the far wall, thick brown curtains were drawn over the window, blocking out any view of the outside world.

Declan didn't glance away from the page in his hand. I wasn't sure he even knew I was here. The dark circles under his eyes made it seem like he'd probably been up all night, and the look on his face wasn't quite like anything I'd ever seen from him.

He looked… sad. Almost lost, even.

"Are you okay?" I asked, breaking the quiet.

He flinched, looking up sharply. Brusqueness dropped over his face in an instant, solid and cold and hinting at contempt.

As if it was armor.

"Excuse me?" he retorted.

I knew he'd heard me. But he just never quit. The asshole. The jerk, as Ellie had called him. He never let up even for a heartbeat.

"I asked if you were okay," I said, heat creeping into my voice.

The barest pause followed my words. "Of course I am. Except, *obviously*, for the fact your little friends seem determined to create a weapon that could wipe us all out."

I didn't respond. I wasn't even sure how.

Because it was true.

Declan's face tightened, just for a heartbeat, just a bit. I paused.

His brusqueness was armor, sure. But that… that had looked like a crack in it.

I checked the hall briefly. No one was there. "Why did you tell them I was a wizard?" I stepped farther into the room. My hand clasped the back of the nearest chair, my fingers wrapping around the cold, smooth wood.

"Aren't you?"

He didn't believe that. I could hear it in his voice.

I waited.

"If they think you're ruanir, they'll be less likely to mess with the rest of us."

"That's what I thought."

He flicked his gaze up to me briefly and then returned it to the paper. I could see the page clearer now. A printout, but with something circled in red ink at the bottom. He kept staring at it.

"You know how to make it work, don't you? The weapon."

He was silent. But he didn't let go of the paper.

Suspicion crept over me. The armor, the crack in it, the way he was awake when no one else was here…

"And you're smart enough to have figured out how to stop it from hurting the other ruanir."

At that, he looked up, one eyebrow arching.

I mirrored the expression. He was an arrogant ass, but screw it, two could play at that game. And besides, my gut was screaming I was right.

It was something in his face. I didn't know what. Something that just—

"Yes," he said.

I waited.

"Yes, I know how to make it work. I know how to kill the judges. All of them. And I can stop it from hurting the regular ruanir in the process. That's how goddamn good I am." Bitterness dripped from his tone, thick and sour.

"Okay. So what's the problem?"

He scoffed. "Nothing."

Yeah, that was a lie. Nobody looked like he had a second ago if *nothing* was the problem.

I hesitated, his words playing back through my mind. "But you're not a regular ruanir."

He didn't respond.

Oh, God. "You're… you're not, right? You're part of that… that Break-something Initiative thing. The ocean magic project.

And the judges—"

He made an irritated sound. "Drop it. It's not your problem. Go back to bed or texting or whatever the hell you teenage magical monsters do these days."

I blinked. Wow. And the world champion of *assholes* award goes to…

Whatever. "What happens to you?"

"I said drop it, get it?" He looked up at me, glaring. "It's not your—"

He cut off, that armor cracking again for no reason I could see. He blinked fast, as if he'd lost track of what he'd been saying, and then dropped his gaze to the paper again. "It's enough. It doesn't matter. It's enough."

My anger drained at the tiredness in his voice. "What is?"

He stared at the paper. Seconds crept past, turning to a minute, then more. And still he didn't answer. In the kitchen, water slipped past a leaky faucet, intermittently plunking into the sink. Beyond the thick curtains blocking the window, birds chirped in mad joy at greeting the morning.

"We're going to die."

My attention snapped back to Declan.

"Me. Veronique. Willa. Anyone who took part in my project who's nearby when the weapon's deployed. Maybe even anyone who's been exposed to the project at all. This thing the landwalkers found… they were closer to an answer than they thought. The weapon targets ruanir with ocean magic inside them. Makes sense; that's what our people would have been, back when the dehaians created this. It targets my people and breaks down the ocean magic inside them like rot, like gangrene. It's a horrible way to die." He shook his head. "The bastards."

He set the paper down. "And it needs someone to deploy it. Someone who understands how it operates, how to direct it. Someone who can use magic. And thus someone *not* your landwalker friends."

A breath left me. So… him. He meant him.

When I didn't respond, Declan glanced over. His face was solemn, almost resigned. He looked older than he'd seemed before. "She would have been about your age, you know."

I blinked.

"My daughter. Almost ready to go through the adjustment. I would've had centuries with her. Watched her grow up. Have a family of her own." His expression twitched, pain fighting to break through. "Instead, I had four years before the Judiciary took her and my wife. Four little years. And I searched. I did. I hoped…" He closed his eyes for a moment. "But the Judiciary never kept them for leverage. I'd hoped they would. They do that sometimes, not that the ruanir masses know it. They keep people for leverage, for experiments," a sickened look flickered over his face, "for all kinds of reasons. But not my family. They never gave me time to save them. In days, my girl and my wife were dead, their twisted—" his voice caught, "—*tortured* bodies displayed on television for all the ruanir to see." Bitterness drew his face taut. "Evidence of my crime of exposing my family to 'ocean magic contamination.'"

Nausea rolled in me. I couldn't imagine. Didn't *want* to

imagine the horror of what he'd been through.

Not when I could see it written all over him.

He pressed a hand to the paper as if to cement it into existence. "But this… this is enough. If it kills them, it's enough. It's not my Breakmire Initiative. It's not ocean magic or beating them at their own game, but…" He nodded, almost to himself. "It's enough."

My mouth moved, trying to find the words. "And the others? Veronique? Willa?"

Declan was quiet for a moment. "I'll warn them. With enough distance, they should…" He couldn't seem to bring himself to finish the sentence.

I stared. He was going to kill himself. Maybe everyone who took part in the project—*his* project—too, if they weren't lucky. To stop the judges, he would—

The sound of footsteps carried from the stairway. Declan glanced toward the noise and then to me, that mask of asshole-as-armor hardening his face again. And I could read the look. The insistence that I damn well better not tell anyone what he'd showed me beyond that couldn't-care-less-about-anybody defense.

I didn't say anything.

"Hey." Robin appeared at the doorway. "God, Baylie, you're up early. This guy wake you up or something?"

I could hear the displeasure with Declan in her tone.

"No, just couldn't sleep."

She nodded. "Right, well, I'm going to get some coffee. You want some?"

I noticed she only made the offer to me. Good grief, how bad had things gotten down here last night? "Uh, sure. Thanks. I'll… I'll be right in."

"Mm-kay." She tossed me a smile and then headed for the kitchen.

I watched her go. Did she know? That Declan had to die, and that other ruanir would too? Somehow, I doubted it. I didn't know Robin, had only met her briefly in the middle of hell, but somehow, I doubted she'd be *that* cold.

Or at least she'd offer the guy coffee.

My stomach rolled. This was madness. I was standing in a room with a man about to commit suicide by proxy, and there wasn't a damn thing I could do to stop it. Change it. Keep him from having to die, because there wasn't any way to—

Change.

My fingers tightened on the back of the wooden dining chair. "You, uh…" I turned back to Declan, keeping my voice low. "You're good at this, right? Research and magic and… all that?"

"I'm the best."

Contempt touched his voice, like everyone in the world should already know that—me included.

Right.

"Well, uh…" God, what was I doing? This guy had been a jerk to us all since day one.

But Veronique wasn't. Neither was Willa. And Declan's atti-tude wasn't exactly a reason to stand aside and let the man die.

Besides, what kind of person would I be if the judges had

murdered *my* family? *My* kid?

"Listen, I don't… I don't know what I am, okay? Or, what I am now. I used to just be an ordinary person. A human, I mean. But…" I felt like I was standing on the edge of a cliff, gambling on whether the murky water below was full of rocks. "Jace thinks I'm sort of like the old ruanir, but different too, because Noah changes things. That's where this came from. The Beast, back before he was Noah. Just the Beast. So if Jace is right, then maybe what's in me can change things too and maybe…" God, I could barely breathe. Dive, dive. "Maybe if you use that, you could change this too, and maybe it would help you not, you know… need to kill yourself for this."

Declan looked up at me. "You want to let me study you?"

God, no.

I gave an uncomfortable shrug. I wouldn't be anything but honest, not when I got the impression this guy wouldn't believe me anyway if I lied. "I don't want to agree to let you die. You're an ass, Declan. A total jerk. But… nobody should die for that, including you."

He stared at me for a moment before he gave a small scoff. I swore I heard respect in the sound. "Okay." He rose from the table. "Then go get your coffee. We have work to do."

❧ 28 ❧

NOAH

I wasn't a fan of this.

Invisible, I moved through the water ahead of the dehaians, Ari, and the strakirin prisoner who looked like a nightmare. Mutters rose from the bound-up strakirin, intermittent and barely audible, and the words were always the same.

The key… the key…

Fury moved through me. It didn't matter if I had no clue what the strakirin meant, or what Shannon had meant, for that matter. Those words were about Ari, and now she was heading toward more of the creatures.

What the hell was she *thinking?*

That she was scared.

Aggravation took the place of my fury. Yeah, I knew that. I'd read that on her face, even if our empathic connection was gone. She was determined and scared, and she needed to end this because it was the only way she'd be free of them.

But if they *wanted* her there…

I wished I was in human form, if only to be able to punch

something. As it was, I couldn't risk even a tiny loss of control, for fear of crushing Ari and the dehaians I was supposed to protect. There were nearly two hundred of them with us now. Kreyus's mercenaries and the survivors of the Yvarian forces combined. To a person, the mercenaries looked loaded for bear, and willing to take one on too. Battle-hardened bodies, even harder expressions, and a multitude of scars that seemed more from survival than ceremony. They made the Yvarian soldiers look like mall cops by comparison.

Which was good. The Yvarians had struggled to hold out against the strakirin's fear-projecting abilities back when I'd captured the prisoner we took to the garrison. Trying to scare these Vetorians would probably only piss them off.

And that was good too. So was the fact that we might see the strakirin coming. Maybe, anyway. Except for how fast they could move, and how they could block any echolocation till they were right on top of you…

God, that was creepy.

Dammit, focus. *Focus*. The strakirin could be out there.

"Where are we?" Ari asked the others softly.

"Sorian Plain." Damerion seemed to remember the fact she wouldn't know where that was. "Wasteland. No one comes out this way, not even Vetorians."

"Because we figured out centuries ago that there are numerous other routes around this place that offer more benefits for trade and defense," Ezio pointed out. "The Sorian Plain is just a useless stretch of desert with no plants, no mountains, barely even a hillside of interest." He gave Damerion a wry look.

"Even *fish* don't bother with this place."

Ari nodded, but her anxious expression remained. "So the strakirin came this way because… they don't know that?" Hope tinged her voice.

Ezio's humor dimmed. "Yeah. Maybe."

Silence reigned.

I turned my attention back to the terrain ahead. Kansas looked exciting compared to this place. Hell, the moon probably did.

God, I wished Ari would have stayed back at the camp with Chloe and Kreyus…

Something changed in the distance.

My awareness zeroed in. Rocks. Tumbles of them, stretching into the distance like some giant had dumped them in a long mound that extended for miles on either side. I wasn't sure if the dehaians had even picked up on them yet, but it worried me.

Everything worried me right now.

Frustrated, I kept going. Rocks or not, desert or not, Ezio's familiarity with the uselessness of this place or not, anything might be hiding beyond those boulders. I could go higher to try to get a view over them, but I didn't want to stretch myself too thin and leave the others exposed. There wasn't any sign of the strakirin yet—not that that meant much—but I hadn't tested how far from Ari and the others I could get before the strakirin could pick up on them.

But then, we could also be heading straight toward them.

I rose higher in the water, blocking the others as best I could.

The pile seemed to end after a bit, but I couldn't tell what lay beyond—

Something felt weird.

In spite of myself, I drew back toward Ari and the others. It wasn't a shape out there. Wasn't a strakirin. It was just…

Weird. And unwelcome. And unnerving like—

Dad picking me up, holding me tight in his strong, greliaran grasp while the warmth of his changed skin lifted steam from my soaked jeans and Captain America winter coat. My small body was heavy with cold from the frigid water of the pond up near our cabin. I'd been playing with Maddox. I'd slipped on the too-thin ice and almost fallen completely through. Residual fear gripped me, made of adrenaline and the knowledge I'd been inches from death by drowning.

"Noah?" Ari called softly.

The memory became mist. The others were ahead of me, stopped at the edge of the boulders. Spikes on their arms, the dehaians studied the area ahead while Ari scanned the water, searching for me.

I cursed myself silently. I'd gotten distracted. I'd slowed down without realizing it—and without realizing what was beneath us. A canyon, black and deep with rocks tumbled down at the sides. It gaped beneath us like a wound in the sea-floor. Like a gash torn in the world.

"In there?" Damerion asked.

Ari nodded.

Trepidation thrummed through me. It took effort to make myself go ahead of them again, swimming deeper into the black ahead of Ari and the strakirin boy and all the dehaians who now had weapons drawn.

This place was wrong.

I felt like I was watching a train wreck unfold, as if I couldn't rip my eyes from the accident playing out before me. Jagged rock walls, sheared sharp like their surface had been split fresh yesterday. Enormous spires of stone, stretched up toward the ocean above us but never reaching the open water. Crumbled boulders piled high and littering the seafloor that was just now coming into view. They all were wrong. Every one of them. The rocks and boulders and the gray-black columns nearly buried beneath the tumbled stones, their carvings lost to decay and time, their surfaces marred by smoke.

By fire.

By blood splashing on the cool white stones and dripping down the marble steps. People screamed as they fled their cities, their villages, and their homes in terror. They had nowhere to go, nowhere to hide. From the skies, I tore them down with lightning that danced from coal-black clouds that pulsed like a heartbeat and storm winds that whipped the blue-green sea into a white and terrible froth. The palm trees shredded up from their rooting, tumbling through the air like the toys of the fallen children who would never play again, never laugh, never smile. And all around, an ink-black darkness chased me, dragging at me, ready to devour—

Crying out, I crushed the edge of a decaying pillar in my bare hands.

And then I froze. I was human. In human form, anyway,

and not the invisible shape of the Beast.

I didn't want to be the Beast.

Frantic, I looked around the shadowed canyon. There was no fire, no bodies, nothing but destruction a millennium old. But this wasn't good either. I couldn't see Ari. The dehaians. Even that strakirin, all bound up and muttering. I'd taken human form without even realizing it, and lost sight of them in this mess of pillars and crumbled mountains.

This nightmarish mess.

I shuddered. I knew where I was now. I knew where the Driecarans and the strakirin had wanted to find.

I'd never wanted to come back here.

I drifted through the dark water, everything that was me trembling. It hurt to be here. Hurt in a thousand ways all at once, and it could easily get worse. If I let my human form go for even a second…

A shudder wracked me. I didn't know. It'd be a mistake. Even being here was a mistake. I'd avoided this place, I realized. The Beast side of me had, long before my greliaran half had joined it, or even before Chloe had woken it a year ago. I'd avoided it since the beginning, *my* beginning. I'd torn it down into the depths of the sea and buried the memories with it.

The island where I'd been created.

I clung harder to my human form, though my hold on it felt weaker than ever. Human shape was protection right now—from the memories or something else, I wasn't sure. The Beast side of me was scared in a way I'd never felt from it. Something was wrong about this place. Something horrible.

They'd tried to kill me here.

The certainty settled over me like the knowledge the monster really was behind you. They'd tried to kill me, back when I barely knew what it was to be alive, back before I'd killed them instead. I'd fought back because I knew they wanted me dead.

I just didn't know why.

My gaze twitched toward the distant canyon top, too far away to be seen in the darkness. I needed to leave. I had no idea why the judges, the Driecarans, and the strakirin were after this place, but I had to get away from here.

But then, Ari was out there. I couldn't leave her. Not to this. And the dehaians were here too.

I moved faster through the water. I'd find her. I'd find all of them.

And then we'd get the hell out of this place.

29

ARI

I couldn't find Noah.

The water was dark down in the depths of the canyon, darker than anything I'd experienced thus far. My heightened vision felt stretched to the breaking point, and even then I could only barely make out the jumbles of rocks around us. Piles of them, like mounds in a quarry, waiting to be pulverized down to gravel. Something about it didn't look right, didn't look natural, though I wasn't quite sure why. The open water overhead had long since been lost to view, leaving us in this pit of destruction where the only noise for miles was our own motion through the water. But worse yet, the ever-so-slight shiver of magic in the water that I'd come to associate with Noah's invisible form was gone too.

Nothing was here. Not fish or plants or even algae. I didn't think I'd ever been in a place that was so… dead.

"I thought you said the Sorian Plain didn't even have a hillside in it," Damerion whispered to Ezio.

"It didn't. At least, at the last survey."

"When was that?"

Ezio was quiet for a moment. "Little over a year ago."

I bit my lip, doing the math easily.

Before the Beast returned.

"Noah?" I whispered.

Silence.

I trembled. I didn't want to keep moving, but alone of all other signs of life, the only thing that had persisted was the impulse to continue swimming. Whether I wanted it or not, I couldn't stop myself from going this way, then that way, weaving down into the canyon and through the jumbled rocks like I had a map in my head that I didn't even know I was reading. I could see the dehaians watching me, and watching the strakirin boy up ahead too, because he was doing the same thing. Turning moments before I did, mere half-seconds before I did.

We knew the way. I just didn't know where that way was taking us.

"Noah?"

There was pleading in my voice. I could hear it. The others probably could too. This wasn't what was supposed to happen. He was supposed to help me, to be here, to stop them from taking over my mind.

This way.

That way.

Turn.

My fingers curled into a fist, clenching down tight. My nails bit my palm, but the pain didn't help. This way. That. Turn. The rocks around us were paler now. Marble, almost. On land, they might even be bright white or a light gray. There were columns too. Carved ones, with designs that had probably been beautiful before time tore into them.

I swam past a tumbled collection of them, one of the designs still clear enough to be understood even after however long they'd been at the bottom of the sea. A dehaian. That was a carving of a dehaian. And a man. A man facing the dehaian with his palm out, a stand of tall plants atop it, while the dehaian held up a bowl that looked like it had something burning inside.

Dehaians. And humans.

My eyes narrowed, something about the plants seeming off. They were too sinuous. They twisted like smoke.

Like magic.

I looked at the figures again. Not humans.

Ruanir.

My heart began pounding harder. I knew where we were. I knew where this was. The island. We were at the island where my people used to live.

What was left of it.

But dehaians weren't there. Not originally. They'd tried to take it over in a land dispute. That's what I'd always been taught. The war had started because they wanted our home.

Why create carvings of someone who wanted to steal your home?

I started to turn to tell the dehaians when suddenly a glow caught my eye. Distant, barely brightening the darkness, it glimmered beyond the tumbled pillars and mounds of stone ahead of us.

The compulsion grew stronger. I bit back a whimper, suddenly scared to even make a sound.

Where was Noah?

"Fan out," Damerion whispered. "Half to the north, half to the south."

I could feel the dehaians move through the water at my back. I didn't turn.

"You okay?" Ezio murmured beside me.

My head quivered back and forth, a tiny shake.

"You could hang back," he offered. "Stay behind the—"

The strakirin ahead suddenly turned toward us. Blindfold be damned, I knew the boy was staring at me.

I faltered, torn between the compulsion to go forward and my desire to retreat.

The strakirin didn't move.

And the compulsion deepened. I *couldn't* go. I needed to be in this place. It wasn't about the judges. It wasn't the Driecarans or this place or anything else at all.

It was about me. *I* had to be here.

I just didn't know why.

"Can't," I gasped, my eyes locked on the strakirin. "Just… can't…"

From the corner of my eye, I saw Ezio look to Damerion.

"Be ready," I heard Damerion murmur.

I wondered for the first time what their orders really were concerning me.

I wondered, if it came down to it, if I'd care.

Ezio nodded slightly, the motion barely discernible. "Okay, then," he said to me.

The strakirin turned like he had been waiting for me to agree to go. The boy swam on toward the light, and I followed him.

This was a bad idea.

Damerion came up beside me. "If this goes wrong," he said in a low voice. "You have the Beast get you out of here, understand? Ezio was right. We need to know what the strakirin are doing, and we can't do that if you're lost to them."

My gaze slid over to him. What about them?

I already knew the answer.

I made myself nod, even as my body kept going. I'd heard what he'd said. I'd heard what he wanted, but I… I needed to be here. It should bother me that I didn't have a reason. It *did* bother me, but that wasn't stopping anything. I needed this. They needed this. The hive mind. The strakirin… entity.

My thoughts slowed. That's what they were, wasn't it? One being. One being… and then me. All on my own, separated from the hive, and somehow that was important but not simply because it wanted me to return. My distance didn't matter—and it was the entire point.

I drifted after the strakirin boy. That didn't make sense.

Nothing did.

Where was Noah?

We rounded the edge of the canyon. The light came into view, a brilliant glowing pyre of blue-white flame in the heart of what must have once been an enormous amphitheater. Traces of the steps still remained amid tumbled columns, collapsed arches, and piles of stone too broken to identify. Row upon row of them waited beneath us, rising easily three times higher than any sports stadium I'd ever seen on land. Somehow the base was mostly clear. And what hovered in the center…

My thoughts stopped entirely.

Osias.

The strakirin.

And Logan.

Up ahead of us, the leashed strakirin swam faster toward the others, hauling at the soldier holding it.

"Let it go," Damerion ordered, not taking his eyes from the strakirin and Osias at the base of the amphitheater.

The soldier complied. The leashed strakirin darted down to join the others, never bothering to take the blindfold or the ropes off. There were at least fifty strakirin still down there, waiting in a circle around Osias and Logan. They didn't look toward the mercenaries and soldiers. But I could hear the drone past my defenses, like a hum of a thousand teeth grinding against my brain.

Osias didn't react. He didn't even glance away from the fire while we sank down toward him. I could see his lips moving, his words inaudible. The strakirin faced him, as intent as Osias himself on the flames twisting in the depths.

But Logan looked up at us. And smiled.

"Well, hey there, Ariabella Moreau." He sounded like this was all some huge joke and we were late in catching the punchline. "Fancy meeting you right where I knew you'd come."

I trembled, making myself stop far enough away that I

could hope to flee before he could reach me. The amphitheater towered around us now, like a gaping maw waiting to close and swallow us all down. None of the strakirin even looked at me, but I could hear the hive like an electric saw in my brain. "What is this, Logan?"

"The beginning. The end. The next chapter. I can't quite decide on a metaphor, but then, semantics aren't really the point. This is the moment where you and all your little friends lose the war you barely had a chance to start fighting. And you're right at ground zero. Or, well—" He glanced around with a mild expression. "Close enough." His smile dropped like a discarded mask. "Get down here."

Deep inside, I felt my strakirin powers stir.

Panic shot through me. No, no, no. He couldn't make me use those. He couldn't control me. I wasn't part of the hive anymore, and I'd die before I let myself become that again.

I retreated in the water, just a few inches, all I could with the compulsion pulling at me.

Hatred crept into Logan's expression. "Now," he growled.

I didn't move. I wouldn't. A gun at my back wouldn't make me come closer to that bastard.

"Enough of this," Damerion snarled. "Osias of Driecara!"

His lips still moving, Osias didn't look away from the fire.

Anger flickered over Damerion's face. He pressed onward. "You and your dehaian associates are under arrest by the royal authority of King Zekerian of Yvaria. You will be escorted back to Yvarian territory to stand trial for crimes of terrorism, murder, espionage, and attempts to incite a war. The strakirin with you will be taken into custody as well, until a decision can be made about their fate." He made a sharp gesture, and on either side of us, soldiers moved forward, weapons drawn and spikes arrayed on their arms. "Stand down your strakirin forces and come quietly, or we will destroy you."

Logan scoffed. "Oh yeah, like that's going to happen."

I felt the order go out. Wordless and utterly silent, it pulsed through me.

A wave of fear rolled into the amphitheater, thick and choking as smoke. I whirled, gasping, because I hadn't known they were there in the shadows. Not till this second. The strakirin had hidden from me.

How?

The dehaians flinched. Their eyes went wide in sudden terror.

And then the strakirin arrived. A hundred of them poured from the darkness around us, twisting like eels, moving fast as lightning. I heard the soldiers and mercenaries shout. Heard the ones behind me scream in pain. The thrill of a hundred minds enjoying the deaths of their prey buffeted me, pushing at my defenses as the dehaians began to die.

Without hesitation, the strakirin abandoned the poisoned dehaians and sped toward the survivors. Green, sinuous bodies wrapped around the dehaians like ropes come to life, pinning them in place. Damerion drew back, Ezio doing the same, till they were on either side of me with their weapons at the ready and spikes standing out from their forearms.

The strakirin rushed toward us. The dehaians wouldn't stand

a chance.

"No!" I fought to push past Ezio and Damerion. "Don't—"

The strakirin racing for us pulled up short. The other strakirin stopped too, spikes on their arms aimed at the struggling soldiers' throats.

Of everyone, only Damerion, Ezio, and I were still free.

I trembled, scanning the amphitheater. Why had the strakirin stopped?

"So," Logan commented, "you were saying?"

My focus darted across the strakirin. They weren't moving, no, but the soldiers and mercenaries were still pinned. There was no way the dehaians could escape and survive. Meanwhile, the strakirin around Osias were motionless, waiting to join their brethren and attack.

Which left the three of us.

And Noah, wherever the hell he was.

Panic pulsed hard in my throat. There were only shadows and ruins around us. Nothing to show Noah was here at all.

"Oh, hello."

My attention snapped toward the base of the amphitheater.

Osias smiling up at us. "There you are. Just in time." He glanced around the amphitheater. "Beast? Oh, Beast? Hiding won't do you any good, you know. You can't stop this. This place will still kill you."

My heart found a way to speed up. "What?"

Osias made a shushing motion at me, his attention still on the remainder of the amphitheater. Nearby, Logan grinned.

"Do you hear me, Beast?" Osias called. "You have only

moments now till this ends. A millennium of trying to escape, and it all ends where it began. Don't you want to say goodbye to your little strakirin girlfriend?"

Something moved in the shadows on the far side of the amphitheater.

Noah emerged into the blue-white light.

My breath caught. He was pale. Paler than I'd ever seen him. Even across the wide expanse, I could tell that his clothes were desaturated and edging toward gray.

An ache gripped my chest.

He looked like a ghost.

"Feels odd, doesn't it, Beast?" Osias called. "And familiar, perhaps?"

"Ari," Noah called, his voice tight. "Get out of here. Please."

I couldn't.

"Aw," Logan said. "How romantic. The monster thinks it cares."

Osias chuckled. "Now, Beast, don't be a fool. She can't do that. We fixed that little problem since you got away."

What?

"We're waiting, Ariabella," Logan called.

Invisible tenterhooks yanked at me, insisting I go down there. I clamped my mouth shut on a whimper. Whatever it took, I swore to myself, I wouldn't move.

Logan's lip curled with rage.

Osias sighed. "It's okay. It won't take long now." He bent down, scooping a handful of the white stones from the ground.

The water shivered.

I looked around sharply, but the others didn't seem to notice. The change was faint, like the memory of a breeze in a place where the world was still.

But my skin prickled with it all the same.

"Such a simple thing, aren't they?" Osias commented. "Little bits of gravel, utterly unremarkable. Of course, they didn't use to be—or so the judges say. They were beautiful once."

He cast a look over his shoulder to Noah. "Do you remember them, Beast? White towers of stone, intricately crafted and imbued with magic over the course of centuries. Archways of marble surrounding them, on an island as close to paradise as anything mortal eyes have seen. Do you remember anything of this place you destroyed?"

Osias let the white stones run from his fingers. "She told us you didn't." He nodded toward me. "Not really, anyway. She told us you hide from your memories, that they were only mist and ghosts in your mind. She said you were nothing but a mere boy with powers he resented as much as feared." He shook his head. "Such a fool. Even now, even as this—" He flicked a hand toward Noah as if to encompass his human form. "—you never questioned a thing."

The stones thudded when they hit the seafloor, as loud as nails pounded into a coffin lid.

No one gave any sign of hearing them at all.

Noah drifted away from the archway, staying wide of Osias and the strakirin. He struggled through the water, kicking a leg here, pushing with an arm there, as if the space around us was filled with sludge more than seawater and he had to fight to keep himself moving. "What was I supposed to question?" he replied.

"What you *were*."

Noah paused, only for a heartbeat, before continuing on. He was circling them, I realized. He was trying to reach us without making the strakirin strike out, and without going across the center of the amphitheater.

Because something terrible was in the center of that amphitheater.

I flicked my tail in the water, fighting to stay where I was when every little motion of my muscles seemed to bring me closer to the other strakirin. Closer to Osias.

And Logan. He'd gone back to watching me. Even while Osias was speaking, his eyes never wavered. He studied me as if I was a puzzle he hated and yet needed to solve.

His attention was like a physical pressure. The strakirin powers inside me shuddered in the recesses of my mind in response, like a crocodile stirring and stretching beneath dark water. A tiny gasp escaped me.

Ezio glanced at me, a sharp look in his eyes.

"Don't…" I whispered, begging the powers to be still. They felt stronger than ever, and I didn't think it was simply because of Logan.

It was more than that. More than him.

My gaze slipped down to the amphitheater floor. Inside me, the strakirin magic paused, heavy and ready like a muscle on the edge of motion. Like it was waiting, listening for something that wasn't me.

I needed to go down there.

My head shook of its own accord. "Osias is stalling." I tore my focus from the white gravel. "They both are."

"We know," Ezio murmured, so softly I could barely hear him. "Wait for Noah to get close. We'll need him if we have any chance of breaking our people free."

I couldn't even nod. I looked to Noah, begging him silently to move faster.

He was changing.

I stared. His body lurched like he was being hit, but still he kept moving around the amphitheater toward us. With every lurch, the water surrounding him swirled, tinged with tendrils of black smoke, like the storm clouds I'd seen of his other form were being pulled out of him, piece by piece.

Never taking his eyes from Osias, he passed over a crumbled column lying on the remains of the stairs. "Dehaians made the Beast to destroy their enemies," Noah said. "I don't need the history lesson, asshole. I was there."

"Not for all of it."

Noah was silent. I flicked my tail, retreating yet again. The water felt worse now. Like it was changing. Like something dark and hungry was seeping from the white stones, even if I couldn't see it.

Osias paid it no attention. "Our ancestors were too fractured by the split of landwalker and dehaian to keep their records well. Families from the rich to the poor were scattered; passing down ancient stories was the least of their worries. But the judges documented their history well. They kept it secret, of course. No need to let the ruanir rabble know the truth. But the Judiciary leaders… oh, they knew. And they told us when we found them last year. After all, we needed to guide their precious pets here."

"What did they know?" Noah growled. I bit back a whimper and the urge to beg him to go faster. We had to get out of here. I didn't know how—if we moved, the soldiers and the mercenaries might die—but we had to.

"The real reason you exist. The reason this place exists." Osias glanced at me. "And the reason they do. I told you that you were something new and ancient, little… well, you're not really a girl anymore, are you? You're an anomaly. A mistake, while your fellow strakirin are simply one product what the Beast's power could have been, if not for the shortsightedness of fools among your ancestors and mine." He looked back to Noah. "Dehaian purists tried to compensate for that shortsightedness, you know. They turned you into the weapon you became. That's what you remember. You weren't precisely alive before that. You were just energy. Powerful energy, yes. The most powerful force in the world at the time, meant to be used up in one wasteful moment, for a purpose that only scratched the surface of what you were truly capable of. But the purists… they saw past that plan and refashioned you into a tool for the defense of my kind, only to fall prey to a monster that ultimately destroyed them. Because even they couldn't control you, you see. You weren't only formed of dehaian magic. You were a creature of wizard and dehaian magic combined."

I remembered the pillars, crumbled and fallen around us.

The ones with the dehaians and the ruanir on them.

Why build monuments to someone you hated?

Because you didn't. Not at first.

Because they'd worked together, once upon a time.

"What purpose?" I managed. "What did the ruanir and dehaians originally create him for?"

Osias chuckled. "Revolution. Pollution. The destruction of us all, dehaian and ruanir alike."

I stared. "What?"

Osias ignored me. "Obviously, after the dehaians took control, the wizards ran." He shrugged. "Even if the wizards did have magic, the dehaians were still stronger. Spikes, strength, speed, and the ability to make their enemies love them meant my ancestors claimed control of this place right from the off, though in the end, they couldn't control what it was meant for, nor did they have the vision to see the possibilities behind the new power at their disposal. And of course, the ones who originally made you tried to fight back. They sought to reclaim the magic in this place and, when that didn't work, to lock you and it away from anyone's use." He chuckled. "A 'land dispute,' the judges told us. That's what they tell the ruanir rabble too. That the war was started by dehaians wanting to claim ruanir land. Of course they don't go into detail, nor mention that they mean *this*." He gestured to the ruined amphitheater. "But didn't you ever wonder why you hunted them both after the dehaians lost control of you, Beast? Dehaians *and* wizards? Why you would crave the magical energy they *both* had?"

Noah slowed.

"It doesn't matter." Damerion drew a knife from his belt. "This is over. Now."

Logan laughed, but the amusement didn't reach his eyes. "Yeah. Sure."

He still wasn't taking his attention from me, and I couldn't stand it. My gaze darted away, only to land on the broken white stones as if pulled by a magnet.

My skin prickled. I couldn't even breathe. The monster was coming for me, and I couldn't see it.

Maybe because I was inside it.

"Noah…" I whispered.

"It's your purpose," Osias said. "It always has been. To take in both, to *be* both, and then to be used in this place. That's all you were, Beast. A magical charge. A combination of magic that shouldn't have existed for any longer than it took to meet your creators' needs."

Noah was only a few yards from me now. He drifted closer cautiously, still watching Osias and the strakirin as if expecting them to attack at any moment.

But could he feel this? The *wrongness* in the water?

"Please," I begged quietly. "Hurry, Noah."

His eyes darted to me and then snapped back to Osias, wary. He looked haggard, and he was still shaking.

Like he was coming apart.

"Why didn't it occur to you, Beast?" Osias called, his voice rising. "Did your dehaian masters hide it from you, or are you merely that foolish, that you never understood that you could *rule* this world if you chose? Magic of the ocean. Empathic abilities to know the intent of your allies and enemies alike. Power to shake the land, to roil the seas, even tear apart the sky itself! You never saw, not for a moment, that you had the power of a *god*."

I stared. And I understood it. In one horrible moment, I understood it all.

"They want to be gods," I breathed. "The judges. They want—"

Osias smiled at me, the expression so satisfied, it seemed to light him up from within. "And they will be. It took centuries, and the Beast's return, to finally develop a spell to use this place to its fullest potential. After all, when a creature of that magic is slaughtering your kind wherever it finds them, that makes things rather difficult. But with the Beast back and yet oblivious to the wizards, with its magic drawn down into a form they can control, with dehaian allies willing to give them any assistance they could need in reaching this place and finally unlocking its power…" He splayed his hands as if to encompass the ease of things now. "The judges had all they needed."

"But…" I couldn't speak. It was too terrible.

The judges, but with powers like Noah's… maybe even *beyond* Noah's…

"This is madness," Damerion protested. "How could they hope to—"

"She knows."

The others looked to me.

"They tested you, little *creature*," Osias said. "Little mistake. Don't you remember?"

My mouth moved, searching for a way to describe my horror. "The poison. The man at Teariad."

"It made him stronger," Ezio filled in.

I nodded jerkily. "The judges were the same. Before I left, they… they had me give them some…" What I'd seen played back through my head. The judge closing his eyes. Smiling like a judge almost never did, as if he'd gotten an adrenaline rush from the poison that should have been striking him dead. "It didn't hurt them." I looked to Noah. "Please. The stones. We have to—"

"They changed themselves," Osias spoke over me. "And us too."

"Are you really this much of a fool?" Damerion called. "Thinking some humans with magic will share the ocean with you, now that they have creatures like these? That they won't just betray you like they betrayed *her*?" He jerked his head toward me.

Osias smiled. "Of course not."

I stared.

"You think that's what this is for us?" Osias laughed, cold malice in the sound. "We want one thing, murderer. We want Yvaria to burn for its crimes. Let the judges have the ocean. Let them have every nation in the seas and let them raze each one down to dust. We don't care. As long as Yvaria falls—and fall, it will, rest assured, in a bloodbath that will be told of in frightened whispers for generations to come—our vengeance is complete. Nothing else matters."

"You're insane," Noah gritted out.

Osias turned to him, all humor vanishing. "You watch your friends die at the hands of genocidal maniacs, then we'll discuss sanity."

The water shivered again.

An edge of Osias' amusement returned. "But then, I guess that's exactly what you're going to do."

He spun back, glaring up at Damerion and the rest. And he spoke one word.

I didn't understand it. The language didn't sound like anything I'd heard, dehaian or ruanir.

But I felt the impact.

Oxygen crushed from my chest. I crumpled like I'd been punched in the gut. My arms grabbed my middle while my tail thrashed in reflexive desperation and my lungs screamed with the need to breathe.

The water hummed. Low at first, then louder, stronger, till the world began to shake.

"What is this?" Damerion shouted at Osias. "What have you done?"

Osias only smiled.

The white gravel began to shift. It quivered away like something was pushing up from below, but what followed didn't make sense. It was black. Nothingness. Darkness with form, and yet to my eyes, it glowed. Burned bright as a star while devouring all the light. It swelled from the ground like a monster emerging from a womb. I could feel it beating on my face, on my mind, with a heat like the sun in the depths of the sea.

An abyss made manifest.

Anti-light.

"Your final resting place awaits, Beast," Osias called. "A thousand years of running will not save you now!"

"Ari!" Noah shouted. "Go! Get out of—"

The blackness exploded. Darkness rushed out, engulfing everything. I saw Ezio grab Damerion's arm, pulling the man back as the explosion rushed at us, but he wasn't fast enough. He couldn't be fast enough. The black wave surged over the strakirin, over their dehaian prisoners. Logan was gone. Osias too. I caught a glimpse of Noah, his back arched, his mouth open in a silent scream.

And then the darkness swallowed me.

30

NOAH

The world was collapsing. I was collapsing. Stretching. My consciousness warped as I fought to stay in my human form and not get dragged into the amorphous, howling hell of magic that drew down and down and down to that point on the sand and rocks where that bastard Osias had been.

Where his ritual had been.

The Beast side of me howled with pain. This wasn't my power. This wasn't me, not fully, not anymore. This was a lie made of magic, a corruption that had promised safety before trying to kill me a thousand years before. And instead, I'd thrown it to the bottom of the sea, fleeing the death my creators had planned for me, and I'd chased the ruanir and dehaians alike for years. Because it was the only way to be safe, the only way to be sure they couldn't kill me. Because the dehaians had twisted me into enjoying pain, so I'd craved that too. And now the world was nothing but pain. Mine.

And they were going to win after all.

Agony filled me. I could feel the power of what Osias had

unleashed building around me, building beneath me. But the energy here was… was a lie. It wasn't what he thought, not fully.

It wasn't home.

My body spasmed, the darkness around me like hungry hands, ripping and clutching to drag me away. The power here was polluted and wrong, but the strakirin had been the Judiciary's way to reach it. Their way to finish what the judges had planned, what I'd escaped a thousand years before.

How did you complete a ritual when the monster you'd made threw the place you needed to the bottom of the sea?

You made a new creature who would go there and be your sacrifice. You made a new creature to take on that darkness for you.

Yet they hadn't wanted me here this time.

I clung to my human shape like a lifeline between here and oblivion. I couldn't understand my own thoughts. I couldn't make sense of what I knew. This place had been part of me, I knew that. I'd been made from it, before they even turned me into a weapon.

And yet this place wanted to kill me.

And yet the judges hadn't wanted me to be here. They'd wanted me dead and my magic fed to the strakirin, and they'd done everything they could to keep me away.

It didn't make any sense.

I thrashed, searching, desperate to escape. The darkness was alive, pulsing with energy. Every survival instinct I had screamed for me to go, to swim for my life because that's what was at stake.

Except I couldn't find Ari.

I writhed in the darkness, human hands turning to wisps as this place pulled at them. To let go of my human form was death. I understood that now. The Beast side of me had chosen to become this for a reason. Not just life. Protection.

I'd known exactly what I was doing a year ago, and I just hadn't remembered all of why. For a thousand years, the only thing that had mattered was survival.

Until her.

A panicked cry rang through the darkness. I whirled, my eyes and the Beast's awareness spotting Ari at the same time. She was a bright light in the black. A gray-white-blue blaze of incomparable power, surrounded with swirls of yellow and green like the aurora borealis. Other lights floated beyond her like flickering stars, a constellation of magic, glowing in the black but nowhere near as bright as her. She was incredible. Breathtaking.

A laugh rumbled in the darkness, and I knew that sound. Logan. The one they'd chosen to claim this darkness, to be the one changed by this hungry maw of nightmares. He was coming for her. He wouldn't let her survive.

To leave my human form was death.

Letting her die was too.

31

ARI

The world was a vice grip of darkness, and from it, there was no escape. Everything was black, like my eyes had changed to human though I could feel the magic still in them. I opened my mouth, calling out, but no sound came. Noah was gone. Ezio and Damerion and all the other dehaians too. Even the drone had gone silent.

But only for a moment.

A scream swelled up, coming from everywhere, rising like the volume was being turned up on the world. I flinched back, trying to flee to nowhere, and then it hit me.

The strakirin hit me.

Other consciousnesses flooded my own, hundreds of them. They pressed on me, burning into my mind's eye like virulent green stars in the black. They were surrendering as the masters had commanded. They were willfully giving in to the darkness.

They were terrified.

I gasped, desperate to hold defenses I had no hope of sustaining. Something was there, beneath the surrender, beneath the obedience.

Panic. Screams. Pleas for help, because their walls were caving in.

They couldn't keep the monsters out much longer.

I couldn't breathe. I knew that terror. I'd *lived* that terror, every second for weeks on end while I tried to keep the strakirin monster the judges had created from killing the last trace of me.

The implications rolled over me. The judges used me as a template. That was what the resistance believed, back when they tried to help me at their bunker. I was the template.

But the judges didn't understand the full extent of what they'd been creating.

The strakirin were like me.

With a single thought, my mind was reaching out to them. Connecting to them, like I had with Noah, like the judges had tried to bastardize into some sort of hive mind.

"Shh," I whispered.

I felt the hive mind turn, but I wasn't talking to it. Wasn't focused on it, because the others were there, down beneath the drone and the surrender. Girls, boys. Teenagers and young twenty-somethings who hadn't yet gone through the adjustment to slow down their aging. The ones the judges had taken.

The ones to whom the judges had lied.

Didn't know…

Told me I'd be helping…

Threatened my family…

The whispers tried to overwhelm me. The pleas and the fear

and so many memories. A desert sunrise. A city street in winter, cold and desolate. A grandmother laughing, and a baby smiling, and a Christmas tree sparkling in the deep black night. Others, more and more.

They were going to crush me. Drown me.

I pushed back, trying to be gentle amid the onslaught. I didn't want to hurt them.

I didn't want to lose my mind.

And the darkness was rising.

I struggled to focus. I could feel it, the magic all around us. It was building. Coming. Even in this infinite moment inside my mind, I didn't have much time.

"Like this…" I envisioned drawing on the ocean. It was easy, sharing the image. Sharing the information. Like the memories Noah and I shared.

The judges had never fully known what they'd created.

"Yeah." Exhilaration thrilled through me. All around me, the strakirin drone stuttered. Stalled. Fragmented into a lonely discordance like the last chorus member who doesn't realize the song has come to an end. "Yeah. Just like—"

That.

I flinched at the new thought. The new voice.

The other strakirin hadn't been the only ones who heard me.

Water shook. The earth rumbled, and the frigid ocean seemed to grow even colder, like the heart of deep space had suddenly arrived.

Logan heard me too.

He rose up before me, in the heart of the brilliant green stars of the strakirin, and he was nothing like before. Not strakirin. Not dehaian. Black, but not like the Beast. Black like the darkness that swallows dying stars. Black like a place no life could escape. Everything could die before him and he'd live from the sacrifice, immortal among the ashes of the world.

Death himself.

This was what the judges had made. What the dehaians and the ruanir could have created a thousand years ago, if not for their war. Death incarnate, but death that would do their bidding. And so much more than that. His power would become theirs, feed into theirs, and then they'd never die. Never, while all the world around them burned and bled and crumbled to dust. This was what the judges' weapon, their Beast, was meant to become.

But where was Noah?

I looked around, frantic, but I couldn't see him. Couldn't feel him. He'd been draining into nothing even before the darkness hit, but surely…

Fear spread through me. Surely…

A chuckle carried through the black, deep and rumbling. Around Logan, the freed strakirin cried out, terrified. Pain shuddered through their minds. Weakness too, like all the strength of their muscles was failing. He was drawing on them. Drawing them back in. Forcing them into the dark and the hive, drowning out every bit of freedom they'd gained and dragging them back down where they would truly die.

In my mind, I reached for them, crying for them to cling onto the ocean magic, to fight back.

Ari…

My name singsonged through the darkness, amused.

Now, what do you think you're doing?

The amusement lasted only another heartbeat. And then he was coming. Darkness like the end of the world bore down on my mind, solid as granite, terrible as a blade. I screamed as it slashed into me, ripping at my mind, my will, dragging every trace of my strength into itself and bearing me down, down, down into the depths where no light could ever escape again. I clung to the ocean magic inside me, throwing it against the black in desperate defense, but it wasn't enough, couldn't be enough. He was too strong.

I was going to die.

No.

A new darkness swept around me, catching my back and engulfing me. Familiar darkness, full of lightning and storm clouds, full of fire and rage. It had torn down civilizations before this monster was even born, and it rang with one thought, one single thought while it wrapped around me like a cloak.

It wouldn't let me die.

The Beast surged around me, past me, through me. Noah's power poured into my mind, setting alight the connection we'd once had with more force than I'd ever felt before. The ocean flooded me, filled with light like a million stars, blazing and brilliant and coursing like fire from the heart of the earth through my veins. And he was in it. Noah's presence filled my mind, dark and light, fire and water, all the things he was and could be. He engulfed me, sheltered me, protected me as he drove Logan back. He wouldn't leave me to this.

He'd promised.

In a rage, he tore into Logan, lashing out and shoving me back at the same time. Logan's presence faded in my mind, forced back by the power of Noah's assault. A few surviving strakirin fled, and the dehaians did too, swimming for their lives while Noah drove Logan away from us all.

But it wasn't going to be enough.

I gasped as the truth resonated along the link between us. Noah's power had been pouring out of him from the moment Osias cast the spell, and it was pouring out even now, draining into the black abyss opened by that ancient magic. Noah couldn't defeat Logan. He could only slow him down.

And his sorrow filled my mind the moment he knew I realized it.

This wasn't a battle.

It was a sacrifice.

"No!" I fought to swim forward, fought to swim for him even if there wasn't a thing in the world I could do. But this couldn't happen. I couldn't lose him. I could feel him in my mind, Logan's magic retaliating and tearing into him, sapping his strength with every blow. There were only seconds now. Seconds till the abyss took him and he couldn't hold Logan back anymore, but it didn't matter. I couldn't lose him like this.

I couldn't lose him at all.

"Noah, *please*! Don't—"

I'm sorry, Ari, he whispered in my mind.

His magic drew down, the last of his strength reaching

out and wrapping around me. I struggled, unable to break free while suddenly water rushed past my body. The darkness turned to a blur of gray and blue. I flew backward, moving so fast the pressure should have crushed me, if not for his grasp.

But then his grip vanished. I tumbled through the water and then crashed down into the sand. Grit erupted around me, and pain spiked through my side, making me gasp in dirt along with the water. I choked, floundering upward.

"Noah!"

I love—

Agony blasted across my mind, whiting my vision, sending every nerve ending screaming. My breath was made of fire, and my blood was too, ripping through me, burning every trace of me till finally darkness found me again and chased me into oblivion.

I'm sorry, Ari…

I gasped, lunging up from the dirt. Pain stabbed through my side, nearly doubling me over. It hurt to breathe, like a knife was wedged in my lungs.

"There she is!"

I turned, spikes rushing from my forearms and poison thrilling through my skin.

Ezio and Damerion raced toward me across the open plain. Dehaians followed them. The soldiers and mercenaries, not as many as before but more than I'd expected to see alive. Flatland surrounded us, full of sand and grit and not much else. The ocean was a vast expanse of gray-blue nothing above my head. In the distance, I could see the tumble of rocks edging the canyon.

And I couldn't see Noah.

"Noah?" I called, looking around. He wasn't with them, but he had to be somewhere. "Noah?"

Ezio and Damerion slowed. The others did too. As I turned, frantic, I could see the pity creeping into their eyes, but I didn't care.

"Noah!" My shout ended in a gasp as something stabbed at my side again.

Silence followed my cry. Cold silence. Empty silence that told you too much because it should have been filled with something. The others glanced around, a pained sort of knowledge already on their faces.

No. This couldn't be happening.

Please no.

"*Noah!*"

"Ari," Ezio started. "He's—"

"Shut up," I snapped, clutching a hand to my side. "No. No, he's not…"

The water didn't change. The emptiness of our connection didn't either.

Sorrow choked me. "He's just…"

Ezio swam closer, holding out his hands like he was approaching a wild tiger. "Ari."

I shook my head, wordless.

"Ari, I'm sorry. When that Driecaran bastard did that spell, he—"

I shook my head harder. I didn't want to hear it. Couldn't hear it. Noah had survived the poison. He'd survived the judges' trap and becoming the Beast and everything else in the past year… the past *millennium.*

He couldn't be gone. He just couldn't.

The silence mocked me, a great gaping maw that had swallowed him whole.

My arms wrapped around my middle, my spikes retreating as if by reflex to keep me from stabbing myself. But I wouldn't have cared. It couldn't hurt any more than this.

Tears joined the saltwater. I clenched my eyes shut, not wanting to cry. I just wanted this to change. For him to not have saved me. For my promise, my *stupid* promise, not to have killed the first guy I'd ever loved.

It was my fault.

"Ari," Damerion said, swimming up next to his love, the one who hadn't lost him, the one who still got to keep the person he adored.

It wasn't fair.

"We have to go," Damerion said.

"I'm not leaving. He's not dead."

"It's not safe here. That thing will—"

The water thudded, shoving me backward away from the canyon. I spun, hoping desperately that my silent pleas had been answered. Noah was okay. He was coming. I couldn't feel him at all, but—

The ground began to crumble beneath us. Sand and grit slid toward the chasm, and then huge chunks of rock did too, tumbling down like the earth intended to swallow the island's remains. The dehaians retreated, and Ezio pulled me with them when I didn't move. The soldiers and mercenaries alike fled toward more stable ground.

Darkness like the depths of space erupted from the canyon.

It wasn't Noah.

"Veil!" Damerion shouted. "Now!"

The soldiers and mercenaries scrambled. Ezio yanked me toward the seafloor, sending a jolt of pain through me. One of the Yvarians grabbed something from the pouch on his belt and swam around us in a blur of speed. The others crowded inward, watching the darkness spreading through the water.

A curtain of bubbles rose around us, meeting at the top to form a dome over our heads. Beneath us, the earth stilled, freed of the monster it had held.

"Quiet," Damerion ordered his people.

No one made a sound.

I stared, watching the blackness, a thing alive but with only the vaguest sense of form. It was Logan. He rose from the remains of the canyon like a cloud, rank with death. I could feel him in my mind, on the edges of my thoughts, huge like a black hole waiting to drag me to oblivion.

But only if he noticed me.

I couldn't take my eyes from him.

Logan turned, heading in our direction but high in the water. I cowered down against the dirt, and pain shot through my side again. I clamped my lips shut, choking back a cry.

Around us, the water grew colder. Impossible crystals of ice sparkled around us. The temperature had to already be freezing at this depth, yet Logan made it grow colder still.

The darkness spread over us. The magic of my vision seemed to lose its strength, as even the murky light I could see faded. Cold shivered through me, setting my teeth on edge. I didn't dare move. Didn't dare even breathe.

And then he was past. The light returned. My warmth did too.

He hadn't spotted me.

The dark cloud of his form vanished over the horizon, fading from my senses and my mind.

"We have to warn them," Damerion said, his voice tight. "Yvaria, the Ivalaen…"

Ezio nodded.

Damerion motioned to the soldiers around us. Cautiously, they arrayed themselves between us and the direction Logan had gone while one of them set to taking down the veil.

I looked back toward the canyon, reaching out with my mind. "Noah?" I waited, willing him to rise out of the canyon too. "Noah?"

The veil of bubbles fell.

I trembled. "Noah, please."

Damerion swam up next to me, Ezio on my other side.

"Please," I whispered.

Ezio rested a hand on my shoulder. "I'm sorry, Ari."

I flinched at the words. They were wrong. All wrong.

"He's gone."

I shook my head. He couldn't be. I'd made that mistake before, thinking he was dead. I wouldn't make it again. Not this time.

"We need to go."

No.

I kicked my tail hard in the water, racing away from Ezio, heading for the remains of the canyon.

"Ari!"

I felt them following. I sped onward, the pain in my side stabbing me with every motion. I made it another fifty yards before I couldn't keep my body moving.

Ezio and Damerion circled around, blocking my path. "Dammit, girl," Damerion growled.

"Noah didn't die for this," Ezio said.

My attention snapped to him. How dare he—

Ezio's expression was implacable. He glanced quickly at Damerion, caution in his eyes.

And my rage faltered. Memory seeped in, filled with the look on Ezio's face when the garrison fell. When he thought the man he loved was dead.

He was being cold, but he also knew exactly how I felt.

Except Noah couldn't be dead. He just… he couldn't…

Ezio swam closer. "He wanted you to live, Ari. I swear to you, he wanted you to live. And if you go back there…"

Damerion joined him. "If any of that magic is still down there, there's no telling what it could do to you."

I shivered.

"We have to go," Damerion insisted.

I couldn't take my eyes from the canyon. I'd never even told Noah, I realized. I'd never gotten the words out, when I should have been saying them to him at every opportunity.

I love you too.

"Noah would have wanted you to go," Ezio pressed.

Ezio's hand came to rest on my arm. From the corner of my eye, I saw Damerion tense, waiting to see if I would lash out at him.

My gaze crept over to Ezio's. "I love him."

"I know."

Grief crushed my chest. I couldn't breathe. Couldn't even cry. It hurt too much. Noah couldn't be gone. Not after all this.

"That thing might come back, Ari," Ezio said gently.

I wished he would.

Something dark and cold stirred deep inside me, beneath the grief and pain and crushing heartache. It wasn't strakirin, wasn't anything the judges had made. And it was everything they'd made, because this… this was rage.

At them. *For* them.

My eyes turned, tracking the way Logan had gone. I couldn't go near the magic down in that canyon, not after what I'd felt there. Damerion was right about that, at least. But Noah would come back. He had to. The world needed him.

I needed him.

And in the meantime, I'd make them pay for this. Osias. The judges. Logan. Anyone and everyone who hurt him, who made me think even for a *moment* that he'd been taken from me. If it took the rest of my life, I'd track every last one of the bastards down, and I'd absolutely make them pay.

Somehow.

"Please, Ari," Ezio urged. "We have to leave."

I nodded and let him lead me away from the canyon, that crumbled chasm of darkness that had buried the boy I loved.

$$\text{\Large 32}$$

BAYLIE

A test tube exploded, propelling glass and droplets of my blood all over the counter.

"Goddammit!" Declan spun away from the machinery by the far wall, raking his hands through his black hair.

I closed my eyes. Test number one million and six, also a failure. Or at least that's how it felt. But then, who was counting?

Declan, probably. Maybe the elders too. We'd been down in the cellar for hours, surrounded by the most random assortment of devices I'd ever seen. The computer monitors, I recognized. Those were easy to guess the purpose of. But the cylinders of metal, the random light bulbs and gemstones dangling from them, and something that looked like the engine of a car sitting off to one side… those were harder.

Countless glass tubes with plastic spirals inside held traces of blood from me now. Those, obviously, were for testing. We'd tried samples of the dark power inside me, but I'd accidentally blown up every sampling device they attempted to use. Meanwhile, an apparatus of copper wires and black crystals hung across the length and width of the ceiling, and that was a defense against the judges detecting this, Declan said.

But as for the rest of it…

"What now?" Robin asked. She'd made her way down here with us after getting the coffee. Olivia was here too, working intently on a laptop over by the leftmost wall. Jace sat next to me, his second cup of coffee held in his hands. He didn't look like he'd actually slept that much last night, though all he'd say when I asked was "weird dreams." I still couldn't quite bring myself to look at him after what had happened yesterday with the magic between us. Meanwhile, Ellie was upstairs, calling her Mom and Dad to update them on the general fact that she was safe, we were safe, everything was safe—or, in other words, lying. Angelica and the others were up there as well. They'd retreated after a shouting match between Angelica and Declan about rights to the research that I was fairly certain Declan had won, at least for the moment.

Declan didn't respond to Robin's question.

"Okay, fine," Robin said into the silence. "Well, now you've tried Baylie's *blood,* for God's sake. Can you think of any other way to get this weapon to work?"

Declan glanced at me briefly, not responding. We hadn't told her. Hadn't told anyone. Not yet. "Can I?" he retorted. "Oh, sure. I've just been putzing around like this for hours because I enjoy playing scientist more than I enjoy killing the bastards slaughtering my people."

I looked away. Yikes.

"You…" Robin set down the vial in her hand. "Screw this."

She turned to Olivia. "I'll be upstairs."

"*Do* you know of another way?" Olivia asked when Robin shut the door to the stairwell.

Declan paused. "I was joking."

Olivia studied him. "I see. Well, perhaps Robin is right and Baylie's blood isn't where we need to be looking. Unless you know something we don't?"

"You're the ones with all the research," Declan retorted. "What would I know that I haven't already told—"

The darkness inside me exploded beneath my skin. My body convulsed, a cry of alarm catching in my throat and choking me. The world tilted, swallowed in black, rushing up from inside me, around me, through the very air.

"Baylie!" Jace shouted.

Pain blasted my cheek, hot then cold. My left arm crushed to my side. The floor. I'd fallen out of the chair and hit the—

The ground started cracking. Rolling. The concrete was breaking beneath me.

"Back!" Declan yelled. "Get back! Run!"

It hurt. Everything hurt. Why did—

Noah.

Oh my God, *Noah*. He didn't… he wasn't…

I screamed. The darkness surged from me, beating out from my skin in waves. Something was wrong, and something had happened, and the pain pouring through wasn't just Noah.

It was the world.

Ending.

Black power surged through me, dark and deep and colder

than snow. I screamed till I couldn't hear my voice anymore, till all that was left was the black-ice heart of a dying world.

Where was my stepbrother? What had happened to my stepbrother?

My strength failed. Whatever power was within me waned, drained to nothing, washing out like an exhausted tide. My skin burned, and my body ached, and slowly, the cold black began to fade.

Thumping then. My heart. That was my heart. A rasp. My lungs, breathing. I was alive.

I was alive.

Oh, God…

The darkness melted away. The blur of my vision cleared enough that I could see the gray ceiling of the cellar.

What was left of it.

Sunlight poured down on my face.

A short gasp left me when I tried to move, my bones and muscles crying out in protest. Dust covered me. Bits of plaster and concrete too. There was dirt under me. Dirt from beneath the concrete of the cellar floor. I'd broken through it, and through some pipes too if the water seeping through the cracks around me was any indication. The cellar walls weren't doing too great either; fissures like spiderwebs ran through them all. Most of the rest of the room was on the ground. The vials with my blood were a shattered mess in one corner. The crystals and copper wires still dangled from a few points on what remained of the ceiling. I could see the living room above me, though. Broken windows and a hole all the way to the roof too. A sofa lay several feet to my right, the legs beneath it cracked from its fall.

But I was alone. The others were gone. Had I killed them? I reached out, pushing at the shattered concrete in an attempt to get out of the hole, and then froze.

Black smoke drifted from my hands, my arms, twisting into the dusty air like a breath of utter midnight.

"*Baylie?*" Jace shouted.

I looked up. Jace appeared near the hole in the ceiling. Dust and tiny debris rained down. He stared, his gaze flashing over me, over the black wisps of smoke drifting up around me like a dream of thunderclouds.

"Be careful, dammit!" That was Declan. He appeared at the edge of the hole in the living room floor for all of a heartbeat. His eyes went wide in shock at the sight of me, and then he whirled fast toward whomever else was in the living room. "Stay back!"

"Baylie?" Ellie called from beyond the opening. Relief made me gasp for a whole new reason. She wasn't dead either. Maybe no one was. "Are you okay?"

"Hang on!" Jace yelled. "I'm going to get down there to you!" He vanished from the hole in the ceiling. I heard his footsteps above me, heading toward the cellar door.

"What happened?" Ellie called. "What was that?"

I didn't know. Not really. I lifted a hand, watching the smoke drift up from my skin, growing fainter now, like the invisible fire was burning out.

Or maybe I just didn't want to admit what I knew.

Tears burned my eyes. A scream pushed at the back of my throat, not of magic but of grief and pain. My gaze slid in the direction I knew was west, even if there wasn't a single window in the cellar. The world felt weird. Felt wrong. Felt dark even though there was sunlight pouring through the gap in the roof and through the windows up above that I hadn't broken.

And I knew the reason.

"Baylie?" Ellie cried.

My fingers curled into a fist. The smoke faded into nothing. My body shook around the impossible words, the horrible words.

"It's Noah," I managed. "He's gone."

❧ 33 ❧

LOGAN

The Beast was dead.

Long live the Beast.

Amusement filtered through me while I sailed through the water, a god, a creation beyond even the scope of divinity. I'd never felt power like this, never known it could exist.

And I'd be damned if I'd give it to the Judiciary.

The water rippled around me, reflecting my humor. In my grasp, the strakirin made no sound, but there wasn't much left of them to cry out anyway. Husks now, barely more than bodies waiting to be filled with a will. There weren't as many as had been in the canyon. The change had been too much for them. Driven to madness, some had fled when I took my true form. But then, I didn't really need them anyway.

Vessels. Broken ones. The judges might have fun poking and prodding to see what good they still were.

Assuming I let them.

The water rippled harder, laughter from a Beast with no form. They'd thought to control me. They'd put it inside me, this compulsion to return once the spell was done. They'd planned for us all to take this power, to turn into this thing, with none of us having an identity or will of our own.

A hive. A creature made of a hundred minds now merged into a single, obedient being. An unthinking monster who would submit to their every command.

To hell with that.

I swept onward over the flat, barren plains. I'd go back to them. I would. We had a new world order to discuss, after all. But it didn't have to be now. Or even soon. I wanted to play with these new powers. Stretch my legs—or tail or whatever—and see what I could do.

And they wouldn't control me. They *couldn't*. Their entire plan had failed because they hadn't seen the one flaw in their system. The one little flaw they'd never spotted in all their examinations and tests and perfected designs.

Her.

A collection of debris appeared on the horizon. A wrecked aircraft carrier. Part of a plane as well, if I wasn't mistaken. But then a shiver in the water like a trace of magic passed by me, revealing something else altogether.

Anticipation spread through me. The judges had meant for me to be a slave. They'd meant for me to be firmly under their control. I'd show them power when I got back to the land, and all the world would cower before what I had become.

But first… some fun.

Thanks, Ari, I thought as I descended upon the city on the seafloor.

ACKNOWLEDGMENTS

DEFIANCE is a novel that, of all the books in the Awakened Fate series, took the longest to create, though the following novel, DESTINY, has thus far proved the hardest to write. But in the time that it took to create this story, there have been a number of people without whom you wouldn't have this book in your hands today.

First and foremost, thanks needs to go to my mother and my sister. They have supported me through good times and bad, and they've believed in me and these books no matter what. The Awakened Fate Series wouldn't be here without their support.

Thanks also goes to my friend, Robin Augsburg, for her support, her encouragement, for her keen insight while betareading, and for the wonderful way she tells everyone we meet about these books (no matter how much it embarrasses me). Thank you for reading, for answering all my last-minute grammar questions, and most of all for being my friend.

Many thanks as well to my friend and fellow author, JC Lillis, for betareading and for all her excitement and great questions about the story. You're an incredibly gifted author, JC, and your insight is invaluable to me.

To Cat Skinner, thank you for betareading as well, and for all your notes and comments and detailed responses to the story.

Many thanks also go to Monica Bogza for her incredibly detailed proofreading, for answering my questions, and for finding the fact we debated commas with each other hilarious. You're a gem and I'm grateful to have your assistance.

Thanks as well goes to Karri Klawiter, the wonderful artist who designed the covers for this story and for all the Awakened Fate series. I have been consistently amazed by your knowledge and skill, Karri, and you have always been a pleasure to work with. Thank you for using your gifts to make this series beautiful.

Last but not least, endless thanks goes to you, the one reading this story. This series wouldn't be what it is without your support in purchasing these books, in reading them, and (hopefully) loving them. Thank you for your time and for choosing to read this series. You make this writing-career thing possible. Thank you.

AFTERWORD

The story continues in DESTINY: Book Nine of the Awakened Fate Series!

Love the Book?

Leave a review on Amazon, BookBub, Goodreads, or your favorite book-related website!

Other Titles by Skye Malone

The Awakened Fate Series
The Demon Guardians Series
The Kindling Trilogy

About the Author

Skye Malone is a fantasy and paranormal romance author, which means she spends most of her time not-quite-convinced that the magical things she imagines couldn't actually exist.

Born and raised in the Midwest of the United States, she dreams someday of traveling the world – though in the meantime she'll take any story that whisks her off to a place where the fantastic lives inside the everyday. She loves strong and passionate characters, complex villains, and satisfying endings that stay with you long after the book is done. An inveterate writer, she can't go a day without getting her hands on a keyboard, and can usually be found typing away while she listens to all the adventures unfolding in her head.

Connect with Skye Malone

Website: www.skyemalone.com
Amazon: www.amazon.com/author/skyemalone
BookBub: www.bookbub.com/authors/skyemalone
Facebook: www.facebook.com/authorskyemalone
Goodreads: www.goodreads.com/skyemalone
Instagram: www.instagram.com/authorskyemalone